Refugee

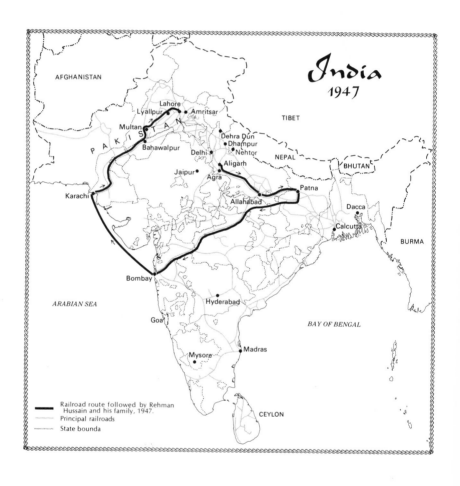

Jndia
1947

AFGHANISTAN

TIBET

NEPAL

BHUTAN

BURMA

Lahore
Lyallpur • Amritsar
Multan
Bahawalpur
Delhi
Dehra Dun
Dhampur
Nehtor
Aligarh
Jaipur • Agra
Patna
Karachi
Allahabad
Dacca
Calcutta

Bombay

ARABIAN SEA

Hyderabad

Goa

BAY OF BENGAL

Mysore • Madras

CEYLON

Railroad route followed by Rehman
Hussain and his family, 1947.
Principal railroads
State bounda

Refugee

LINDA and KHALID SHAH

THOMAS Y. CROWELL COMPANY
New York   Established 1834

The authors would like to thank the governments of India and Pakistan for their cooperation.

DESIGNED BY JUDITH J. WORACEK

MANUFACTURED IN THE UNITED STATES OF AMERICA

Library of Congress Cataloging in Publication Data

Shah, Linda.
  Refugee.

  I. Shah, Khalid, joint author. II. Title.
PZ4.S52665Re [PS3569.H315]   813'.5'4   74-8820
ISBN 0-690-00556-3
          1 2 3 4 5 6 7 8 9 10

HISTORICAL NOTE

After two hundred years of British rule, India won its independence on August 15, 1947. The only significant militant uprising during the colonial period took place in 1857, and thereafter rule was transferred from the East India Company directly to a viceroy appointed by the King of England. In the ensuing century the revolution was fought day after day and from year to year by hunger strikers in the scantiest of clothing, by cotton spinners and bread bakers, by Gandhian Congress Party workers who repudiated violence.

With freedom, however, came partition. India as it had been for twenty-five hundred years was divided into India and Pakistan, with Nehru and the Muslim Mohammed Ali Jinnah as the respective leaders. The vagaries of a vote in 1946 created Pakistan out of India's western and eastern states, separated from each other by over one thousand miles.

Within the last half of 1947, as the British prepared to relinquish power, twenty million Hindus, Muslims, and Sikhs fled in either direction across the lines of demarcation drawn through India's fields and villages, and the anger repressed in a century of pacifism erupted into a fratricidal chaos. Over a million died in the span of four months, and only the shock of Gandhi's assassination in January 1948 dampened the hysteria.

The late nineteen-forties were a time of upheaval for many people, the tremors of the Second World War. Israel, China, India-Pakistan, Southeast Asia, partitioned Jerusalem and Berlin, each defined itself differently in the new geopolitical sphere, but the experience for the individual has always been identical.

To the uprooted of the world; and to our son,
ADAM SYED AWAZ HUSSAIN ZAIDI SHAH—
may he never be a refugee.

Contents

1

Twenty-Two Steps

AUGUST 1947

The rains of India were falling on them. Hundreds, thousands, of refugees were already standing at the cordoned entrance to the Bombay wharf, their feet sore and cramped together on the uneven cobblestones. Women waited erect beneath shapeless sacks that perched heavily on their heads. Small children carried bundles in their arms and babies too young to walk. Old men and adolescents with new moustaches clutched boat tickets and bits of documentation to their chests, yellowed deeds to their lands scrawled in Persian and fixed with British stamps, that said "I am Syed, Mohammed, Khan, Hussain, and this was my home, and this was my land."

Before them was the customs shed, a vast airy hall, dim in the sporadic light of naked electric bulbs. Rehman Hussain lifted his wife, Apaji, and each of their eight children from the rear of the open lorry that had brought them to the dock area. Their frail wet bodies shivered in his arms, and water ran in greasy streams down over their dark, gaunt faces. Rehman led them into the sea of drenching people where they huddled together like monkeys for warmth and to ward off their fear of the soldiers and the angry men cursing behind them and jabbing their knives and sticks through the fencing.

1

The sirens for curfew had blown three times since sunset, but the battalions of police lining the roads in their trucks were making no move to clear away the mob that beat on the fencing with their fists and kicked it with their feet. They were loud and drunk and continuously cajoling the police to let them storm the docks and take whatever the refugees had brought with them. "Muslim traitors," they shouted. "The meat eaters have divided our country and now are running like jackals." The soldiers glared back at them in impassive silence.

No one beyond the fencing made a sound. Rehman knew that if the police shot into the crowd there would surely be a riot. The police had rifles, but so did the mob. Their guns were clearly visible in their hands. Rehman felt his own pistol strapped against his thigh beneath his soiled tan pants. The air was rent by the screeching of trucks, which stripped their gears as they lurched through the gates and disgorged an endless stream of people in their midst. Old men in white pajamas, women wound tightly in the thin cotton of their saris and draped in their shawls, all waited patiently trying to discern some hint of the ocean they had traveled so far to reach, looking for someone to come through the customs shed and give the order for them to leave.

The rain abated while they waited. It drifted out of the sky in thin sheets and then was blown away by the wind. The late waning moon fluttered wanly among the clouds, and Rehman could feel his clothes soggy against his skin. His children stood around him in a knot, supporting each other with their bodies and swaying on their rubbery legs. He tried to hold the younger ones by turns, rocking them against his chest, murmuring in their ears, and kissing their eyelids which would not close. His mind was filled with questions, but no one spoke and no one asked. The two eldest sons, Gappu and Gerrar, were still wearing their black school blazers, but they were torn, and the emblems and epaulettes, which their mother, Apaji, had sewn on for them, were crusted with dirt. Apaji, standing beside them, was staring straight ahead at the shed, with the baby Sara curled into a ball of cloth, sleeping beneath her neck. Rehman's mind reeled at the thought of his wife's delicate, perfumed skin gnarled with cold and rain. He knew it was only a matter of time before her strength gave out. Her recent fainting spells were only a symptom of the exhaustion and the tension and the hunger he also could feel gnawing within his own body and flooding his senses and his veins.

It seemed as if they had been waiting for hours, but Rehman knew that the midnight siren had not yet blown. Finally over the heads of the people, he saw the electric lights of the shed spring on through the screens. Police officers and soldiers flooded out of the building and took up their positions, ringing the refugees. Everyone pressed forward, and Rehman felt himself enclosed by a thousand bodies and feet pinching together. As the refugees began to seep through the shed, the mob behind them in the street started chanting in unison: "Keep the traitors here. Don't let them go." But India was already behind them as they filed through the empty customs shed, kept in line by rows of Bombay police, their southern brown knees peeping between their green shorts and military socks, bayonets pointing at the soundless children clutching one another's hands and the shuffling women holding veils between their teeth.

No one looked back. The wharf was an island between the swirling water and the lives they were leaving. For many it was the first time they had seen the ocean. Those who came from midland, from rivers' edges ringed by jungle growth, and those from plains of blowing wheat and singing sugarcane twice the size of any man, and those who came from the hills and fruit gardens laden with mangoes and the perennial singing of cuckoos, and ridges of coffee plants and tea leaves, saw their first ocean at the boundaries of this teeming candle-lit city, staid and solid, that had housed them for days and weeks in crumbling corner mosques and at the dead end of a twisted street. Before they saw it, they sensed it, smelled its salt and sewage mingling, heard the clanging of buoys and the shouting of fishermen pushing off to find a run of fish now that the moon was up.

The long wide wharf stretched out into the bay, and all the refugees sat among the ropes and pulleys on the wet wooden planks of the dock. They hunkered together in small family groups, shoulder to shoulder and back to back. The moon made pirouettes of light on the waves that slapped the wooden moorings beneath their haunches. Here and there people were building fires from bits of rope and charcoal they had brought with them, to cook their grains of rice and lentils, and fill their hollow stomachs. Without his glasses Rehman could barely make out the darkened bay from the middle of the dock where he had told his family to sit. He had to seek the help of his eldest son to find out if the ship was coming or not.

Gappu stood up and looked over the mass of people at the sea. "Is anything there?" Rehman asked.

Gappu scanned the dark water which was tipped white with froth and churning in the gusting monsoon winds. He looked for the lights of a ship, but the bay was silent and empty. Only fishermen's junks gave off a glimmer of kerosine light, their wooden masts keening deeply in the wind. Gappu sat down, looking sorrowfully at his father's face. "No, Abu," he answered. "There is no ship." He could see that his father was tiring; he could hear it in his voice. The tall body that had killed a seven-foot cobra bare-handed was showing signs of the final strain.

Apaji was trying to nurse Sara, who was not yet six weeks old, and holding on to the others with her eyes. On every side, families like their own were spread out along the wharf. Body was pressed into body, knee locked to knee, as they crouched wet to the bone beneath the damp cloths they hugged around their heads.

Throughout the night they waited for the ship to come into the harbor. A distant siren tolled the hours from midnight to dawn. Squatting on the boards of the old wooden dock around the dying charcoal fires where the last morsels of food, scrounged and cooked, had long ago been eaten, it seemed as if the whole city of Bombay had come to camp in their dark shrouds and tattered veils. The entire mass of people gazed out over the rippling bay. In the silence they could hear the aged water come and go against the stones of the city. Behind them from the sleeping streets, they heard the bell of a temple calling for morning ablutions, the creaking of a milk cart, a lone lantern, whisperers up for breakfast. It seemed that the mob waiting for them at the gates had grown tired and were asleep or perhaps had finally gone home.

Their silence was complete. Nobody made a noise for fear they would be detected and the cursing crowds who had haunted them for weeks would gather and swoop down on them again. Even the police, whom they could see through the screens of the shed, were nodding over the rifles between their legs, and sprawled out on the floor and benches. Dead weight surrounded their helplessness. A child whimpered, but not for long. The palest of moons had gone behind the monsoon clouds before the night ended and the darkest of mornings blinded them. They sat sleepless but motionless, all facing the water, all waiting for darkness to melt into shadows, and shadows into silhouettes.

Rehman stood up to stretch his legs. The dock was so tightly packed with people that it was impossible to take a step. Apaji and the children were lost among the multitudes seated in front and behind and on every side of them, from the screened windows of the shed to the water's edge, as the hazy morning light sifted through the fog on the water. Although at sunrise Rehman never missed his morning prayer, here on the threshold of his native land, there was no one to call the morning Azan. Slowly he could feel the warmth of the sun drying the crushed cotton of his clothes, and the gathering heat crawled beneath his collar, itching the graying stubble of beard at his chin and on his cheeks, and obliterating the memory of the chill night rain. His eyes were strained from looking out across the bay for the ship to appear. The stooped fragile backs of the refugees seemed to ache in his vision, pulsating with the squalor of their once fine clothes. The saris of the women were limp and soiled. The pajamas of the men were frayed and faded, and even those who wore Western suits seemed crumpled beyond recognition, faces pocked with beards, hair greasy and running rampant on their foreheads, eyes rimmed red. Rehman could identify people who had come from every corner of India by their clothing. Madrasis in their brightly colored cloth were seated beside Punjabis in traditional baggy pants and long cameez blouses, but all were uniformly riven with a gray despair. Rehman's own clothes were streaked with perspiration, and blackened by the charcoal soot from trains. The slim lines of the pants, which his Delhi tailor had fitted to his rugged body, gaped from his legs, and his shirt seemed to have retained all the stench of the rioting and killing, the urine and defecation of the waiting rooms, the sickness and filth he had seen around him on the month-long journey from home.

It seemed impossible that they were still waiting. All anyone could do was stare ahead into the rocking waters of the bay, which were empty and forbidding as long as their ship did not appear. The horizon was etched on Rehman's mind, ringed by the bare brown rocks of islands that blazed in whiteness as the sun grew and mushroomed overhead. Boats plied in and out of the harbor, foreign tankers and cargo ships along with double-masted schooners and fishing vessels hardly bigger than canoes. Off the farthest edge of the dock, little dinghies were buffeted by the waves, while the oarsmen slept inconspicuously in the hulls.

One ship, white and stacked with decks, seemed to hover in the water like a bird poised to fly. Slowly it turned landward, and Rehman held his breath. A murmur of voices spread among the refugees as they recognized their boat. "It is the ship," they whispered to each other. "Our ship has come."

They watched as the boat sped directly toward the wharf, growing larger and more distinct as it churned head-on through the water. The tension was almost audible as everyone craned his neck to see over the heads in front. How big the ship looked riding over the waves! Fishermen's junks scattered like crows in a rice paddy before its wake. And then suddenly how small it was as everyone's eyes scanned the yards and yards of multitudes waiting at the water's edge. We will never fit, an entire population, an entire race.

There was a commotion at the farthest end of the dock. People were standing up, waving hands and shaking fists. Excitement rippled through the crowd, and everyone was standing up and pointing and shouting. The boat seemed to have stopped. It hung just before the wharf, its white decks deserted and its smokestacks silent. The only movement was that of the dinghies fluttering at its sides like scavenger gulls.

"Why has it stopped?" someone near Rehman asked.

"Haven't we all waited long enough?" another shouted.

"Haven't we all paid fortunes for our tickets?"

"Maybe some of these Chamars haven't paid."

Everyone looked from neighbor to neighbor. Rehman thought of the gold coins brought in bundles and laid on the shipping agent's desk, the deeds and promissory notes slapped into the open palms of minor clerks and semiliterate dockworkers to ensure his family of passage, of a seat, of sleeping room, or standing room only as it now turned out. Sagged muscles straightened and fists clenched. Grandfathers with white beards, many hunters of tigers and geese and quails, felt the familiar coolness of their smuggled pistols under their tensed fingers once again. If the boat hesitates a moment longer, that's it. The vision of a turning boat, gleaming white in the new sun, welled up behind the bloodshot eyes of every man, woman, and child on the dock. The dream which so often had become not a dream but a reality in recent times, might turn again into the nightmare of hot air pierced with screams, a midday collage of blood and torn flesh, the crack of guns and the flash of knives pulled from chests and thighs and head coverings, as frustration and grief would explode into a murderous and suicidal anger.

There was a high-pitched blast, a rumble, and steam poured blackly from the ship's towering smokestacks. The boat moved, and the doubted future inched toward them again. Men stooped to gather their belongings; women called frantically to their children to stand still, to hold the baby tighter, to try to move closer to the water, and never to look back.

Rehman extended his hand toward Apaji. A smile flickered on her face, but Rehman could see the beads of perspiration clinging to her upper lip, and her cheeks were gray and drained. He grasped her by the wrist, but he could feel her arm trembling and all the weight of her small form resisted him. She pulled herself up slowly, but suddenly her eyes rolled up behind her heavy lids, and she collapsed back onto the dock in a heap. Raheel let out a scream and fell over her mother's body. The younger children started to wail and pull at her arms and her face. Rehman and Gappu tried to push the children from her body, and Gerrar and Karim picked the youngest babies up in their arms.

"Abu, Abu, do something," they were all crying. "Apaji has fainted."

Rehman grabbed one of the jute bundles and began pulling its contents out of the bag and throwing them on the floor. All around him the refugees were standing up, moving in place, their shouting, anxious voices and their swirling clothes a cacophony of sound and color. He found the small lacquer box containing smelling salts and doused a portion in water from a flask he wore at his hip. Hurriedly he held the salts beneath Apaji's nose. Her head jolted, and a low moan escaped from her lips. The eight children sat wide-eyed around their mother's form, pressed together among the tangle of legs stepping around them, although there was no place for anyone to go. It was the fourth time she had fainted since they had arrived in Bombay the week before, and still she refused to eat. She would not take food from her children's mouths. Rather she would leave the food lying in her lap where her oldest daughter, Raheel, placed it. In turn, the children refused to take food from their mother's mouth. Even Piari, who was only three and the most demanding, followed her brothers' and sisters' lead, and finally the food, little as it was, went to another mother, frailer and more distraught than she, or to the young girl still in the remnants of her bridal dress, seeming alone and coughing tubercularly, or to the priest shivering in his incongruously white suit who cried and offered her a prayer.

Slowly Apaji began to revive. Rehman held her hand clasped between both of his and studied her face. The taut smooth skin that always used to glow with health and high spirits was yellow and sallow, and her round childlike eyes were mere slits. She pulled her hand out of Rehman's grip and tried to rise, but her head was reeling and the sun seemed to blind her vision.

Their neighbor on the dock leaned over the prostrate family, clucking his tongue. "You had better get some food into her, or she'll never make it onto the ship," he advised.

Rehman looked at the stranger frantically. "I don't know what to do. All we have is uncooked grains and raw flour."

The man took off his head covering and unwrapped a hanky where a few warm and dried chapati were pressed together. He peeled off one of the flat breads and handed it to Rehman. "It is all I can spare," he said, shaking his head.

Apaji smiled weakly. "Thank you for your kindness. I will always remember you," she said. The neighbor shrugged and pushed among the people standing closest to them. Rehman looked up and watched him make his way toward the edge of the wharf and disappear in the crush of bodies milling nervously about the dock. The boat was turning heavily into the wharf, scraping its sides with a shrill whine as wood contacted wood. Coolies were shoving through the crowd, leaping onto the ship and clinging alongside the lower deck. The refugees straining toward the boat left no room for them to grab the ropes and heave the ship forward.

"Move back, move back," officials were shouting from the decks, and the police had reappeared behind them along the walls of the shed.

As the side of the boat heaved toward them and the ropes were lowered, the crowd surged forward with the name of the boat on their lips. "S.S. *Shiralla*," they were all shouting.

"Move back, move back," the officials called.

The crowd moved forward again as one mass. Bodies pressed into bodies. Voices called, necks craned to discover severed children, husbands, brothers.

A shot was fired, and in the immediate silence one voice was heard, a piercing whine: "It's the wrong ship."

"What? *Kya?*"

"What?"

"Impossible!"

"It's the wrong ship," the man wailed again. He tore his ticket in a fit of hysteria, and flinging it into the air, he sank into sobs as the yellow bits of paper fluttered over his head. "My ticket is for the S.S. *Ravi*," he cried.

Everyone checked his own ticket.

"S.S. *Shiralla*," a thousand voices said, "S.S. *Shiralla*"; and they heaved ever closer to the ship, fortresslike and majestic in the water, attached to the land only by massive ropes that the coolies struggled and grunted to secure, cursing unintelligibly in colloquial Maharathi.

The phantom ship *Ravi* had come and gone a week before. Rehman had tried to book passage on it as soon as he arrived in Bombay but to no avail. Now the *Ravi* was no more than a torn ticket lying in a sobbing man's matted hair. The man could not go forward and could not go back, for back there was only death.

Slowly a single wooden gangplank was being raised to the ship, and orders were being shouted by officials on every side. Coolies were clambering up the half-raised plank, hoisting themselves by the ropes that seemed to be the only protection on the steep plank. Desperate to leave the country, several young men and women at the head of the crowd leaped onto the plank, clutching babies and lumpy baskets.

"We are going to Pakistan," they yelled as they scrambled on all fours along the wooden slats. The sure-footed coolies ran up the plank after them, their bare legs full of strength and muscle, and they kicked the bodies over the side with their calloused feet.

"We must have order," officials pleaded through the ship's loud-speaker. Members of the Indian crew ran from side to side in front of the refugees. No one moved. No one pushed them in. Everyone looked for some way to create order, individually, in the chaos, and then pushed forward again. On the highest deck bathed in sun, young British officers in white shorts leaned over the railing, flinging cigarette butts into the water and observing.

The first passengers seeped up the gangplank. The narrow incline was suspended at a steep angle over the water. There should have been room for only one person at a time, or perhaps for a woman and a child, but they were moving three and four abreast, squeezed between the loose sagging ropes. Soon the gangway was clogged, and movement ceased. Thousands upon thousands of women were crying while the coolies rushed through the crowd, making deals and bargaining with customers. Often a coolie, hired and paid in advance from dwindling stores of gold coins and bangles, would drop a load of cases for a better offer.

Rehman could not find the coolie he had reserved many days before along with the tickets. Since Rehman had bought first-class tickets, the coolie had seemed very pleased and promised to see the family safely to their berths. "No problem," he had told Rehman. "First-class passengers, no problem." Now it was clear that there would be no first-class accommodations for refugees and the coolie was nowhere in sight.

Rehman clapped a passing coolie on the shoulder, a wrinkled wiry man who smelled of turmeric and fish. His eyes squinted, and his smile was full of blackened teeth. Rehman shoved half his remaining gold coins into the coolie's fist. "Double this when we are on board," he promised.

"Follow me," the coolie smiled.

The children gathered their belongings, the jute and cloth sacks, and the tin trunk, and Apaji rose painfully to her feet. The coolie waited for them with twinkling eyes, and when they were ready, began snaking the family through the crowds of people and their bags. A few yards later they stopped again. The children stood in a bunch, their arms loaded with possessions. Apaji swayed on her feet, her jaw set, her lips colored gray.

"You can't take all that," said the coolie, pointing to the children with their bundles. He squatted down to make a deal, and Rehman bent over him trying to decipher his dialect mixed with a little English in all the noise and pleading and shouting. A hundred shoulders closed in above their heads, and Rehman's body was pressed against the leathery black calves of the coolie. Gappu leaned over his father's shoulder, watching the filthy black coolie suspiciously.

The coolie spread his open palms between his legs, trying to explain. "It is dangerous on the plank. Too crowded. Too much people. Bad men are waiting in their canoes. No good. If you fall one-one time, finished." He made a gesture of a knife at his throat. "Leave those bundles here, and I will carry the children up the plank. I am a friend. Bundles are too much."

Rehman rose slowly. Gappu waited to hear his father's thundering voice, to see his massive hands grab the coolie's skinny neck and send him spinning into the crowd.

"You don't understand," Rehman sighed. He tried to make this coolie with his impassive face understand what it meant to have

11

come this far. The house abandoned, full of furniture and art, the legacies of his ancestors, the fields that needed harvesting, the contracts torn from his wall safe on the run, the money and the gold suddenly worthless, paid out and paid again, to buy life. Gappu waited for his father to speak as he was accustomed to hearing him speak, but looking at him closely Gappu could see that the long journey had exhausted the man, and the strong body sometimes swayed from side to side.

Rehman turned to his son. "We will have to do as the coolie says. You keep your mother and the children in the middle. She is weak. If you see her fainting, put these smelling salts in water and hold it to her nose as you have seen me doing. I will walk ahead."

Gappu did not have more than a moment to reflect on his responsibilities. Suddenly he was set apart from the others. The "children" would walk between. He and Abu would watch them and protect them. Gappu had to hold the prized salts in one hand and the flask of water in the other. He laid down his last bundle, full of those things he had prized before, but now would murder to keep if he had his way, for his mother, for his sisters, for his own wife someday and children.

"Above all, Gappu, do not fall yourself." They both looked toward the plank. Hundreds of people were still waiting in front of them. There was no siding, and the single rope was flaccid and only waist-high. Many children had slipped underneath it, and their parents jumped over after them. One barely noticed their screams any longer. Those at the top were engaged in discussion with the British officers. Those at the bottom were pushing to get on. Everyone had someone on the boat or halfway up the plank, and on the other hand, someone else had been left behind, some to protect property, some to look for a relative lost in the journey, some to wait for a brother who had not arrived. The mothers were crying. The children were crying, and this never-ending repetition of bodies was moving up the plank an inch at a time. Whenever a suitcase fell over the side, someone panicked—an angry man, a screeching child—and perhaps the owner would follow his belongings into the water where he would drown.

Gappu understood. They would have to walk up the plank as if in a circle, keeping Apaji and the youngest children in the center. Raheel and Gerrar and Karim, the middle brother, would walk on the outside and keep the others safe. Abu looked at him closely and repeated his instructions: "I will walk in front and you will be in the rear. Hold your mother tight and try to shield her from the sun. We could have put the luggage on the coolie's shoulders and the babies on top of the luggage. But that is not the best way, I have decided. The children will walk, and we will leave everything behind. The coolie is a poor man, poorer than we."

Rehman looked at all his children, round-eyed and frail, jostled on every side by the shouting, pushing people. The boys still wore their school blazers which were torn and caked with dirt, and the girls seemed lost in the cloth of their old long skirts and thin shawls. For over a month they had not had a full meal, and Rehman prayed that their strength would not fail them here. Already Apaji had fainted and could hardly stand, although she clutched Sara in her arms, and the three smallest children were clinging to her skirts. Rehman stood on top of the tin trunk to scan the heads of the people still waiting before the gangway. At the foot of the plank a woman was screaming hysterically, struggling in the arms of three coolies who were holding her by her legs and chest as they tried to drag her away from the ship.

"No, Babbu. *Mere bete*, my babies," she wailed.

Rehman stepped down from the trunk and grasped Gappu by the shoulders. "You have had no chance to use your energy, but I have prepared you to be mentally strong. I never disturbed you from your sleep, because I knew when the time came you would have many sleepless nights. My father took care of me, and I wanted to do the same for you. I thought I could keep you as a child for many years still, and I thought that there is much suffering in this world that there was time yet for you to see. I kept you away from it, but the world would not wait for you to reach manhood."

Rehman spoke to Gappu without pausing for breath. The words tumbled out of his mouth, and Gappu thought that this conversation would never have come, if it were not for this. The father and son might otherwise never have exchanged such thoughts or knowledge or understanding.

"Only one thing," Rehman continued. "I want your solemn promise that you will use all your energy to keep your mother in the middle and to hold onto these last of our family belongings."

He took a package wrapped in cloth out from under his own shirt and thrust it beneath the shirt of his son. Gappu felt it there and knew immediately what it was, just from the warmth of it, the throbbing feeling it gave his insides and his being.

It was the golden forehead jewel, the tikka that fell delicately and glitteringly through the deep part in his mother's curtains of hair. He had seen Abu wrap it in the old lace hanky before they left their home in Aligarh, and many times he had seen it lying on his mother's forehead, a diamond set in gold surrounded by stars of emeralds and rubies. It turned his mother's rich brown skin to velvet, and when she wore it, she moved with a special grace.

Gappu did not know the value of the tikka, but he knew that when his mother wore it, she was beautiful. He had been told many times that it was the oldest heirloom in his mother's possession, and had been Apaji's ultimate gift to her husband in her dowry, which no one in the family of Rehman Hussain knew she had until the first glimpse of her face during the wedding ceremony. It was the gift of the riches of the land of India to the man of the world, the merchant and the trader. It was said to bring good luck. The girl who wore it would have many sons, and it was true, one after the other, barely two years apart, four sons had been born with only a girl or two dropped in between like a flower.

Apaji had worn the tikka only two months before at Uncle Tariq's wedding. Gappu wondered if he would ever see her wear it again. Whether she would ever again enter into gatherings of people, dripping in jewels and shimmering in transparent saris like the ancient ones already lost. Gappu could not meet his mother's sad eyes, although he could feel her standing close beside him in her brown dirt-stained sari. Only his mother had remained slim after marriage and eight children. Apaji's father had seen to it that his only daughter, Munir Jehan, born late in life and after many years of waiting, would never have to bend over a stove or bear water or carry a chair. Every day two servants had stretched her hair across a table like the finest silk sari and combed it with four silver brushes. Her hands had never known a scratch, and her fingers worked only across the ivory keyboard of a harmonium or stitching silver *gotas* on to cloth. Apaji's jewels were the finest in their village of Nehtor. There were whole suitcases full of rings and bangles, anklets, brooches, hair ornaments, and golden ropes, but of all her jewels, new and old, antiques and heirlooms hundreds of years old, the tikka was the most important.

Gappu tingled as he felt it beneath his shirt. Besides the tikka, the little cloth package also contained the family's miniature Koran, the holy book whose name should never be spoken. Gappu and Gerrar and lately Karim, who had just learned to read Arabic, spent hours avoiding the priest, or Mulvi, in his mosque where they were supposed to recite the Koran until they knew many passages by heart. Even though Gappu found the Arabic still unintelligible, he was glad to have the book there against his heart.

Rehman tapped Gappu on the chest. "See what has happened to our possessions," he said. "The Koran tells us not to pay attention to worldly goods, and if we had not paid that attention, if we had given more to the people, this day might not have happened to us. A bad kismet has caught up with us, and it is for the culmination of our guilt that we are seeing this day."

Gappu did not answer his father. It was not his place either to answer or to disagree, and all his life he had kept any skepticism to himself. Gappu thought, however, that his parents had always been good. He remembered how his grandfather refused to eat any food until an equal amount had been prepared for the local beggar. Why then should it be culminating like this?

"Our possessions are gone," Rehman said to all the children. "We had a very simple decision to make. Should we stay behind and try to save some of our wealth or should we keep the family together? We are near the end of the journey, but now it is more important than ever that we stay together and protect each other."

All the children nodded, their faces solemn and their eyes riveted on Abu, in spite of the noise and the movement of the people swirling around them.

"If I did not trust you, I would stay behind and protect your mother who is not well," Rehman continued. "I want you all to remember that as we go up to the ship."

He looked again at the steep narrow gangplank, so filled with shouting men and women and screeching children that the plank itself was not visible. The people seemed to be suspended by themselves over the water, a blazing whirl of cloth swept by the wind. Although at times Rehman's hands ached to fight, his decision had been made and was final. He went sore and then numb with the sensation of loss that crept from his fingers all the way up his arms to his massive shoulders. Instead he shouldered the last remaining trunk out of the twenty original cases and valises with which they had left Aligarh, and signaled for the rest of the family to move. The coolie heaved Piari, the next to youngest child, over his head and held her legs around his neck. "Ummy, Ummy," Piari screamed, holding her thin arms out to her mother, but the coolie started to walk. With his free arm he began to thread the family through the masses of people toward the foot of the steps.

It was all decided, but Rehman went over the plan once again to make sure it was the right one. I am to be in front with the tin trunk. I can use it as a battering ram at the final steps if need be. Gappu will be behind, watching us all. God, let him be stronger than his fifteen years. On the sides will be Gerrar and Karim. Rehman closed his eyes at the thought of their tender bodies taking those next steps, hovering over the water where so many had failed. The children still did not know that below the deck scavengers were waiting with knives and moon-shaped kirpans to decapitate the drowners and steal their belongings. Raheel, his first flower, would also have to stand against the ropes, next to Apaji, his bride, and then Apaji in the middle, surrounded by five-year-old Moïd and seven-year-old Mona, who were shaking so they could barely walk. They had been clutching onto their mother's sari for the last two weeks, refusing to let go even for an instant, while the infant Sara was adhered to her breast as if she had not really been born yet. And finally Piari, with no place else to go, would sit on the shoulders of this barefoot, bony-kneed coolie, half the family's remaining coins already in the pocket of his shorts.

Rehman glanced back at Gappu as they began to walk. He felt like telling it all to him again, but there wasn't time. He wanted Gappu to understand how he and Apaji had sat for hours, huddled in corners of rooms and railway stations, deciding what to do, but if it wasn't all told by now, perhaps it never would be told.

Gappu caught his father's eye and nodded his head. He did not really know why he was here, and he did not really understand why they were going to Pakistan, but after all he had seen, he knew there was no turning back. He knew that the angry people swarming around the entrance to the customs hall would still be there to curse his family and pummel him if he tried to escape. And anyway, escape to what? His father had told him that everything they had was here. Aligarh was no more. Delhi was no more. Their villages of Nehtor and Milak, and the five hundred others that Abu governed and profited from, were no more.

There were so many instructions, and these last steps to the S.S. *Shiralla* were the most unconquerable. Although they had already traveled a thousand miles from Aligarh to Bombay, their destination had never seemed farther away or their voyage more impossible. Even when they had been forced to flee their home, or in the very beginning of their trip, the first time their train had been rerouted and they were herded into the waiting rooms of the small station at Allahabad, Gappu had not felt as hopeless as he did looking up the steep steps of the gangplank, frenetic with movement, with cloth and hair flying, and people screaming each others' names. He had thought nothing could be as bad as the trains, the constant threat of ambush, the waiting in obscure stations, not knowing where they were or where they were going. It had seemed certain that when they reached Bombay the danger would be over, but here at the last port, before the last steps, the killing was still going on.

Why should I not disappear? Gappu thought to himself. Why should I not kill? Why should I let them cause me to suffer and not be the cause of their suffering in return? Apaji can take back the tikka and have another son. She does not need me. He could not bear to look at this lady with her eyes full of tears and her heart full of love for her eldest son. Indiscriminate love. Love caused by accidents of nature and accidents of circumstance. Who asked her to give up half her food for strangers, so that now she was weak and fainting? Why had she cared all her life for distant cousins and the relations of servants, and why had she gone outside the railway station in Allahabad, a city nobody knew or cared about, risking her life to bury someone's dead infant when her own sons needed her so much? He remembered so many times when child after child demanded her affection, when strangers held her attention, and he the eldest had to hold his own. He was torn between the desire to fulfill the responsibilities and trust Abu had given him and his longing to fly into the city of Bombay, vanish in its anonymity, and cling to India which he loved.

"Gappu, keep moving," Abu said sharply over his shoulder. Gappu started. Abu still had the small trunk across his back. Every time Gappu looked at his father during the past month, the trunk seemed to be heavier than before, and those shoulders more and more stooped.

At the edge of the dock the coolie stopped in front of the family group and told them exactly how many steps there were on the gangplank. The coolie said, "Each step is important. When you are standing still, nothing will happen to you, but when you take a step, remember it is important where you put your foot down. There are twenty-two steps. Count each one as you go. If you do not put your foot down in the right place, if you put your foot down where somebody else is putting his foot, your next step may be in the water." The coolie was not smiling as he spoke.

"Gappu, don't falter now," Abu cajoled. "I am depending on you."

Gappu, who had been praying that his father would not falter, wondered how Abu could be saying that Gappu should not falter himself. Suddenly Gappu wished he could see himself in a mirror, wondered if at the age of fifteen he had already acquired a lifelong stoop, whether he had lost the fat, pink-cheeked look which had earned him his pet name, Gappu. He did not know if he was prepared to carry the burdens Abu had given him, the tikka, the Koran, the smelling salts and water in case Apaji fainted. He did not know if he was ready, now that there were only twenty-two steps, the last steps in India.

Gappu recited his instructions to himself and reminded Karim, who was holding onto his jacket. He did not want to forget a single word that Abu had told him during the long morning wait for the boat. Now was the time. The gangplank loomed up before them, and they took the first steps.

Karim and Gerrar were on the outside of the family group as had been planned. As soon as they were on the gangplank, they could feel the hot wind of the bay blowing against their cheeks and the crumpled cotton of their shirts. They had not realized how steep the plank was until they were actually on it, nor how far below the water was nor how filled with bodies and litter. They each saw the blood-stained water in a glance, peripherally, and the dinghies guided by ravenous-looking men, and then never dared to look again.

From the plank they could hear the commotion on the wharf more clearly than when they were down on the dock in the middle of it. Sounds of crying and pleading voices assaulted their ears. Children were being dragged up the steps after their parents, and there was no room to turn around. All the feet were stamping on other feet, especially the big ones of the porters loaded down with luggage. Everyone was telling everyone else, in the name of Allah to have mercy, and the little ones screamed every time their feet were crushed by the shouting adults.

It was difficult to see up the gangplank to the entrance of the ship. There was nothing to do but wait, take a step, and wait again. Their eyes were closing from the sweat and the heat and the light. Gappu's greatest fear was that his mother would faint and fall into the water before he had the time or the strength to hold her. He kept his arm outstretched and tried to hold onto Apaji as tightly as he could, but instead it seemed as if Apaji were holding onto him, and he was continuously screaming that she should not drag him close to her. She kept trying to clutch him toward her breast with Moïd and Mona hanging on beneath his arms, while he was holding the smelling salts and the flask of water and supporting Apaji all at the same time. His tiny delicate mother, whom he already towered over, was encompassing him when he was supposed to be holding her.

Gappu saw his father looking down at them. He knew Abu was saying, If you let your mother go, I will be next. How could his mother hold on to him like that when she knew Abu's final instructions? When she knew that Abu had said he would rather stay behind in Bombay than risk Apaji's life on the gangplank? Apaji was too weak to walk up the steps alone, and Gappu had been given the responsibility of supporting her.

Gappu could do nothing. Every time they moved, they were crushed against the press of people in front, and when they stopped, all the people behind began pushing upward. The tin Indian trunks, or *sandooks*, became torturous weapons on the heads of the porters. They used the trunks to push through the middle of the gangplank while everyone clung to the swaying ropes. The sandooks with their pointed edges, were slicing into the heads of the children in the coolies' arms, and all they could say was "*Baba, Baba,*" but there were no fathers to be found.

Abu was at the head of the family, and Gappu was behind. He kept remembering with the sharp sandooks in his back and the coolies calling, "Clear the way, Babbu, clear the way, *Aeh-Babbu-Oh-Babbu,*" that all the comfort his father had given him and all the mental strength were going to bear fruit now, even if there were none left later on.

Abu had been the tallest man in the entire district of Nehtor where five hundred villages were in his safe-keeping and under his administration. Abu used to dress in an immaculate khaki uniform and safari hat to take the three older boys hunting. Gappu wore plus fours. Abu would often prove how strong he was by climbing straight up rocky hills and by tearing down the young rooting branches of banyan trees for firewood.

The children loved taking long walks in the jungle with him.

20

They hunted for deer and wild boar and even tigers, stopping over-night at government rest houses in isolated places where the managers knew Abu and provided the coldest purified water from mountain springs in the foothills of the Himalayas.

They stopped in rest houses that hung over the sides of cliffs with green vines dripping past them and monkeys everywhere, so that Abu had to keep the doors locked or the monkeys would come right inside and steal the most valuable possessions—a Swiss watch or a gun. Abu taught the children how to lure a monkey into exchanging the stolen trinkets for a banana, keeping their fingers crossed that the monkey would not drop the watch in his excitement over the banana or perhaps shoot someone's head off with his own automatic.

Gappu thought Abu was the strongest man. He was well over six feet tall, with broad shoulders and beautiful, thick, black curly hair. He never told Gappu until they were safely home that a place was infested with snakes. Then he would say that such and such a field they had visited was crawling with cobras, or that he had seen the hugest of all pythons dangling from a tree. He loved to repeat the story of how he had killed the cobra he found lurking beside Gappu's cradle when he was an infant. Apaji always took over the story, saying that the snake was more than seven feet tall, and when your father tried to kill him, the snake stood up.

Apaji never called her husband by his first name. Usually she referred to him as your father, or more rarely simply, Abu, father. To her nephews and nieces she referred to him as your uncle. To the servants she would say such things as "Get the water for Bare Bhai," or older brother, but she never said Rehman Hussain. Sometimes Gappu thought, "Maybe they had me just so she could refer to him as Abu, so that she could say to others, 'His father is at home' or 'his father is on tour.' " There was only the ultimate politeness between Abu and Apaji, never a voice raised, never a tear shed.

In all his life, Gappu had never seen Apaji lose control. She was so unlike her cousins and her own mother, Nani, who was prone to hysterical fits. When other women went into hypnotic states of prayer, keening to the floor, weeping and tearing at their clothes because of illness or misfortune or someone's death, Apaji always remained outwardly calm, her fine-honed jaw and chiseled features firmly set. Gappu remembered how often she had set an example for other women, at funerals, and how she never even fainted the year before when her nephew died at their home in Aligarh.

The boy was the only son of Apaji's oldest brother. Bhai Jan, his family called him, which meant brother life, but to his cousins he was only Waji. On their summer vacations, he went with them on snake hunts and swung with them from the tallest banyan trees, and flew kites from rooftops from which they all periodically fell, shattering several bones apiece. Every autumn Rehman took his family back to the city. He sent the children to the best boarding schools and colleges India had to offer, in Aligarh and Dehra Dun and Delhi, despite the children's protests that they would rather stay in their ancestral village of Nehtor and run in bullock-cart races with their cousin Waji.

Finally the tables were turned, and Waji wanted to leave the countryside and the village girls and the long dreary days of winter lessons on the mosque floor with the senile old Mulvi. Uncle Reaz had felt no need to give his son a formal education. He did not feel it served any purpose for a son of the land, one who had to know the times of the coming of the rain and the seepage of the fields and the quality of a mango by its smell and the touch of his fingers. Reaz detested the British educational system, and had himself left joyously after two years of college to come back to the lands and ride over the muddy roads in his father's canopied tonga behind two gleaming white horses.

Waji was different. He loved to listen to the stories his younger but better-educated cousins would tell him of the city, and the movie houses and books like the Kama Sutra that described in poetry the ecstasies of sex. Gerrar, who swore he would be a doctor, taught Waji anatomy and the theory of cross-planting fruits and hybrids. Waji told his father that education could help the farmer, but Reaz was unconvinced. Finally Waji showed up in Aligarh, against his father's will. He just packed his valise, boarded the train with the help of his confidante and servant, Moonah, and arrived on Rehman Hussain's doorstep ready to be educated. The next day, after a delicious feast in the market of pani ke patashe, a pastry filled with spice-water, he was dead of cholera.

Waji had come to their house in Aligarh just before the school term began with fresh notebooks and a pot of India ink under his arm. The children were all over him with questions about the train journey, and how he could have left Nehtor all by himself without anyone knowing, and without even the stationmaster at Dhampur sending word that Waji was making his escape.

"I went by horse with Moonah to catch the mail train late at night," Waji explained. "No one saw us go. I waited behind the train for it to leave and jumped on as soon as it started moving."

"No one knows you're here?" Apaji repeated incredulously.

"Nobody."

"There is nothing to do now," Abu said. "We will send a message tomorrow morning and see if they will let you stay, now that you have come this far."

The next morning, however, there was no need of messages. After running all evening through the bazaar of Aligarh, Gappu came to his parents' room, ashen and shaking. "Waji has been throwing up, and he has diarrhea," he announced.

No one knew what was happening, but a doctor came and forbade Waji to drink any water. It did not matter that Waji cried out that he was thirsty until he tried to lick his own sweat off his hands and threw up again. Apaji kept running to his room, but what could she bring him? She seemed close to hysteria, and every time she reappeared, the children asked, "What is it, Apaji? What is happening?" All she knew was that her tall handsome nephew, with the black hair and dark eyes and skin shining with the healthiness of the village, was reduced to screams of "water." There was no water to give him except a herbal concoction that the doctor left behind, and Waji did not want that. It made him throw up even more, and it seemed as if his insides were flowing out of him.

At dawn the children were taken next door for breakfast, and Apaji remained behind with Waji, who looked like a skeleton. His arms and legs were reduced to bones. Apaji massaged his legs, but

23

Waji kept rising from the bed, dazed and delirious, and all he could do was cry and pull at his chest that gulped the air with all the force left in his body.

By ten o'clock the children were ushered back into Waji's room. The stink of vomit hung in the tight air, and as they filed past him, they could see the plea for water in his dried eyes and the veins standing out on his strong neck. Apaji was crying quietly, doubled over on a chair, her head buried in her sari. Waji who had been silent for hours let out a piercing scream with all his energy, and Apaji leaped to her feet. She started to run in desperate circles around his bed. Seven times around meant that she had asked God to take her life instead of her nephew's, who until that day had the breath and air of Nehtor in his voice, and milk and honey in his body, and now after eating *gol gappa* and *chat* and a whole variety of sweetmeats, in the bazaar of Aligarh, was lying in the bed with his own vomit and sweat, dead of cholera.

Raheel and Abu begged Apaji not to make the seventh circle for the sake of her own children. "It is too late," they pleaded. All their pleas seemed to fall on deaf ears.

Again the children were hustled out of the room. There was blood in a corner of the living room where a sacrificial goat had been slaughtered, and the butcher was humming prayers to himself as he skinned the animal and carved its flesh.

Although they had only just returned from Nehtor themselves, the whole family was loaded into a caravan of black taxis, and they brought Waji's body back to his parents' home in the village. The entire journey Apaji cradled Waji's long shrouded form in her arms, and delivered him silently to Nani and Uncle Reaz and his pink-cheeked wife, whose soft skin was pudgy like butter, and all Waji's sisters, who collapsed in a heap of mourning which claimed their laughter and their songs for the next year. Through it all, Gappu remembered Apaji's ghostlike face, weeping only when she thought the others could not see, holding locked up inside her the guilt that she, who had never lost a child, had allowed her brother's only son to die.

Standing still on the gangplank, Gappu could feel Apaji's back, warm and moist beneath his hand. The thin material of her sari blouse heaved up and down as she gasped for breath in the hot air. Karim and Gerrar, pressed up against the ropes on either side, watched her face. Her eyelids dripping with perspiration fluttered heavily over her rolling eyes, but they could see her fighting to stay alert, to keep Raheel, who was one step ahead of them, and Moïd and Mona, who were practically standing on her feet, within her line of vision. Gappu prayed that she would not faint, that she would stay strong just a few minutes longer.

He could see that his mother was using all her strength not to collapse on the gangplank. They were almost at the top, and Gappu kept saying, "Apaji, you made it through the trains, you made it through Waji's death, now just make it a few steps more, and you will never be sad again."

They were close enough now to the main deck of the S.S. *Shiralla* to observe what was going on at the final gate. They could hear the twanging voice of the British officer who stood at the top examining tickets. He was arguing with the family up ahead, and every time the officer spoke the tips of his red-tinged walrus moustache twitched on his upper lip.

"Sorry, old man," the officer was saying. "But you do see my position now, don't you?"

"But it's only a printing error, I tell you," the distraught man was insisting.

"Here let's have a look at it again." The officer took the ticket and scanned it over the bridge of his nose. "If only it were a different sort of printing error, but I really cannot permit a man with a Hindu name to get on a boat full of Mohammedans heading for Pakistan, now can I?"

"But my name is Shah Nawaz."

"It says here Sri Nawaz, now doesn't it? That's a Hindu name, I believe."

"Yes, but my name is Shah Nawaz, and that's a Muslim name."

"My good man, I am acting in your best interests. If I let you on this ship, there is no telling what might happen. A Hindu among all these Mohammedans. The British-India Shipping Company simply cannot take the responsibility."

The man looked up at the officer helplessly. His wife and two daughters had begun to cry, and the man was losing his grip on his valises. "What am I to do?"

"Well, I guess there is nothing to do but go back where you came from." They all looked down the gangplank at the dock, crowded as ever, with the real or imaginary hordes of angry men waiting behind the police lines for any victim who dared to stray backward once he had decided to leave India for good.

"I have no place to go," the man said, close to sobs.

"Now that's not the responsibility of the British-India Shipping Company, and I am afraid there is no more time to argue now. You will have to move."

The family of Shah Nawaz, or Sri Nawaz, made an almost imperceptible movement away from the entrance to the ship.

"Unless," the British officer said.

"Unless?"

"You might purchase another ticket under the name of Shah Nawaz."

"You mean right here? From you?"

"Yes, but quickly, quickly."

"But I sold everything to buy this ticket."

"This ticket is no good," the officer said, and seeing he could not make a sale, impulsively grabbed Shah Nawaz's ticket from his hand. "How do I know why you want to go to Pakistan? You might be a Hindu spy, for all I know. Now move fast, or you'll be pushed. We have to bring back a batch of your kind from Karachi."

Hands seemed to materialize from nowhere—coolies' hands and the hands of other British petty officers—and they started pulling him down the gangplank, hanging onto the ropes. They pushed into Raheel and Gerrar, who had to squeeze tightly together in the center of the plank against Apaji and the children. It was miraculous that no one fell overboard. Shah Nawaz was calling out prayers and curses all at once, and his wife and daughters were sobbing loudly.

Several times Rehman opened his mouth to speak out in favor of this stranger, but he bit his tongue and thought of his own wife and his own eight children, and the possibility that their tickets, too, might be invalidated by some preposterous logical fallacy. He could see that the officers were willing to disqualify anyone they could from passage and pocket the profits from a second sale.

One more family remained, and then his own. Rehman felt for the tickets under his shirt. They were secure, pages and pages of pink and yellow paper, for each child and for Apaji and himself. He watched the officer's bulbous face, the pale blue eyes where he felt he could read no emotion, could discern no flicker of recognition. From the bottom of the gangplank he could hear Shah Nawaz's cursing voice shatter into wails. Rehman could see him over the heads of his children, and the tightly packed mass of bodies twirled together on the gangplank. He felt his tongue thick in his mouth with arguments for the officer. It was so obvious that the man was Muslim: the flowing cloth of his white pajama suit, the neat black beard sculptured onto his sharp-boned cheeks and chin, the white prayer cap tilted on his thick mass of curls, the lucky talisman *tabeez* with a prayer from the Koran at his neck, the haunted look of disinheritance in his eyes and empty naked hands—everything about the man identified him as Muslim. Rehman knew he should have raised his fists, grabbed the whole family by their arms as they fell against him and looked into his eyes, but he had also seen Apaji below him, Sara clutched in her trembling arms, and he choked on his words of protest until it was too late.

Gappu had also been hoping his father would not speak; he should not even breathe. They were so close to their goal beyond which there were no other goals. Still, if Abu did not speak, who would speak up for them when their turn came? The answer was a resounding no one. No one had spoken when they disposed of their home, and no one spoke when they left half their luggage at the railroad station, and no one spoke when they went through the customs hall, dragging and kicking the bundles that remained, and no one would speak now even if they were told to dispose of half their family.

27

Only the tikka and the Koran were left. The night before, Abu had thrown a bundle of valuables in the face of a customs official who had demanded a tax for their departure, but he had hidden the tikka and Koran and slipped it to Gappu in the morning. It was still there under his shirt. Abu had said, it is the same Koran that your grandmother Dadi kept with her when we crossed the river Indus. When I married your mother, Dadi gave it to me and said this Koran saved your life when you were a child, and someday it will save the life of your son. The river Indus was in Pakistan now, but then, when Abu was only three years old, it had been in India in the desolate western portion of the Great Indian Desert, tearing open the sands with its waters from the Himalayas.

Dadi had told the story often on hot summer afternoons in Nehtor when the children were forced to stay indoors for naptime but were unable to sleep. Although Dadi kept the air circulating with huge green and purple fans made from peacock feathers which her thick country wrists wound and wound in the air over the bed, the three brothers lay coiled with excitement, waiting for the wrist to stop and Dadi to fall asleep, so they could escape to the courtyard and over the wall and into the gardens and fields of their village for endless adventures. They only had to be careful that they did not come reeling home, yellow with sunstroke or scratched or muddy or bitten by a snake.

Dadi ordered servants to bring water in the silver tumbler reserved for Abu, which made the water taste coldly metallic. She sent Bashir, the servant child who was their own age but did not have to sleep, out of the white shaded sanctuary of the house and down to the baking brick streets for ice to crush with salt into tall glasses of spicy milk. She read them poems and showed them secret chests filled with coins from faraway places like Saudi Arabia and Tashkent, but the only thing that could keep them still on especially restless afternoons, when a race had been planned and the bullock fed well in advance and washed down so he would be ready for the run, was the story of the river Indus.

All day, Dadi told them, she and her husband Mubarik and Abu, who was then a small child, had hidden along the river's edge, their bodies wet with perspiration on the dry planks of the wooden boat. The sails were down, and Dadi watched the masts for hours, tipping toward the water as gusts of wind got stronger and the rains began to come. The sandbanks, with spiny growths of cactus and sand snakes wriggling out of the desert like animated shadows, kept disappearing as the surge of tide vomited them miles back into the valley of Dera Ghazi Khan. The flooding continued for three days and three nights, and as she lay in the bottom of the canoe, with Abu on her lap, Dadi sometimes heard the slow ringing of camel bells, which might be a trader, uninvolved in local politics, en route between Afghanistan and Delhi, loaded with cloth and hides and dried fruits, or it might be a scout from the private army of the Nawab of Bahawalpur. Dadi waited for hours after the camel bells faded into the distance for the sounds of horses and men who were hoping to divide her husband's flesh.

As she told her story, the children watched Dadi's long oval face fade into the masses of her gray hair, which she let hang like a tapestry about her shoulders and into her lap when she was hidden in the women's quarters where no man above the age of ten, other than her own offspring, was allowed to see her face. Her voice was deep, and the desert winds were in it and she seemed to moan like the sound of the storm and she rocked back and forth cross-legged on the ground between their beds, as the boat had rocked when the lightning came, and the oarsmen pulled down their sails. They were searching for a fordable crossing, sailing all night and hiding by day in coves, which they would wake up in the cruel sun to find had disappeared.

The westerly winds kept pushing them back and widening the river between them and Rajputana where the local Maharajas did not care that the family was of the highest caste and did not believe the superstition that pieces of their flesh and hair were lucky talismans.

The highest caste, the Syeds, were direct descendants of the Prophet Muhammad's only daughter, and the desert tribespeople coveted them as much dead as alive. Dadi's husband, Mubarik, was also the only man who could read and do calculations in the entire valley of Dera Ghazi Khan, where the Nawab ruled his sands with armed men on camel- and horseback. They tore their meat like tigers and collected taxes from the peasants, who carried water for miles on their heads to scratch pale vegetables out of the land and feed their spindly goats.

Dadi told them that she and Mubarik had lived within the old walls of the Nawab's palace for several months. Shortly after Abu was born, they had gone to Tashkent, which was now in Russia, to settle the matter of their ancient lands. On the long journey back to India, the Nawab had allowed them to rest in his palace. As payment their grandfather had served the Nawab, writing letters and documents and deeds, but he missed the fields of Nehtor, and the mango gardens and the fresh streams pouring through the land. He was always missing India and its crowded roads filled with singing children and its cities filled with merchants and its universities filled with books. One morning he had told the Nawab, he was leaving with his wife and his only son, and he ordered the camels to be prepared. That night his servants came to him and in whispers told him the Nawab had decided not to let him go. They advised him not to wait and litigate but to hurry. There was no time. Camels were too slow. The Nawab's horsemen would catch them before sunrise. "Quickly, quickly," they all told him, packing his coins and papers into boxes. "You must leave by the Indus River."

"But monsoon has begun. There will be flooding."

"That does not matter. It is your only chance."

They told Dadi that an educated man was a rare enough commodity in the valley of Dera Ghazi Khan, but a man of the highest caste, the Syeds, would never be allowed to leave: "Instead, they will carve your flesh and pass it out among all the members of the Nawab's clan and wear bits of you around their necks. There is nothing so precious as the flesh of the family of Syed."

When they were seated in the boat, someone dropped the miniature Koran into Dadi's lap. She did not see who gave it, but its tiny crisp pages were all illuminated with golden flowers, and the Arabic words sang in her ears. Dadi kept the pages open in her lap for the entire three days they spent on the river. She had to feed opium to Abu to keep him from jumping about, and with his sleeping head resting in her lap, she read and reread the book, moving her lips with the words. On the third night when the moon broke through the cloud-cluttered sky and seemed to light a passage across the swollen water, Dadi thanked God and swore the book would be passed on from generation to generation to protect all her sons as it had protected Abu.

Gappu felt the Koran against his chest, and knew that of all their possessions, this was the one thing that must not be lost. This book was their ultimate security. Gappu did not understand why his family seemed always destined to have to flee and hide. It could not be because of anything his father had done or his grandfather, whose only desire had been to live and die in Nehtor. Now so many others shared their fate. The whole of India, it seemed, was on the move, and half of the Muslim population was here on the gangplank. He thought that in Pakistan, which had been given to them, fresh as a baby, this would never happen. Never again would half of Punjab and half of Bengal empty out as if earthquakes and tidal waves had rifted their lands wider than the river Indus.

When Abu had slipped the Koran and the tikka into Gappu's shirt, he had said, "You carry this, so that I can lead your mother onto the ship. If we are lost, you should still bring the tikka and the Koran to the promised land." Gappu had looked into his father's tired face. Abu had been eating animal fodder while the children sometimes had bread.

"I have no energy, Gappu. When we climb up the gangplank, you will be behind the rest of us. You will have the tikka and the Koran. You will watch your mother to make sure she does not faint, and you will watch the children so that they do not drag her into the water."

Gappu felt his trouble-making days were over. He knew he had been responsible for half his parents' anxieties. He had dragged his best friend, whom he called Kali Soori, the black pig, into the canal when he knew Kali Soori, son of the postal clerk, could not swim, and when he almost drowned, the entire family had sat with the postal clerk until Kali regained consciousness. They had to pray and sacrifice a goat, and they offered many gifts of atonement to the family. They finally had to take Kali Soori into their house like an adopted son whenever they went to Nehtor. Gappu remembered hiding with Kali Soori behind a stall in an alley of the marketplace, and eating pork, the most forbidden food for Muslims. He had watched Kali sucking the grease on his long dark fingers, and that night he cried and threw up all over Dadi's courtyard. He knew that Abu had despaired of him as a student, and each year he had brought home failing marks in at least one subject. Abu shouted at him and told him he was good for nothing but quail shooting and bull racing. Every summer he led Karim and Gerrar into the woods and fields on snake hunts, and into river rapids for swimming and fishing. Time after time they sneaked home with fractured wrists or deep gouges where a bull had gored their legs. Dadi let them do everything under the sun, and afterward Apaji would bandage them, her tears dropping on their cheeks, and tell Gappu never to play with his younger brothers again. Gappu remembered making Karim go with him into Dadi's chests and handing over fistfuls of coins and bangles to a beggar. Dadi had always told them, Whatever you give to a beggar you will get ten times back in this life and a hundred times in the other life. Gappu had wanted the world, and he had believed he was buying his fortune with Dadi's gold. Gappu wished he could tell Abu that now he could be trusted. He prayed he could live up to Abu's faith and help make Apaji strong.

Gappu saw his mother faltering. He was being pushed from behind and then from in front by the nimble coolies swinging along the ropes and rushing down the center of the plank as if no one were standing there, crashing into their heads and legs, for another load and another payoff. There were five more steps. Apaji was drenched in perspiration. Gappu could feel it on her back, but she was not saying a word, trying not to let her eyes close, and clutching on to

Sara with every ounce of strength in her arms which were now throbbing with numbness.

It had all been decided before they left Aligarh that the whole family would go or else none of them at all. Dadi and Nani would be waiting in the village of Nehtor for their children and grandchildren, not knowing they had decided to go the other way. It was all decided again when the tickets were bought for the train and the ship, and the luggage was exchanged for the passage and food. It was all decided with every step up the gangplank that they were going together, and no one must fall.

Gappu remembered seeing a little Sikh boy, his long hair spilling in streams out of a handkerchief tied around the topknot on his head, walking around in circles on a railway platform with his mother's breast in his hand. Gappu and Karim had seen him together, in a flash as if in a mirror, as their train lurched and creaked through a riot-torn station somewhere in the middle of India. It was not something he and Karim could discuss, although Gappu could feel his brother's narrow shoulders quivering against his own. Now the memory rushed into his mind with the sun glare in his eyes and the blood-stained water gushing below the gangplank and Apaji's back hot and wet beneath his straining fingers. He wanted to remind Karim of the little Sikh boy, tell Karim to help him with Apaji, so that their mother would not end up like that, her breast slashed off by a knife, the breast that had fed all the children, the breast that had strained to feed a dying infant at the railroad station in Allahabad. Gappu shook his head and tried to clear his mind of all the thoughts that were clouding his vision. With the back of his hand, encumbered by the objects he was carrying—the flask of water, the smelling salts, the tikka and the Koran he was trying to protect beneath his shirt, Abu's pistol, and the last hundred rupees Abu had given him—he tried to wipe the perspiration from his eyes. They were all going together or not at all.

Suddenly Apaji's back was heavy in his hand. Gappu lunged toward her, and the flask of water slipped from his hand, splattering on his feet. There was no water, and the smelling salts would not work without water. He could not even bend his knees in the crush of bodies to soak the salts in the water lying on his sandaled feet. Raheel grabbed Sara from Apaji's arms, and she was shouting frantically at Gappu. They were all shouting at him: "Do something. Apaji has fainted."

Abu seemed so far away, though he was just ahead of them. In desperation Gappu smeared the salts on his face, so that the perspiration would wet it, and in a frenzy he stuck his fingers inside his mother's nose, rubbing the salts first on himself and then on her.

Rehman was already facing the British officer at the top of the plank. The square bulk of the Englishman's pink body filled up the entire entrance to the ship, firm and neat beneath his trim white shorts. Rehman prayed that the officer had not noticed Apaji in the middle of the plank, covered by the children in their frantic attempts to revive her. Rehman knew that the British had a simple system. If there was the slightest infraction of the rules, if they could bump someone off for any reason at all, they just stopped the person then and there and sent him back down the gangplank.

Everyone had been warned in advance that they would have to slip a packet of cigarettes to the officer at the entrance to the ship, and it should be filled with enough money to pay for the number of people in the family. Rehman proffered the package stuffed with bills to the officer, hoping to distract him. If someone fainted, that was it. No amount of money was enough for someone who was stupid enough to faint on the gangplank, and Apaji had fainted. Now it was certain they would not be able to get on board.

Gappu saw the officer point to the coolies just below their family group and heard him say they should take Apaji back down. He heard his father's screams, and for the first time, Gappu was crying, "Please, please, make it just two more feet up," and Abu was making frantic gestures to hold the coolies back while shouting instructions at Gappu, and Raheel and Karim and Gerrar were telling him what to do until it became unbearable.

The vultures had found their way not to let the family of Rehman Hussain get on the ship. "Let us on the ship," they all shouted. The parents had been convinced that if they all were together, all ten of them, they could act as a cohesive force. "Let us on the ship," they all shouted again.

Apaji should have eaten, instead of praying all the time and taking care of the children. All her life she had eaten the best food; the freshest of wheat was slapped into breads right over her fire, and mangoes had come from the village in bullock carts and poured into her kitchen, and all her servants came to her in her marriage contract, which stipulated a new one for every child along with a baby water buffalo bought while it was still inside the cow's stomach. How could she protect her children from a scavenger's knife if she had not eaten and her frail body was fainting? Filthy-looking men in tattered clothes were waiting below the boat. Their tiny canoes were bouncing on the churning waves, and the water was bloody, and their knives were flashing.

The coolie was coming toward Apaji; Piari was still on his shoulders. As he touched Apaji, she suddenly revived. "Get away," she shouted. Gappu's hand was still supporting her soaking-wet back, but he felt the energy snap into her muscles. "I will strangle you with my hair," she hissed at the coolie and screamed as he touched her, so that he lurched backward and Piari almost fell from his thin naked shoulders.

"We cannot let a sick woman come on board," the British officer told Rehman.

Rehman roared. "Listen. I am leaving behind everything. I used to own a hotel for the English where I had to put up signs that no colored man was allowed, and I could not show my own children the rooms since they are dark-skinned. Even that I have left behind, and I have had enough. I have nothing against India. It is you who have forced us into this position."

"Let me see your tickets," the officer said, and he examined them as he had all the others. He counted the family of Rehman Hussain, moving his lips.

"There are ten of you."

"Yes. Yes."

"This ticket is for nine."

"I don't believe it. Let me see."

"Take my word for it. Only nine are coming on this ship."

Rehman roared again. "What can I do?"

"My advice is that you leave the oldest one behind. That is always best."

"No. No. My wife will not part with one of them, and I will die for them. Let us on this ship."

"Not a chance."

Rehman remembered why the ticket was only for nine people and not for ten. "Look at the rules and regulations and see for yourself," he said. "One of them says that children under the age of three are allowed passage free. This baby is only one month old."

"Not a chance," repeated the officer. "Every passenger must have a ticket; otherwise we will not be able to supply the government of India with the information. We are keeping very accurate records."

"And, sir, are you keeping records of the extra profits you are pocketing by denying us passage and reselling our space?"

The pushing from behind began again. No one was interested in the discussions at the top of the gangplank for long. If you discussed too much, the crowd pushed, and that took care of you. Apaji had already decided that if she died, there was a better chance that all her children would make it to the promised land.

Rehman had always won by argument. He was hard on the officer with the walrus moustache, and he did not know how far he could push him. He had nothing left but logic; the officer had power. "Have you ever had a mass migration from London?" he asked the man.

"Are you going to reduce your number, or should I throw one overboard?"

"Babu Sahib, forgive me for all the sins we have committed by keeping you in our country. You came empty-handed looking for food, since you have none in your country, and your black iron and coal were not worth the dirt they were buried under. The fact is you came empty-handed and hungry. You took diamonds from our country, and you gave us guns. What more do you want of us? Now you send even the people of India out of India, and you take our possessions and occupy our houses. I curse your country, and I pray for a thousand revolutions to divide your British Isles, like the severed limbs of the Hindu and Sikh and Muslim children I have seen in my land."

"That's enough of this rubbish," the officer commanded, but Rehman could see by the distorting of his red face that the man was shaken. "There is only one thing that will get you aboard this ship."

Rehman could see that the officer was afraid of him, afraid even though he had nothing, even though his power was nowhere but in the energy of his mind. "What is that?" Rehman asked.

"You can buy a ticket for one more of your bloody brood. If you've got the money, hand it over. Otherwise you've got thirty seconds to decide which one to leave behind."

Rehman felt the gold coins in the belt strapped around his stomach. They were the last of his fortune, worth at most a thousand rupees, the price of a passage, but he had promised them to the coolie. He looked at the coolie with Piari on his shoulders. If he reneged on the gold coins, the coolie would drop Piari into the water or run with her and abduct her into the streets of Bombay, where she would be raised as a slave and a prostitute if she did not die first. A fair-skinned child was worth a lot to a pimp, and a coolie could be anything—charas smoking, fenny drinking, a hand in every sordid activity Bombay could dream up in all its back streets and hot rooms. Each of the older children had a hundred rupees tied in a cloth around his arm, but four hundred rupees was not enough. Even if it were, then what would they do for food? They would surely starve. He watched the coolie who himself lived half starved on the wharves of the city like a sea gull scavenging for a few annas and crumbs of food. He saw his daughter clinging to the coolie's head with her fragile hands.

"Well, have you the money or not?" the officer demanded.

"I don't know," said Rehman, searching the face of the coolie, the narrow slit eyes and coarse brown skin wrapped in an old torn and dirty rag which served as a bandanna. The coolie was Indian, too, which meant that he had to hustle to survive, but could he throw the family at the mercy of this white Sahib, whose skin and nasal garbled accent had become so despicable?

The coolie moved a step toward Rehman. "Take the child, Bhai Sahib. You have given enough already."

Too dazed to speak, Rehman hugged Piari to his chest while unstrapping his money belt with his other hand. He let it fall at the British officer's feet, who pushed him headlong onto the deck of the ship. "And take your bloody litter with you."

2

Summer Largo

The beginning of the summer had been so long ago: it was remembered like a dream more vivid than reality.

June was always the most exciting time of the year. The last painful days of school finally came to an end, and Gappu, Gerrar, and Karim returned to their home in Aligarh. But vacation never truly began until the family packed their trunks, locked up the big house, and left for the countryside.

The three brothers could hardly wait for the family to unload themselves of winter and head for their villages of Nehtor and Milak. There had been vacillation enough during the spring, and now that the decision had been made to leave Aligarh, there was no time to wait for furniture to be wrapped in cloth, for objets d'art to be stored in the room-sized closets, or for saris and summer clothes to be ironed and packed into the huge wooden trunks.

The servants had to be instructed: one placed in charge of the house keys; another given possession of the keys to the closets and safes. Once again an intricate system of checks and balances would be worked out, so that if a servant on Apaji's side of the family caused a disturbance, another servant would inform Rehman Hussain, and vice versa. The banks were notified; business contacts invited for a last tea, and some told to come to Nehtor for a week of hunting and rest.

This year Abu had almost decided not to go to Nehtor. India was passing through momentous times—freedom from British rule after two hundred years. Contracts and treaties had already been signed, and the day of independence was looming before them.

Everyone was talking about the new government of Pandit Nehru and the parliament that would make its own constitution and laws. It seemed to the children that Abu's conversations with professors and lawyers and business friends would go on forever. Each afternoon they moaned to see a new caller come up the long circular drive in front of the house to sit with Abu over tea, and probably remain for dinner and long into the night, discussing politics and religion and the new country, Pakistan, that was being created for Muslims only. It had been impossible to pin Abu down about leaving for their summer vacation. As soon as his guests left each night, Abu went to sleep, and in the morning he was gone from the house before anyone else was even thinking about getting out of bed.

Already school had been out a whole week, and there was nothing to do in Aligarh but sit under the ropelike roots of the banyan tree that sprawled and branched all over the front lawn. Moïd, Mona, and Piari played in the grass, running up and down the shaded garden walks and picking jasmine and rat-ki-rani petals from the flower beds, which Raheel wove into garlands for their hair and wrists. Half the city, it seemed, had shut down for the summer season. The Aligarh Muslim University was closed. The students and professors had gone back to their country homes and villages. June was the best part of the summer, before monsoon, when the countryside would be full of quails and ducks for hunting, and the waters of the canals, a cool respite from the long heat of the day. Aligarh was dull. There were no parades or speeches, and important men were deciding issues in other cities. The excitement of independence was elsewhere.

In May, at his boarding school in Delhi, Karim had been let out early one day, because it was said that Gandhiji would speak before a crowd. It was only two weeks before the end of the term, and the professors had practically despaired of teaching the fourth-grade students another thing. Like his classmates, Karim was given a rupee for transportation to New Delhi. Rather than waste the money, he and several of his companions bought sweetmeats instead and jumped onto the back of the most crowded bus, stuffing halvah into their mouths as they held on to the careening bus with their sticky fingers. As soon as the bus passed the Red Fort on the outskirts of the city, they saw streams and streams of people heading toward New Delhi, the capital city of India. Nobody was going in the opposite direction, and traffic was completely clogged. Everyone was heading for the darshan, or sacred glimpse, of Gandhi. The boys jumped from the bus and ran and walked down the broad boulevards of New Delhi and through Connaught Place with its shops and colonnaded walks, past gardens and fountains and big colonial houses, where brown-skinned girls pushed little English babies in prams.

In the distance they heard a great roar from the people. The crowd was in clothing of a thousand colors, from dazzling oranges to the deepest purples, violets, reds. All the arteries that converged on the square were seething with cheering, singing people. They were standing on the lawns and wading in the reflecting pools and fountains that stretched back from India Gate—the Roman triumphal archway in the center of the enormous square—to the red domes of the capitol building gleaming in the distance. Some boys, who had climbed to the top of India Gate, unfurled the flag of the Congress Party with its symbol of Gandhi's spinning wheel in the center of the green, white, and orange tricolor.

"Jai Hind. Jai Hind. Hindustan Zindabad. Long live India," they shouted, and the crowd burst into the national anthem, screaming it, rather than singing, "Jai jai jai jai jai Hind."

It was truly One India, *Ek Hind*, and Karim shouted along with everyone else and threw his emblem cap into the air, never to find it again. He felt his blood pumping through his body at the thought of India, Free India, One India, India my love. He kept moving closer to the India Gate. The crowd was bursting with energy and joy. Arms entangled him and embraced him: "I am Indian. No more will

41

I read *K* for King and *Q* for Queen in the *King's Reader*. I will go to my father's hotel. I will burn the sign that says Colored Not Allowed. I will put Mahatma's picture in every room of Abu's hotel."

He found himself separated from his companions, and he was hurled from stranger to stranger, his countrymen, his friends. The crowd parted for just a moment, and jumping to look over the heads and shoulders still in front of him, Karim saw the tiny man in a white loincloth pass silently on his bare feet. Gandhi smiled but his eyes were stern. The crowd quickly enveloped him again, and everyone went crazy yelling, "Gandhiji ki jai. Long live Gandhi."

Two weeks later, school was out, but Karim still basked in the glow of having been inches away from the most important man in all of India. Gandhi had seemed to greet him, to touch him personally, as the brown body moved serenely through the swollen mass of people, the delicate bald head glinting in the sun and the furrows of skin resting on his neck and naked bony shoulders.

Every afternoon since he had come home to Aligarh, Karim was forced to sit at tea while his father's business friends questioned him. Abu would come to the verandah of the house and call his three older sons inside. On this particular afternoon, Zamir Hakim was visiting. The rich lawyer wore a new set of crisply starched white pajamas each day and gave the old ones to the poor. The finest embroidery was filigreed at the neck and wrists. He raised his teacup carefully between two fingers and sipped over the cuff of his ample white beard, which he flattened against his chest with his other hand. Both hands were festooned with diamond and sapphire rings, and a gold watchband gleamed beneath the soft transparent weave of his sleeve.

"What did Gandhiji say?" Zamir asked, smiling benignly at Karim behind large black-rimmed glasses.

"He said we are all brothers."

"What else did he say?" Rehman coached.

"I didn't hear him say anything else," Karim said, embarrassed. No one had asked him before what the Mahatma had said. It had not seemed important. Most people only wanted to know what Gandhiji looked like, how he smiled, who was helping him walk on his stick-like bowed legs.

"Karim is stupid," Gappu piped up. "He didn't listen to what Gandhi was saying."

Karim was furious and would have punched Gappu for being fat if they had not been sitting properly at the long dining-room table for tea with the "oldies."

"I could hardly hear Gandhiji's voice; it was so thin and squeaky," Karim told them. Zamir continued to smile at Karim, and Rehman rose from the table and ushered his guest out to the verandah.

Gappu, Gerrar, and Karim followed and sat among the pillows on the floor at Zamir's feet. He was a distant cousin from Apaji's side of the family—the oldest, the most aristocratic and educated. Although his huge white house was just a mile away at the end of the street, his visits were rare and considered an honor. Apaji sat quietly in the far corner of the verandah, which wrapped around the house, watching the younger children play, and Raheel passed quickly in and out with bowls of cashews and oranges. The boys nibbled sweets from a bronze tray that one of the servants rolled out onto the porch. A fan whirred overhead.

"What of Pakistan?" Zamir asked Rehman.

"We have no reason to leave India," said Rehman, curling up in his favorite chair. "I did not vote for Pakistan. For those who did, I am happy they can go there."

"All my Muslim friends at school left for Lahore months ago. I was practially the only Muslim left in Dehra Dun," Gappu said, sitting cross-legged on the cool stone floor.

"Did anyone speak to you about that?" asked Zamir.

"Of course," said Gappu with surprise. "We talked about politics all the time. Most of my school friends are the sons of ministers and congressmen. They showed me the new flag of India which will be raised on the day of independence."

Rehman dismissed Gappu's remarks with an impatient wave of his hand. What could his children tell him that he did not already know? "We have all seen India's flag many times."

"But this is a new flag," Gappu protested angrily. "Instead of Gandhi's spinning wheel in the center, there is a picture of Ashoka's wheel."

"I don't see what importance there is in a flag," said Rehman. He had invited the lawyer to his house to discuss the meanings of the riots he had heard about in Bengal and Punjab. He had a family and many interests to protect, and did not want to waste any more time talking about schoolboys and flags and parades. "Why don't you take your brothers to play?" he said to Gappu.

Gappu was angry. "Send the others to play. I have finished with playing," he snapped.

"Then find other things to do. You know ways to amuse yourself, I am sure." Rehman turned his soft white pajama-clad body away, and Gappu marched off the verandah with Gerrar and Karim, his hands thrust deep into the pockets of his knee-length shorts.

Out of habit, Rehman reached into his silver box for a cigarette, but reminded himself in time that he must not smoke in front of his distant cousin and wiped his wire frame glasses instead. Zamir was a Haji many times over, which meant he had made several pilgrimages to Mecca. He had also been around the world and studied in England for his law degree.

Zamir smiled over a glass of water and adjusted his smooth beard that was tucked neatly at the ends into his white dhopi cap. "There is more significance than you imagine in the flag your country chooses for itself," he said.

Rehman looked up, abashed. He felt rebuked for having dismissed his son, who had obviously impressed the learned man more than Rehman realized, but he still pooh-poohed the notion. "Flags are for waving in parades," he said.

"They are also a symbol by which people express themselves. They are like anything else that is painted on a wall or worn in a lapel. They are the signs of the times."

"And what does this new flag of independence mean then?" asked Rehman.

"It is the symbol of a united India, the same India that stretched from ocean to mountains and desert to jungles two thousand years ago under the emperor Ashoka."

"I believe in that," said Rehman.

"It means there should be no Pakistan, even though the people voted for it."

"That's just the problem," said Rehman. "Now that the people have voted and Pakistan will be a reality by the end of the summer, Pakistan must be. We are morally and legally bound to Pakistan. Yet I cannot understand the fear of the people that One India will not be a secular state. There are many people who fear that in the name of democracy, which Mr. Nehru advocates, powerful and middle-class Hindus will take Muslim land and keep it for themselves, instead of distributing all the land, Hindu and Muslim alike, among the people. Many landholders who say they would be willing to give up their lands to move India forward into the modern world are now afraid it will not be accomplished equitably. I do not know if those people are going to Pakistan to preserve their land or to create a democracy where Muslims will not be forgotten."

The lawyer nodded. "As you say, Pakistan has been voted into reality. I think that as long as Pakistan exists, a unified India symbolized by the empire of Ashoka cannot be. With this new flag, I do not think India will rest until all the diversity of peoples and languages and customs on our subcontinent becomes a single economic and powerful force in the true sense of nationhood today. We will continue to fight among each other, and every state with a grievance will look for nationhood as have the Muslims who are going to Pakistan. The British have played a King Lear in encouraging our differences and contracting to us a divided house."

Rehman looked out over the lawn. Apaji had joined her children and was sitting in the shade of the banyan tree, her fingers working over bits of deep red satin and threads of gold and silver, preparing dresses and blankets for the new baby that was expected in August. Although it was already June, there was not a sign of protuberance beneath the folds of her bright green sari, which whispered in chiffon around her body and splayed out on the grass. He knew that it was customary for the children of his family to be born in Nehtor, on special sheets that both grandmothers, Dadi and Nani, kept in their secret storage rooms and at the hands of the same midwife whose family had brought generations of Nehtoris into the world.

Zamir rose to go, extending his hand to Rehman. "There is no reason for you to go to Pakistan," he said. "I think you should take your family to Nehtor. I know they are anxious to be leaving."

After seeing Zamir to the gate, Rehman strolled over to Apaji. The children were all stretched out around her in the shade of the banyan tree, and the glaring white sun leaped through the broad leaves. The children were lethargic, and the only respite from the oppressive heat of the low-lying town was the endless round of cold water that their servant boy Bashir brought from the icebox, where at least ten bottles were kept filled all the time.

Karim looked up at his father accusingly. "When are we going, Abu? When does the packing begin?" he asked.

Gappu was morosely pulling up blades of grass and clover from the lawn. "I have heard rumors that it may not be safe to leave a house all locked up in the hands of servants during these times," he said without looking up.

"What's wrong with these times?" said Karim, jumping to his knees. "I think that these are the best times, and summer is the best of all."

Apaji was laughing. "You should not question your father like that. He is busy thinking what is best for us, and maybe he will tell us when he makes up his mind."

"I have been speaking to your cousin Zamir at length," Rehman said. "He thinks there is no reason to alter our plans. Nothing can happen in Aligarh. We are too strong here. Tomorrow we are going to Nehtor."

Nehtor, Nehtor—it was the place all the children of Rehman Hussain dreamed of going. Every summer after school their ancestral village represented a haven of complete independence, even from the restraints of their parents. They had learned from infancy how to play one set of grandparents off against the other. Although both grandfathers had died during the last five years, both grandmothers, Dadi and Nani, were still there to see that the summer passed slowly and dreamily for them as the bird-filled orchards and the broad flat fields ached in sunlight.

At the tiny railroad station of Dhampur, where only one train a day managed to stop, Apaji's father, Daroga Mumtaz Hussain, Chairman of the entire district of Nehtor with its five hundred villages, as long as he was alive, had always had everything prepared for the arrival of his children. The servants continued his practices. The Darogaji had several horses trained to go to the railway station by themselves and pick up visitors.

Gappu's horse, Yellow, was the best of the lot. Shining and cream-colored, he always led the rest of the pack. When Gappu was coming he was tense with excitement. Usually Moonah or one of the other servants would whack Yellow on the rump, which was the signal for the horse to go to the station seven miles from Nehtor and wait. When strangers were coming, Moonah knew he had to hit Yellow with the stick well in advance, because the horse did not take orders to pick up just anyone, and he would walk most of the way, munching the tall grasses and wild flowers and breathing the air just as Gappu liked to do. When Gappu was coming, it was a different story. All Moonah had to do was to whisper in Yellow's ear, "Gappu is coming," and the horse would take off, kicking up his hoofs and galloping the whole seven miles.

One time, just for a joke, Moonah had whispered "Gappu is coming," when there was no Gappu at all. All night Yellow had waited in Dhampur, and the stationmaster complained that nothing would shut the horse up. He whimpered the whole time like a child. He balked and kicked the stationmaster, and finally Moonah was made to walk all the way to Dhampur to retrieve Yellow, who was not likely ever to forgive him.

The three oldest boys and their sister Raheel jumped from their compartment as soon as the train pulled into Dhampur. For twelve hours they had been confined with their parents and the little ones in their second-class compartment. First class was reserved for British only, and third class was a weltering mass of people going for short stops, carrying their chickens, cloth, and a myriad of merchandise. Wandering saddhus in their saffron robes, carrying nothing but a stick and possibly a sack, camped on the floor. Bangle salesmen with ropes of glass bracelets of every hue sat beside traveling magicians and flute players. There were troupes of entertainers, dressed in patched motley, with painted faces. Snake charmers led their mongooses on a rope and their heavy sacks with the sleeping cobra inside were bulbous on their shoulders. There was always music and loud arguments, sometimes about politics and sometimes because someone was taking up too much room on a seat. Second class was the dullest place to sit—betwixt and between, neither luxury nor life. At every station the boys got off the train to watch the endless show that India unwittingly staged.

At Dhampur, however, few people descended onto the sleepy country station. Everyone knew the family, and the stationmaster came to smile and tip his hat and exchange the greetings and pleasantries of summer.

"Where is Yellow?" Gappu asked. He paced the dusty road among the horses and tongas and bullock carts bringing loads of sugarcane to the train. "That Moonah must be off in the woods somewhere."

"Here's Yellow," said Karim, pointing down the road where the horse was coming at a trot. The three brothers and Raheel took off to meet Yellow and the two other horses following behind.

"There's no horse for Raheel," said Gappu. Raheel complained loudly, but it was explained, she was now too old at twelve to ride a horse, and she would have to wait and come in one of the tongas with the rest of the family and their trunks full of clothes and presents.

The boys leaped onto the horses and were off before the luggage was even loaded into the bullock carts or the slow procession of tongas was ready to start. It was not long before they left the road, where their passage was thwarted at every turn by lumbering carts loaded with produce—rice, mangoes, sugarcane—and pulled by slow grunting bullocks and oxen. Gappu, who was a superb and fearless horseman, led his brothers through the maze of footpaths that twisted through the fields and woods from village to village, ducking beneath the low hanging mango trees, where the first fruit had already begun to turn ripe yellow or green and pink. The boys took the opportunity to stuff themselves full of the half-sweet fruit before any adult could warn them that they would break out in hives, which they always did.

The outlying Hindu villages dotted the fields in small clusters of tan clay. It seemed as if each village were an abstract sculpture, conforming to the contours of the undulant earth. Each hut merged into the next, turning corners as a single coil and embracing miniature courtyards in their midst, filled with chickens, cows, and small children. The dry mud walls were painted at the entrances with figures of gods, birds, and animals. In the paddies, water buffalo hot with fatigue shared the labors of planting with the farmers, sweat pouring from their taut skin as they rode the wooden blades of their plows. Girls in sun-colored saris padded lightly across the furrows in the marshy paddies, balancing clay water urns on their swaying hips.

The first brick houses of Nehtor were ringed by the jute huts of the bhangis, or sweepers. They were the so-called Untouchables, the outcastes, Gandhi's children. The dry mud and dusty flats over which they lived swarmed with children, and young mothers who juggled their bright wedding saris, petticoats, and shawls, so that there was always one article of clothing being washed while the other was worn, until the color was sun-bleached to faded brown. Gappu and Gerrar were always surprised to see the smiling teeth, the clear skin, and dancing eyes of the painfully young faces already tending several babies. Gerrar, especially, who had left Nehtor the summer before with a new abiding interest in girls, peered into their deeply brown faces as they looked up from the well where they had gathered to draw water, wash clothes, and gossip.

The boys guided their horses over the canal that separated the center of Nehtor from the countryside. Along the banks the dhobis,

49

or washers, were pounding cloth against the rocks. Buffalo were nosing heavily through the water, and almost naked children in loincloths were swimming among them.

Nehtor was a wilderness of orange brick. Every house, or mahal, created its own mahalla, including within its walls, gardens, courtyards, stables, and the quarters of shopkeepers. The narrow brick streets and alleyways, twisted among the walls, under archways, and opened out occasionally on tree-rimmed ponds. Ducks and swans floated among pink-flowering lotus pads in the clear water. The rich Muslim families of Nehtor considered sewage their first priority. Since there was no modern plumbing, the severest penalties and even whippings were imposed on anyone caught defecating in the ponds or urinating in the streets.

For the first week in Nehtor, the boys did nothing but eat. An endless round of relatives, from the oldest uncle to the most distant fifth cousin, was waiting to entertain Rehman and his family, to hear about the city and be able to bask in the honor that the favorite grandchildren of the favorite child of the Chairman of Nehtor had sat in their house, complimented them on their sweets, and had a second tea. The only trick was not to be caught overeating by Abu or Apaji, and at this they were very adept. It was with good reason that Gappu had earned his pet name, which meant fatso. His round cheeks were a golden tan, and only over the past winter had his limbs begun to stretch, his nose become slightly firmer and elongated. A light brown fluff of hair had sprouted on his lip and sideburns, but it only seemed to accentuate his pink glow.

As their horses' hooves clattered over the cobbled streets, the people of the town came to their doors and ran out of their houses to watch the fabled children come. Young girls, already observing purdah, peeped from windows and accidentally let the black veils slip from their faces, so that they could smile at Gappu and Gerrar, who was so handsome with his shining black curls and delicately boned features that he had recently learned he could have any girl for the asking. Karim called out to everyone, waving his arms and swiveling on the bare back of his horse with exuberance. He kept lagging behind to chatter with women, who greeted him from behind their veils, and to laugh with shopkeepers. Gerrar and Gappu had to warn him to keep up. The children were truly the patriarchs of Nehtor. Apaji was the only daughter of the Darogaji, and by Indian law she had inherited one third of all his lands. By their marriage, she and Rehman had brought together virtually all the surrounding lands and villages for miles and miles.

The streets and alleys of Nehtor were barely wide enough for the wheels of a bullock cart, and during the monsoons when they gushed with water and mud, there was no navigation at all. Everywhere the high walls converged on narrow passageways. The tiny orange bricks had been baked centuries ago in the families' own factories under acres and acres of soft moist clay. After generations of intermarriage, almost every building belonged to them. This, combined with extrafamilial marriages, linked the entire community together in an intricate clan of Nehtoris, which Persian scholars found difficult to decipher as they poured over the lacy scrollwork of family trees and ancestral record books. Even the few Hindu families were related. Before his marriage to Nani, the Darogaji himself had married the daughter of Lala-ji, the rich Hindu moneylender, from whom it was said the children's grandfather had stolen a large amount of gold and almost demolished his empire in the ensuing fight.

Even when they were not related, the Nehtoris were tied to the family by generations of continuous service. The local tradespeople had come in the sixteenth century with a great-great-grandfather as horse traders and arrow makers. Finding peace in the circularity of life on the Indian plains, they bent their forging instruments to other purposes. The arrow makers became iron forgers who made tools and the sharpest plows and wheels for bullock carts. The *teergars*, or bow makers, opened shops for firecrackers, which were used to celebrate marriages, engagements, and births. Cloth weavers utilized the cotton crop to pattern decorative sheets and blankets. An oil maker crushed mustard seeds on an iron tablet, which was rotated hour after hour by a drowsy bullock. The air was filled with the crying sounds of the mill where wheat and grains were crushed into flour.

Obediently, all the tradespeople and shopkeepers and farmers waited for the Darogaji to tell them which field was in need of fertilizing, and they went there to defecate. Old men and tiny children wandered from the surrounding walls of the mahalla every morning and at sunset to crouch in the appointed field. Together they all ate the rich produce of the three yearly harvests, and they were all buried in the same graveyard, and in time were washed back into the devouring earth.

Gappu pulled up Yellow at a strategic point where two alleys turned, the blindest, most secluded spot in all the streets where on moonless nights the ghosts of their ancestors were said to gather, and no one dared to walk.

"Where should we go first?" he asked his brothers. The choice was a difficult one. No matter which grandmother they picked, the other would complain that the children had not come first to her. Dadi's food was the best, because she insisted that no servant should feed her sons or grandsons. She alone, and her two daughters when they lived at home, were allowed to touch the food that would make the men in her family as tall and strong as she. On the other hand, Nani was always quietly respectful, in her proper austere way, and she was sure to give them some prized trinket or let them go to the market with an extra allowance. After much debate they decided to go to Nani's first and leave the feast with Dadi for later.

Nani's house was called The Nest. It had been built for her by the Darogaji when she became his fourth and last wife. Not only did Nani have the fairest skin and a body as slim and graceful as a child's, but she brought with her the mango gardens, the crowning jewel in the Darogaji's fortune. The Nest formed an estate in itself. Tucked into the surrounding walls were the homes of a cloth weaver, an iron forger, and a miller. Around the periphery were fishermen's clay huts. The fishermen went every morning to the nearby tributary of the Ganges and brought the best catch to Nani. Their wives sat in the shadows of the rooms behind the open doors and windows, knitting coils of jute string into nets, and in an alleyway a small rough-hewn canoe was waiting for repair. The wives served the Darogaji's family in various ways. While they were still

52

young and childless, they had danced for the old man. Late at night their sullen songs could be heard.

The Nest itself was constructed around four large courtyards, and settled within a still larger garden laden with trees, flower beds, and duck ponds. Gappu, Gerrar, and Karim entered through the deep brick archway. The garden was glowing in sunlight. The boys dismounted and left their horses to wander among the flowering bushes. Everything was quiet. Since their grandfather's death two years before, few villagers came to the huge courtyard which had always been accessible to anybody and served as a sort of Diwan i Am, or hall of the people. One judged his own status by how far he could proceed into the inner sanctums of the mazelike house where its many courtyards were bounded by the private studies, bedrooms, salons, and dining rooms of the immediate family.

As always, the garden was in perfect order. A servant was dousing the hot bricks of the courtyard with water from the severed neck of a goatskin pouch. Nothing had changed, and it seemed as if their grandfather would come riding up at any minute, standing bareheaded in his tonga behind two white horses, his dyed orange hair brushed to wisps of fluff around his deeply tanned face. Nani still never used the public courtyard since she practiced purdah and entered only through her own garden, adjacent to the men's. Her maids and women who came to call followed suit. It was an unthinkable invasion for a man to wander into the private garden of the women, filled with the substance of feminine afternoons, silk-embroidered pillows, and musical instruments.

Karim raced along the colonnade off which were rows of little storage rooms and outbuildings, all trellised with vines. He ducked behind the khus, a curtain of sweet-smelling desert weeds that were sprayed with water and continually blew their musky perfume through the inner rooms of the Darogaji's private quarters.

"Come quickly," Karim called, motioning to his brothers to follow. "We can have a look at Nana Darogaji's rooms before anyone finds us." Gerrar dashed after him, and Gappu followed behind, giving Yellow a pat on the rump.

53

Their grandfather's formal sitting room was bathed in the perfume of the khus, and the half-light from the heavily draped curtains
made shadows across the large brocaded sofa, the deep plush armchairs, and lamps made from Chinese urns. Delicate Mogul minia-
tures—oil paintings of courtly musicians and palatial scenes—hung
on the walls. Darogaji's old gray mastiff, who had outlived his master, was snoring steadily before the massive fireplace.

Karim stopped to admire the poem framed on the mantle. When
Nani married Darogaji, besides gold, jewels, silver, cloth and servants, factories and land, her father had bequeathed the poem. It
had been hand painted by the most-renowned poet in Delhi and
sung up and down the streets of Nehtor and in every village, praising her forever as the diamond sitting on her father's knee, the song
in his ears, and the joy in his heart. The poem ended by ad-
monishing Nani never to forget the poor.

Behind the sitting room was Darogaji's private entrance and
courtyard. It was completely secluded behind a brick wall, and only
Darogaji's study, bedroom, salon, and bath opened onto the small
rectangular garden, which was lush with flowers and a row of willow
trees. It was just large enough among the bushes and vines for his favorite chair, a bench, and an oversized charpoy, a bed of jute rope
strung tautly over a frame of mango wood.

Gerrar had already entered Darogaji's bedroom, where even
these favorite grandsons had rarely ventured before, and never without their grandfather. He called to Karim and Gappu to come inside.
Everything was exactly as Darogaji had left it, and the boys felt
afraid to breathe as if at any moment the old man might descend
upon them and discover them snooping through his things. A clean
sheet of woven cotton was spread on the charpoy, with a myriad of
pillows, and over these hung the sheerest of mosquito netting, rolled
back on one side to look like the canopy over a throne. A lantern was
lit on the Persian prayer rug where Darogaji had knelt at every
sunrise and sunset. It was almost as if they could see their grandfather sitting there, kissing the floor between his sculptured moustaches, just as the muezzin called the Azan through the freshly stir-

ring air, and everything was tinged with orange like the color of Darogaji's hair.

On a nightstand, gleaming from a highly polished silver frame, was a photograph of Darogaji sitting sternly on his horse beside his most trusted friend and servant, Moonah's grandfather, Allah Baksh. The servant held the highest position in his own hierarchy, and in his own way wielded almost as much power among those he dealt with as the Darogaji himself.

Allah Baksh had grown up with Darogaji, and it was imagined that they must have played together, if one could ever think of the two old gentlemen playing. Slim and willowy but muscular, their delicately boned faces were ringed by their graying hair which was freshly dyed each week in a preparation of hinnah. The orange hair gave the dark-skinned men a torrid, continuously ironic, expression. The only noticeable difference between them was the deep scar wedged into Darogaji's brow, inflicted by the first of twelve men he had killed, all distant cousins, to avenge his father's death in a land dispute.

The two men had rarely been seen to speak. Perhaps words were not necessary. They had both known their positions and their roles, and one inspired as much fear as the other. When the two legitimate sons of the Darogaji went off to college in Aligarh, Allah Baksh's son, Mollah Baksh, went to college, too. While Darogaji's sons studied philosophy and Western literature, living in the finest hostels, entertaining and buying Italian suits and English bowler hats, so that after six years the first son had dropped out and the second had to pay a huge sum to his professors for his degree, Mollah Baksh studied agriculture.

He came home on vacations and brought basketloads of mangoes into his room, which was studded with flower pots and piles of treated soil. By the time he graduated, he had elevated the mango gardens to the point where Darogaji could sign the largest contracts in all of India for the export of mangoes. Mollah Baksh could crossplant mangoes with any kind of fruit, other than banana, coconut, or dates, and every tree bore fruit of a slightly different flavor. Some hinted of peach or plum; others, of apples and berries. The mangoes were sent to places as far distant as South Africa and Turkey.

The relationship between Darogaji and Allah Baksh continued until Darogaji's death in 1945. Half servant and master, half friendship, half business. It was a total interdependence. The one owned the land; the other held its secrets—both owned allegiance.

Allah Baksh accompanied Darogaji on the week-long trips each month to survey his villages and lands, except during monsoons. Darogaji would clatter through the streets, standing bare-headed in his tonga, the sun glinting off his red hair, and the reins of his two white horses whipping through his hands, while Allah Baksh sat behind with the week's supply of food. Every village bore their offspring, for with the exception of his four legitimate wives, every girl whom Darogaji desired automatically became the wife of Allah Baksh.

When they returned home, the household retinue scattered before them like a flock of frightened birds, and the women hastily vanished into their own quarters, drawing their cumbersome burkas tightly across their heads, and peering out like caged mice. Darogaji would disappear immediately into his private bath, where he heaved the frigid water in his *ghara* over his hot dusty brown skin. The large iron pot was still kept filled with fresh water.

Beside the charpoy was Darogaji's hookah, which Allah Baksh had prepared for him every night. He made sure that the stone was properly grinded for the chillum—a triangular bowl of slightly glazed clay—and filled it with home-grown tobacco and molasses prepared from Darogaji's own sugarcane fields in the factory on the outskirts of Nehtor, which was managed by Darogaji's eldest son. It was imagined that the two men smoked, passing slowly and wordlessly the long snakelike cord bound in silk and larded with silver, through which the smoke was filtered.

In a corner of the room, Darogaji's weights were stacked against the wall. Allah Baksh had reported that even on the day of his sudden death, Darogaji had grasped the forty-pound weights in either hand and swung them over his head. Now Allah Baksh polished the black iron weights each day when he cleaned the quarters, but he never lifted them himself any longer.

The only other thing in the room was a life-size portrait of Nani, which hung directly in the line of vision from Darogaji's bed. She was a silent but beautiful woman with black hair braided to her knees, nervous deep-set eyes, and a quivering mouth. Nani's marriage to Darogaji negated his first three, and all those earlier offspring were relegated to brick homes at the edges of far-flung villages of clay huts and sugarcane fields. Nani had quickly produced two sons and the prized daughter, Munir Jehan, who all her life was called Apaji, or first sister. Apaji looked exactly like Nani, and was the only female child born to the Darogaji in all his marriages.

Nani derived her power from her aristocratic heritage and the fortune she had brought her husband relatively late in his life. No one knew much about her first adolescent and childless marriage. Most said it had never been consummated and it ended in divorce with the sad husband disappearing in shame from the entire state of the United Provinces. A few of the boldest relatives said that the first husband had died and that Nani's hand was not unsoiled by his death. The rumors were never permitted to reach Nani's ears or the ears of her daughter, but it was also believed that Darogaji himself had been well aware and also implicated. Whatever the case, even the children knew that Nani had brought her own lands to her second marriage, plus the lands of her first husband who had been an only child.

The fifteen grandchildren of Darogaji were the only ones who dared to call the two landlords Nani and Nana. They rushed through the house and into every corner, sat upon their knees, and pulled their clothes. Karim remembered when he was only five, sitting at tea with the Darogaji, gorging himself on mangoes and sweets. "You eat too much for a black-skinned boy," Darogaji told him in his smooth voice.

"My skin is only as black as yours," Karim answered. "And my hair is not orange." They all laughed, and Darogaji took his grandson on his lap and covered him with kisses.

Gerrar yanked Karim who was staring at the portrait of his grandmother, fresh and young in her bridal clothes. "We can't keep Nani waiting any longer. She will wonder where we are," he warned.

Karim nodded and followed his brothers out of the little room that seemed to him like a living museum, and through the half-sized wooden door that connected the two grandparents' gardens. Nani was presiding over her courtyard. A group of women in their best saris squatted on the benches and on the ground, while Nani whooshed here and there, ordering tea and responding to conversation with an occasional nod and her endlessly darting and probing eyes. She wore a satin *gorara* of forest green bordered with silver thread, six yards of cloth sewn into a voluminous skirt that blew about her ankles. She chewed thirty pans a day, leaving a trail of shells from the betel nuts she cut with metal prongs. Her hands were constantly busy working the nuts into a deep green betel leaf to which she added a mixture of sweet herbs from her *paan dan*, a special silver filigree box, where the pink and green and brown and yellow ingredients were separated into neat compartments. There were rose petals and jasmine buds, dried nuts, cumin seeds, and jelly made from a combination of flowers, along with calcium in a white paste, and a pile of moist aged tobacco, gleaned daily from her husband's humidor.

She was so adept at chewing paan that her lips never showed a trace of the blood-red juice which oozed from the betel nuts, and she showed no affect from the strong mixture which made the children drunk when they tasted it.

"Good! I am glad you have arrived," she said as soon as she saw her three grandsons. "What took you so long? I have been waiting."

Gappu, who was already a foot taller than she was, twirled her around and around and made her laugh, and Karim ran to her arms for a hundred kisses. Gerrar hung behind, waiting until the excitement was over. In the latest manner he had learned at boarding school, he brought her small hand, with rings on every finger, to his lips and bowed in the English style.

"Gerrar," she said, "my son. I have needed you most of all. What have you been learning in Dehra Dun?"

He smiled and said, "Nothing useful, Nani. I have more to learn from you."

She ran her fingers through his thick curls. Gerrar was the smallest and most fragile. He reminded Nani most of her own family. Unlike Gappu who was only one year older, Gerrar showed none of the awkwardness of early adolescence. His olive skin was fair by Indian standards, and his eyes were shining brown ovals fringed by long black lashes. Nani could see her northern Kashmiri ancestry in his chiseled face. Although Gerrar was the quietest and most remote, he was charming with girls and women whom he feasted on. Gerrar's main goals in life were to please Nani and quietly to cause enough damage and destruction, so that he would be banished to the village of Milak where he knew every farmer's daughter intimately. Some said Gerrar had become a man at the age of six, and the public ceremony of his circumcision some years before had aroused the greatest curiosity among all the female relatives of Nehtor. Nani's goal for Gerrar was for him to become a doctor, and she had him practice on any sick child that came to her attention in the villages. "Your great-grandfather willed you to become a doctor," she reminded him. "Have you studied any medicine," she asked as she did every year.

"Not yet, Nani. They don't teach medicine at boarding school."

"But you have decided to become a doctor?" she insisted.

"Not yet, Nani. But I will let you know."

"No matter," said Nani. "There is time to discuss that later. I have been waiting for you, and I need you."

All the women who had come to call on Nani in the courtyard rose to go, but she motioned to them to sit again. No one really wanted to leave. They knew that the real excitement was just beginning. Any grandmother with any sort of dowry worthy of the name had a trustee, who alone among all the other members of the family knew the secret hiding places of the lady's treasure, and knew the contents of that treasure and its worth. The trustee was never a son or a daughter, but always a grandson and usually the favorite son of a favorite child. Dadi's trustee was Karim, for Dadi complained that Gerrar was too quiet and did not appear manly. Nani called Gerrar's silence determination, and prized him as the only one trustworthy enough not to spill her secrets into every anxious ear, of which there were enough to fill an entire city. Gappu could never be a trustee. As an eldest son, it was understood that Gappu's first loyalty must be to his own father, and this would never do, not considering the intricacies and politics of the families, or more appropriately, the mega-family of Nehtor, where husbands and wives, brothers and brothers, and certainly sons-in-law and cousins were not safe from each other's desires and needs.

Everyone knew when Gerrar disappeared with Nani, they were going to some portion of her treasure. It was the same when Karim disappeared with Dadi, who prized his innocence, his sense of humor, and his fighting spirit, which she called loyalty. At the same time there was no tangible reward for being the grandson selected as trustee. The grandmothers tried to be fair to the hilt, and superiority came only from the distinction that the particular grandson had been chosen and that he had knowledge that no one else possessed. From then on, it was the object of every relative, servant, and associate to try and pry the information from the trustee, because information was almost as useful as possession of the treasure itself. Every trick was employed, including suspicion, bribes, and threats.

As soon as Nani and Gerrar disappeared into the innards of the house, the courtyard buzzed with comments and questions. Nani's maid, Saddiquan, who in Nani's presence had not said a word but had passed out water among the ladies with a half-concealed sneer on her lips, now flung out her skirts and sat down in the center of the courtyard, laughing. She pinched Karim's cheeks and rubbed his arms with her fingers. She was the only one besides Nani to wear a *gorara*, and the cloth made a wide arc around her form as she sat. It was obvious that Nani and Saddiquan did not like each other. Still the woman remained year after year, serving sullenly and laughing behind Nani's back.

Saddiquan had the family of Daroga Syed Mumtaz tied three ways. First, it was a known fact all over the mahalla that Saddiquan's fourteen-year-old daughter, Jilla, was the child of Darogaji. There were very few things that were known with such certainty of fact even in the relatively closed circle of the Daroga's estate, and it was probably known beyond that, in the other houses of Nehtor where such matters were usually never confirmed beyond firm suspicion. Jilla looked exactly like the old grandfather, from the broad forehead, high cheekbones, and slender lips, to her startling height in an otherwise short servants' family. It was also said that Jilla's older sister was the favorite of Nani's son Reaz, for he never permitted any harm to come to her, and Jilla herself was known to play with Gerrar. She had been delegated the role of nurse to his game of doctor.

Saddiquan was also the chief cook, and had been as long as anyone could remember. The family tried other cooks, but no one else would do. Only Saddiquan could prepare the chick-pea bread, so that it did not become chewy, or cook the rice to fluffy perfection, or not stint on butter, in order to save some for her own family. Besides, Darogaji's principle had always been, "A thief known is better than a thief unknown," and if Nani defined sex as thievery, the principle was as applicable here as anywhere.

All the boys liked Saddiquan's daughter very much, and they wanted to know where she was. Jilla's particular job was to massage the legs of all the children between the ages of six and fourteen, after their baths and when they broke their limbs playing in the fields. It was customary among Indian families for growing children to be massaged by their servants, but the boys considered Jilla the most expert and lovely masseuse. It did not matter that Nani hated Jilla as much as she hated Saddiquan. When Nani was around during the day, or on warm nights when she lay in the courtyard, not too much attention was paid to the maid servant and her daughter, but there was quite a bit of mixing during the long darkened hours of monsoon nights when rains slashed the courtyards that separated the rooms of the massive house.

"Has Gerrar decided to become a doctor?" Saddiquan asked, laughing.

Gappu and Karim were furious at Gerrar for having disappeared with Nani before they had a chance to eat. Their purpose in coming here first had been to eat with Nani quickly and then leave for Dadi's house before their parents and brother and sisters arrived and tied them down. They knew Gerrar's doctor game very well, and they were getting sick of it.

"Gerrar will never be a doctor," Karim told Saddiquan.

"We know what he's up to," explained Gappu. "He doesn't lift a book all year and then pretends to Nani that he is a serious student."

"Your Auntie has been praying in the mizar for him, you know," said Saddiquan. "Your Auntie wants him to marry her daughter Rosey, even though she knows Apaji is against marriages of cousins. Your Auntie thinks because her son, Waji, died in Apaji's house, she can make an arrangement at least with Gerrar, and she went for a whole month to a mizar far away from Nehtor. The Mulvi does not like it."

They all knew that the subject of Gerrar was a very touchy one in the family. It all began, Saddiquan explained, when Gerrar was born, and the old great-grandfather had said, "This child will be a doctor." His own son by a former marriage—one that was discredited—had studied to be a doctor. The dispensary was all built with marble floors and waiting rooms, and supplied with the latest Western instruments, including a table for surgery. The day the son returned to Nehtor with his diploma in hand, he died of cholera, and had never even set foot in the new dispensary or used the instruments. Nani said that her stepbrother should not have become a doctor and that nobody in the family should ever try this again. Yet the old great-grandfather, upon seeing Gerrar in his granddaughter's lap, proclaimed that this child would be the new doctor and would inhabit the dispensary, and commanded Nani to see that it should be so.

Apaji had cried and said she would not let Gerrar be a doctor, but it was as if Gerrar had heard and understood the decree even from his cradle, and for as long as anyone could remember, Gerrar became the Doctor Sahib. It was now the task of all the female members of the family to pray that Gerrar would not die if he really decided to become a doctor. Trips began to mizars all over the district and the state, to which they brought offerings of cloth and grains. When Apaji took a sheet to one mizar, Nani brought two sheets to another mizar, but the local mizar of Nehtor had the most powerful legend of all, and it had grown rich in offerings of blankets, jewels, and animal skins the women had left there through the years, making wishes and above all hoping to thwart the curse that prevented any Nehtori from practicing medicine.

The mausoleum of yellowed marble stood ghostlike and solitary in a field of towering sugarcane, just at the bank of the old canal. When the water was high and the sugarcane ready to be cut, the empty fields seemed to cry in pain, and the canes creaked as they swayed, threatening any man who dared to walk among their knife-sharp edges. It was said that a hundred years ago an old man, Mungo Peer, passing through the district, had seen the water of the canal rising, until with freezing fingers it trickled over the mud banks of the dam and ran in red streams through the brick streets of Nehtor. Everyone slept while a gale drenched their houses, and farmers lay huddled beside their hearths, watching their thatched roofs and praying they would not blow away. Mungo Peer ran through the town pounding on the iron doors of the estates, but no one came, and his voice was silenced by the wind and the hailstones that clattered to the ground.

Finally he ran to the dam and held it all night with his work. He piled stones half his own size onto the melting walls and packed dirt against the sides. He shivered with cold, and the next day when the people of Nehtor found him, he was covered with red clay and was practically indistinguishable from the walls of the dam themselves.

Mungo Peer, whose name meant "begging priest," settled in Nehtor and waited for his payment. At first the gifts of rice and grain were abundant, but soon Mungo Peer was forgotten, and no one knew or cared how the reclusive stranger nourished or clothed himself. When he died, he called the Mulvi to his side where he slept in piles of old rags and rancid sheepskins. "Since I was not paid for saving the people of Nehtor, I curse them and their children and their homes and their fields." As news spread of the curse, the elders gathered together and offered Mungo Peer in death the payment they had forgotten to give him in life. They built a mausoleum, or mizar, at the highest point along the canal, so that he would watch over the waters as he once had done so long ago.

The Mulvi from Nehtor stayed by the grave for a week, praying and accepting the offerings of cloth and semiprecious stones, but on Thursday night a lion appeared and clawed the Mulvi to a pulp and devoured all the gifts. Now it was said that if a woman went on Thursday night and placed gifts upon the grave, the lion would come and take them and her wish would come true, but the woman had to be very careful that she was not caught by the lion or she would be finished off, too.

Saddiquan told them that the present Mulvi of Nehtor had advised Auntie to weigh Gerrar in wheat and leave the offering at the mizar. "Your auntie will be coming soon," Saddiquan laughed. "With that daughter of hers to cover Gerrar in flour and pray that he will survive, so that he can marry Rosey and make her the doctor's wife."

"What are you telling them?" Nani snapped as she appeared in the doorway with Gerrar behind her. "You are always frightening the children when you should be feeding them."

Saddiquan sneered, as if to spit, but hoisted up her skirt, so that Gappu and Karim, seated on the floor, could see right up to her thigh, which was long and pale and silky.

"It was only the story of Mungo Peer," Karim explained.

Saddiquan tossed her hair and her hip. "I was telling them that Gerrar is going to marry Rosey." She laughed again. "Would you like that, Gerrar?"

"I'm not marrying anyone," said Gerrar, and Saddiquan winked at him as if to say, "Not when you can play with my daughter Jilla on those summer afternoons in Milak by the electric tube well. My daughter is also the child of the Darogaji, just like you and just like that brat Rosey."

Nani did not like Saddiquan's wink, and she picked up a broom as if to sweep her away. "Don't you see these children have been traveling all night? They have not been fed properly in days. Why do you sit and chatter when there are breads to be made and milk to be boiled?"

"Yes, yes." Karim cheered her on. "We want food."

"You talk too much, Saddiquan," said Gappu. "And you are as lazy as ever."

Gerrar said nothing, but Saddiquan was satisfied. As she entered the kitchen, she called Moonah, the servant child, to her side and told him to run to Milak with a message for her daughter Jilla. "Tell her that the Doctor Brother has arrived and that she should prepare herself and rest. No more work," she whispered.

Dining in Nani's home, even breakfast, was a formal affair. Saddiquan appeared in the courtyard, all seriousness and subdued, and announced that the meal was prepared. All callers and guests left quickly, and Nani ushered the children into the main room where the sixteen-foot English-style dining table was laid with cloth and bowls of fruit. Piles of chapati, or flat breads, were wrapped in lace napkins, and the steam made them moist. Each child sat lost in a cushioned armchair while Saddiquan and her entourage of young girls, usually the daughters of the fishermen who lived beside the house, brushed past them, serving omelettes mottled with herbs and spices, poured their tea and milk, and peeled their fruit.

The girls had a very short tenure. They worked only from the time they first began showing signs of breasts until their first pregnancy. Their faces were always the same—dark and hidden, with wet shy eyes and half smiles. They had the odor of spices in their skin, and their hands were stained pink with herbs.

Forks and spoons were laid at each place, and Nani cut her omelette into small bits before wrapping it in pieces of bread. No one ever saw her chew. It was not proper to speak during a meal, and the children obediently filled their mouths with the delicate morsels, waiting for the passing out of candies at the end of every meal. When the Darogaji was alive there was often music with the meal, and male servants also would come and go, bearing messages and papers to be signed. Now men were banished from the dining room.

Only Allah Baksh still dared to enter, as he had always done. He stood just beyond the door to the cool room which was covered on every side with shades of sweet-smelling khus. Allah Baksh lifted the khus and stood outlined in the white sun. He looked for a moment so much like the old Darogaji that he gave Gappu a start. He wore the same tight trousers, creased just up the middle, and a long red scarf of Dacca muslin around his neck, covered by the orange hinnah-dyed beard. His feet were slender and pointed in black velvet slippers with gold threads, and his face was browned by the sun, with a thousand wrinkles and a million secrets in his mind. He coughed before entering the room, and Nani turned toward him with a frown. She never got used to his sudden entrances, and she did not like to have to hold her shawl across her face while she was eating.

Karim ran to him immediately for the trinkets he always carried in the deep pockets of his peasant's blouse. He had so many children and surrogate children wherever he went, that he always had to be prepared. Gerrar and Gappu at fourteen and fifteen were too old for trinkets, but they wanted to see what he had brought, and he showed them tiny lacquered figurines of farmers with plows and bullocks with leather reins.

"I was sent by Apaji," he told them. "Your family has gone first to the home of your Auntie and Uncle Reaz to pay their respects, and you should meet them there later."

Nani looked sideways through her shawl at the old servant.

"It is only to be expected," he explained. "After Waji's death last year."

"We won't speak of that here," Nani warned Allah Baksh, in her sternest voice. "Why did they send *you* with the message?"

Allah Baksh observed her mood and stepped backward from the dark mahogany table, his hands folded neatly behind his back.

"It was Rehman Bhai's wish that the children see the Mulvi before they proceed any farther in the town. The Mulvi has sent word that he expects them to come immediately to the mosque to learn their lessons. He feels there is not a moment to be lost with trouble brewing in Aligarh, and times such as they are."

"What trouble in Aligarh?" Gappu piped up. "There was no trouble in Aligarh. We were there yesterday."

Allah Baksh ignored Gappu's question. "The Mulvi heard that Karim has been to see Gandhiji, and the children have been singing 'Jai Hind' and pledging themselves to the flag."

"And what is wrong with that?" said Nani. "India is a free country now. It is their country, and it is your country, too."

"Muslims should not be praying to a flag."

"A national anthem is not a prayer," said Nani. "I do not think you should put ideas like that into the children's heads. The Darogaji would not have approved."

"It does not matter what I think. It is the Mulvi who says these things."

The servant and the grandmother glared at each other, but she knew she would have to let them go. The Darogaji might have been in favor of sending the grandchildren to the Muslim University in Aligarh. He had even bought his daughter and son-in-law the house in Aligarh for that purpose, but that did not mean he was not loyal to the government, and it did not mean he did not wholeheartedly support the Free India movement once it became clear that the British would soon be leaving their land. Darogaji had always moved with the times. He had been friends with the English Sahibs to the point that they had visited his home in Nehtor and even offered him a knighthood, and Nani herself had had the unheard-of-distinction of having a white English nurse take care of her first-born son, who was at least two tones darker than she.

Darogaji had felt that India was inevitable, and so it was here upon them. If they could work for the English occupiers, they could work for the government of Nehru, and no power on earth would force them to leave their lands, not even the Mulvi and his treacherous prayers for Pakistan, a Muslim state. Still, in matters of religion, the Mulvi had the last word, and in matters of education, her son-in-law would decide, and she would pay for her grandsons to go to

67

universities in two-years time since that was what Rehman Hussain wished.

"Well, as usual you have come at just the right time. Take the children to the mosque," she said and rose to go. She kissed each grandson on the head. Gappu, she noted, had to bend way down to reach her now. He would be taller than his father soon, and the fat would stretch into extra inches of height. It had been true of all the males in the family of Rehman Hussain. That was one of the reasons she had consented to her daughter's marriage with this upstart from Dera Ghazi Khan and Tashkent, whose family had been in Nehtor for no longer than four or five generations.

As soon as they were outside, Gappu hit Karim across the back of the head. "It's your fault, you know. We have to go to the Mulvi because of you. He is going to have you circumcised this summer."

"Oh, no. Not me," said Karim.

"Why? Do you want to be a messy brat for the rest of your life?"

"I don't care," said Karim.

Gerrar did not care, either. He would spend a week or so basking in Nani's favor and eating Dadi's good food, but already he was laying plans for his escape to the village of Milak, with its endless fields of sunlight to lie in, and the water spilling from the electric tube well to swim in, and Jilla's legs.

"Allah Baksh," Gappu persisted. "You are not really going to take us to the mosque are you?"

Allah Baksh nodded.

"Really, only Karim must go to prepare for his circumcision."

"The Mulvi asked for all of you," said Allah Baksh.

"I could tell you something you want to know," said Gappu.

"No, you can't."

"I can tell you where Nani has hidden her gold."

"No, you can't. Only Gerrar knows that, and he is not talking.

Gerrar is a good boy. Besides, I don't want to know where your Nani has her gold."

Gappu was disgusted. Everyone wanted to know where Nani hid her gold and her contracts and her deeds, especially the servants. He was annoyed that Allah Baksh did not act more like a servant. He might have sent his son, Molla Baksh, to school to learn more about mangoes than anyone else, but his grandson, Moonah, still had to run messages and his son still had to water the gardens and pray for rain to come at the prime time, or everything would wither and nothing he had learned at school would do any good. If there was no rain just at the time that the bunches of white flowers appeared on the mango trees, the bitter fruits would die in their pods and never sweeten, and even if they did sweeten, it was Gappu's grandmother and mother and uncle who would reap all the profits— not Allah Baksh. Gappu would have said these things if Allah Baksh had not looked so much like the Darogaji.

Furthermore, Gappu's Uncle Reaz, Nani's son, had proven that Allah Baksh was not all that smart. When everyone was praising Allah Baksh for the mangoes his son produced, Uncle Reaz went to Aligarh and bought every publication he could find on sugarcane. Soon he had the tallest sugarcane in the entire state of United Provinces and opened his own sugarcane factory. Mangoes weren't everything.

"Allah Baksh," he said. "I'm not going to the mosque."

"Yes, you are," said Allah Baksh.

"If we go, will you teach us to kill a snake?" asked Karim.

"No," said Allah Baksh, and there was no more discussion.

For two hours Gappu, Karim, and Gerrar sat cross-legged on the floor of the mosque and recited the Koran. They vowed that they would never be caught like this again. They knew enough escape routes through the alleys of Nehtor, so that people like Allah Baksh could not trap them. They did not need an escort, and Gappu would complain about that to Abu as soon as he saw him. Once they were able to get into the fruit gardens, they could bribe the Mulvi out of lessons for a basket full of plums or bananas. The old priest was much easier to bribe than Allah Baksh.

When they finally arrived at Dadi's small white house for their second breakfast, it was already time for lunch, and Dadi was fuming mad.

"Skinny and sickly," she called them. "I know what your Nani feeds you, those skinny omelettes with too much pepper and dried-out chapati that you have to eat with a fork."

She had paced the floor of the inner courtyard all morning, going in and out of her kitchen to keep the fire crackling and adding more pieces of wood to her stone stove. The shadow had already moved from the east side of the courtyard to the west, as the house was strategically built to always be half in brightest sun and half in coolest shade no matter what the time of day. Her milk came from her own water buffalo, who inhabited a huge enclosure just beyond the walls of the house and stable. Her husband, Mubarik, had sent all the way to Punjab on the borders of the valley of Dera Ghazi Khan for a water buffalo he had purchased there, and the servant had walked the five hundred miles back to Nehtor, feeding the buffalo in every field and village before he ate himself.

To this day the old servant was known as Buffalo Man, and he tended all the offspring of the prized buffalo, carrying fresh grass and fodder on his head from Milak every day even when the rains turned the footpaths into rivers that circled about his shoulders and climbed into his face. This was Buffalo Man's only job, but it earned him quarters in Milak for his family and a special room in Nehtor adjacent to Dadi's house. He fared better than most of the retinue that accompanied Dadi and Mubarik from the valley of Dera Ghazi Khan. Those tough traders and camel riders and gun makers from Kashmir and Afghanistan found no use in the farming lands of the United Provinces, and they could not understand why the old man had settled there, never to move again. Only that Mubarik had been born in Nehtor and like an old elephant he crept back there with his only son to die. Except Mubarik did not die. He went on to purchase salt lakes in Jaipur Province and exported salt all over the world on his own ships. After he tired of ships, he bought hotels in Delhi and Agra and even in the sophisticated city of Calcutta. He developed so many interests, no one really knew where he got his money. The mountaineers and desert fighters, who had come with him from Tashkent and Kashmir, had to try to blend into the farms, but many of them moved away.

The animals remained, and Mubarik who had waited patiently for seven years for his beloved wife to bear their first son, soon had two more sons and a second daughter. His patience was vindicated along with Dadi's prayers that he not divorce her. She had visited every mizar that came to her attention and left fortunes behind at crumbling graves and at Mogul tombs in Agra and Fatehpur Sikri. Dadi was taller than her husband, and as large-boned as her spirit. She worked constantly for her three sons, feeding them four times a day with her own hands, grinding spices into powder for curries or massala, separating the whey from butter with a long wooden spoon so that only the clarified ghee remained and the rest was given away. Her two daughters worked by her side as soon as they could walk, because to her, daughters meant trouble, and a girl showing her legs at the age of six was naked and provocative. Apaji only brought her own daughters to Dadi's house at most once a month, whereas the grandsons were practically permanent residents there throughout the summer.

Dadi used all the local vegetables in a variety of dishes. She made her breads from grainy chick-pea flour, or from spinach leaves so that they appeared the palest green. She preferred pilaf soaking in mutton fat and studded with peas to the fluffy white rice that Nani used and Apaji grew up with.

At the birth of each grandson she gave Apaji six tolas of gold buttons for the baby's suits. Nani complained that Dadi neglected the granddaughters only because she was hoarding her gold, and Nani often questioned Karim, who was Dadi's trustee, as to her real worth. Karim knew that except for gold coins and many, many papers he did not understand, Dadi hoarded very little compared to what she gave away or used herself. While Nani wore delicate rings and bangles and fine thin earrings, Dadi wore cumbersome gold anklets halfway up the legs of her pajamas, which she liked so tight she had to sew herself into them every morning. She had heavy chains that covered her chest, and earrings so big they caused her ear lobes to stretch down the sides of her neck. Whatever treasure Dadi had, she seemed to wear it on her person for all the world to see.

Dadi wasted no time in stuffing the boys full of food. She sat them down on a carpet in the courtyard with their Uncle Salim, who never left his mother's home, and ordered milk still warm from the buffalo to be brought to them while she chattered away from her kitchen. She wanted to know if their father was mean to them. Had they ever been hit? Did their mother send them sweets and corned beef when they were away at school? Soon the warm chick-pea breads came dripping with fresh butter, and clay bowls were filled with milk.

"Eat faster," she complained. "If you don't eat fast, the food will jump up and bite you."

The boys were gulping the milk and the sweet breads, but not fast enough before whole shanks of mutton appeared saturated with tomato sauce and almonds, lying on a bed of brown buttered rice.

"See how your uncle eats. You cannot even see his jaws move before he takes another bite."

The boys' faces were smeared with grease. They could not even speak, with Dadi hovering over them and throwing food onto their plates. They licked their fingers, with butter dribbling down onto their wrists and forearms.

"Clean the bones, and then eat these mangoes," she said, plopping a whole basket down in their midst. Gerrar took out his pocketknife and carefully began peeling the outer skin.

"Who taught you that," Dadi demanded. "Eat them like this." She bit off the stem and stuffed a whole mango into Gerrar's mouth. "Now suck like I taught you to, and don't waste the pit."

Karim laughed at Gerrar with the big mango hanging out of his mouth and the juices washing over his chin. "What is for dessert, Dadi?" he asked.

"Dessert." Dadi hit herself on the forehead. "I forgot." Her fair color turned scarlet with embarrassment, and she rushed around the courtyard, calling for the servants. "Rashid, Babu! Where have they all gone to?" Finally she discovered Buffalo Man sleeping in the cool hay by his water buffalo's side in the outer courtyard. She aroused him with her foot and told him to hurry with the grain to have it crushed at the mill. Buffalo Man winced at the thought of venturing out into the 110-degree temperature, but Dadi warned him not to walk like a buffalo as he had learned to do, but to hurry back with the flour, so she could mix it with sugarcane juice and serve it to her skinny grandsons who had been deprived of food all year.

It was a joy to Dadi to see the grandsons sitting there today, eating so willingly. When Mubarik was alive, it was impossible to get them to sit still. First, they wanted to eat exactly what Mubarik was eating, and that was not the custom of the house. They wanted to know why they could not eat his extra portion, which was always put aside on a plate before anyone else could eat, but they were told that the portion was meant for a beggar. Her old husband would sit benignly smiling on his charpoy, blowing mellow gurgles of smoke through the water in his hookah, until he retired to his room and left it up to her to solve the problem of the children saying, "I won't eat this" and "I won't eat that." They had probably learned such nonsense from their maternal grandmother. The three boys would watch the servant outside their grandfather's room, pulling the string that worked the huge ceiling fan over the bed where he slept. The servant had been brought home because of his blindness, but Gappu was certain that hiring the old man, who always fell asleep, was a good trick on his grandfather's part. He could be no teller of tales, and it was Gappu's belief that his grandfather was not really sitting in his room smoking his hookah or lying on his bed, and not in the house at all.

Dadi had no way of knowing since she never entered her husband's private room, and had not left the confines of her white house and its courtyards and its stables in over thirty-five years, not since she came home from Dera Ghazi Khan, after the three sunstroked days passed in the bottom of a canoe on the river Indus, to discover that seventeen members of her family had died of plague in the course of a single week. Only she survived of all her brothers and sisters and first cousins, and she never left again lest her absence would bring another sickness down upon the lives of her loved ones.

When none of the family was left in Nehtor, and they were all off in Aligarh at school or in Delhi on business or Jaipur tending to the salt lakes, she still felt her presence in the house was essential to everyone's survival and continued good health. Mubarik had almost convinced her in the last years of his life to accompany him to Mecca to perform Haj, the duty of walking around the sacred stone from Heaven three times, after which a pilgrim must pray five times a day for the rest of his life or face eternal damnation. Even if a man who had been to Mecca lost the faculties of speech and all his limbs lay paralyzed in a heap, he must pray five times with his eyes or he could not be saved. Dadi, who was supposed to be so religious, really had considered going, but when all the bags were packed and they had said good-bye and given final instructions to the servants left in charge of the house, she remembered her months of captivity on the relentless sands of Dera Ghazi Khan, and the plague that had finished off her entire family in her absence, and the three days on the river Indus, and she never even crossed the threshold of the house. Only once a year she visited the graveyard, not far from her house in Nehtor, to pick up bits of the diminishing clay from her family's old graves.

By the middle of the summer, Dadi knew, the children would be restless during long meals and afternoon rest, because there would be other attractions like their female cousins and that vicious Jilla, the Darogaji's shameless bastard. Today, Dadi was relieved to see the children had been hungry, and she could berate the other relatives for their lack of concern and personal preoccupations. The children were all tired out from the train journey and from leaving Aligarh in such a hurry with all that she knew was going on there, and from riding to Nehtor on those wild horses the Darogaji had kept for them, and sitting with their Nani in her strained household and reciting the Koran for the Mulvi in the mosque. It was no wonder they made no fuss when she left them sitting in the courtyard without dessert to go to sleep.

74

Dadi remembered last summer and Karim's kite-flying. He had sat up all night, crushing bits of glass until his hands were cut and bleeding, so that he could make the best string. Then he led his poor tiny brother, Moïd, up to the roof, and they both fell off, breaking their wrists, despite the fact that she had ordered the wall to be built another foot higher and had watched her son Salim laying the bricks to be sure he did not stint or run off to play carom and chess in his room with the pretty teen-aged girls he obviously preferred to his own wife, who had finally divorced him.

She also remembered with a wince the day she had found all three boys taking turns on each other's shoulders to peep through the window where their cousin Mia was taking a bath. She had heard their giggles and their comments about the fact that Mia had so much hair growing between her thighs like a dog's tail.

Dadi did not know if she had been more shocked by their comments or by the fact that Mia had not yet begun to shave herself, as all Muslim girls were supposed to do. Still, what could she expect from the daughter of Nadir Tasildar, the tax collector, who lived with the offspring of his four wives in the four-sided house adjacent to her own. She was sorry to say that Mia was the second cousin of her own grandchildren on Darogaji's side. Nadir Tasildar lived off bribes and dowries. That much everyone knew, and the stricter the purdah he imposed, the more his daughters flaunted themselves in secret in front of men. Mia's mother had her eye on Gappu for marriage, and when the Tasildar was away for a fortnight at a time collecting taxes from the peasants and shopkeepers who lived on his land, she invited Gappu to sleep overnight. She must have known, as Dadi knew, that Gappu waited for the moon to go down and then crossed the courtyard from one end of the four-sided house to the other, even though his cousin had warned him that snakes lived there. Dadi knew he had crossed when Mia came to the window shining in candlelight, wrapped only in a huge shawl of the sheerest muslin, and signaled to him to climb the stairs.

Karim and Gappu were determined to fight off the midafternoon drowsiness that threatened to imprison them in Dadi's sleeping rooms before dessert was prepared. It was already late in the day, and the sun poured down in unflinching whiteness into every corner of the town. Only Dadi's courtyard remained cool. It smelled perpetually like a spring day just after the rain. The flagstones seeped up the water that hourly was tossed from the water bearer's goatskin. In one corner a pump dripped continuously, and Dadi's child-servant derived his greatest pleasure from bringing the special silver cups filled with water to Dadi's grandsons.

Here in their Dadi's courtyard Gappu, Gerrar, and Karim felt the ageless security of their youth, the never-ending cycle and recycle of summers that were made just for them. The troubling rumors of Aligarh, which they pretended to ignore but which they heard nevertheless in bits and pieces, were behind them. Friends who had already left for the new country of Pakistan no longer plagued them by their absence, and their big houses with padlocks on them were not a continuously subtle threat. Here in Nehtor they reaffirmed their Indianness, their lands and the food of the land and the soil that was in them.

Also, Gappu did not relish the thought of going to Uncle Reaz and Auntie's house to meet up with Abu and Apaji. This year games like spying on girls in the shower were overshadowed by the certainty of mourning for Waji's death last fall. Who could fail to mourn the death? Gappu realized with a shiver that this was the first summer without their cousin Waji. Last fall, when they brought Waji's body back to Nehtor, Apaji had only a week to mourn with her brother and sister-in-law. The family wept together for the entire seven days, but then Abu took them all back to Aligarh and sent the boys to their schools, but Apaji had it on her conscience forever that she had killed the son of her older brother. That was the reason, Gappu knew, that she had gone directly to Uncle Reaz and Auntie's house upon the family's arrival in Nehtor for the summer, and that was the reason the three grandsons were anxious to prolong this reunion of grief as long as possible.

Gerrar had already curled up on a charpoy and was fast asleep. Gappu noticed that Karim was sinking fast and poked him in the ribs. "If you go to sleep, I am leaving you behind," he hissed. "Don't think that I will keep you company if Dadi makes you take a nap."

Karim jumped up from the carpet where he and Gappu were sitting cross-legged, their fingers and shirts thick with grease from the lamb and curry. "I'm not sleepy," he proclaimed. "I'm going to the kite-maker right now and see if he remembered to make me the best string."

"You can't go now," said Gappu. "We haven't had dessert."

Karim laughed at him. "Always thinking about food," he said, as he had heard Abu complain a thousand times. "I don't care about that. I am going to the kite-maker." He dashed to the door of the courtyard and ran right into Abu, Apaji, Moïd, and all his sisters, who were finally traipsing into Dadi's home.

Abu caught Karim around the middle with his big pawlike hands. "Running off again?" Abu demanded.

"He was going to the kite shop," Gappu reported.

"No," Karim protested, but he knew all was lost, and Abu sent him back to the charpoy with a wave of his hand.

The family flooded into the courtyard. The younger children were all tired and whining, and Dadi scooted about after them, offering treats to Piari, water to Mona, and kisses to Moïd, the youngest son, who ran to her side complaining. They were followed by a huge retinue of servants and onlookers.

Every stop Abu made on his way to his mother's house brought another group of solicitors and well-wishers, all ready with smiles and eagerness to report on the ills of the last winter and to ask for favors. Dadi was horrified to see her daughter-in-law and granddaughters surrounded by so many men. They were all the hangers-on of Nehtor, distant relatives, and the like. She knew in Aligarh such improprieties went on with Apaji's consent, but not in Nehtor and especially not in her own courtyard, which was meant for the seclusion of women, for napping and cooking over the stove. Dadi knew her stone stove, which was nothing more than a clay mound at the side of the courtyard and permanently blackened from the wooden logs she used as fuel, would never command the subservience of Apaji and her daughters. Raheel, who was sprouting breasts,

77

should have come immediately to her to make sure that the food for her brothers was well prepared, but such was not the case with her overeducated, citified granddaughter.

Dadi refused to let her thoughts soften her features toward her oldest son. She had not seen him in almost a year and longed to extend her cheek to him for a kiss and to bless his head with her hand. Rehman could do what he liked in Aligarh. In Nehtor he should know better than to bring the entire mahalla stringing along behind him, right into her private courtyard of purdah. She glared at him over the top of five-year-old Moïd's head, but Rehman strode into the courtyard with barely a glance at his mother. At his shoulder a stooped old man in dhoti and cap was speaking continuously into Rehman's ear: "Meer Sahib, we were not expecting you to come this year. There are many matters for discussion, but we did not give up hope. I said Rehman Sahib cannot forget his factories and his lands, now that he has inherited Darogaji's mango orchards and villages."

Rehman saw his mother's face glowing red. He did not salaam her, but turned to the man at his elbow and all the others chattering behind him. Apaji and Raheel were in the center of the group holding the bundles of halvah and sweetmeats they had brought from Aligarh as gifts along with new cloth for Dadi. They were at pains to cover their faces with their long dopatta scarves as they were expected to do in their ancestral town.

"You know better than to come into this courtyard," Rehman Hussain boomed at his following.

"Ji Hazoor. Yes, sir," the man at his elbow said. "Only give us an hour of your time."

"Yes, yes," said Rehman impatiently. "We have only just arrived. There is an entire summer ahead."

"Ji Hazoor," the man repeated. "We will be expecting you." He backed off, bumping into Raheel, who turned away drawing her dopatta across her face. It was a great nuisance to have to observe all the strict rules of purdah.

As soon as the courtyard was cleared, Dadi came to salaam her son, his wife, and Raheel, who was too old now to be cooed over and pampered.

"I am going to teach you to make chapati this summer," Dadi warned Raheel, who bent her head obediently.

Karim was happy to hear this news and ran over with glee to taunt his sister. "Yes. You must learn to cook, so you can take better care of us." Raheel stamped her foot at him.

"Munir Jehan," Dadi said to Apaji, extending both hands to touch her daughter-in-law's bowed head and shoulders. "I see you are expecting your baby in two months."

Rehman laughed. Only Dadi could tell when his lithe graceful wife was expecting a baby. Most people were surprised to learn she was pregnant at all. Her stomach never protruded from a sari, even up to the last month.

"You should know that I am an expert at such things," Dadi said. "I have delivered children and baby buffalo and foals. I've bound splints on broken wrists, cured snakebites and fevers. What can a doctor tell you that I don't know?"

"Now that we are all here," said Rehman, "you should prescribe rest."

Dadi ushered Abu and Apaji into one of the cool inner rooms off the courtyard where a charpoy was spread with cotton sheets. A curtain of khus was hanging at the door. She nudged the old blind man, who was sleeping beside the door, and he jumped awake, startled. He began to pull the long string of the ceiling fan at a furious pace, so that the room was filled with the flapping movement of the air.

Dadi left them together, and Apaji stretched out tiredly on the charpoy. Rehman was too restless for the long sleep that settled over Dadi's house every afternoon. He gulped cup after cup of the strong tea that Dadi brought him while he leafed through old worn documents on rice paper that had yellowed with age. The sun was lingering possessively over the land. Rehman could not wait for nightfall to bring a respite to the hungry dust-drenched roads and lanes, so that he could ride out to the fields and inspect the nearby villages and the mango orchards.

Rehman had many changes to make in his administration of the lands. He had inherited five hundred villages from Darogaji, perhaps

79

even more he was not aware of, but he was not interested in assuming the lordly role that had been his father-in-law's very being. He would not ride through the narrow twisting streets of Nehtor on a white horse, beckoning all to see him while he saw no one. He would not go wagging a tail of servants, or use the farmers to tend his feet with their earth-encrusted hands. He planned rather to organize the farmers to reap their own profits from the rice they harvested twice a year. Rehman was satisfied with his businesses, his hotels and factories, where he paid a man for the work he performed. He did not need the work and lives of others, and was determined to manage his lands in the manner of the New India, until they were his lands no longer.

Everyone knew the stories of Darogaji's forays in the villages, and the people were probably anxious to learn what their new Chairman would expect of them and what he would offer in return. Rehman imagined that some of the more favored farmers and servants would not be happy with his new ideas. In the village Milak, Saddiquan's father never went to the fields to use his hands himself any longer. Only when Darogaji came, did the farmer spring into action, washing the old man's feet delicately with his own hands, bearing tea, and sometimes walking the four miles back to Nehtor for a dish that had been forgotten. It was payment for his daughter Saddiquan, who lived in Darogaji's house and bore him a daughter, and the farmer was still procuring unmarried girls for Darogaji on his visits right through the year he died.

Rehman knew that similar behavior was expected of him. They would say that Rehman Sahib was not up to his job of Chairman of Nehtor. They would discredit him and his marriage and say that the dowry which had changed him from a mere businessman's son into a landed aristocrat had fallen into incompetent hands. Rehman was determined not to listen to idle village talk. He knew, however, that any change—even change meant to better the farmers—would not easily override the centuries of acceptance which everyone called tradition.

He had after all been Darogaji's choice as husband for his daughter, Rehman reminded himself. It had been Darogaji's cherished idea that his prized daughter, Munir Jehan, should marry someone of great potential but lower than she in status, as he had done by marrying his fourth and last wife. This, he had felt, would secure for his daughter lifelong respect. No dowry could protect her from the Muslim law that allowed a man to take four wives. The fact that Darogaji himself had married four times meant nothing. Darogaji considered his first three marriages merely stepping-stones to his fourth wife. Nani had brought him the true power and status he had been seeking, and his daughter by that marriage must be honored accordingly.

Darogaji had been right. Even after seventeen years of marriage, Rehman was overwhelmed with feeling for his sliver of a bride as he stared at her sleeping form on the charpoy. She was bathed in a soft half-light that touched her cheek, which was resting smoothly on her ringed and braceleted hand. Her round nails were polished with the palest rose, and her hair, which was washed by two servants every week, was twined up from her knees into a crown atop her head and adorned with the tiniest jewel and petals of jasmine.

His body hungered incessantly for the feel of her silken flesh beside him on their bed, which was permanently scented with the garlands she braided several times a day around her wrists and ankles. Over and over again, he infused her with children, and then waited in anguish for the forty-day period of abstinence after childbirth to come to an end, watching her skin spring back to its girlish place, strong and tense as a young animal. With each child the celebrations on the fortieth day grew more lavish than the one before. Seven times he had regaled her with dresses and saris from Delhi. He bought French perfumes and 24-karat-gold bangles from Jaipur, and all new bedding of the finest, soft woven cotton. Sweets of dried milk dripping in rose water were offered to friends and strangers alike in Aligarh when he brought his bride back from Nehtor, the village where she was obliged to give birth, and he could consume her again with his huge nervous fingers and mouth.

The sun was finally sinking all around him. It settled a pale glow within the rooms and courtyard of Dadi's house. Apaji's body on the charpoy was languid, and he could see her breasts rise and fall over the small mound of stomach that was stretching and taut with their next child. He tiptoed outside, where the children lay strewn about the courtyard on charpoys and small Persian rugs. Dadi's stove in the far corner seethed with smoke from the burning logs, and several female relatives squatted around their iron implements, grinding, chopping, and stirring the evening supper into existence. Dadi's large form appeared through the smoke, and she came after him.

"You are going," she said.

Rehman nodded.

"You cannot wait the night?" Dadi asked, pursuing him into the animal shed beyond the courtyard. The clay earth was growing cool in the evening, and the air smelled fresh and pungent with moist hay and the vines that grew up every inch of wall. The cattle were moaning gratefully as Buffalo Man relieved them of their milk, hunkered on his little stool. The bullocks had already been fed and were ready for the journey.

"I must go tonight before the wind starts up," Rehman said, inspecting the cart that had been loaded and hitched up to the bullocks. Mollah Baksh, who was to accompany him, turned from the alley into the shed, calling out to Rehman, and began to lead the bullocks toward the street.

"I think you are going so quickly because of the trouble in India," said Dadi.

"What trouble?" asked Rehman, turning toward his mother with a smile. "What have you been hearing in your little courtyard in Nehtor?"

"I hear everything," she said. "They say there is trouble in India."

"You speak of India as if it were a foreign country," said Rehman with a laugh.

"To me," said Dadi. "It is. This house is my country."

Rehman bowed his head for his mother's traditional blessing. "I must go. There is no trouble in Nehtor. Nothing more should concern you."

Dadi was satisfied. She had prepared enough food for many

days, and it was already loaded into the bullock cart. There were blankets, pillows, changes of clothing, and Mollah Baksh, whom everyone trusted, would accompany her son. There was nothing more to say. She offered her blessing.

"Salaam Aleicum," said Rehman. "I will be gone for no more than five days, and we will enjoy the rest of the summer together."

After seeing to it that the brick floor of her courtyard was doused with water once more for the evening, Dadi slipped between the charpoys where her grandsons were sleeping and gently massaged their feet. She sat for hours, fanning away the occasional flies that threatened to buzz in their ears. There is time, she thought, for their sleep to be disturbed, but not as long as they are with me and not as long as they remain in Nehtor. That, she swore, will be forever.

Although two important events were planned for the summer—namely, Karim's circumcision on his ninth birthday at the end of June and the wedding of Rehman's youngest brother, Tariq, the following week, Gerrar's one aim in life was to find a way to get to Milak. It took an explosion of firecrackers in a clay pot that practically blew away the entire door to Uncle Reaz's house, but he was finally banished from Nehtor and on his way to the village with its tiny brick houses on the edge of the irrigated fields.

The explosion had the desired effect. Immediately rumors started that Gerrar had lost his mind with passion for his cousin Rosey. They said he had been watching her through binoculars for days and that the female cousins were not safe as long as Gerrar remained in this state of mind. Abu did not believe the silly gossip, but he packed Gerrar off in a bullock cart with Moonah to guard him, because he wanted to get his son out of Nehtor until every one piped down.

Soon Gerrar was sitting in the small brick house which he shared only with the caretaker, his stepuncle, Chacha Zulfiquar, who spent all day feeding the water buffalo and bullocks and supervising the irrigation of the fields. It was the nicest time of day. Moonah had disappeared, and the pretty face of a farmer's daughter was looking at him through the darkened window. Every time Gerrar turned on his bed under the mosquito netting he saw the angel face reappear at another window. He could hear the early summer rains falling on the roof, and whooping cranes calling as they dashed from the fields to their nests. "She will be a dream tomorrow," Gerrar thought. "But today let her look at me while I am sleeping so I can smile and she will not even know."

It was the first time Gerrar had come to Milak alone. The clouds were so low they seemed to have descended to earth, and the lightning that darted between them seemed just beyond his hand's reach. He dreamed of the games the children all played in the pool of the tube well, where the water was blocked up by stones before running down the gulleys to irrigate the fields. The pool was always littered at the bottom with fresh mangoes. Gerrar was only half asleep, and in his dream he knew he must be very small, because he was afraid to drop into the tube well to fish up the fruit while the water was gushing over his head and roaring in his ears. It was the coldest water, and doves were cooing in every tree. It was difficult to tell what was part of his dream and what was reality as his heavy eyelids fluttered over his eyes and the moist air sensuously caressed every inch of his warm body. He saw a peacock strut across the path and the bull in its shed was lit up by the flashing lights deeply embedded in the clouds. All the shadows that fell from the maze of trees seemed greener than the leaves themselves. The women, who always came to watch the children play, were turned away beneath their white shawls like a row of silent marble statues that had not yet been unveiled. The children were as free as birds to bathe together, and the girls lifted the hems of their long skirts and dipped their legs into the swirling water. They waded up to their waists and called to Gappu and Gerrar to remove the stones that would allow the water to rise higher and higher, and with the first touch of water to the thin muslin of their blouses, their gorgeous skin was visible, and the games of pushing and pinching stopped as all the boys riveted their eyes on Mia's breasts, the size of oranges, with two stems protruding sharply in the cold water.

Suddenly a door slammed, and he dreamed he saw a hundred doors in the city of Aligarh all wrapped in black banners and fastened with huge iron padlocks. Someone was removing a body from his home, and he thought it was the body of his cousin Waji. Then, with a start, he thought it was his own. That was why Apaji was crying. But he could hear his own breathing, and he was struggling up into consciousness, saying, "I am not dead. I am only sleeping."

Gerrar smelled the food his stepuncle was preparing, wafting through the cozy room. A hazy light filtered through the window, but the pretty brown face was gone. The rain had stopped. Someone was lifting the mosquito netting, and Gerrar jumped halfway up in the bed into Jilla's hair laced with flowers of jasmine, which fell around him.

He saw Jilla's smile close to his face and felt her breath warm with the dried mint she was chewing. With Jilla's cheeks almost brushing his own, no one could worry about the world and Aligarh and death from cholera or anything else.

"Hello, Gerrar," she breathed. "Do you know how to milk a goat?"

Gerrar laughed, but her whisper was serious.

"My goat needs milking, Gerrar. Wouldn't you like to help me?"

"You don't milk goats, Jilla. You're a girl. Who would make you do that."

"Oh, yes, I do. I am very good at it, too. I would like to show you how, Gerrar."

"Jilla," he laughed. It was funny to be sitting in the half-light of the little brick room, all lit up and rose-colored, saying each other's names as if they had never said them before. Only last year, right in front of Abu and Apaji, they had played a game of jumping from bed to bed until they both fell together into a heap and Abu sent Jilla out of the house.

"I do milk goats, you see, from time to time," she continued. "It is a wonderful feeling, and I think you would like it very much."

"I don't know much about it," he said, rising from the bed. He was skeptical about milking the goat, but definitely willing to follow. Jilla took him by the hand, carrying a water pitcher in the other one, and led him out into the evening. The sun was sinking all around them as they passed along the soft clay ridges through the flooded fields. Along every path, women in red and orange skirts were walking slowly home, the grasses they had gathered balanced on their heads. A few still bent over the rice paddies, transplanting the pale green stalks beneath the water, one by one. Jilla and Gerrar passed farmers riding on the edges of their wooden plows, their brightly colored turbans floating in the air. She led him through marshy fields where white cranes were standing erect on one leg in the water. The grasses were soft and spongy beneath Gerrar's bare feet, and the sweet fragrance of fertilizer mixed with decaying sugarcane hung warmly in the rain-washed air. They walked through the deep green mango gardens. Jilla lifted the edge of her skirt to climb over the mango roots knotted under a blanket of fallen leaves, and Gerrar could see her ankles laced in silver rings. Bits of orange sunlight hung through the trees like bubbles.

They came to a shed full of bleating goats, prancing restlessly at the end of long ropes. Their narrow eyes darted nervously in their miniature faces. Jilla sat down on the thick grass, letting her shawl slip from her shoulders, and pulled the goat into her bare arms. Quickly she released the sack tied around the goat's teats, which was used to prevent the kid from drinking up all the precious milk.

"After we milk the goat," Jilla explained, "we will let the baby drink. We always see to it that there is enough milk to feed the kid."

She took Gerrar's hand and held it against the warm udder. He was surprised at the human feeling of the goat's flesh, and he pulled back his hand.

"Not like that. You'll frighten her," Jilla reprimanded. From the pitcher of water she sprinkled the goat's teats to wash them. She put down the best fodder for the goat to munch. Again she took Gerrar's hand and pulled him down, so that he was sitting beside her.

"Softly, softly," she said, "like this." She placed her hand firmly over his, on top of the goat, so that the skin squeezed in his hand. Together they were moving their hands firmly along the elongated tube of the goat's udder, which was swelling and filling with liquid beneath their grasp. Gerrar felt the teat become bulbous, and it quivered in his hand as if it had a life of its own.

Jilla released his hand and turned to him. Slowly she undid the buttons of her blouse while Gerrar continued working on the goat. Her breasts stood out firm and long.

"The milk isn't coming," he complained.

"Don't worry; the milk will come. Give me your other hand." Obediently he let her place his hand over her breasts which were soft and leaped between his fingers.

"You see," Jilla continued, "the goat has two, and I have two. You do the same thing to me. You squeeze and pull them with your hands until they fill with liquid and life, and then the milk is sure to come."

"Like this?"

"Yes, yes," said Jilla. "Keep working." She was working on the goat's teats, and Gerrar was working on Jilla.

With her other hand Jilla loosened the cummerbund of Gerrar's pajamas. He felt frozen with her cool hand against his stomach, and the hand was going around his waist, but Jilla was still talking about the goat, and her eyes were staring into his. For a moment he felt an intense urge to laugh, but before he could, he felt for the first time in his life, despite all the rumors to the contrary, a girl's hand grasp his penis. "The goat has two; I have two. And you have one," she said. She rubbed him and said, "The milk is coming. You can feel it. Soon it will be all over your hand, and you will see how warm it is."

Drops of milk began to form at the end of the long tight tube. Jilla was talking continuously, and Gerrar felt her words slide over his body as her hand worked his flesh. He felt himself becoming hard and elongated just like the goat's tubes. "It is so dry," he said.

"First, we must wash the nipples with water, so the milk will come out clean." Gerrar saw Jilla's tongue slip between her lips like a pink fresh date. "We don't have to use our hands. We can take the milk right into our mouths." She bent the tube against her lips, and a long squirt of thick white milk bathed the orb of her mouth. He felt her hands pushing him upward along his thighs, which were quivering, and he did not think he could stand up. His pajamas fell in a heap around his ankles, and Jilla pressed against his thighs. The long pink tongue washed in milk licked him in a circular motion all around the inside of his thighs, and he felt himself becoming tighter and warmer with a milkiness of life inside. Jilla's mouth was filled with a warm white substance, and he could not tell if it was the goat's milk or his own liquid welling up and coming out. The lick was warmer than her hand, which was still holding on to his stomach.

Jilla tried again to get some more liquid from the goat. She made a gurgling sound in her mouth, and again she stuck her tongue covered with the white foamy spittle onto his penis, like a sweet mango floating in cream. Finally she squirted his hand with the goat's udder, and it was sticky and warm with the substance drying quickly between his fingers.

"Now you do the same thing to me, too," she said, and dipped his aching fingers beneath her skirts into her opening, which was warm between her crouching legs and also gushing wet with liquid. She held tight to both his forefingers and placed them deep inside the folds of flesh, opening like a thousand suckling baby mouths, biting onto him like soft gums. He felt his fingers being brought deeper and deeper between her legs, lost in a tunnel of flowering flesh and silk skirts, and he felt there was nothing to grasp on to, nothing to hold to prevent his sinking right up through her body.

"Don't bend them like that," said Jilla, but he felt his fingers fighting the swallowing flesh that was like tongues and foliage. She took her own finger and put it inside herself, too, directing his fingers and holding them stiff. Jilla was holding onto the goat's nipple with one hand and directing his fingers with the other. She continued to wet Gerrar's penis with her hand straight from the goat's teat, and she had her other hand inside herself, and was stretching with endless elasticity until she lost the feeling of fleshiness and became rubber.

Suddenly she released him, and with her groans coming fast between her lips, she arched her neck backward and rubbed her own breasts with her open palms. "Stand up, Gerrar," she whispered, and he stood again with the pajamas still trailing at his feet. She made him look at her lithe naked body twisting and contorting on the grass. The silver anklets on her legs tinkled like bells. Her long braid of hair was knotted with leaves and crawled through the grass like a huge muscular snake. Her nipples were stiff and wet and shining. Everywhere was the slightly sour musty smell of gushing milk.

"Let the milk come," she ordered him. "Don't worry. I will help you." Again she put her tongue on his bright and shining penis, which by now was throbbing with pain, and she was saying not to worry, it will come. But Jilla was as restless as a grass snake.

"Don't you know how to milk the goat?" she asked over and over, and he saw that she was putting her own hands into her mouth and then stuffing them inside herself with the fresh growth of pubic hairs standing on end as she arched her back, and she was crying.

"Is something wrong? Jilla? Jilla, tell me. Is something wrong?" He bent over her form, and he thought that he was crying, too, and something felt dead and heavy around him. His penis was sticking out into the air, ridiculous and heavy, but he could not touch himself with his own hands. Why did Jilla ignore his hands that were desperate to touch her? Why did she turn and writhe and seem to forget him standing there over her with the evening air turning him hot and cold all at once. He crouched beside her, and asked her to come to him.

She fell against his chest, and her long tangled hair whipped across his neck. He folded her in his arms.

"Jilla. This is horrible," he said. "It is not like this. Do you know what you are doing?"

"Milking the goat," said Jilla, and she broke into sobs coming out of her mouth all thick and sour with milk.

"You don't know what you're doing, do you?" Gerrar still could not believe it himself. He stretched her out gently on the ground and covered her quivering little body with his own and found her skin of jasmine petals with his mouth while she was laughing and crying.

"Jilla, child cousin. Don't make it so." He found himself hard and strong above the wreckage of her body, and he needed no one to tell him what he was doing, with Jilla's body moving slowly under his and the tears pouring out of her, as they rolled and rolled about in the thick leaves, one form entangled in the other, and sobs and laughter wracking their bodies all at once. Poor goat and her kid the only witnesses.

They sat together in the moonlight, which poured all around them. The air hummed with crickets and choked with the sound of frogs. He wrapped her in an old blanket he found in the goat shed and lit a fire. They watched the kid suckling greedily on his shaky legs from the she-goat, and he held her bangled hand in his.

"Why, Jilla?" he asked.

She turned away from him.

"Cousin, child. You are beautiful. Don't be afraid."

The tears were gushing from her opaque eyes, heavy with smudged mascara like a wounded fawn's.

"Tell me, Jilla. Don't be afraid," he whispered again and again into her tangled hair.

"My mother told me to," she said.

"Saddiquan, that bitch," Gerrar hissed. He held her back and looked into her eyes. She was so lost.

"No, no. Don't do that."

"Your mother told you to," he repeated.

"I imagined all the rest."

"And have you never done this before?"

"I have practiced," said Jilla, smiling slightly.

"With whom?"

"With everyone," she said, and she looked directly into his eyes.

They walked slowly back to the village where the rows and rows of clay huts lay silently in the moonlight. "I am afraid of snakes," she said. "They come out on nights like this."

"Don't be. I will kill them."

She laughed. "You were afraid even to come here before."

"I am not now. We will come again maybe," he said. He offered to take her to her own house, but she made him leave her beside the lake where all the courtyards of the village with their mud floors and freshly lacquered doorways opened out onto a communal garden. His food was waiting for him at home, sent by Apaji all the way from Nehtor. The four-mile journey to Milak took even longer than the usual two hours by bullock cart, because the paths were flooded by the afternoon monsoon, but the food had already been reheated. Moonah served it to him, and they ate together without uttering a word.

The village of Milak was also a place for playing. Gerrar felt he no longer had any need of Jilla. He had done only what the old Darogaji had done a million times before. He had taken Jilla by the hair, after watching her foolishness, and thrown her into the leaves where he climbed onto her and forced himself into her. No woman, not even the daughter of Saddiquan, would ever be so disrespectful as to acquiesce. No matter how much a girl led the way in a seduction, no matter how she flirted and teased, love making was a man's prerogative. If she had a baby, so much the better for her. It was all Jilla or Saddiquan could possibly ask for. It would mean food and clothes and shelter for them for the rest of their lives. Gerrar had cousins littered all over the district.

Almost every night he listened to the music from the wedding feasts that went on throughout the months of June and July. When he heard the wooden string instruments, the tablas and flutes, he knew the Darogaji would have called the bride to him, and taken her there on the floor, before her own husband had a chance to lift her veils and peer into her face. It was an honor. He was the Doctor Sahib, grandson of Darogaji.

Gerrar saw Jilla rarely during the next week. He spent his time fishing in the pond, where the ducks swam all day through the lotus reeds and mud, and just before the rain he watched the cranes come whooping down, white and dazzling in the hot Indian sun, raising their beaks up and down in the rice paddies where they ate the tender stalks. Since the farmers were all Hindus, there was no one to disturb the birds or gun them down, not even the watchman who slept all day in a thatched-roof lean-to, high above the swamped paddies on stilts, a living scarecrow who scarcely had a thing to eat himself but would not kill a breathing creature.

Gerrar and Moonah swung from the vines of the banyans, leaping from tree to tree like monkeys. They replenished themselves with sugarcane which they hacked down with their knives and chewed between their teeth. They flew kites and raced on horses, while Gerrar did atonement for having blown up the door to Uncle Reaz's house. It was really a pain, this deportation—making love to Jilla and stuffing himself with milk and mangoes. Gerrar's only problem was that he needed money to buy a new kite. His own kite had been cut down and sailed away in a kite fight with Moonah. He sent three baskets of mangoes, stolen from his uncle's gardens, to the market. He gave them to Buffalo Man, who brought sweet rice every day from Dadi. He warned him not to walk too slow and waited impatiently for the new kite, so he could beat Moonah to a pulp.

Buffalo Man returned slowly the next day when the sun was already sinking. He brought a terrible sluggish kite, and also a letter from Rosey telling him to come home and quit fooling around with Jilla. Gerrar liked his status. She also told him that Karim had broken her front tooth with a cricket bat and that she had socked Karim in the nose, so that they both came home crying and bleeding. Gappu was playing up on the roof again, and his friend Kali Soori had fallen off, smashing the same leg as last year. Nani spread it all through the mahalla that Dadi was reckless with the grandchildren, and Raheel was caught at the movie house three times in a row. All the children had sunstroke and nosebleeds. It was clear that banishment was imminent for all of them.

That certainly would never do, and Gerrar immediately set in motion his plan for returning to Nehtor. He stopped drinking his milk and sent the hot food back to Apaji untouched in the tiffin carriers, sending shock waves through all the female relatives in Nehtor. Secretly he fed himself on fresh vegetables and fruit, and accepted milk right from the hands of a farmer's daughter, who met him among the tall sugarcane and massaged his legs and let him touch her breasts. He tasted vegetarian dishes late at night in the farmers' courtyards while they smoked their pipes and listened to his stories of the city and the latest gossip in his family. Two days after he sent home the message that he was no longer eating or drinking any milk, a bullock cart arrived from Nehtor loaded with enough watermelon for a final feast with the entire village of Milak and a message from Abu to return immediately to attend the ceremony of Karim's circumcision.

For three years Karim had put off his circumcision. Until the age of six, a Muslim child—boy or girl—was permitted to run about the villages and the house with the bottom half of his clothing missing, and only the gentlest remarks about his nudity as he approached the age of six. At the time of birth there was no need to remove the little piece of foreskin, and it seemed an unnecessary intrusion on a small child's innocence. By the age of six, however, there was very little innocence left, and Dadi, for one, saw to it that little girls wore long skirts, or goraras, or pants. Girls even began to wear a dopatta, a three-foot piece of cloth that was supposed to drape around the neck, across the shoulders, and down over the breasts. That was also the time that the boy would have his piece of foreskin chopped off by the barber, or Nai, while the Mulvi recited a prayer.

The barber was a very important man. Not only did he see to it that a boy's sideburns and forelocks were properly maintained, but as a boy approached puberty, he also began pulling down the boy's pajamas to see if pubic hairs had begun to grow. He then shaved these hairs, too, with an expert flicking of the wrists. His eye was very sharp, and he always warned Abu when one of the sons had begun playing around and it was time for a lecture on the dangers of venereal disease.

Karim had witnessed the circumcision of his older brothers, and was in the shop when the Nai opened their pajamas and grasped them on their private parts for a close examination. Karim was determined to have none of it, but now at the mature age of nine, he was sorry he had put it off, for the humiliation was going to be even greater.

Dadi could not believe her eyes when she came to examine him. "*Ai hai hai hai hai.* He is still running around with an uncut penis," she exclaimed, barging in on him with lantern in hand while he was crouching over the stone toilet. Karim quickly pulled up his pants around his waist and slammed the door. After that, he went into a week of seclusion, attempting to bring on all sorts of fever and diseases, but nothing came. He lay all day prone on the hot bricks and watched the sun climb over his head in utter dizziness and nausea. He even managed to produce a faint and a nosebleed in front of Apaji, but that was worth only one day in bed with an agonizing headache and no appetite.

Gappu laughed at him. "There's no getting out of it this time."

One morning Dadi came into the room and told him she had to measure him and give the information to the barber. "Nine is very old for such a thing. It will be a delicate operation."

"No," Karim screamed, but Dadi was too quick and she caught him by his shirttail and had his pajamas down around his ankles in no time. She held his penis in her fingers and measured its thickness with a bit of string.

"*Aarre* Allah," she exclaimed. "He will have difficulty having it cut off."

Karim was crazy with fear that he was going to have his penis cut off. He went about holding himself and looking for a place to hide. He agreed that Gappu looked much better than he did when Gappu let him see, but that was small consolation for the thought that part of his own flesh was going to be hacked by the barber's razor in public with all the women watching, and Abu and Apaji who were supposed to be proud of him, and everyone giving gifts that amounted to a sort of mini-dowry. How could anyone enjoy a celebration when he was sliced in half and maybe ruined for life by a tiny slip of the barber's hand?

Everyone asked Dadi if Karim was a good size. "Oh, ho," they all said. "Gerrar was so nice."

Dadi answered coldly that Karim was the biggest of them all.

On the morning of the ceremony, which was to take place in Dadi's courtyard, Karim remained in seclusion in his room, holding himself and nursing the wound that was soon to come. He refused to see anyone or eat. Apaji came into the room and told him to wear his oldest clothes, because they were bound to get messed up. Karim flung himself at his mother's feet and burst into tears. "Messed up? Messed up with what?"

"It's not as bad as all that," Apaji said. "After it's over, you will have a new set of clothes from top to bottom."

"I don't want new clothes."

"There are velvet slippers, and your shirt is all brocaded in silver."

"No, no. I don't care about all that," he whined.

"That's enough," Apaji said, leaving the room. "It will all be over in an hour or so. You will be a man."

"God," Karim thought. "The first minute I am a man, and my own mother turns away from me. My own mother sends me out to face a knife, and all she can offer me is a new set of clothes. I don't want to be a man."

He heard giggles at the door, and he opened it angrily. Raheel and his cousins Rosey and Mia came flying into the room. They were wearing new goraras; their hair was piled up on their heads, and they even had on mascara. "What are you all dressed up for? You look ugly," he told them.

"Not as ugly as you're going to look," Raheel said, and Rosey burst out laughing.

"You shut up, or I'll break your other tooth, too," he said and shoved them out of his room.

When he was ushered into Dadi's courtyard, he could smell the food cooking in the oversized iron pots used for celebrations. A rug was on the floor, and Abu and his uncles and the Mulvi were kneeling there with white prayer caps on their heads and Korans open on their laps. Gappu and Gerrar were there, too, smirking surrepti-

95

tiously. Incense was blowing to disguise what Karim was certain would be an awful odor, like the goats he saw slaughtered on the Muslim holy day, Bukra Id, or when someone was dying like Waji last year. He saw the chopping block, and the barber with his wild black moustache, and his soiled working clothes, and he counted his steps forward: "One, two, three, four. Oh, no. I am too old. My time is past. I won't go any farther."

There were no women in the courtyard, but he knew they were all lined up on the roof, just behind the wall, and peeping through the cracks he had often peeped through himself when there was something worth spying on. Then after he was finished, they would all come running down and devour the meat and the sweets.

As he approached the chopping block, he saw it was really a big Indian straw basket with orange colors woven through it like snakes, and it was turned upside down. He tried to look back at Abu, but the barber clamped him down on the basket. The Mulvi moved closer and held his head while the barber pulled his pants down around his ankles and forced him to sit with his knees up and his legs spread, so that he was looking down at his own penis shaking madly in its little case. Karim wanted to close his eyes, but he could not take them off his own skin with his skinny legs wedged up under his chin. The he saw the knife, and he began to scream. The thousand curses that were in his heart were now on his lips. Karim yelled at the Nai, "If you touch me with that knife I'm going to sleep with my dick in your daughter's mouth and leave it there all night."

The Nai was unintimidated. Karim saw the knife flashing in the air, and he screamed a loud piercing scream as the knife bit into his flesh, and his blood squirted so hard it hit the Nai on the front of his shirt. "Din Din Muhammad," said the Mulvi. "Din Din Muhammad," all the men repeated. "Now you are a Muslim." The skin was taken by the Mulvi to be buried in some graveyard, and Karim, a mass of wails and tears and blood, was led stumbling and naked to the bed in Dadi's room for rest.

All day and night he lay moaning in bed, the sore penis limp on his naked thigh. At first he did not dare look. He was sure three quarters of it was gone. When he finally felt it gingerly with his fingers, there it was, sure enough, straight and arrowlike, if a little limp, just like Gappu's and Gerrar's.

Abu was the first to visit him with a prize of gold coins and money. He was amazed at his young son's vocabulary of curses. Karim even told his father to go suck, but Rehman reminded himself that Karim was older than his other sons or nephews, who had gone through the ordeal usually at six or seven. "That's some way to make money," Karim told his father.

Apaji came next with a cooling herbal ointment left behind by the Nai. She rubbed it into Karim's thighs and groin while he sobbed and clung to Apaji's neck. "Oh, oh," he moaned. "There is bound to be infection, Apaji. I am too old, and it is so sore." She covered him with kisses and told him he was not as old as all that.

"But I am a man now," he said, sitting up in the bed. Then he flopped back down, clutching his penis with a new flow of tears.

"Don't touch yourself so much," she said. "Or there *will* be an infection."

"Send Gerrar and Gappu," he commanded her.

His brothers were very sympathetic. "Don't worry, Karim," Gerrar told him in his best bedside manner. "I will send for Jilla tonight. She will come and massage your legs, and she will make you feel very good."

"She did the same for both of us," said Gappu.

"I don't want any girl here."

"You will," Gappu told him. "Din Din Muhammad. You are a man now."

Rehman left Karim's celebration with a strangely heavy heart. Even the innocent rituals of life seemed to him to have profound and ominous overtones. While his sons played and experimented in the village, and his daughters whispered with their cousins about marriage and movie stars in the films they were not supposed to see, and Apaji handled the politics of the extended family, which twisted around every generation with games of intrigue and speculation and

97

revenge, he received the mounting news daily from all parts of India with a sadly deepening understanding.

For days Rehman had been expecting a close business associate from Delhi to arrive in Nehtor. He had invited him to attend the wedding of Tariq, Rehman's younger brother, at the end of the week. Every day Moonah sent Yellow and the tonga to the station to pick up the guest and his wife and children. Every afternoon the horse and the tonga returned alone. Not even a messenger came. Finally Rehman decided to go to the station at Dhampur himself and send a telegram.

Hitching up his father's old horse, Rehman set out at a slow walk along the red clay road. Since the monsoons had begun, the deep dried furrows and ditches were muddy, and bullock carts sometimes had to leave the road to circumnavigate deep patches of flooding. Several brightly colored canopied tongas, filled with summer visitors to Nehtor, were stopped along the marshy road while groups of servants heaved their bodies against the carriages to push them through the mud.

Rehman did not mourn for the passing of the old. Yet how could he accept the coming of the new when it seemed that already millions were being destroyed and even his own family and children were threatened? The news from Delhi was more rumor than factual account, but in these days one was learning more and more to rely on rumor. What other communication was there? And besides, the Indian grapevine was intricate and personal. The newspapers did not describe what Rehman managed to hear by word of mouth, since most of them only pursued their own party line.

Old Delhi, it was said, was becoming a huge ghetto for Muslims fleeing from the countryside. The narrow streets were clogged with cattle, and houses already overcrowded were teeming with new arrivals. People were sleeping on the streets, and every day more and more came, sitting on the tops of buses, crammed into the back of trucks, walking for miles on foot, and riding in bullock carts. In New Delhi people were barricading their houses and buying ammunition by the truckload. Every day Sikh and Hindu refugees came from industrial cities like Lahore and Lyallpur that were to become part of Pakistan on August fourteenth, the Day of Independence as well as partition of the two countries. It seemed as if the land itself was dying of a kind of cholera and spitting up half its people like so much waste.

Riots were not unknown in India, Rehman knew, and he had often seen their results. They flared up, usually in small enclaves, neighbor fighting neighbor. Caste Hindus, themselves illiterate, who had to work day and night to harvest their lands with wooden plows that had only the smallest strip of sharpened and resharpened metal, who had to heave water up from a well with ropes and wooden levers and carry it home in clay pots for miles upon their heads just to do the day's cooking, who sat idle for months at a time while the monsoons slashed against their almost naked bodies and their fields became infested with snakes and their village walks ran deep with sewage and the seasonal plagues of cholera and smallpox, who themselves knew hunger and thirst and were driven from their homes in great upheavals of the earth or the intrusion of the oceans and the rivers, often were known to slaughter an entire settlement of Harijaans, the garbage sweepers and shit cleaners, just because a woman, cracked with thirst, dipped a gourd into a Hindu well to moisten the lips of her grandchild when all of India was a parched plain and the eastward winds blew fistfuls of red sand even through the streets of Delhi.

Rehman knew that the sounds of drums in a distant village at night often signaled the war cry from one mound of clay huts to another. The next morning both villages would be found charred heaps of burned thatching and pieces of broken clay urns, perhaps only because a daughter from one village had eloped with a son from the other. Once, when he had been passing through a fishing village in the Christian colony of Goa, he had seen two funeral parties standing sullenly before two mass graves. Thirty-six bodies were laid out on stretchers in neat white shrouds, while a black-skinned priest intoned a Latin prayer mixed with the singing words of Konkoni, the local dialect, half Portuguese, half an indigenous language which had never been recorded. He asked if there had been a plague, but he was told that these were the thirty-six bodies of two families, both of which had been entirely wiped out in a bloody brawl. The eldest son of one family had died in a raging madness, after having been bitten by a dog. He clawed his hair and screamed and barked. Just before he died, he had told his family that a neighbor's son had appeared to him in a dream in the form of a dog. Naturally it must have been the neighbor's son who bit the fisherman, and one household attacked the other with knives and sticks. They fought until every member of both clans was dead.

Sometimes, it was true, Indians got together with Indians and fought off their more profound oppressors, but even then the death had a gruesomeness difficult to equal elsewhere. Rehman had often heard the story of the Black Hole of Calcutta, during the uprising of 1756, in which five hundred English soldiers were locked into a tiny room and found the next morning suffocated in frozen attitudes of struggle for breath and air.

Now the riots that had been raging in the eastern- and western-most corners of the infant yet ancient country were threatening to sweep across the entire north of India and converge upon those in the middle. These riots were on a scale no one had ever imagined before. For almost a year, Rehman had heard horrifying tales of burning, looting, rape, murder, and mass migration out of Bengal in the east and Punjab in the west. Both states had been slashed down the middle in order to create the new nation of Pakistan for the Muslims of India. Conveniently the states had been divided so that the jute mills were separated from the jute and the tea gardens severed from the processing plants and the textile mills from the cotton crop. But just because he was a Muslim, did that mean he was no longer an Indian? Rehman did not like that sort of talk. The politicians and theoreticians, the land-hungry and power-craving, all intellectualized the Muslims and said they were a nation within a nation—one with their own dress, their own language, their own customs, their own religion and calendar. But in India where every village was the microcosm of a nation, and every man defined his religion differently, and the people of every state spoke a different language and used a different script, how could one state be more homogenous than another? Rehman did not really believe in Pakistan, yet in a way he realized that his identity was being labeled for him regardless of his own beliefs.

It did not seem to matter that several years before, he and other members of the family had shouldered their way through a cursing mob of Muslims to make a speech in support of Nehru, who had been due to arrive in the district that morning by train. The men in the crowd clutched rocks and bricks in their fists, and many, it was known, were carrying guns. An advance detachment of police was visible everywhere in the surrounding hills. Rehman's cousin-in-law, Nadir Tasildar, tax collector for the entire district, mounted the podium constructed for Nehru and answered jeer for jeer and curse for curse, but the Muslims shouted him down, even though previously they had always listened to him and his word had been law. They called him stooge, and they chanted, "Pakistan Zindabad. Long live Pakistan." They tore down the flag of Nehru's Congress Party, but still Nehru arrived and gave his speech and left safely on the next train. Rehman and his relatives had to hold the crowd back with their own bodies, screaming a barrage of threats, cajoling and bribing. They had done it for free India—religion or no religion, Pakistan or no Pakistan. They had done it for the sake of their lands and their children and each other.

As Rehman rode into Dhampur on his horse, the activity of the little market town temporarily stilled his thoughts. The stalls of the market, flanking the railroad station and the tracks, were laden with merchandise, and he stopped to have a thick hot tea sweetened with milk. He left his horse to wander in the dusty road, and went in search of the telegraph clerk, who was not in his office or anywhere on the station platform. Rehman found him napping on a charpoy outside the stone quarters of the railway officials. The clerk roused himself slowly, rubbing his heavy stomach beneath his open khaki shirt, and led Rehman back into his small office which was cooled by an electric fan and buzzing with flies.

"I see your horse Yellow bringing the tonga from the mahalla every day," he told Rehman. "I know Sahib is looking for somebody, but if there were any news, I would have come myself to Nehtor."

Rehman nodded, smiling. "I'm sure it's nothing serious, but I am concerned that my guest may be having trouble in Delhi."

The clerk unlocked the drawer of his big wooden desk and assembled his forms and stamps for Rehman's telegram. "No, Sahib. I don't think you should worry about your friend. It is only the people on the borders who are having trouble—and poor people." The clerk shook his head smiling broadly. "I see the train from Delhi come every morning, and the mail train comes at night. People say Delhi is very crowded and prices are high, but this is a hardship that will pass."

Rehman examined the clerk's expression closely. The man seemed to be his only link to the rest of India. Rehman felt confined in Nehtor, isolated from news sources and events. "Have you heard anything about riots?" he asked.

"Rioting is only on the borders, where it is to be expected. They say it is dangerous to travel to Lahore and Bengal, but the Delhi train comes and goes as usual. Sometimes there is a delay because the trains are carrying refugees back and forth. The express is a little more crowded than usual, but other than that, I have seen nothing extraordinary."

Rehman scribbled a message on the telegram form and handed it to the clerk. "Let's hope you're right," he said.

"I know I'm right." The clerk smiled and raised his hand in the Muslim gesture of greeting. "Assalaam Aleicum."

"Namaste," Rehman answered in Hindi, and left the station, feeling somewhat reassured.

As he stepped into the blinding sunlight in the road he heard the high distant whistle of a train. He ran around the stationhouse and climbed the embankment to watch it pass. He could tell that it was not going to stop because it was clattering along the track at a tremendous speed under a huge cloud of black smoke. Sparks were crackling out of the coal smokestack, and the rushing iron engine seemed to be eating up the earth. As the train sped by, Rehman could see that every car was filled with people. They were shoved up against the windows and hanging from the doors, their hair and clothes flying in the hot dust and wind. All along the roof hundreds of families squatted together, a blur of white robes and cloth.

Rehman was amazed at the telegraph clerk's flair for understatement. He had said that the express trains were a little more crowded than usual, but Rehman had never seen so many people on a train, not even when there was a religious Mela, and everyone was going to do ablutions in the Ganges. On the one hand, it was true that the trains were running, but on the other, there was the vision of the train and its human cargo speeding through India and his consciousness.

Rehman found his horse sleeping on three legs among the stalls of the market. As he mounted and rode out of Dhampur, he felt completely frustrated by his lack of information and ignorance, but he felt there was nothing he could do for the moment but wait. Perhaps his friend had been mistaken about the date of his arrival and would still come in time for the wedding. Rehman could not believe there would be no news at all, and surely when his friend arrived, there would be an explanation.

The day before Tariq's wedding, Rehman called a meeting of all his relatives. There was still no answer to his telegram, and each day his concern and feeling of isolation grew stronger. They all met in Dadi's courtyard: his younger brothers, Salim and Tariq, who was about to get married, Apaji and her two brothers and their wives. They sat about on big armchairs brought into the courtyard for the occasion. Rehman wanted no servants about, so Dadi served them tea herself. They spoke of nothing but the wedding, and Rehman could see that only he was in possession of any news about Delhi and riots. Their carefree attitudes made him feel that perhaps he was in possession of only rumors after all. Nothing could be verified with any certainty. Perhaps he had let his imagination carry him away. They were laughing and asked Tariq how he felt about his bride. Had he sneaked a look yet at all the preparations? Had he managed to see her face since she went into seclusion two years ago after the signing of their engagement contract? Perhaps all that sitting around in her mother's house for two years had made her fat and pimply.

Rehman cleared his throat, and they all looked at him expectantly.

"Has any one had any news from Delhi?" he asked the assembled group.

"Delhi?"

"Why, no."

"Nothing at all."

Rehman stood up and began pacing the courtyard. It was his habit to pace, and no one took any notice of it. "I have heard that there is a mass migration of Muslims into Delhi, as well as of Hindu and Sikh refugees who have been uprooted from their homes."

"Of course. From Bengal and Punjab. That should be obvious," said his brother Salim.

"I was thinking that in the light of recent events, we should leave for Aligarh immediately following the wedding."

Dadi let out a cry. "There is no need to do that. Why cut the summer short?"

"We don't get any news here," Rehman explained to his mother. "The trains are running sluggishly. They are jam-packed with refugees. By the time August comes we may not be able to leave at all, and the children must be enrolled in school. Besides, I think we should go there to make sure the house is safe."

"Why not make sure your children are safe first?" said Dadi.

"The children are always safe with me."

"They would be safer in Nehtor," she said.

"Now, now. Nothing will happen in Aligarh. Everyone there is Muslim. Who is going to fight whom in Aligarh?" said Salim in support of his brother.

"Then who will stay with me?" complained Dadi.

"I will be here," said Salim.

"You. What good are you?" Dadi snapped at her second son. "Unmarried. Couldn't hold a wife. Can't produce any children." Salim slunk down into his seat.

"Salim is right, nevertheless," said Rehman. "He will take care of you."

Dadi's face was turning redder by the second. They knew she was capable of hysteria, and they wanted to avoid that at all costs. Tariq jumped up and gave her his seat; Apaji started massaging her legs.

"And you? What have you to say?" Dadi said, turning to her daughter-in-law.

"I believe your son has already decided," said Apaji.

"What else would a wife say in front of her husband!" groaned Dadi.

Everyone laughed. It was not that serious, after all. To each member of the family except Dadi, Aligarh was a second home. It was no less familiar than Nehtor. They had all gone to school there or sent their sons there or lived there while their fathers and brothers attended the university. It was the most prestigious Muslim university in all of India.

Dadi sighed. It really was decided then. No one would dare suggest that she leave Nehtor and go to Aligarh with them. She had not left the house since coming there from Dera Ghazi Khan, not even to go to Mecca. Salim would stay with her, filial as ever, haunting his room with all his friends and presiding over the house, the only man left in Nehtor.

"So then, let's get on with the wedding," said Rehman. "We will make it the biggest, most beautiful wedding Nehtor has ever seen."

The children were all excited by the news. First, Tariq's wedding, and then back to Aligarh in time for Independence Day. It would be a month of continuous celebration, and they were going to be in the thick of it. All the unhappy relatives who had tried for years to marry one of their daughters to the last son in Mubarik's family, even after the engagement contract was signed, were finally resigned and going to have a good time.

The wedding procession was preceded by a band of reed instruments and drums. Dressed in his ordinary clothes, Tariq walked behind them to the bride's house, which was already filled with close to a hundred guests. They would sleep there all week during the ceremonies. In the outer courtyard a single bed was laid out with a new suit of clothing for the bridegroom. It was prepared by the bride's parents for the wedding night. All the things one could imagine were included—pajamas of the finest white cloth, a silk blouse with gold buttons, a brocaded jacket, velvet shoes, stockings, and even underwear. There was also a shining turban, a sash of silver threads, garlands sculptured from sandalwood, and a wreath of silver flowers to be hung from the turban over Tariq's forehead, lace handkerchiefs, a pot of hinnah to paint his hands and feet with petals and designs, perfume oils, soaps, and an empty bucket for Tariq's last bath as a bachelor. On top of these things was a miniature Koran that would hang from Tariq's neck, and a leather billfold filled with money.

Tariq gathered up his wedding clothes, with many exclamations of pleasure from the men who accompanied him, and took them back to Dadi's house for the first feast of the celebration.

The next day at noon Tariq's preparation began. He was given a bath in the courtyard with the new soap and bucket, wearing only a loincloth in full view of all the ladies. Piece by piece he was dressed in the fine new clothes. His own wedding party of well over a hundred had now assembled, and the evening meal was brought from the bride's house by a procession of servants.

Everyone sat on the floor to eat, each at his own lacquer table, just inches off the ground. The food was served piping hot on clay dishes that had been lightly greased with clarified butter. The mutton had been specially killed from prized goats, saved and fattened all year just for the wedding. The meat had the aroma of cardamom and cinnamon and an abundance of the freshest black pepper.

Next came the Korma, another dish of mutton prepared with thick yogurt and a variety of spices and herbs, and in the end the servants passed out a new set of clay dishes just baked by the potter, and sweet rice was served, covered with the thinnest silver leaf and sprinkled with rose water and powdered pistachio. The greatest fear of the bride's family was that an adverse comment would be made, for that would ruin the entire meal, and the bride's parents had warned all their servants not to serve too much water as that would ruin the appetite. They made certain there was plenty of everything, and that the mutton was soaked with butter, so that everyone's fingers were sweet with grease. There were many loud belches from the assembled guests, which was a sure sign of approval, and spirits were so high that even blatant flirtations were not frowned upon.

After the meal, the guests dispersed to their rooms to dress. The women's quarters were a frenzy of silk cloth and jewels and laughter. Dadi was near hysteria. It was the marriage of her last son, and her husband was no longer alive to help her. She put on a long orange scarf and ran into the women's room constantly to make sure all the girls were properly covered—neck, shoulders, and breasts—by their own dopattas.

"The marriage contract had better not be changed," she told everyone she could find. "I will bring the boy back if there is not enough dowry, or if the bride is demanding too much alimony in case of divorce. I've been through that once already," she added. All these matters, she knew, had been arranged previously, two years ago when Mubarik was alive to supervise and they signed the engagement contract, but now she was alone, and the marriage contract was the ultimate agreement. It would not be signed until the ceremony, and there was always the possibility of a last-minute switch. She sent several of her relatives over to the bride's house three blocks away to extract a few last promises. If the proper assurances were not given, she would delay the wedding party for hours if necessary.

Dadi went into her bedroom to look at her surprise gift to the bride, a four-tola golden tikka. She thought she had left it in her wooden wall safe, but it wasn't there. Frantically she ripped the bedding off her charpoy, thinking she might have hidden it there. She searched through boxes of papers and even in her silver betel-nut box. The hairpiece was as big as a plum and hung from a chain of black pearls, which was to be threaded through the bride's hair.

Dadi ran out into the courtyard, shouting to everyone that the tikka was missing. All the men scattered about the house looking for the ten thousand-rupee hairpiece.

"How do I know what else is missing?" she shouted at all her relatives and servants. "Karim," she called. "Where is Karim?"

Everyone started calling for Karim. They all knew he was Dadi's trustee, and she needed him to take her into her secret attic rooms to look through her treasure. Only Karim had access to her closets full of multicolored baskets and boxes. Dadi had difficulty climbing the ladder and stooping beneath the low roof where she hid the gold and stones that had been in her family for generations. Now she had to find Karim to go to the inner storerooms and look for the hair piece and count again all the gold coins she had saved for her last son, Tariq, whom she still called Chunua, or Baby.

Karim, however, was deep in consultation with his older brothers. In the confusion of the last two days, Gappu had seized the opportunity to be alone with his cousin Mia. The glimpses through the bathroom window had proven too much. The brothers were hiding in the back of the men's room, where Tariq was putting the last finishing touches on his suit. The servants were running in and out with third and fourth portions of food and carting away the used clay plates, which would be left outside all night for the neighborhood cats to lick clean. Tariq's friends were telling him how to behave on the first night. They told him not to try anything too daring because they would be next door, listening in the guestroom where thirty beds were laid out.

"Is your heart beating, Chunua," they asked laughingly, now that they had finally discovered his nickname.

"No."

"Not even a little bit?"

"Shut up," Tariq told them.

Karim, Gerrar, and Gappu had better things to talk about. They had been on the lookout for Mia for two days. Finally Karim saw her walking alone between two houses. He called Gappu who dashed outside and took her into an empty room. Gappu was determined to find out about the hair he had seen growing between Mia's legs through the bathroom window.

"He's scared of her," Gerrar said in disgust.

"No. I put my hand through her pants and I got a hold of it."

The story was enough to cause a near ejaculation in the three brothers. Even when Gappu had slept the whole night in the four-sided house and sneaked up to see Mia after everyone else was asleep, he had not dared to go so far.

"What is the good of all that hair?" asked Karim, but none of the brothers knew. There was a mad dash to find the Kama-sutra which would surely give them the explanation. Karim was appointed to find the old copy, since he knew all the corners of Dadi's house. Karim peeped out the door into the courtyard. He saw Dadi running around in circles among the guests in their saris and silk pajamas, and thought she was much too near hysteria to notice him slipping past her and into the inner rooms. He took a glance into the women's quarters where he saw Mia hiding her face in another girl's lap, since she felt she might get pregnant after Gappu had touched her.

"Karim!"

He whirled around. Dadi was descending upon him, her gray hair flying beneath her orange shawl.

"Move," Gerrar hissed, looking at him through the door to Tariq's room and waving his arms frantically. It was too late. There was no chance for Karim to get away. Dadi held him firmly by the hand. She led him through her rooms to the ladder of the trapdoor.

"Climb up," she ordered. "And look into the box with the gold pieces. Go into the yellow box inside the pink box, but don't touch the red box because there might be a snake in there."

Karim rummaged around for a few minutes until he found the box. He looked in and saw the hairpiece lying in a pile of gold coins, closed the lid, and started climbing down again.

"What are you doing?"

"It's all there," he told her.

"How many coins?"

"I don't know."

"Well, go back up and count them," she shouted, pushing him up by his leg.

Karim had already forgotten which box it was, and he had to lift all the lids again.

"What are you doing?" Dadi called up to him.

"Looking for the right box again. I found one with a lot of colored stones. May I have one?"

"No. None. Hurry up and find the right box."

"Not even one colored stone, Dadi?"

"I will give you one when I find you a bride as good-looking as I was."

"Here they are, Dadi," he said.

"Count the coins," she ordered. "Then bring the box to the door, so that it will be near the ladder when I want them."

Karim pretended to be dragging the box across the floor, but instead he looked through the other boxes for the Kama-sutra. He couldn't find it.

By the time Karim and Dadi returned to the courtyard, his two older brothers had left in the tonga for the wedding ceremony at the bride's house. Karim's yells were louder than a tin drum, and Dadi and everyone else came running.

"Why is he crying?"

"Who made him cry?"

"He has been left behind, and now he has to ride with the ladies or walk with the old men." Karim let out another yell. Dadi felt so guilty for making him miss the tonga she did not know what to do.

"Karim will ride with the bridegroom on his horse," she decided. Karim was all happiness; Tariq was all smiles. "Come, Karim. You can ride with me."

The old gun maker, turned firecracker man, announced the beginning of the procession with an explosion from a bazooka. The white horse was draped in red and gold, and Tariq hoisted Karim up into the saddle in front of him. All around them bazookas were booming and trumpets were blaring. The music of the shahnai pipes began to wail, and the Mulvi was chanting the Koran. His lips were moving although he could hardly be heard over the sound of all the music and drums and explosions.

The entire town turned out to watch the procession, especially the beggars. A second Mulvi was carrying a cloth sack, and he kept dipping his hands into it and throwing small coins over the heads of the bridegroom and the beggars. The gas lamps on every street were lit from torches as they went, and the copper coins shimmered in the street as the beggars dashed among the members of the wedding party and in front of the horses, to scoop them up. Some women were using their dopattas like butterfly nets to catch the coins as they flew through the air.

The women in the bridegroom's party were dressed in new saris and goraras supplied by the bride's family, and they, in turn, were bearing the clothes they had prepared for the bride. Dadi, at the front of the procession of women in their tongas, carried the golden tikka for the bride's hair. Behind her came Apaji and her daughters with the bride's gorara in reddest satin with golden borders, a cummerbund, underwear, bangles of gold and blown glass for the arms, a whole sack of pearls to be beaded through the hair, hinnah to be painted on the palms, shoes of filigreed gold, and last of all, the huge red silk dopatta as delicate as spiderwebs and large enough to be draped over the bride's entire body, arms, head, and face. The dopatta alone had taken four tailors a month to complete. The older men came next on foot, in starched white suits with their Korans in their hands. Then followed the youngest children, tended by their ayahs, in open carriages drawn by horses.

By the time Tariq's party reached the home of the bride, the number of the wedding guests had swelled to well over two hundred. The bride's parents were in a state of panic because the wedding party was late and they were afraid something had gone wrong. The two families greeted each other with much bowing and a thousand compliments and explanations. Everyone was fed sherbet and shown to various rooms in the house, where the whole huge assemblage went to sleep.

In the morning a wedding breakfast was served, and buckets of

111

the finest Darjeeling tea were brought right into the bedrooms. After breakfast the parents of the bride and groom had their final conference, and examined the dowry, laid out on tables covered with silk and lace cloths. As soon as it was approved, the guests would be allowed into the courtyard to see the jewels and riches for themselves. It was understood that the dowry would include seventy-two dresses for the bride. There were customarily so many that the average girl never had a chance to wear them all before she became pregnant with one child after another and would put the unused clothes away into her own huge trunks in secret storage rooms, for her daughters' dowries many years later.

But for now, the bride was everything, and her body ached to wear the silk and satin saris in every color under the sun, in every shade of pink and violet and every shade of blue and silver, which no unmarried virgin was allowed to wear. She wanted her arms to jingle with the fragile glass bangles, twenty on each wrist, they could only be put on with soap and much squeezing of the palms, and would be replaced as soon as one broke. Only when her young husband died would she dash all the bangles onto the floor and never wear glass again.

Along with the seventy-two dresses came twenty-five pairs of shoes, so that the colors would never be mismatched. It was also understood that the bride would be equipped with everything necessary for setting up a home—from the deed to a new house in Delhi to the rope and bucket for pulling up water from the well to sets of wooden spoons and china dishes and at least three personal servants. Of course, there were seven sets of clothes for the groom, including handkerchiefs and gold cuff links for each shirt, a Swiss watch and Parker pen, and a deed to some especially prized lands. In Tariq's case there were a million extra sundries, including a new motorcycle and a commitment in writing from the bride's parents to pay for the rest of Tariq's education, including a year at an English university. Finally, already stitched and prepared were the clothes for the first-born child, and inconspicuously on the far side of the room, the wooden coffins for the bride and groom.

Tariq's main interest was the motorcycle, shining and new and imported from Italy, on which he would ride through the streets of Delhi. He felt that the dowry adequately matched all his expectations. He was surprised to learn that Dadi was very upset.

He burst in on the family conference, all aglow from his first glimpse of the new motorcycle, to find Dadi pacing the floor and throwing her hands in the air, her orange dopatta streaming out behind her as she walked.

"I knew they would try to take advantage of me," she shouted at Tariq.

"What is the problem?" he asked his mother.

"They are demanding too much alimony."

Tariq was dismayed—who could discuss alimony an hour before a wedding?—but he did not say anything.

Tariq's future father-in-law rose with a harried expression on his face and took him by the arm. "You don't have to concern yourself about all this, son."

"I'm not concerned," said Tariq. "I will never divorce your daughter, sir."

"That's fine," said Dadi. "Already he's taking sides with the other family."

They all explained lengthily to him that alimony was traditionally set at ten times the value of the original dowry. This, they said, had been done. Dadi, however, was of the opinion that the dowry was valued too high. Almost double its worth, she complained.

"The second problem is that your fine new bride won't sign the marriage contract unless it is specifically stated that you will not marry another woman so long as you are married to her."

"That's the modern way," said the bride's father.

"You can't expect us to allow our daughter to become a servant to a man who can have as many wives as he wishes," said the bride's mother.

"No, no, no," said Dadi.

"Your husband only married once," they reminded her.

"That is because I was obedient, and I signed the marriage contract the same as all Muslims have done since the time of the Prophet."

"Well if you want to get into a religious dispute," said the bride's father who had been a magistrate. "I can point out to you that the Koran does not condone polygamy. It merely designed a means of protection for women who in those days were being sold as slaves and prostitutes because they had no husband. The Prophet never consummated his second marriage."

"But he married more than once," Dadi argued. No former magistrate would intimidate her!

"That's enough of this," Tariq interrupted. "I don't plan to marry a fourth or a third or a second wife. I don't plan to divorce. So let's leave the contract as it is."

Everyone protested.

"My daughter won't sign."

"The alimony is too high."

Tariq raised his hand. "Enough. I think we should ask brother Rehman to settle this," he said, and everyone agreed.

Tariq brought Rehman into the sitting room from the outer courtyard, where he had been enjoying cold drinks with the relatives he had not seen for years. Dadi was sitting uncomfortably in a deep velvet armchair facing her son's future in-laws. The whole room was festooned with tall flowers in slender vases, enlivening the heavy teak furniture and dark red carpet. Tariq hastily explained the argument while Dadi sent him stern looks and the disgusted father of the bride leaned tiredly against his mantlepiece.

"You must find us a compromise," Tariq said.

Rehman folded his arms across his chest. "If you want to go by religious law, the Koran sets alimony at thirty-two pennies."

Dadi settled back into the chair, smiling.

"What nonsense," the bride's father said. "That is clearly impossible."

"Of course," Rehman continued. "The Prophet also gave a single sheet to his daughter for her dowry, and that is also impossible, so I think we should leave the Koran out of this, and do the sensible thing. Tariq can sign the clause your daughter wishes, but the alimony must be reduced."

"Never! Tariq will never sign such an agreement," Dadi shouted at him.

The bride's father threw up his hands and started to pace the floor. "How much lower? What are you asking?"

Rehman sat down on the sofa to settle the remaining issue of the amount of alimony based upon the evaluated worth of the dowry. It would be a long discussion, Tariq knew, but he was smiling because the main problem had been settled and soon he could take his position beside his bride under the ornate canopy for the ceremony.

Rana, Tariq's bride, was well aware of the furor she must be creating. Dressed for over an hour, the tall shy girl stood in her room, surrounded by her cousins and sisters, with her eyes transfixed on the door. She was not going to sign her sovereignty away, not to a boy whom she had not seen in two years, whose education did not outshine her own—Koran or no Koran, tradition or no tradition. The Mulvi did not agree with her. He had harangued the family all day yesterday, saying, "I am the man who whispered the first prayer, the Azan, in your daughter's ear the instant she was born. I slaughtered her first goat on the holy day, Bukra Id. I am not going to sign a marriage contract that is not based on the Koran." Finally her father banished the Mulvi from the wedding ceremony for talking too much.

Now she was dressed, and the marriage party was already assembled and had slept all night in her home. The girls who had just gotten married buzzed with stories and helpful hints in her ears. The others lifted her hands and painted swirls of tiny flowers and stems all over her palms and fingers, with orange hinnah herbs which would not wash off for the next month. A hundred fingers dropped heavy pearls into her waist-length hair. Her eyes were dabbed with soft charcoal mascara, and her face filled with powder. Every finger was covered with rings, and these were connected by a golden chain that ran across the backs of her hands and was fastened at her wrists. Her arms were roped in bangles, and Dadi's tikka as large as a guinea was pressed into her forehead. She held the tiny mirror numbly on her thumb through which her husband would have his first look at her in two years, when she allowed him to lift the veil of her dopatta ever so slightly, and see the cosmetic that was her face. She could hardly move in all her armor. While the girls chattered excitedly about the transformation of the plain willowy girl into a luscious ornament, a jewel, a bride, she thought only of that clause in the marriage contract. Without it, she would not sign.

After an interminably long wait, the bride's mother slipped through the curtain that divided her daughter's garden from the rest of the house. The handmaids all stood back for the bride to be examined and admired.

"Rana, queen, you are very beautiful," her mother breathed, running her hands gently over the long red dopatta.

"What is the answer?" her daughter whispered.

"It is all right. Tariq will never take another wife."

The girl almost burst into tears of relief, and had to hold herself back or the mascara would run. She could not fling herself into her mother's arms for a last embrace or her hair would fly and her satin skirts be crushed. Already her cousins were lifting her veil over her head and shoving her toward the door.

The guests did not notice the delay. They were too busy eating food, ordering servants to bring water, and spitting red betel juice on the floor and into spittoons from the paan they were chewing. The paan was filled with a specially potent kind of tobacco, something like cannabis, and everyone was feeling high. Even the children chewed it, and they were very happy, and inspected every inch of the nuptial bedroom while they had a chance. Next door to it thirty relatives would be sleeping to make sure no one bothered the newly married couple on their wedding night. The bed had been sprinkled with aromatic oils of jasmine and musk, and mogra incense had been blowing all day. The children found the scents very exciting.

Food was circulating continuously in every room, and a Brahmin cook had been hired so that only his hand would touch the special halvah and sweetmeats prepared for the Hindu guests. They ate from separate dishes, made by the potter, and gave a lot of money to the groom and left before the ceremony.

Little by little, the assembled guests began to sit around the courtyard where a huge red tent, or shamayana, was erected. In front, the bridal altar was strewn with flowers. As the Mulvi began to read the genealogies of both families, the bride was led in, completely veiled with red silk, amid blasts on the bazookas. Tariq took his place on the raised dais of the altar, and the young couple sat cross-legged, facing the guests. The butcher touched their clothes with a knife with which he would slaughter a goat to make the meat kosher, or hillal, before it was distributed to the poor, waiting outside the mahalla. Prayers were read for hours, and vows exchanged. Fireworks blazed across the moon-filled sky, and all the guests approached Tariq and handed him money. He made a deep salaam as he received each packet of crisp bills. Finally the bride gave all her money to the groom, and he in turn gave all his money to her, and they salaamed each other with a gentle nodding of their heads.

As the music of the reed instruments, the shahnai, wailed loudly through the air, every woman in the courtyard burst into tears, and it was difficult to tell which was crying louder, the women or the shahnai. Four men lifted the bride, who was close to hysteria, crying "Mamma, Mamma," and brought her out to the waiting sedan chair. Tariq was hoisted in after her, and his scarf was tied to the end of her dopatta. Eight of the strongest bearers raised the long poles of the carriage to their shoulders and waited as Rana's father appeared under the brick archway of the mahalla. All the guests had flooded into the street, but they fell into silence as Rana's father raised his voice to sing his poem of farewell.

"You are going as a bride to the house of Mubarik, married in riches and tied in love," he sang. "Though the gold may vanish and the silks be torn, may you merge with him such, that only your coffin returns when you leave that house forever."

There was a blast from the bazookas. Rockets flew into the sky, and the pipes began to sound. Tariq pulled a silken cord; the red curtains fell over the carriage, and the bearers began to walk, with all the guests following behind, through the streets of Nehtor.

3

Partition I

JULY-AUGUST 1947

Kanti Lal Shah watched the family of Rehman Hussain return to their house in Aligarh, across the street from his own home. He could not belive his eyes. Standing just behind the trellised gate to his garden, he peeped through the vines and counted them—seven children; Apaji as pregnant as a cow. His old friend and neighbor Rehman Hussain was leading them with his booming voice as usual. The servants were scurrying here and there with trunks and valises from the tongas and buggies, all except that lazy Bashir who was always fooling around with Karim and never doing any work. He had watched Bashir all month living in the big house across the road as if he owned it. The other household servants lived elsewhere in their own houses, but Bashir stayed on Morris Road, passing Kanti Lal every day with a wave of his hand and leaving the gate before Rehman's circular driveway wide-open half the time. "Tomorrow," Kanti Lal decided, "I will go over there and have a word with Brother Rehman about the boy."

The old Hindu salesman scratched his shaven head and tugged on the string of white hair growing from the center of his dome. He remembered. It might not be the best thing to go into a Muslim home at a time like this. There might be reprisals. Maybe he would send a message.

Nothing had happened in Aligarh. Not yet. But Kanti Lal had been to meetings that he did not really want to attend. He went for business reasons. Half his customers were leaving for Pakistan. He had to find new contacts. Friends he never really had, but for business associates, he would travel anywhere and invite anyone into his home.

Kanti Lal had discussed the Muslim question in great detail with the other Hindu businessmen of Aligarh. They had gathered at big meetings in each others' houses, dismissing the women after tea was served because they became too emotional. Kanti Lal was uncomfortable in large gatherings, but he went nevertheless and sat unobtrusively, eating sweetmeats with his dainty fingers and listening. The older leaders of the Hindu community were all for peace and order in the city. There were many new upstarts, however, who came into their big flowering gardens without ever offering a fruit or a handful of flowers to the household shrines, and still they called for justice. This, the outsiders defined as retaliation for the deaths of millions of innocent people in the western part of Punjab and Sind and the eastern half of Bengal. Other Hindus, they pointed out, who had been living in homes as fine as theirs, had been forced to flee from their lands to make room for the partition of the country. Everyone knew there had been rapes and that thousands of the young flowers of their land were committing suttee—a horrible practice, young mothers flinging themselves onto the funeral pyres of their dead husbands. There had been far too many deaths. The Ganges was flowing with their ashes.

No one, of course, wanted bloodshed. All through June and July the Hindus of Aligarh had argued among themselves: "We do not kill living creatures. We do not even touch the meat of animals or birds or fish, so how could anyone harm his brother or cause blood to flow?"

"At the same time we must see that others who have been uprooted and forced to flee to the motherland shall find a haven among us," an old Brahmin priest reminded them.

"And those who voted for Pakistan should go there where they belong," shouted a young Bengali student. He had come recently from Dacca to live with his uncle after the university there had been closed down.

"Not all the Muslims voted for Pakistan," another businessman protested.

"They supported it all the same," the student shouted, growing red in the face. "After ruling India for four centuries, they sold us out to the British rather than relinquish power to Hindus."

The young man's voice added a new note of urgency to their evening discussions, and Kanti Lal looked at him guiltily over the rim of his teacup. The boy was hardly older than his own son, Muni, who might be speaking the same way in someone's garden in Rawalpindi. Kanti Lal had already sent urgent messages to his son to come home from his boarding school immediately, before the rioting made India impossible to traverse. Every day his suspicions mounted and Kanti Lal watched the student's taut nervous face, the young smooth skin turned livid with anger over his fine bones.

"What you say may be true in Bengal and Punjab," said a doctor whom Kanti Lal knew well. "In Aligarh it is different. I have Muslim friends who are members of the Congress Party. Men who have met Gandhiji and spoken for One India from the beginning."

"But now it is the end, and they have severed our country, taken our jute and tea gardens, our textile mills and half our rivers," the student argued. "The Holy Ganges will soon be flowing through a foreign state."

A student from Aligarh jumped to his support. "They have taken our brothers from their homes and looted their possessions. The khans have raided villages way beyond their sphere of land and forced thousands to convert to Islam."

"I say the Muslims of Aligarh must go to Pakistan—just like the Muslims of Delhi and Calcutta. Their homes rightfully belong to the refugees from Punjab and Bengal who are coming here," the Bengali student demanded.

Kanti Lal cleared his throat. "I haven't seen any refugees in Aligarh."

They all glared at him. He knew he should not have said that in his high voice, which usually made him embarrassed to speak in a gathering.

"What do you mean no refugees?" they demanded.

"It is true. Aligarh has been peaceful. It will remain peaceful."

Everyone said he was wrong. "They are coming, I tell you," someone said. They asked him if he had not seen the trainloads of suffering people that stopped every day in the station at Aligarh. He had believed those trains were filled with Muslim faces, but he did not dare to say any more. They told him it was wrong to believe Aligarh was any different. Hindu refugees were flooding every city of India. They were looking for homes.

Kanti Lal looked again through his gate at his neighbor Rehman Hussain's home. Nothing had been resolved by the meetings Kanti Lal attended, but every day more and more people came, and the discussions were growing louder and more intense. On his long evening walks Kanti Lal noticed that more and more of the rich and intellectual Muslims of the university were padlocking their doors, and suddenly an old acquaintance would be gone without a word of farewell. If Aligarh were no different from Delhi, where riots had already broken out, then what was Syed Rehman Hussain doing here fresh from the railroad without a scratch on him, lugging all those children and thousands of rupees' worth of belongings? Why had Rehman come to Aligarh when everyone else was seeking safety elsewhere? Kanti Lal decided he would have to find a way to talk to Rehman and ask him these things. Perhaps all was not the way it seemed.

The children thought the return to Aligarh was exciting. They had left Nehtor full of gaiety, singing the songs of Tariq's wedding. They had gone slowly in tongas and bullock carts, in order not to upset Yellow and the other horses by their departures. The seven-mile drive to Dhampur had been filled with the fording of rich streams that flowed across every road, since the monsoon rains were coming almost daily now. The air hung with the silence of the countryside, the creaking of wooden wheels, and the calling of parrots like bunches of green flowers in the mango trees. The station at Dhampur was empty, and the stationmaster who had not expected their arrival was caught sleeping on his charpoy behind the thick screen of musty khus in his room. He accommodated them easily in the second-class compartments on the slow passenger train to Aligarh, which rumbled into the station almost empty for an Indian train, and hardly anyone else got on at Dhampur. They slept most of the way, still dizzy from the food of Uncle Tariq's wedding and the adventures of the summer, shortened though it was.

Gappu, Gerrar, and Karim had learned from their father with great pleasure that this fall they would not be sent away to boarding school but would attend the colleges and day schools of the great Muslim University in Aligarh. No questions were asked for fear the decision would be altered.

In the next two weeks an educational atmosphere pervaded the big house in Aligarh. They were determined not to let Abu regret the decision to let them stay at home, instead of facing all those narrow little dormitory beds and the disciplinarians who gave them no freedom and understood nothing. Gerrar was finally enrolled in the premedical course at the college, and Gappu decided to enroll in pre-engineering, largely as a matter of default, since engineering would prepare an Indian for practically any future in government service. Apaji was busy putting the house in order. She had to call the tailor to fit the new school jackets—black for winter and white for summer. The boys wanted the university emblem—a palm tree and a crescent—to be stitched onto the high-necked collar. Karim, of course, demanded one, too, and the trip to the university shop to purchase the emblems and the regulation cloth turned into a whole day's excursion for the three brothers.

Since Waji's death, they were no longer so anxious to eat the spicy snacks sold at open-air stalls in the market, but that did not stop them from looking. The market was filled with the noise of haggling. Overhead, yards of printed cloth, sheets, and saris stretched from shop to shop, and each lane had its own specialty. Some had row after row of terra-cotta pots, and others had trinkets and perfume in neat glass cases. Women stooped over piles of vegetables—four-foot-long cucumbers and eighteen-inch bananas—stuffing their saris between their legs and tossing their purchases into oversized baskets which bearers, hired for the day, carried two or three to an arm with one on top of their heads.

Bearers and beggars alike lived in the market like scavengers, and both went about their business in the same way. The bearers, thin and bony but sturdy and succinct on their bowed legs, and the beggars, crumpled and filthy with their minds and teeth blown away from smoking charas and chewing raw tobacco, chose their victims with care and then followed them through the market, haunting them with a stream of pleas and warnings: "You will do much shopping, memsahib. Let me lighten your load. Here, put those stinking fish in my basket. You will soil your fine sari."

"Memsahib, I wish long life to your children and your children's children. I praise your beauty and your motherhood and your fairest skin. For four annas I will pray for you five times today, and I will have your name constantly on my lips."

"If you ignore a poor beggar, memsahib, I know you will have three accidents today."

Money was exchanged at every turn. A fight developed when a fat bald-headed man in a long white loincloth, or dhoti, which hung in drapes and pleats almost to the man's shaven ankles, refused to give baksheesh, the little extra tip, to a wizened old man with a tin trunk on his shoulders. The bearer let the trunk fall on the ground with a bang and threw the coins given to him at the fat man's feet.

Gappu kept pushing his brothers ahead of him and exchanged banter with all the money seekers who approached him. "Find your bread elsewhere," he told a young mother with an infant on either hip, who thrust her pleading face breathlessly into his own from under the tattered border of her sari. Karim bumped into her and fell. The woman laughed and laughed, hoisting the blank-eyed babies higher onto her hips. "You do not take care of your brother, Baba." She had won. Gappu gave her four annas.

"Now we will not be able to buy three milk shakes," Karim complained.

"It's your fault for falling. I will let you have a sip of mine."

Karim argued with Gappu all the way to the milk-shake shop. Vats of milk were fermenting into yogurt, and sweet cheese balls sizzled in woks of clarified butter. They ordered two peach lassys of yogurt buttermilk and sugar into which were crushed two whole peaches. Karim had to share his with Gappu. Then they raced away down the twisting alleys with saris fluttering overhead to the sports shops where they examined cricket bats and tennis rackets and football shoes. Finally they decided it was getting late, and they had better get a rickshaw and go to the university before the shops closed for the afternoon and the heat became unbearable.

As they approached the university buildings with all its faculties, colleges, primary schools, and residences, their rickshaw was stopped several times by large bands of ralliers. There was a profusion of political parties, and some were waving the red banners of the Communists; some had the green banners of the Muslim League; others, the green, white, and orange tricolor of the Congress party flag with Gandhiji's spinning wheel in the center. A small group of hunger strikers, barefoot and dressed like Gandhi were sitting to one side of the big entrance archway, behind which rose all the Gothic spires and clock towers. They were listening to a speaker raised slightly above their heads on a makeshift platform. Sitting cross-legged and bare-chested, he told his followers that Gandhiji was threatening to fast unto death if the trouble between Hindus, Muslims, and Sikhs did not stop.

Gandhi's voice calling for unity could be heard throughout the university halls, even as Gandhi sat in his tiny village in the remote state of Gujarat nourishing his birdlike body on only an orange and a glass of milk. Gandhi's voice was saddened. *I gave you independence from the British without shedding blood. Now in independence you are creat-*

125

ing armies. It was said that Gandhiji planned to go to Delhi and isolate himself in the Birla Temple to fast and write letters of personal appeal to his people.

"Gandhiji is too old and weak for another fast," the speaker cried. "He will surely die. As it is he cannot walk unless his granddaughters are at his side, holding him up in the air. Still, Gandhiji lives by many rules he will not break. Nehru has pleaded with him to give up his walks and his days of silence, when one word from his lips could have altered history or saved a politician from execution by the British."

The voice sounded sad and disillusioned. It fell from the lips of his followers on every street and in every marketplace. "Let us not forget the reason for India's independence," the speaker was shouting to all the passersby. "Let us not forget the self-sufficient village for which India is being created. Let us not sell India from the slavery by government to the slavery of business. We free ourselves from the British masters one way, and we bind ourselves in another. The village is everything. The spinning wheel is the answer to our economic survival."

Gandhiji's voice was quiet, a whispered prayer like the tinkling of temple bells: *Pakistan has been created. We must live in peace.*

The speaker's voice was drowned out by the insistent pounding drums as a procession of Muslims marched by, banners waving and men and women shouting, "Hindustan Zindabad." Karim jumped from the rickshaw to join in the procession.

"Where are you going?" Gappu shouted. "Come back here."

"We can sing the national anthem. Come, come," Karim answered.

Gappu and Gerrar jumped off, too, and they all marched and chanted, and then they sang, "Jai Jai Jai Jai Hind." They did not even know whom they were marching with, but they sang until they were hoarse and nearly fainting from the heat. They had to run almost a mile back to the university shop and pound on the tin door that the merchant had already lowered halfway, pleading with him to let them buy their three school emblems.

As soon as they came back outside, they saw another group of marchers and joined in the procession, yelling slogans and cheers. All afternoon they listened to speeches, walked and sang, until early evening when the sky began to fill with threatening gray clouds.

'I'm glad to see you are enjoying Aligarh so much," Abu said to them when they finally reached the house and were sneaking up the wide circular driveway. They darted from tree to tree, trying to make it across the lawn and up to their rooms before someone saw them and realized how late they were coming home. How could they have missed seeing Abu sitting right there in front of them in his favorite lawn chair? Bashir was watering the rose and jasmine and rat-ki-rani bushes. He glared at Karim angrily for having had a whole day of fun without taking him along.

"Come inside. There is news," said Abu.

"There is always news," said Gappu. "Is it good or bad?"

Rehman glanced at his oldest son. "Good news, of course. Have I ever given you bad news?"

"That is only because you are the one to decide what news to give us. We always find out the other things, too."

Rehman scowled, but he was glad to see that Gappu was definitely ready for an education at Aligarh University. They went inside to Apaji, who was sitting on the floor of Raheel's room, sewing a blanket for the new baby.

"You will have a sister or a brother any day now," Apaji told them as they entered. The boys looked at her stomach which was finally protruding under her sari. Apaji was so used to having children that they would never know she was pregnant until the last month, if it were not for all the baby clothes being sewn and collected in a new valise for months in advance. "Everything is good," she said. "Your father plans to leave for Sambhar on business."

They all looked at Abu. The news was sudden, but everything was made in the form of startling announcements these days.

"Yes," said Rehman. "I think this is the proper time to leave. School is opening. We have been in Aligarh for two weeks now, and everything is peaceful. A little politics maybe, but that is healthy. Everyone has something to say."

"It's fine with me," said Gappu. "You have nothing to worry about."

"Your cousin Zamir is an administrator at the University, and he will watch over you at school. My big sister, Phopi Fatima, will come from Delhi to help Apaji when the new baby is born and see that you don't hang on her too much. We have hired extra servants, and they will take Karim and the girls to school."

"No one has to take care of me," said Karim.

"If no one takes you, you will be spending more time in the market with Bashir than at school," said Gappu.

"At any rate, it's all decided," said Abu. "Now come with me for a walk before I have to leave for the station."

Outside, the street was quiet. Kanti Lal was seated in his garden behind the open gate so he could get a good view of the street, but nothing much was happening. A lone vendor pushed his cart of vegetables along the road, and the candy salesman and betel-nut salesman were both asleep on the grass under their stalls, which stood against the outer wall of the big houses.

Rehman raised his hands in the prayerful greeting of the Hindus. "Namaste," he called to his neighbor.

Kanti Lal bowed his head in the Muslim fashion of salaam and greeted him with the Arabic words, "Assalaam Aleicum. Peace be with you."

Rehman was surprised that Kanti Lal had been so reticent in the two weeks since they returned from the summer in Nehtor. He would have liked to have asked him to keep his eye on the house while he was away in Sambhur. Kanti Lal's eyes were always on it anyway from the vantage point of his garden directly across the street. Rehman knew it was not the best of times to travel, but all the trouble with the trains and the refugees was in the north. Most of India still lay stretched out lazily and untroubled on its forested footpaths and luscious fields and jungles in the south. It was only in the big ancient Mogul cities that minority groups came into such vicious conflict. It seemed that the population of northern India was not only trying to wrench itself out of the grip of British colonialism, but also from the memories of the Mogul Empire, which had crumbled a hundred years before. Aligarh, however, was safe. It was not really an ancient city, and had gained fame and prestige around the walls of the infant university, which was founded by Sir Syed Ahmad Khan in the last century, because he felt that Muslims were intellectually far behind the rest of the population of India. The current president was still willing to dance before a gathering for five-rupee donations as Sir Syed had when the university was being formed. There was never any danger in Aligarh, where the Muslims supported India and the Hindus were friends. Rehman had been to meetings every night, and he was convinced.

The lamplighter was coming along Morris Road early, filling each lamp with fresh oil, even though the sun still outlined the heavy rain clouds and reflected on the street. Gappu and Gerrar lagged behind, and Karim, prancing at his father's side, had to take double steps to keep up. Rehman prided himself on his ability to walk great distances without breaking his stride. His strong legs kept pace with his thoughts, and he did not feel that walking was the time for lengthy conversations. Only Karim did not respect that tradition. With his hands busily weaving images in the air, he chattered on about the political processions at the university and hunger strikers as thin as Gandhi, sitting on the sidewalk.

Rehman listened with only half an ear, his head cocked but his eyes sweeping the road and the white brick walls that surrounded each house and the occasional stalls erected like tents over three-wheeled carts. Several children in bright skirts and short pants were leading their goats through the grass-filled plots that straggled among the houses. Rehman and Karim walked almost a mile, as far as the big house of their cousin, Zamir. He had Zamir's assurances as trustee of the university that the children would be well supervised in his absence. Rehman glanced through the wrought-iron gate, which was slightly ajar, to the garden but only a gardener was about, spraying the spacious lawn with water from a hose. Without stopping, Rehman twirled Karim around, and hurried back down the road toward home. Gappu and Gerrar, who were blocks behind, waited until they caught up and then strolled slowly after them.

As soon as he brought the boys back into the house, he raced up to his room and changed from his lounging pajamas into a Western suit and shirt for the journey to Sambhar. He packed his valise with pajamas, shirts, and bedding for the train and riffled through the papers in his briefcase to make sure everything he needed was there. After poking his face into each room, he joined Apaji who was sitting on the verandah for a late tea. She offered him a cup, but he waved it away.

"I will try to be back before the baby comes. If not, my sister, Phopi Fatima, will be here in a day or two to help you."

Apaji nodded. "I will manage very well," she said, pulling her sari tautly across her small swell of stomach.

Rehman was pacing nervously. "Where is that Bashir?" he growled. "I sent him to fetch a tonga an hour ago."

"It could not have been so long," said Apaji, checking her watch. "You only returned from your walk fifteen minutes ago."

"That is still enough time for Bashir to get back here," said Rehman. "I have never missed a train." He kept on pacing and glancing down the driveway and across the lawn where the children were playing cricket. Finally the horse and buggy pranced through the gate with Bashir riding peacefully behind the driver. Rehman turned and took Apaji's hand in his. "I'm sorry to leave you at a time like this, but you understand that events press upon us and business will not wait."

Apaji laughed. "The child is strong and restless, and will not wait for business, either."

Rehman gave his wife's hand a pat. "Assalaam Aleicum. You know how to send a message if you need me." He hoisted up his large leather valise and his attaché case, and jumped into the tonga, scowling at Bashir who ran into the house.

The children looked up from their game and waved at Abu as the carriage drove past them. It was not unusual for Abu to be away on business trips for weeks at a time, and none of the children even bothered to see him off. They were more interested in homecomings because there were always presents and Abu would not be all nervous about missing his train. The rain clouds were gathering into knots of silver, and the children could barely see the cricket ball as it cracked off the bat into the shadows and was lost in some bushes.

Apaji called to Raheel to come upstairs to practice her crocheting, and she raced across the lawn with Mona at her heels. Raheel's chiffon dopatta was flying from her shoulders, and both girls needed a bath after playing with their brothers. A few big droplets of rain were splattering onto the driveway, making deep red stains on the hot clay. Gerrar could not find the ball anywhere in the bushes, and Karim was making so many runs that Gappu had to raise his hands and call the game off. He led them back into the house with Karim whooping noisily that he had won. Gappu whopped him across the back of the head and warned him that with Abu gone, he must be especially good and quiet so as not to upset Apaji. To keep the children calm, he allowed all of them to come into his bedroom and let Moïd and Piari tear through his closet full of games, since he never used them much any longer.

Bashir went from room to room turning on the electric-light switches, which to him were the most remarkable aspect of the city house. It was the one chore he never grew tired of performing. Dinner was already prepared, and the cook, the gardener, and the washerwoman had all left for their own homes in another section of Aligarh. Bashir hurried through the rooms, hoping nobody would see him, so that he could take a nap before it was time to serve the evening meal. He finished the upstairs first, where the family was all scattered in their bedrooms, and did not bother to fluff up the deep pillows on the couches in the living room or to clear away the teacups and dishes from the verandah, but ran quickly off to his charpoy in the rear garden, which was his own personal domain. In the distance he could hear the sound of drums signaling yet another procession that he had watched amusedly all over Aligarh during the summer. He dragged his charpoy under the enclosed portion of the patio and sprawled out, his head on his arms, to breathe the aroma of the flowers which was heightened by the rain.

Suddenly Bashir jumped up. He thought he heard someone running along the verandah. The front door slammed shut, and Abu's voice could be heard booming through the house. Bashir leaped off the charpoy and raced through the kitchen into the reception room. He thought Abu must have missed his train and that he would get a scolding for sure now. Everyone came running to the head of the stairs. Apaji and Raheel were already in the reception room, and Abu was waving them back. "Inside, inside. There is no time to talk."

"What happened?" asked Apaji. "Why are you back?"

Rehman was breathless, and he no longer had his valise with him, only his briefcase which he was clutching tightly against his chest. The pocket of his suit jacket had been ripped away. His black hair was tousled and his usually neat moustache was disheveled. He did not answer their questions, but kept waving them back. "Bashir," he called. "Take these keys and open my closet. Bring the guns."

Bashir grabbed the keys and leaped up the stairs three at a time.

"Guns?" they all asked incredulously. "What for?" They could hear a lot of muffled voices coming from the streets. Far away the incessant drums were pounding, but they were used to the sounds of drums and processions.

"There is no time. Gappu, Gerrar, gather all the long sticks you can find. Bring them quickly. I want everyone to have a stick and a gun." They could not believe what he was saying.

"Don't stand there gawking like that. Move."

Raheel and Mona were crying, and Piari and Moïd were jumping up and down.

"Karim, take the children out of here. Put them in the storeroom."

Karim grabbed Piari and Moïd by their hands, but they, too, started crying. "No better leave them here," Rehman said. "Just keep still everybody."

Bashir dashed in with the guns—hunting rifles and pistols—and Gappu and Gerrar brought a stack of long sticks that they had pulled down from the grape arbor outside.

"Abu, something is burning in the bazaar. We can see the flames," Gappu told him. He was shaking. With that, Apaji ducked past her husband, swung open the door, and ran out onto the front lawn. Sounds of screaming pierced through the garden, and she could see the sky lit orange in the distance. Rehman ran after her and pulled her struggling back into the house and slammed the door.

"They are killing. They are burning, and they are killing," she said over and over. Rehman dropped Apaji into Raheel's arms. Raheel was still crying. Everyone was crying except the three oldest sons and himself. His family was collapsing around him in a heap. Bashir was moving furniture to try to barricade the doors and windows.

"Quiet. Quiet." Rehman demanded. "We have to think."

Everyone stopped frozen. There was a hush, and the room seemed to be shrinking and closing in on him. "We must be calm. Not excited. There are riots all over the city. The train to Sambhar was attacked. It was filled with refugees, and people were charging at each other with sticks in the railroad station. There were no policemen to be found anywhere. We have to barricade the house and make it into a fortress. We are going to have to protect ourselves. The rioters are miles away, but, my dear wife"—he turned to Apaji—"they are coming."

Apaji straightened herself up. She set her face and looked determined. "Is there any way we can get back to Nehtor?" she asked.

"We will try to do that. I have already sent someone to look for a lorry. Now I want you all to stay together in this room. Later the children will hide in the trunks. The boys should put air holes in them so they can all breathe. When the lorry comes, we will have the children carried out in the trunks, and we will follow."

They spent the night barricading the doors and drilling holes in the trunks. No one talked as they worked; and dinner was forgotten and grew cold in the iron pots on the stove. Raheel and Piari fell asleep with their heads on Apaji's lap. Mona slept on the floor at her feet. Apaji sat as still as she could, praying the baby would not come until this terrible night was over. She had visions of giving birth to her child in a burning house surrounded by flames, or in a lorry on some deserted roadside with all the children crying and not understanding.

Throughout the night the long periods of silence were interrupted by far-off screaming. At times the screaming seemed to be getting louder and coming closer. Sometimes it was close enough to make out the Hindu and Muslim prayers of Jai Ram and Ya Allah. Then there would be silence, and the next screams seemed to have receded into the distance again.

Once they heard footsteps running by the gate of the house. Everyone sat holding his breath, and Apaji's hand was on her heart. It sounded as if a hundred people were running but not saying a word. Rehman whispered that the children should get out of the room and hide in the trunks. Gappu, Gerrar, and Karim began to lift the younger children gently, so they should not cry out, but before they moved, the sound of running was over. They all listened sharply. Everything was quiet, and they sat down again with their guns and sticks. Since they had been brought up hunting with Abu, they did not feel strange holding guns, only none of them dared to imagine what they had to use them for.

The night dragged on past midnight and into the early hours of morning. The rain had stopped, but there was no moon, and they sat in total darkness in the living room. The only sound hour after hour was the soft crackling of static from the large floor radio, which Abu tinkered with hoping that All India radio would broadcast some news about Aligarh, but there was nothing, not even a mention in passing.

Again the air burst with screams and running. It sounded as if the rioting had reached their own block. This time the boys picked up the younger children and carried them quickly from the room. "Stay there until I call you," Rehman said, without looking back, his eyes trained on the heavy door with a table in front of it and his fingers on the triggers of two pistols.

There was a knock on the front door. Rehman waved Bashir toward the door and aimed his pistols. "Stand to the side of the door and say no one is home and ask who is it," he ordered.

Bashir stood where Rehman pointed and pressed his lips to the wall.

"Sahib and his family are gone," he said in a high shaky voice. Rehman looked at him for an instant and reminded himself that Bashir was just a child, little older than Karim.

The knock came again. "Let me in Rehman Bhai. It is your neighbor, Kanti Lal Shah."

Rehman waved at Bashir again. "No one is home," said Bashir.

"I promise you, neighbor, it is truly I. Let me in quickly."

"Step back and unlatch the door," said Rehman.

Bashir moved the table. The door latch snapped, and the door swung open. Rehman was facing the blackness of the early morning. He could see the glow of a fire reflected on his front lawn. He was pointing his pistols at the diminutive body of his neighbor Kanti Lal Shah, who had also been concealing himself against the wall on the other side.

Kanti Lal slipped into the living room and quietly closed the door. He put his fingers to his lips. "Do not let the children cry," he said. He looked around the room. Only Rehman and Apaji were there, and Bashir half hidden behind a curtain.

"Where are the children?" he asked.

"They are hidden in the trunks," said Abu. "I am waiting for a lorry to take them to Nehtor."

Kanti Lal shook his head. "You can't get out of Aligarh. The entire city is barricaded and blocked."

"Do you think this will spread any farther?" Rehman asked.

"I think it is spreading everywhere."

"What should I do?" Rehman asked for the first time in his life.

"I have a proposition. Do not send them. Do not step out of your property. You must hide in the servants' quarters in the back garden and leave the house in my hands."

"They will come looking for us," said Rehman.

"No. No. The people will respect my caste. They will not come in when they see me. I will not let them go to the back of the house. I will tell them—"

His voice was interrupted by a loud wail from Rehman's own front lawn.

"They have set fire to the house next to mine," Kanti Lal said. "Hurry! There is no time. One more house and yours is next."

"Who is in your house?"

"There are people. Don't worry about that. You must hurry."

Abu nodded and grabbed Bashir, who had frozen rigid with fear. "What are you doing here? You will give us away. Come."

The wailing outside was louder. They recognized the voice of their neighbor, the lawyer, although it was distorted with hysteria.

"Dead, dead, all dead," he was wailing. "No, no, no, no! I supported you—I supported all of you."

Apaji turned ashen. "Rehman," she gasped, saying the name she had never said before. Again she dashed to the door.

"Stop her," Rehman screamed at Kanti Lal Shah, but it was too late.

The lawyer next door was standing naked on their front lawn with a dead baby in his arms. Another child lay moaning at his feet. The lawyer, Syed Munir Haider, defender of the British Raj, was turning around in circles, mad with hysteria.

"I supported the Hindu," he said as he circled.

"I supported the Congress Party.

"I supported Nehru.

"My father supported.

"I asked all of you people to support it."

There seemed to be people hovering around the outer wall and about to come over the wall. Apaji ran to the child moaning in the grass. One hand was missing. She picked up the child and hid her in her sari. "Drop that child," ordered Rehman.

She glared at him with the ferociousness of a lion, her eyes red with fire. Rehman pulled the moaning lump from her grasp and dragged her inside. "Your own children will be killed," said Kanti Lal. "Please, I beg you. Hide in the servants' quarters." Rehman pulled Apaji and Bashir from the room.

When she picked up the lids to the three huge tin trunks with their contents spilled out over the floor and saw her children's faces looking up at her, Apaji snapped into action. Bashir had disappeared, but she took the children with her and in less than five minutes put everything of value into their arms, including her jewelry and gold coins and whatever else they could carry. There was nothing to understand. In a few minutes' time, part of their house was burning. They could hear furniture being dragged across the floors and out onto the lawn. The whole family met in the kitchen in the back of the house. "Quick," said Rehman. "Everyone into the servants' quarters." They dashed through the garden at the rear of the house, and into the small detached room where Bashir was supposed to sleep. It was concealed behind a row of flowering rosebushes and a clothesline, where an old white sari was flapping in the breeze.

Everyone sat huddled together in the little room, which was only big enough to hold a single charpoy, a chair, and a chest of drawers. The older children leaned against their parents and each other on the floor. The room was musty from disuse, and with the small wooden door locked and barred by the bureau, and the single window shuttered tight, perspiration hung like oil on their faces and on their arms encircling each other. Apaji laid Moïd, Mona, and Piari on the charpoy and kept pressing their foreheads with her fingers. No one dared to make any noise or even whisper.

All morning they listened to screams that went past their house, down the street, and around the block. They could see a ribbon of sunlight crack through the slats of the shutters, but still they did not move. Although they could hear doors of the main house opening, and two men actually tramped through the flower beds in the rear garden, no one came into the servants' quarters. They listened incredulously while the two men in the garden discussed the quality of the roses and dug up several small bushes to replant for the Independence Day celebration, they said. It was hard to understand how anyone could stop to pick flowers when everything was burning down around them. But it seemed Kanti Lal had done the job. The family was saved.

Hours passed, and still Abu and the three older boys clutched their guns in their hands. Their eyes were ringed with red but unblinking. It seemed impossible that they could not move. Although there had not been any screams, or drums or running since dawn, they were imprisoned and immobile on the earthen floor of Bashir's room with the sun beating down on the tin roof and the heat welling up like a moist bath.

They had never gone into the room before. Since his father died, even Bashir rarely used it and usually slept outside in the garden surrounded by the soft smells of the night-blooming flowers, or managed to sneak up to spend the cooler nights in Karim's room. If he had asked, Bashir would have been given a room of his own in the house, and Apaji often urged him to take one, but Bashir had been quite content as he was, and did not wish to lose his freedom to the confines of the house with all its locked doors and keys, which Apaji wore on a silver hook from the waist of her sari.

No one knew where Bashir was now. Karim was very worried, but Apaji assured him that Bashir could take care of himself. She said they all knew he often slipped over the garden wall late at night and went into the forbidden districts of the city to amuse himself and hustle money. Karim could not believe his mother knew about that. The younger children started crying for food. There was a stink of goat droppings and no toilet, only a bucket of dirty water standing in a corner and the warped jute armchair covered by a reedy quilt.

At midday, Kanti Lal crept quietly into the room. He brought a cup of lukewarm tea. Rehman jumped up and handed the cup to Apaji. Kanti Lal looked as if he had not slept all night either. His dhoti hung in limp folds between his legs and about his ankles. Normally it was starched to shining white, and Kanti Lal carried the edge of the cloth gracefully in the crook of his arm.

"One cup is all I could get. I promise to bring more later," he said, hanging his head.

Apaji gave the tea to the younger children, a sip apiece. They did not ask Kanti Lal why all he could procure was a single cup of tea when their own larder was filled with a whole year's supply of commodities just brought from Nehtor and Milak. Perhaps everything had been looted. They wondered why Kanti Lal had not been able to spare a little from his own supplies of food. They assumed there must be a reasonable explanation. Perhaps too many people had come to his house and questions would be asked.

Helplessly Rehman looked around the room for a place for Kanti Lal to sit, but there was only the chair with the woven seat half torn, and his children covered every inch of floor, staring up at him with wide frightened eyes. "What is the news?" he asked, turning to Kanti Lal.

"They came, and they have gone," Kanti Lal said. "I saved what I could. There are very few people left in the neighborhood."

"Did you know any of the looters last night?"

"No. Even if I did there could be no way to report them. You are listed as missing. Everyone in your family is listed as missing."

"Can we get out of Aligarh?" asked Rehman.

"There is no way. No trains are stopping in Aligarh, and the roads are far too dangerous. Besides, they will never let you out of the city. When they find you, they will arrest you. You are supposed to be in Pakistan."

"But that doesn't make any sense," Rehman argued. "We are here."

"To the police, you are a Pakistani national now. You are not supposed to be in India."

"No court would abide by that. I am here, and I never left for Pakistan. Pakistan is not even a country yet."

"You speak of courts, when I tell you of killings."

"And the house?"

"I am taking the house," Kanti Lal said, clearing his throat as he always did whenever he was embarrassed. "You must hide here. You should forget about the house. There is no other way. If they find you here, they will arrest you or kill you."

Rehman did not answer.

"I am only being blunt with you. I will keep you hidden until it is safe for you to leave the country. That is the most I can do."

"What about food?"

"I don't know. I can't bring you food."

"Why not? There is a whole storeroom filled with food, we just brought with us from Nehtor. Isn't it still there?"

"Some of it is there, but I cannot bring it to you. I need it to feed my own people."

Rehman was amazed. He thrust his hand into the pocket of his suit but found it torn and folded his arms restlessly across his chest. He could hardly believe this was the same shy Kanti Lal Shah, his neighbor for over ten years, who went about his export trade so politely, and sent his children across the road to play and invited Rehman to festivals of Durga Puja and Holi when his house was strung with colored lanterns and images of the gods. Kanti Lal was leaning against the door, and his soft pink skin looked sallow and spent.

"What *can* you do?" Rehman asked him.

"I can sell it to you," Kanti Lal blurted out.

Rehman saw that Kanti Lal had been doing his business. He could understand the house, but the idea of buying back his own food was too much. "Come back tonight, and I will see if I can do something," said Rehman.

Kanti Lal left, closing the door as quietly as he came. "I am sorry," he said, once he was outside.

That evening Tariq arrived. The family had not eaten all day. Rehman could feel the hollow of his stomach rising dizzily into his throat with a choking sensation. No one could sleep from the hunger, and they sat uneasily together, not daring to speak about the riot but unable to talk about anything else. They stared blankly at the walls and ceiling, nervously avoiding each others' eyes. Only Piari complained, climbing over Apaji's shoulders and squirming in her lap. When they heard a scratching at the door, everyone stiffened visibly, and Gappu's fingers reached for the gun that lay at his side.

Rehman tried to hold the door closed quietly with his fingertips, but Tariq grabbed it with all his might, flinging it wide and hurling himself headlong into the room with a sob. Apaji and the children jumped up and threw themselves on their uncle with a hundred questions.

He was weeping so hard that he was doubled over, and he struggled away from their arms and crumpled against his brother's chest. Rehman supported Tariq and stretched him out on the charpoy, rubbing his shoulders and trying to calm his weeping. Apaji held Tariq's limp hand in her own and felt the tears flood to her eyes at the sight of the young bridegroom. He was still wearing one of his new wedding suits, but the satin of the blouse was torn and stained, the black shervani spattered with mud and the trousers crumpled and sagging.

Apaji could not look at Tariq's face, filled with tremors and hollow-eyed. His black moustache was wet from crying.

"Where did you come from, Uncle Tariq," Gappu asked, breaking the shocked silence.

Tariq sat up, swinging his legs over the side of the charpoy and buried his head in his hands. "I do not have words to tell you," he moaned. "I was in Delhi to supervise the furnishing of my new house when the rioting broke out. I only went to Delhi for the day. I tried to make it back to Nehtor. I did not even look back at the house when I decided to go, but I could not get through Old Delhi. The Red Fort was completely blocked off, and Muslims are going there for safety. People pulled me from my motorcycle. There were hands all over my body and my face, and I could feel the bike slip out from under me. There were so many hands."

Tariq looked up helplessly at the family who surrounded him with looks of horror on their faces. "My bride is in Nehtor," he wailed. "My sweet little girl. I left her there. She may be pregnant, for all I know, right now. Suppose the riots have reached Nehtor!" He wailed so loud the children jumped backward and Rehman had to clamp his palm over Tariq's lips, because he still did not know the situation in Aligarh and whether rioters were still lurking about.

Tariq pulled his brother's hand away, shaking his head. "No, I will be all right," he said, raising his hands. "Just let me tell you what happened. I must tell somebody, or I think I will lose my mind."

Rehman nodded, and the children crouched on the floor or sat beside Tariq on the charpoy. "I could not leave the city," Tariq continued. "So I went to our sister Fatima's house in Old Delhi. The mobs were running through the streets in every direction and buildings were burning all around. I was not in Fatima's house more than ten minutes before people stormed the building and broke into Fatima's rooms. They said they were a refugee relief team and hauled us all down the stairs—Fatima and her husband and her four children. We were loaded into lorries and driven to the Red Fort where a million Muslims are already living on the grounds. It is amazing to think that in this same place Akbar and Shah Jehan were kings and ruled India, and built the Taj Mahal, and now their children are drinking infected water from the sewers and dying in the mud around the palaces."

Tariq stopped for breath, trying to hold back a new flood of tears. He could not understand what was happening to him. He hardly had time to notice the room in which Rehman and his family were hiding, yet here was brother Rehman as strong and forceful as ever, while Tariq was crumbling like a woman. He bit his lip so hard he could feel the pain jump in his otherwise numb face.

Rehman put a hand on Tariq's arm. "Rest now. You can finish telling us later, after I find something to eat."

"No, let me speak," Tariq protested. "Fatima's son, Achan, is lost. He did not get into our lorry, and Fatima looked for him all over the Red Fort. We walked all day and all night through the encampments of families on the grounds. Many people pulled at our clothes and begged us for food, but of course we had none for ourselves, either. Fatima cannot find her son anywhere. I told her that he was a young man now, and that she would probably find him in Nehtor, but Nehtor is more difficult to reach than London, and Fatima could not sit still. Her husband wants to go to Pakistan. There are airlifts from Delhi to Karachi and Lahore, but Fatima refused to leave the Red Fort. She says she must wait for her son there. She says that is the only place he will come, unless he is dead. I tried to get her to leave, but when she would not, I climbed over the walls late at night. I thought I would try again to go to Nehtor, but the only roads I could reach were going south, so I thought, I must go to Bhai Rehman. As it was, I had to hide in fields by day and walk at night along the roadside through marshes and swamps. I thought surely you would know what to do, but when I arrived in Aligarh, the city was smoldering from fires. Many of the houses on Morris Road are burned and scarred. Your front lawn was trampled, and your gate was broken on its hinges. Half the verandah is charred and burned away."

Rehman winced as Tariq described the house, which he had not been able to visualize since they had come to hide the night before. Apaji hid her face in her sari, and the children began to weep quietly.

"I thought, Rehman and Apaji have disappeared. There is nothing left for me to do, but take my own life right here on my brother's lawn. At that moment your Hindu neighbor crossed the road, looking frantic. He said he knew he should never have left your house unguarded for a minute, and he whisked me back here to you. Oh, brother, what is happening to India?"

Rehman took off his suit jacket and covered Tariq's trembling shoulders. "None of us have slept or eaten in over twenty-four hours. I am going to the market to see if I can buy food. If Tariq could make it here, dressed in Muslim clothes, I can make it to the market in a Western shirt."

Apaji stood up, hoisting Piari onto her hip. "Please don't go," she pleaded. "Buy the food from Kanti Lal Shah. I am afraid for you to go."

Rehman opened the door. "I will only see what the situation is. If it is too dangerous, I will not leave the grounds. I promise you."

Apaji reached out to the door, but Rehman closed it and left her to try to put the children to sleep. He went toward the market the back way, climbing over garden walls and slipping through alleys and side streets. He barely glanced at the silent houses of his relatives behind their gates as he ran furtively across the broad paved roads toward the center of the city. Evening was settling over Aligarh, but the gas lamps had not been lit, and Rehman could sink into the shadows as he traversed the almost empty streets. There was no traffic on the main thoroughfares, but bands of looters were running noisily from house to house.

Before he reached the bazaar, Rehman passed a street where there was a smaller market of stalls under canopies of jute. Very few people were about, and Rehman walked quickly, afraid he might be recognized and stopped. He saw a merchant seated on a carpet among his scales and piles of peaches and melons. The salesman was following Rehman with his eyes, and finally lifted his forefinger and signaled to him to come.

Rehman ducked under the tenting and crouched beside the merchant, who whispered in his ear, "I have some grains I can sell you but only at black-market prices."

"What about the fruit," Rehman asked.

"I cannot," the merchant mumbled, shaking his head. "Tomorrow the government is bringing ration cards. I am allowed to sell nothing without the government's permission, but grains no one will notice. Wait here. I will bring it to you."

As the merchant slipped behind the stall, Rehman had to press his fingers tightly into his palms to still the urge to grab some of the fine plump peaches and deeply ripened plums. He felt he would have taken them without thinking twice, if it were not that his whole family was waiting like sitting ducks for some one to detect them and swoop down on their little hiding place. The merchant reappeared and handed over two small sacks in exchange for ten times the price just the day before. Rehman did not even know what was inside the bags, but he slid them beneath his shirt and slipped stealthily into the street, heading toward home.

Nine male relatives arrived in the next three days, but when they saw the overcrowded conditions in the servants' quarters, where there was not enough room for another soul to sit down, they decided to keep moving. None of them knew where they were going. Some said to Pakistan; some said south. Everyone agreed it was impossible to reach Nehtor. The state of United Provinces was untraversable. They all agreed Rehman should wait. One man alone might make it, but a wife and children, never. They, of course, could not take refuge in the house. The big elegant edifice was occupied by Kanti Lal Shah. Although they felt free enough to walk out into the rear garden during the day, no one ever looked in the direction of the house anymore. Kanti Lal had the prize for saving their lives and the weapon for their disobedience. All of a sudden the house and the lawn and the doors and the verandah had become nonexistent.

By the fourth day, masses of black flies had gathered in the room. They covered the chair and the bed and the makeshift table which Rehman had constructed. Apaji closed her eyes as she put the food she had prepared down on the two planks her husband had tied together with an extra piece of jute rope. The children sat on the bed, clustered together and hugging each other's bodies despite the heat. They eyed the food hungrily, but they did not make any move to eat. Apaji did not call them. The little rice and dal which Abu had brought her was finished, and she could not bear to tell the children what she had cooked for their breakfast. She merely left the food and disappeared again into the corner of the garden, behind the bushes and the clothesline, where she cooked over a fire of leaves and sticks.

"What is that?" Karim asked his brothers, pointing at the food.

"Don't ask. Just eat it," said Gappu. "Apaji prepared it—that is all that should matter."

"But what is it?" Karim went toward the lumpy brown food and picked it up disgustedly. Moïd and Piari started to cry again. They were always crying. It did not even pay to try to stop them.

Gerrar got up from the bed slowly and went to examine the food. It was warm and pasty like cereal but dark-colored, and it had a strange pungent odor. "It is animal fodder mixed with grain," he announced. "Eat it."

"No," said Karim.

145

"Eat it," said Gappu.

"No, no, no."

Gappu put a whole handful of the mixture into his mouth and swallowed hard. "It is not so bad. You try some."

Gerrar measured out a portion for himself, and ate the feed in large gulps. Then he and Gappu fed the younger children. Karim was in a state of frustration, and near to tears. He had told himself that his circumcision was the last time he would ever cry. He refused to cry now.

"How can you eat it?" he demanded.

The other children ignored him and continued to swallow their meal.

"I won't eat it," said Karim.

"Then don't eat it," Gappu shouted. "But God will punish you if you curse the food your mother made."

"How can we just sit here and let them take our house and all the food we brought from Milak?" Karim demanded.

"We have to do what Abu tells us to do," said Gappu.

"I am going into the house." Karim went over and stood with his hand on the door. Everyone pretended not to notice him.

"I am going," he said again.

"Then go."

Karim ran out into the garden. The sunshine, the birds, the flowers. Everything was as it had been except for the rosebushes, decked with thorns but barren of roses. Apaji sat alone, leaning against the side of the little house, her only pot empty above the dying fire of leaves and sticks. She had used bricks for kneading, and her fingers were rough and tired. She did not see Karim, and he slipped through the bushes and felt the grass between his toes. The big house was not a shelter now. Its high walls seemed forbidding and distant. He thought he heard a whistle, along with the calling of the birds, but it was faint. He walked to the far edge of the garden, near the chicken house, and listened. The whistle came again, low but distinct.

"Karim. Quick. Over here."

Karim ran to the chicken house and peered through the wire netting. "Who's there?"

"Bashir," the voice answered.

"What are you doing there?"

"I have been hiding," said Bashir.

"What for? Come out."

"I can't. I'm afraid. You come in here."

Karim climbed through the netting into the coop. It was dark and empty inside, save for his friend Bashir, and old chicken droppings dried all over the floor.

"Where are the chickens?" asked Karim.

"I don't know. Gone."

"Why are you afraid?"

"I killed a Hindu."

Karim searched the close darkness for the eyes of his friend. Bashir had told him a lot of fantastic stories before, stories that he half believed, half only wished were true—about the night people in Aligarh, the dancing girls who sent him to find strangers in the town for a rupee and a feel of their breasts. Karim was not sure about the rupee, but he could imagine what a feel of the breasts was like, and Bashir always described it in vivid detail. Several times on the way home from school, when Bashir was supposed to meet Karim and carry his books, he had shown him the house where the girl with the biggest breasts in all Aligarh lived. It was a doorway no different from all the others on the street, too low and too narrow, with children defecating in the sewer that ran just below the single step. Behind the doorway the woman was always sleeping, but the smell of her hot perfume lingered in Bashir's words and in Karim's mind.

"Didn't you hear what I said?" asked Bashir. He was crouched into a corner, and his whisper was cracked into a little squeak. Karim could barely make out Bashir's face, gone pale in the shadows, and only the whites of his eyes shone, swimming in his face.

"You killed a man," said Karim.

"Yes. Don't you believe it?"

147

"Yes," said Karim. Anything was believable now.

Bashir looked as if he had killed a man. He was so distraught with fear that he only came out at night as far as the garden wall—to scavenge berries and eat leaves. He was throwing up all the time. Bashir told him that the night of the riot he had run into the city looking for help, and had to stay out all night hiding in an alley because everything was burning and people were running with knives. Then he had looked all the next day for food to bring to Apaji. Bashir always kept a long knife tucked into his pajama belt, but he never really thought of using it. He just had it there and had practically forgotten about it. He had searched all day for friends to give him food, but no one came to the closed silent doors when he knocked on them. That night as he was climbing back over the garden wall, he saw a man, just distinct enough in the moonlight not to be the shadow of a tree. The man grabbed Bashir down off the wall and put his face very close—Bashir still had the scrape on his leg from falling onto the bricks. "Where is Raheel," the man hissed into Bashir's face. "How do you know her name?" Bashir asked, but the man only laughed and said he wanted her. He said he had come back for her.

"I knew he was very drunk," Bashir told Karim. "He could hardly stand up. So I pointed toward the house, and when he turned around, I took the knife out of my belt and put it into his back. It came out right here." Bashir jabbed Karim between the ribs.

"Don't do that," said Karim, jumping away from his friend, so that he bumped his head on the low sloping roof of the chicken coop. "Where is the body?"

"I buried it."

"Where?"

"Right there." Bashir pointed a few inches beyond their toes to the floor of the coop.

Karim jumped again. "Let's get out of here."

"No. I have to stay here and guard the body."

"Don't be stupid," said Karim. "We ought to tell Abu."

Bashir was afraid he would be arrested and shot, but Karim argued that there were no police. Abu would not be angry. He would understand. He would thank Bashir, but Bashir was not convinced and refused to leave the chicken house.

Karim reached out and tried to grab his friend, but he jumped backward, like a frog, on his haunches.

"No, no," Bashir whispered. "It is a sin to kill. Abu Sahib will punish me." He was trembling all over, and his body looked frail in dirty, stained pajamas.

"I'll think of something to do," Karim promised. "At least, I will bring you food."

Bashir nodded, but slunk deeper into the coop as Karim raised the window to climb out. Karim knew as soon as he told Abu about Bashir, everything would be all right, but in the three days since the riot, Abu was almost impossible to find. Karim never saw him eat or sleep, and the long walks he took through the city every day, looking for food, lasted from morning till evening. When Abu did come home at night, Karim did not dare disturb him. Abu ordered complete silence after sunset and sat himself, all wilted, over his guns in the bushes of the garden. Even though they all slept together under the small tin roof of the outer room, it seemed to Karim he had said fewer words to Abu than when they were separated by all the rooms of their big house and by their different worlds of school and business.

Rehman needed gold. Money was useless now. People wanted only gold, or deeds to houses and lands as payment for anything at all. A day's supply of grain was worth a bangle of 24-karat gold. A train ticket commanded a whole pouch of gold coins. He walked all day looking for friends. He had to slink along catlike on the balls of his feet, always clinging to the rear walls of houses which he knew only from the front, stepping across heaps of garbage in the alleys where cats were picking. The sounds of pedestrians on the thoroughfares hummed in his ears. Occasionally there were drums and sloganeers passing on the other side of a wall, but mostly the houses were quiet. Everytime he saw another figure coming toward him in the shadows of an archway or from the far end of a long alley, his heart pounded against his hot perspiring skin. It took hours just to cross from the suburban section to the market with a corner of the university in between.

The sun was unmerciful, and Rehman could feel his shirt adhering wetly to his chest and back. He felt squeezed in a vise. They could not remain as they were, but they could not leave. They were banished from their own house, but they were unable to walk off their property. He could not afford to squander whatever gold Apaji had brought with her or the few deeds he had hurriedly grabbed from his safe. Most of them were in banks which were closed. Yet food was either sold at a higher rate to Muslims, on the black market, or exchanged for ration cards which he could not obtain. He was not on a list. He was missing. Rehman had not even been able to obtain any substantial information on the cause of the riot. Kanti Lal was making himself very scarce and only came on his twice-daily rounds, like a sentry almost as afraid of guarding his prisoners as letting them go.

Rehman turned a corner sharply, his back pressed against the wall, into an alley just wide enough for one man to pass. At the far corner, a man dressed in a Western shirt and pants was urinating against the wall, looking guiltily from side to side. Rehman realized that he was a Muslim dressed as he was in Western clothes, but it was an obvious disguise. What Christian or Parsi businessman would be pissing in a litter-strewn alleyway in the middle of Aligarh? The man turned and stared at Rehman. It was a face he recognized from social visits, maybe card games at his club. The man threw out his arms, and they greeted each other like long-lost friends.

"I have been looking for someone I knew all morning," Rehman whispered.

"I, too," the man said. "I know you well, Rehman Bhai. I am Jamil Adam. Where are you living?"

Rehman swallowed hard. "I am hiding in the servant's quarters behind my house with my family. We have had no news."

Jamil shook his head. "It goes very hard," he said. "I have been in the home of a Hindu friend. We are making arrangements to go to

Bombay by train and then take the boat to Karachi. It is the long way to reach Pakistan, but it is the only route that is safe."

Rehman nodded. "I have not been able to decide what to do."

"Go to Pakistan," Jamil advised. "We are not wanted here. The government has sent trainload after trainload of Hindu refugees, coming from Lahore, to Aligarh, rather than letting them get off in Delhi, which is crowded to the bursting point. It is not the people of Aligarh who are making us leave. It is all of India."

"When are you going?" Rehman asked.

"Tonight. That is why I ventured outside today. I know it is dangerous, but I had to find someone to tell that we are going. I could not just disappear."

Rehman gripped Jamil's arm in his two hands. "Assalaam Aleicum," he said. "Go carefully."

Rehman turned and crept back along the wall. "I will try once more to throw myself on the mercy of Kanti Lal Shah," he decided. "Surely he will spare a little of the food I brought from my own village. There must be an explanation for his behavior, when Jamil Adam's Hindu friends are helping him."

When Rehman finally padded up the long brick walk to the entrance of his own house, the bricks felt forbidding beneath his feet, as if each one were saying, "You are not wanted here; you are not needed here anymore." They jabbed at him through his sandals as if he were a strange man on foreign soil, a beggar coming to the home of an important powerful master, who might not understand his words or his language. Kanti Lal was no longer the neighbor who came across the road with hands folded prayerfully before his chest, taking his sandals off at the doorway and stepping gingerly onto the carpet with his clean pink feet. He was no longer the cautious friend who traded respects before offering a business proposition, or the father who allowed his children to come into a Muslim home and eat on plates that meat had touched and play with sons who had been circumcised. Karim and Gerrar had told him how they in turn placed offerings of flowers at Kanti Lal's little temple to the elephant god Ganesh and rang the bell and made wishes that always came true.

Kanti Lal came to the doorway, diminished and stoop-shoul-dered. He ushered Rehman into the house with a tired wave of his hand. "You see what I have inherited?" he said. "All this."

Rehman looked at the gaping reception room, which had been almost completely emptied of furniture. Here and there an armchair stood in vague isolation. The wall beside the part of the verandah that had burned was charred and smoke-stained. The deep wine-colored rug had been removed, and instead a small cluster of pillows lay in the middle of the marble floor, beside which were Kanti Lal's prized books of poetry and his hookah. Candles burning on the man-tel surrounded a small icon of Lord Krishna and a silver filigree box, which Rehman knew was used to hold the ashes of the dead. Kanti Lal's eyes were red. Rehman could see that he had been crying.

"What does this mean?" Rehman asked him.

Kanti Lal tiptoed to the mantelpiece and gently took down the silver filigree box. "We were friends, but now we must be enemies. It is beyond our control," he said.

Rehman could not speak. He was afraid to learn what was in the box.

"These are the ashes of my son, Muni," Kanti Lal continued in his soft singsong voice. "When there is peace again, I will take them to the Holy Ganges and let them drift where they belong. Then my son will flower again into India and grow strong with our country. Until then, I have sworn, I will keep this house for him. It is the only justice I can offer him."

Rehman sank among Kanti Lal's pillows on the floor. He had not eaten all day, and with this last piece of news, his legs would not hold him any longer.

Kanti Lal joined him and offered him the hookah.

"How could such a thing happen?" asked Rehman.

"I don't know why it happened. I only know that those Mus-lims who are creating the state of Pakistan out of our country came to his school, Ghora Gali, which is in their country now, killed the students, took their belongings, and those who escaped brought to me the ashes of my Muni Lal Shah, my eldest son."

They sat in silence sharing deep breaths of the water-cooled smoke through the long stem of the pipe which the two men passed between them, until it was finished. "It is no longer a question of possession but one of identity," said Kanti Lal finally. "I do not know how long I will be able to stay here, or when you will return with knives and anger to tear me out of this house. I know it is yours. I say that to myself all through the night as I sleep within your walls. But my son, my Muni, was Gappu's age. I worked and lived for him. Now he is dead. Who will marry my daughters? I know your children, who played with mine, are living in this garden with insects and filth and eating animal fodder. I have seen your wife heavy with child hiding behind the bushes, to prepare bits of grain, when only last week servants brought her platters of rice and almonds covered in silver leaf. But this is what I must do. What else can I do?"

"I will bring you a piece of jewelry to pay for the food," said Rehman. "I don't understand everything you feel. But I know we have brought our children to these days of pain, and we will have to leave for Pakistan, because there is no other way. As soon as my child is born and strong enough to travel, we will leave India forever."

"There is no meat left," said Kanti Lal. "Your storerooms were ransacked, and the grains which I could pick up are all mixed together in the sacks. You will see for yourself. I don't eat your food, Rehman Hussain, but I cannot give it to you without a price. I must collect my price."

Rehman walked with Kanti Lal into the cellar storage rooms. The floors were slippery with grains, and the huge jute sacks, each neatly labeled for rice, chick-peas, different kinds of dal and wheat, were ripped open and spilling out their contents. Ten-gallon pots of oils and butter were cracked open, and smelling rancid. The icebox was bare and hot. Kanti Lal loaded Rehman's arms with small sacks which he filled with grains from the large bags at random. He explained that they were all mixed anyway, so it did not matter. Rehman also took an old suit he found hanging on a rack, so that Tariq could change from his Muslim wedding clothes to Western dress, which would serve as a less conspicuous disguise.

When they returned to the living room, Kanti Lal stood embarrassed, looking up at Rehman, who was almost a foot taller.

"I can help you leave for Pakistan. Come back and we will discuss many things."

Rehman shook Kanti Lal's hand and walked quickly out onto the verandah. He could not be sure whether he would be thinking of a price if the situation were reversed. Rather than trouble himself with further thoughts, however, he decided to believe Kanti Lal without understanding him.

Apaji was sitting beside the bricks she was using for a stove in the rear garden. Silently Rehman placed the sacks of grain at her feet and told her about the death of Muni Lal. She put the edge of her sari over her head as if to say a prayer. "Hi Allah. Why is everyone being punished?" she murmured.

Rehman looked away. "I promised to pay Kanti Lal for the food. Jewels and gold will not bring back his son, but he does not know what else to do."

Apaji rose without a word, smoothing down the folds of the printed cotton sari she was still wearing, and brought the small sacks of grain to the chilren in Bashir's room. She returned with a heavy brooch of pearls and gold which she placed in Rehman's outstretched hand. Their eyes barely met. Rehman knew it was not the value of the jewels that brought the tears to the borders of his wife's lashes, or even the fact that the piece had come from Nani's mother, and perhaps even earlier generations of the old proud family. It was the thought that the treasures had hardly been worn, and saved instead for the dowries of their daughters, and without this assurance neither of them dared to think what future they could expect.

"I will have to ask you for much more," he told Apaji. "There will be train tickets to buy, and food every day."

"I know," she answered. "Only promise me you won't take the tikka." He could see that she had already hidden it beneath her blouse.

"I promise," he said. "And I promise there will be much more, twice the amount we give away now, when we get to Pakistan."

Right now, however, Rehman knew he needed gold for everything, and lots of it. It was needed for the train to Bombay since that was the only safe route left. Gold was needed for food, and huge amounts for the boat from Bombay to Karachi. The journey from Aligarh to the city of Lahore, just over the border in what was to become Pakistan, was filled with stories of terror, of trains being stopped in the woods and raided on either side by Sikhs and Muslims seeking revenge for other trains that had been cut down a few days earlier. Everyone said the other side had started it, and neither side was willing to stop. Thousands of Muslims in Delhi had been evacuated to the acres and acres of old palaces and eroded fields in the Red Fort. Cholera epidemics had broken out, clean water was completely unavailable, and everyone was looking for a train out.

Rehman knew they could not stay in Aligarh with the whole family sitting on one charpoy and no one sleeping but lying awake all night thinking about the rioters, and the little girl without her hand, their neighbors missing or dead, the houses in flames, and the drums of the rioters. The Bombay route was the safest, although it was circuitous and extremely expensive. Trains crossing the borders were often redirected without warning to distant cities to avoid a riot or to pick up a whole station full of evacuees. Many border areas had not yet even been defined. But in Aligarh communications had completely broken down. There were no newspapers. The university was closed. Business was carried on behind closed doors in the bazaar, and news travelled only by word of mouth.

Rehman did not have to explain anything to Apaji, or even discuss it with her. She followed him into the small dark room where the whole family sat separating the rice and lentils and wheat he had brought from Kanti Lal Shah. Rehman barely had time to notice the children bent in work. Karim tried to get his attention to tell him about Bashir who was still starving in the chicken coop, but Rehman immediately grabbed Tariq off the floor, made him change into the Western suit, and set out again with his nervous brother in tow, to make inquiries about their passage to Pakistan.

They sorted the grains all afternoon in the suffocating closeness of the heat while Abu and Tariq were gone. As she worked, Apaji's face squeezed into lines of sudden pain as she felt the contractions of childbirth knotting her uterus, her chest, and her legs. Finally she said quietly that she thought the baby was ready to come. She told Raheel she would have to help her, but Raheel was scared and started to cry.

Apaji gathered up her skirts and grabbed Raheel by the hand.

"Where are you going?" Gappu asked.

"Into the garden," said Apaji.

"No. You can't have the baby in the garden," they all protested. They stopped separating the rice and lentils, and Gerrar, who felt that he must act as the doctor now or never, began giving orders.

"Raheel, you take Mona, Moïd, and Piari into the garden and start boiling water. Gappu, you go and make some clean strips of cloth out of the sari on the clothesline, and a wrapper for the baby."

Karim ran outside.

"Where are you going? You help me with Apaji," Gerrar shouted.

"Bashir is in the chicken coop," Karim explained. "I am going to send him to look for a doctor."

Gerrar did not have time to wonder about Bashir. Apaji was leaning heavily on his arm and breathing rapidly. He had never seen the birth of a baby, but he had watched breathlessly a buffalo calf being born in Milak, and Saddiquan had told him stories about her own midwifery. Silently praying that Abu would return in time, he worked diligently on, and gently transferred his mother to the charpoy, all laid out with the cleanest clothes they could find, and transformed into a mass of soft pillows and sheeting.

"Everything has to be clean," he ordered, and the boys swept the room and doused it with water that they drew hurriedly from the well. Raheel brought the boiled water which Apaji used expertly on herself, with Raheel kneeling and holding her hand, and the boys turning their backs until she called for them again. Apaji was experienced. This was her eighth child, and she had little pain or trouble.

Together they all brought their sister Sara, the firstborn refugee, into the world.

Rehman returned home that evening dazed with joy yet full of tears at the sight of his newest flower lying in the white sari wrapper by Apaji's side on the charpoy. Cradling the sleeping infant in his arms, he carried her out into the amber light of the early evening and walked with her back and forth among the denuded rosebushes and gently blowing fruit trees. He watched Raheel, who had never cooked in her life before, as she stooped by the fire to prepare chapati. She pounded them with her fists and the flat of her hands, and he could smell them sizzling on the almost greaseless pan.

As he was walking beneath the grape arbor, peering into the raw fresh skin of his new daughter and gently rocking her back and forth, Bashir slipped over the wall at the other side of the garden. The boy hung there for seconds by his long thin arms, his soiled pajamas gaping from his chest and falling below his stomach, and he dropped among the bushes. Rehman felt a chill run up his arms. He had completely forgotten about Bashir. Still holding Sara, he rushed over to the bushes, and looked down at Bashir who was crouching against the wall.

When Bashir saw the infant in Abu's arms, he burst into tears. "Forgive me. I could not find a doctor," he wailed. "I walked a few blocks, and I was afraid. I hid all afternoon."

Rehman pulled Bashir up with his free hand. "Thank God, you are safe. Where have you been?"

"Didn't Karim tell you?" Bashir asked, looking up at Rehman and shaking from head to toe.

"No, he hasn't told me anything," said Rehman.

"He didn't tell you what I have done?" Bashir covered his face with his hands and was flooded with sobs.

Rehman put his free arm around Bashir's shoulder, still rocking Sara with a swaying motion. He could see that Bashir was terrified, and he looked as if he was starving.

"It does not matter what you have done. It only matters that you are here with us. Come inside. There is food to eat."

Bashir looked mournfully up at Rehman through his wet lashes. "I want to go to Nehtor," he moaned. "Why can't we go there?"

Rehman did not answer, and Bashir followed him into the room. The family were all seated around the table, gazing at Raheel's dried-out chapati and a pot of rice. There were no mats on the table. There was no butter or silver bowls, like the ones Nani always used to dunk the bread into the spiced clarified ghee. The eight chapati had to be divided so that Tariq, who was the guest, could have a whole one for himself. That left seven for the family that was now ten in number, plus Bashir, who hung back in the rear of the room staring at the scene in wide-eyed disbelief.

Rehman cut the eight chapati in half with his pocketknife. "Every one should try to eat a little more slowly than usual. That way it will not seem like so little." He did not lift his eyes from the chapati as he cut them, and tried to seem very busy. This was the opposite of what he had been telling his children for as long as he could remember. It was the opposite of what Dadi told them; she always said to eat fast so that they could eat more.

"I will eat only one quarter," said Apaji.

"Nonsense," said Gerrar. "You must eat a whole one, so that your milk will come, and you can feed Sara."

"You must fill your stomach," said Raheel, pushing little pieces of the dry flat bread into her mother's mouth.

The whole family sat on the floor, because they insisted that Apaji lie on the charpoy with the sleeping baby tucked warmly in her arms.

"This is our first bread, and it is a celebration for the new baby," Raheel told her mother, and she began to sing a gentle lyric from a song that was popular in a voice so quiet it was only a whisper. "So ja, Raj Kumari. So ja" she sang. "Go to sleep, Princess. Go to sleep."

Only Tariq was going crazy. He could not decide whether to go with his brother's family to Pakistan, or to try again to reach Nehtor where his bride and mother were waiting for him, or perhaps to go back to his sister Fatima in Delhi, and take the airlift to Lahore from there. He knew he could not stay with Rehman where he was an outsider and could not act like a man. Evening was usually the most horrible time of all, and he dreaded the darkness encroaching through the door and windows and closeting them in the shadowed light cast by a flickering hurricane lantern. Evening always brought bad news from friends and distant relatives who dared to venture out through the streets to come to the little house, speak their piece and disappear again into their futures and fates. Many were taking the long route to Pakistan through Bombay. They said that the trains to the north were being raided, that those who were not killed often had to walk hundreds of miles or go to refugee camps where cholera epidemics were rampant and smallpox had started. They said that water was being sold at five rupees a gallon.

Tariq could not listen to the stories without visualizing himself butchered in his own blood or wasting away with disease, blind with thirst and mad with fever on some rain-slashed field. The friends who came in the evenings said that there were only white British policemen to guard the refugees and that they demanded heavy payment for protection. Tariq wondered how their protectors would feel if suddenly they had to escape to Manchester from London and go via Le Havre or Rotterdam with only Indians to protect them. Even then the distance would be shorter. Bombay was a thousand miles to the south, while Pakistan lay only three hundred miles to the west. From Bombay they would have to travel the same thousand miles back to the north, first by boat to reach the port of Karachi and then by rail to the city of Lahore. Tariq knew nothing about Karachi, only that everyone was saying they must get there before their lives would be safe.

Tonight, however, no visitors came, and Tariq thought this was even worse than the other way. He kept jumping up and going in and out of the garden, although there was hardly any room to sit, much less to move around.

"What a horrible place to have a baby," he kept saying.

Rehman tried to ignore him.

"I can imagine where my son is going to be born. Here I am with a bride of scarcely more than a month, and for all I know she is not even in Nehtor where I left her, and I can't get back to her. The house in Delhi is surely not ours anymore. We never even had a chance to live there."

"That's enough," Rehman told his brother. "You are upsetting the children."

"They should be upset," said Tariq. "Look at this place. They have had to watch their own mother give birth to a girl in a place like this. What kind of a child is that going to be?"

"Are you going to shut up?" said Rehman, rising. "Or do I have to take you outside and make you shut up?"

"You don't have to make me. I'm leaving," Tariq said, opening the door.

Everyone looked at him, stunned.

"I'm going to Nehtor," he said. "I can make it alone, I'm sure. It's madness to sit here. Why should I? What sense is it for me to go to Pakistan with you?" He ran into the garden, and Rehman followed, grabbing his arm.

"Don't try to stop me," Tariq shouted.

"I only want to be sure you will be safe," said Rehman.

Tariq backed away from him. Rehman's old Western suit swam on his younger brother's slighter form and Tariq's once immaculate beard was growing in stubble all over his cheeks.

"Why don't you eat something first," Rehman insisted, pursuing him through the garden.

"No, no. Leave me alone," Tariq protested. He pressed his fingers against his temples. "Oh, God, I think I am going mad," he moaned.

Suddenly Bashir burst through the door of the little brick room. "If Sahib Tariq is going to Nehtor, I am going, too," he announced. "I know the way better than anyone else. Let me go, too," he demanded.

"I can't do that," said Rehman.

"Why not?" Tariq said, grabbing Bashir by the hand. "Do you think I won't look out for Bashir?"

Rehman shook his head sadly. Pushing Bashir ahead of him, Tariq turned on his heel and fled from the garden.

Rehman stepped back into the shadows of Bashir's room. The

children all looked at him questioningly, and Tariq's uneaten chapati lay on the table where Rehman had set it aside.

"He's gone," Rehman said helplessly, and sank onto the charpoy beside his wife. "Bashir left with him."

Karim buried his head in his arms, which were folded across his knees, and tried not to sob.

"I think we should all go to sleep," said Apaji, and Raheel sang the ballad again, as they lay on their backs, looking up at the blackened tin ceiling.

In over two weeks there had been relatively little excitement. News came less and less often from the hurried evening visits of emigrating distant relatives and friends and was more and more readily accessible in the marketplaces and offices, from clerks and salesmen who had relinquished their newfound taciturnity for their usual garrulousness, although the friendly cup of tea was no longer proffered. Rehman had been able to arrange for train tickets to Bombay. They were sold only at the stationmaster's house for gold, since the railroads were in chaos. No assurances could be given about specific seat reservations, but Rehman made them anyway as far as Allahabad, where they would have to change trains. Kanti Lal had agreed to bring to the railroad station as many valises and trunks full of belongings as the family could carry and have them held there in his name. Rehman was only waiting for Sara to be strong enough to travel. Milk was coming to Apaji's breasts in little niggardly dribbles, but far off in the quarter where the Bhangis or untouchable noncaste Hindus lived, Gappu had found a streetsweeper with a cow who was willing to sell his entire supply of milk and who would accept cash at almost uninflated prices. Gappu brought home a small clay pitcher filled with the warm milk every day. It was hardly watered down at all, as he always went at the proper time to observe the milking process. He told his father that the Bhangi family was very appreciative of his patronage as if nothing had really happened, nothing changed. Gappu realized that before the riots turned Aligarh upside down, a Bhangi selling milk might easily have been shot. Rehman told his son that the so-called Untouchables were Gandhi's children, and it was for them that the New India was being made. Rehman had often debated with other Muslims how much like a new religion Gandhi's preachings were, in which the caste system was abolished and equality was sought, along with a new asceticism and appreciation of India, and acceptance of India on its own terms, which no imported system from England or Communism from Russia as Nehru seemed to dream, could possibly cope with.

On his daily trips through Aligarh, the purposes of which were mostly unknown to the family, Rehman had learned to steal through the narrow, tightly populated areas of the city. Since Kanti Lal had let him take whatever he wanted from his house, he sometimes disguised himself by wearing a dhoti, or loincloth, instead of the white pajamas associated with Muslims or the Western suit that seemed no less obvious when he peered around the corner of an alley into the broad boulevards of the suburban sections of the city, where he and all his friends had lived and life had generally centered. It was not that the streets bore witness to any kind of upheaval or violence. On the contrary, they were unusually peaceful, devoid of the customary morning vendors calling out their wares in treble and bass octaval tones. Windows were boarded over. No one was sitting at the entrances to their gardens, or buying vegetables from a cart stopped before a house. Tongas and horses and motorcycles did not zip down the street; no children were playing on the broad lawns; and no migrant workers with bags of earth on their heads were repaving the streets or fixing sewers or taking afternoon naps under the hanging roots of the massive banyan trees. Aligarh was a city in silence.

Rehman crossed to the far end of Morris Road, about a mile away from his own house. Glancing quickly down the street, he was surprised to see the large gate to the house of his old friend and cousin, Zamir, standing slightly ajar. There was something strange and inviting about the gate, half open in this street of padlocks and barricades. He thought someone had told him that Zamir had left for Pakistan weeks before. He passed into the still garden. He felt he was the only one left living on all the earth. The lawn was lush and growing in abundant clumps over the walks, since the grasses of India needed constant pruning or they would grow rampant in a matter of days. Imported palm and banana trees dotted the lawn, heavy with unpicked fruit, and banyan trees lined the driveway, filling the garden with patterns of light and shadow.

As soon as he opened the door to the house, he was overcome by a wave of nausea from the heavy stench of rotting flesh. He adjusted his glasses, wiping them as if they were dirty, and he saw there was dried blood splattered on the carpet. In the center of the room was the body of Zamir's favorite son, Rashid, who had been going straight through medical school, training his delicate hands to be a surgeon. He had been disembowled by a kirpan, and his left hand was lying several yards away from his body on a velvet sofa. The vultures had killed the son of one of the most prominent men in Aligarh, but still they had not had the nerve to occupy the house. Rehman tried to enter deeper into the untouched, fully furnished, silent house, but there was the stench of the soft pajama-clad boy with his olive skin and tender body and his open mouth through which a whirring nest of hornets entered and exited again at the bowels. His nose had been eaten. He used to carry a soft hanky always. It was his custom to have the hanky doused with perfume and ready to hold to his nose as he passed through the city with its sudden smells of rancid meat in the butchers' market and its open sewage. Sometimes he wore the hanky at his neck, where it was folded neatly to protect the collar of his shirt from being spotted by perspiration. When he held the hanky in his hand, he often twisted it and then would catch himself sharply, reminding himself how unattractive the habit was. He used it delicately, after he had been offered a paan, to wipe the juice off his lips. He used it on his head in the hot sun, folded three times over his silky hair, and he used it to dab his nose with perfume.

Rehman came out of the house and just stood in the garden. He felt a huge roar welling up in his stomach and his chest, but he did not let it out. He searched all morning like a haunted man through the wide empty boulevards to find a tonga, which finally he was able to steal from an abandoned stable still filled with horses. He also stole two horses. He galloped back through the streets and clattered into his own driveway, where he leaped from the tonga and stormed into the living room. Kanti Lal was still keeping vigil over the ashes of his son and reading prayers.

"I'm leaving. This is the end," he shouted.

"What happened?" asked Kanti Lal, pursuing him through the house to the rear garden.

"Oh, God! Don't ask me," Rehman roared. "Just meet us at the station in an hour. We can still make the noon train."

Looking at Rehman's determined face, the strong jaws clamped tightly under his moustache, the thick curls of uncut hair disheveled around his face, Kanti Lal hoisted his dhoti and ran out of the house to go to the station.

Rehman ran into Bashir's room and called the whole family together. "We're leaving right now," he commanded.

In a flurry of excitement he grabbed three of his guns and herded the children ahead of him. He was in such a hurry he barely allowed Apaji a moment to grab a sari from the clothes-line and wrap it around Sara. Raheel and Mona scooped up the little satin purses with their small collection of earrings and bangles that were hidden beneath the charpoy. They ran through the house without a glance at the dusty barren rooms, to the tonga waiting in the drive. Rehman put all the children into the tonga with Apaji. He told Gappu to ride on the second horse, in front of himself, and they started to move toward the station. The children did not ask, Apaji did not ask, what he had seen. They only grasped their remaining belongings in their laps and left for the station without a word of farewell to Aligarh or their house or anyone they might ever have known in other days.

Kanti Lal was waiting on the crowded platform at the railroad station surrounded by twenty of the family's valises, trunks, and bundles. Rehman had already handed over to Kanti Lal the deed to the house in exchange for the belongings. Kanti Lal fully realized the importance of the trunks. They were not merely a matter of property or possession, but for the purpose of bartering on the long jour-

164

ney, which was certain to be filled with unforeseen hazards. Only with valuable property could a man negotiate his way out of India.

Kanti Lal's overriding purpose was to see that the family of Rehman Hussain went to Pakistan. He did not want their death, and he did not really need or care for their wealth. It was only the insurmountable passion to see justice done for the death of his son on the other side of the Himalayas in Punjab. To Kanti Lal this meant the exile of the Muslims to Pakistan, and to Kanti Lal, his old friend Rehman was the Muslims, and the religion and the race and the people. The train had already arrived, and he stood waiting on the platform, buffeted on every side by Muslims clamoring to find room in the already crowded compartments. Harried train officials and British soldiers dripping with perspiration were running up and down the platform, trying to squeeze people through the doors and windows and hoisting them to the roofs of the cars or bogies, which were covered by a wriggling mass of children and women in saris and men clutching lumpy sacks full of belongings. Kanti Lal had to stand on one of the trunks to search the crowd for Rehman and his family. As soon as they arrived, he shoved them into the vacant compartment he had been guarding with his life, and together with Rehman, dragged and kicked the valises and trunks up the three steps and into the narrow corridor of the bogie.

The children were amazed to see Kanti Lal leaning up against the window of their compartment, full of instructions and advice. They had thought that he was the cause of their present situation, the thief of their house and their food. Now he was standing in the railroad station of Aligarh filled with evacuating Muslims dressed uncomfortably in saris and dhotis to disguise themselves as Hindus, certain to be concealing guns and other weapons in the ill-fitting drapes of their makeshift clothing, certain to be full of anger, sorrow, and vengeance. Yet here was Kanti Lal saying to be sure to keep all the doors and windows locked, especially while the train was in a station and even more so if the train stopped unexpectedly anywhere in woods or fields or beside a river bank. Never look outside, he warned them, and do not let anyone into your compartment or even into the bogie if you can help it.

Rehman had not told his family that Kanti Lal Shah was now in possession of the deed to their house, which he had formally signed over to him in exchange for the twenty trunks, valises, and bundles that were crushed like miraculous gifts of newfound wealth into the small compartment. They also did not know that the choice was not between keeping the house or giving it to Kanti Lal Shah, but between giving it to him or to the agent of a British shipping company who had come to Rehman to exchange ten passages on a charter flight to Pakistan for the deed to the Aligarh house.

Rehman was glad the house had gone to Kanti Lal instead. He had felt an overwhelming hatred for this effete relic of the British Colonial Empire in his neat summer suit and boater, with his narrow tearing blue eyes and light-brown moustache tinged with blond from the Indian sun. Suspiciously he had given him a copy of an old deed and waited for the promised news of the charter flight. He searched British companies and agencies for any knowledge of such a flight at all. When there was none and the British agent did not return, he and Kanti Lal quickly had a new deed drawn up, artfully backdated by an obliging Indian government official to read two years earlier, and the transfer was legally made to Kanti Lal Shah, rendering the earlier deed given to the swindling English Sahib null and void. Whatever the case, charter flight or no charter flight, swindle or no swindle, Rehman felt he would always sleep easier, knowing the house he had built himself would be occupied by his Hindu neighbor and the ashes of his son, rather than with the remnants of the British Raj who seemed to be living in and among and through all the torment the two infant countries, India and Pakistan, were experiencing.

The train began to move. Rehman could see Kanti Lal raising the palms of his hands together in prayer as he disappeared behind the heads and bodies of the thousands of people on the platform. Aligarh and Kanti Lal Shah and the Muslim University and the brick houses of Nehtor and the fields of Milak and the schools in Dhera Dun and Delhi, and the vacations at hill stations and in jungle rest houses, all was behind them as they heard the familiar sound of grinding charcoal, and the heavy coal dust filled their hair and eyes and lashes and the creases in their hands. Soon the train was rattling through the glistening hot fields of India's plains. The family was crushed together in the small compartment with its stiff wooden benches and iron-slatted windows. With all their luggage pouring out of the room and into the corridor, there was barely room to sit, and the smaller children had to curl up on the trunks and narrow planks of the upper berths. The electric wires had been jarred loose by the thousands of people sitting on the roofs of the different cars, and there was no air from the fans or lights in the room.

Karim pressed his face against the window, watching the familiar terrain of huts and fields, marshes and farms that were slashed by the metal shutters. He was still mourning the loss of Bashir, whom he felt should have come with them to Pakistan. He thought if only he had told Abu immediately, when he found Bashir hiding in the chicken coop, his friend would not have become so anxious and left so frantically with Uncle Tariq.

Everyone assured Karim that it would be simple for Tariq and the wily boy to slip through the roads and villages of India, buying food as they went and sleeping by the roadside. The roads were nothing for a young man and a boy alone, they told him. It was only large families, with women and children, who were easy prey. He would not be harmed. Karim was no longer convinced by verbal assurances, and anyway he wanted Bashir with him. The monotony of the passing fields and the hot wind on his face were rocking him to sleep. Apaji was trying to nurse Sara, whose eyes had not yet fully opened and who was whimpering slightly. Her milk strained through her breasts like the driblets of liquid from a lone cactus in a parched land. The other children were draped across the trunks and lying on the overhanging berths, their legs dangling down just over Karim's head. He pressed his face against the dusty wire screen across the window and peered through the outer slats.

All of a sudden his eyes opened wide. The train had slowed down almost to a standstill, and as it rounded a wide curve, Karim could see a long bridge with dirty river water swirling far below. He knew the river must be the Ganges.

In the middle of the bridge another train was parked. It hunkered menacingly in the distance and seemed slightly askew. As their train started across the bridge, which thundered and shook beneath the wheels, Karim pressed his cheek against the screen and tried to look down the track, but he could no longer see the other train, which was now directly in front of them. Karim remembered the last words of Kanti Lal Shah as they were pulling out of the station at Aligarh: "Be particularly careful if the train stops between stations, in woods or fields or beside a river bank." Why was this other train parked here? Perhaps they were permitting the Hindus to get off and bathe for an hour or so in the holy water of the river. He scanned the yards and yards of mud flats directly below, which only in floodtime could the swollen unpredictable river ever hope to claim. They were deserted. Not even washerwomen were bent over the dhobi ghats, where they usually pounded wet clothes on wooden planks to beat the dirt out of them. Besides, Karim had crossed the Ganges many times before, and he had never seen a train stop to let anyone say his prayers, even though the whole train seemed to tip as Hindus leaned far out over the water's edge, yelling *Jai Ram* and *Hare Krishna* and throwing coins into the river.

As their train inched across the bridge, Karim could see the rooftops of the stopped train striated through the slats of his window. The other train was no more than a hundred yards away. There were bodies on the roofs. It seemed impossible that their train would not stop, but it continued to sway and lurch toward the hulk of black engine standing in a veil of steam. Then the whole world was blocked from view except for the sooted train, which filled Karim's eyes and his ears with moaning and shrieks. Bodies were lying like slaughtered goats on the holy day Bukra Id. Mothers were half covering the bodies of their children, and many were on the tracks underneath the train. It was all visible. There were the bloated stomachs of starved babies, and the wrinkled faces of children, and the skinny legs of old women lying spread and bare across the roofs of the train. Along the metal rail, the strongest were lying in heaps next to each other, as if they had tried to escape. Karim could see that their extended limbs had been severed, cut off in flight, and some sat dazed and smudged in blood, coddling the stump of a leg or an arm that twitched in their hands.

A loud shrieking of a thousand tongues rose up from their own train, and everyone was pounding on the roof and on drums until the very air vibrated. Abu tried to pull Karim away from the window, but the two trains were standing inches apart, and Karim's eyes were fastened on the bodies sprawled and motionless so close to his window he felt he could touch them. Gerrar was practically climbing on Karim's shoulders to look out. Behind him he could hear Raheel screaming hysterically and Apaji started to recite the Koran as if in a trance. Abu was trying to clutch all the children at once. For imperceptible seconds their train stopped, and a white officer standing on the tracks looked up at Karim, and for instants Karim was certain their eyes met. The officer seemed to be waiting for the train to pass, and Karim realized that there was a white officer in every compartment of the parked train. His own train was inching along with sudden starts, and the air seemed to whistle and creak with pain, and the thudding on the roof was like a deafening heartbeat in answer to the scene of death below.

Compartment after compartment rolled by, each unfolding its contents of twisted limbs and necks with faces frozen in terror and eyes open wide. Most were dead, and the few living stared back in dumb shock, or lay limply on the floor, or squatted in a circle of bodies, just screaming with wild wet faces. Karim was dizzy with nausea, but he could not tear his eyes from the window. He felt Gerrar's hand trembling in his own, and Abu and Gappu pressed mutely against his shoulders as they struggled past the train with the engine screaming and the roof thudding, and all the girls crying and hugging each other tightly. Only Moïd sat alone, dumb and frozen on the wooden plank above.

The train lurched forward, and Gappu, Gerrar, and Karim fell into each other's arms. Slowly their train was gaining speed. The last car drifted by them, and they were looking into the waters of the vast river Ganges, filled with bodies floating in billowing cloth, as the water rolled away between the distant banks of mud and palm trees.

Someone was standing in the doorway to their compartment. Rehman grabbed one of his guns, and the children whirled around with a gasp. Karim felt Gerrar's hand tighten around his own. A white officer was waiting in the corridor. A man in a turban and two women were alongside him. The women were inexpertly dressed in saris that were all askew, as if they had put on the complicated pleats and drapings for the first time. Their eyes were full of tears, and their eyelids were swollen and red. Rehman went out into the corridor to talk to them, and Karim heard the man in the turban say in a tremulous voice, "Indians did it to Indians."

Karim did not understand. He could not imagine why these people were wearing turbans and saris, when they obviously did not belong in them. Besides, Karim knew that the wives of Sikh men who wore turbans rarely wore saris but the tight pajamas and long dopatta scarves like Muslim women. Only the most sophisticated Sikhs and Muslims wore saris. Karim had not known that dress made such a difference. All the people looked the same to him. He had had little time to think about the other religions that surrounded his daily activities, but he knew he had no difficulty entering a home where there was a cow instead of a water buffalo in the courtyard, and he had often gone into homes in Delhi where strong little Sikh boys wore long hair piled up on top of their heads in a knot and fastened with a hanky. There was no difference to him.

Karim thought that all the hiding under clothes and disguises for protection was of no use. All the women who had taken off their Muslim veils for the first time exposed their shy frightened faces to no avail. When all was said and done, the telltale circumcision of Muslim men gave them away. Karim gulped at the thought of his own circumcision, performed just over a month ago, and thought angrily that if they had left him in one piece no one would know who he was when they raided his own train and pulled down his pajamas.

The man in the turban and the women in saris were only going another two stops. Rehman let them sit in the corridor of the bogie while the white policeman stood guard at the door. Karim thought they must be very important people to have a personal guard and for Abu to break the first rule, not to allow anyone into the bogie. They left the door open, and the whole family listened to the story of the train that had been cut down. The story was not new, but it was the first time any of them had seen with their own eyes the death of a thousand people. Karim tried to listen to the story, but instead his eyes were filled with the vision of the parked train, the compartments loaded with dead and wounded, and the sight of a baby with slashed throat and dripping blood.

Their own train had hardly crossed the bridge when they saw thousands upon thousands of turbaned men armed with guns and knives and kirpans and hatchets. There were swarms of them on both sides of the train, which was picking up speed. They were running and walking across the mud flats to the river and wading fully dressed into the water to wash off the human blood splattered on their clothes and faces.

"I was on that train," said the English Sahib, leaning on the butt of his rifle to look out the window. "Those are the men who did the killing, and now they are washing their weapons, so they will be ready for another one. You chaps are lucky that your train came to this spot just when it did. You are a lucky Mohammedan. Can you imagine picking the Ganges to do their killing?"

"How far are you going," Rehman asked the Englishman.

"I am taking this family two stops. Then I will go back and see what I can do to help."

Before long, the train pulled into a small country station. There was a lot of pushing and shoving, and everyone was running in a different direction. The platform was filled with British soldiers, whose only concern seemed to be to shove everyone into the train as quickly as possible before an incident could occur. The stationmaster jumped into their bogie and announced to no one in particular that they had found the missing train.

Everyone looked at him.

"You must have seen it," he said. "The train came from Bombay with recent immigrants from Karachi. They have been looking for its arrival at every station. It passed through here hours ago."

"You mean those were not Mohammedans who were killed on the roof of the train?" asked the Englishman.

171

"No, no, they were recent arrivals from Karachi," the station-master insisted, and he hiked up his uniform and straightened his hair to talk to the English Sahib.

"Then who were all those men in turbans cleaning their weapons?" asked Rehman.

Everyone realized immediately the mistake they had all made. Those were Muslims ambushing new arrivals of Sikhs and Hindus. Karim was certain he had seen the bare circumcised groins of several men sprawled out on the tracks, but the Englishman explained that Muslims often circumcised their victims before killing them and called it a sacrifice to Allah. He felt that was probably the explanation.

Karim was convinced more than ever that everyone had lost their identities. The turbaned men were disguised to kill men without turbans who were disguised in order that they not be killed themselves. You weren't safe no matter who you were, and sometimes the disguise could be more dangerous than the actuality. Now Karim was glad he had been circumcised in his Dadi's courtyard with all his sisters and female cousins looking on and bringing him new clothes and silver when it was over, rather than by accident in the compartment of a train at the end of a deadly kirpan. Only the Englishman seemed safe in his own identity and his own skin.

"Would you consider accompanying us to Allahabad where we must change trains?" Rehman asked the Englishman.

The officer plunged his hands into the pockets of his tan trousers. "I don't know," he said, looking down at the floor. "I've been traveling this route for days, and I'm dog-tired. My assignment's just about done, and I'm out of money."

"I'll pay whatever you ask," Rehman said quickly.

The officer searched Rehman's bloodshot eyes with his own paler ones. Apaji climbed across the valises to Rehman's side in the corridor, clasping a large cloth sack to her chest.

"It's not that I would take your money," the officer explained. "Only I have no way of getting back to the post."

Apaji dug into her sack, which was camouflaged at the top with odd pieces of cloth, and fished up a necklace, which she held shimmering between her fingers. The officer nodded and took the necklace from her hand, stuffing it into one of his hip pockets. "Also cash, so I can get back to Delhi," he said.

Rehman took a wad of bills from the money belt beneath his shirt and started counting off rupee notes in hundred denominations. The officer watched Rehman's fingers slipping the bills off the top of the pile. "That should do it," the officer said, stopping Rehman at a thousand. "I'll stay out here. You can relax now. Nothing will happen."

Rehman sent Apaji back into the compartment, but he felt weak from heat and hunger and from slowly being stripped of his belongings and his position in the eyes of his family. He opened the door in the corridor and swung down onto the empty platform, which was baking in the white light of the early afternoon. Although the station had hurriedly been cleared of passengers, and the train was loaded and ready to go, the engine was silent and had stopped emitting steam. Rehman knew that an Indian train never turned off its engine, because hours of stoking coal were required to build up enough steam for the train to move. He saw the yards and yards of people who were riding on the rooftops of the train, drained and wilted under their thin cotton coverings which could not protect them at all from the sun. The heat caused the whole earth to smell slightly rancid, and the bricks of the platform burned the soles of his feet right through the leather of his sandals. The stationmaster was running toward him, blowing his whistle and waving his arms.

"Everyone must stay on the train," he shouted. "There are no exceptions. None." He stopped in front of Rehman, wiping his oily brown face with a frayed gray hanky. The shirt of his official tan uniform was a pattern of wet streaks, outlining his underarms in deep circles, and the mound of his stomach, which protruded between the buttons.

"Why are we standing here?" Rehman asked.

The stationmaster kept waving him back into the compartment and followed him up the steps.

"It is too dangerous to travel by day," the stationmaster explained. "Once a train is as overcrowded as this one, it cannot move until after sunset. The government has sent out circulars, and we are holding you here."

"Why don't you make an announcement, so the people will know?"

"I can't. My electricity isn't working."

"Well, you can send the *titis* from car to car and tell everyone how long we will be here. It is not fair to let us just sit and wonder."

The stationmaster nodded worriedly. "Yes, yes, I know you're right," he said in a hushed voice. "But I am afraid the people on the roof will panic. It is very hot. There is no food or water. I can't let them off. There are worse things than thirst."

Rehman crossed his arms across his chest. "I think you are making a very bad mistake, and I advise you to make your announcement. There is nothing worse than ignorance."

The stationmaster looked frantic. His face was flushed a deep scarlet, and he kept smearing the grease across his fleshy cheeks with the soaking-wet cloth. "I suppose you are right. It is difficult to know what to do. In all my years as stationmaster I have never had such a responsibility."

Shaking his head and mumbling, he lowered himself onto the platform, and Rehman climbed across the suitcases in the corridor and back into the compartment. A deep hollow sensation of hunger was pounding in his chest as he calculated the length of the journey. It seemed the distance just to Allahabad might take five or six times as long as usual. After one hour of slow travel, stopped first by the train riot, they were stopping again for the rest of the afternoon. It was at least another five hours to sunset, and at this rate the normally twelve-hour journey was bound to be extended to several days. He would have to ration sips of water to his family from the one flask he had brought from Aligarh. The only other source was the nonpotable tap water in the toilet and shower which was just an invitation to contamination and cholera. They had brought almost no cooked food, and there was no place to cook the rice and raw lentils they were carrying in sacks. His children were all staring at him silently. The family that had joined them were sleeping exhaustedly in the corridor, and even their British protector had no recourse but

174

to wait out the hot hours, unless he wished to spend days stuck in the inaccessible country town, surrounded by marshlands, fields, and the huts of farmers.

Rehman rummaged through the bundles, praying he would find something they could eat. From the bottom of one of the jute sacks, he fished up a fistful of gur wrapped in old newspaper. The raw brown sugar, which was used for sweetmeats in the country, was flaking and warm in his fingers, and he passed out handfuls to each of the children and a double portion to Apaji. At least, the sugar would give them temporary energy, but he did not know how they would nourish themselves for the next few days.

Through the window Rehman could hear the *titis* and the stationmaster walking beside the train, calling out the news that they would not move until sunset. There was not a stir from the roof, not a single answer or protest, as the minor officials moved along the dust-swept platform, chanting their instructions over and over in high-pitched voices.

For hours they sat closeted in the little compartment. The air was still and heavy, and the heat was swollen to a crescendo so thick it was tangible. In the fields across the tracks, Rehman could see the patchwork of planting and harvesting, left in the hiatus of the endless afternoon. No animals were plowing, or women walking along the rutted brown furrows of the paddies, or oxen rotating the wooden lever of the irrigation well that stood silhouetted on the horizon.

As the first breezes picked up and the sun began its descent, a parade of bullock carts, donkeys, and farmers bearing bales of produce on their heads wended their way toward the steaming train and descended upon the station. The local farmers had been preparing all day to sell their vegetables and breads to the trainload of starving people. Probably never in their lifetime would they be able to sell so much at once, Rehman realized, and it seemed as if several entire villages had come, hauling a feast from heaven on their shoulders and in their crude two-wheeled carts.

The station became a mass of activity, and despite the officials' frantic attempts to keep everyone inside the compartments and on the roofs, people were swarming through the windows and over the sides of the train. Leaning out his window, Rehman bought everything he could fit into the compartment. There were long white radishes, cucumbers, oranges, and roasted flour, because there had not been enough time to make breads. Rehman wanted to buy enough to last any number of unforeseen events and days, but he did not want to waste a penny more than necessary, because already he had lost thousands of rupees and a fortune in gold.

By the time the sun was sinking over the fields, the farmers' carts had been completely emptied, and everyone was packed again into the train like chesspieces in a box, waiting for the signal to move, listening to the condensing steam, which dripped from the train's pipes, and to the engine huffing strenuously to get its fires started, until finally the wheels shuddered beneath them, the brakes released, and the train moved slowly forward into the dusk.

The train pulled into Allahabad late at night, and the city seemed lit by fires and explosions. Three nights of painful, slow traveling across India seemed lost in a hazy sleep, punctuated by two long days of waiting, once exposed to the scorching sun in the middle of empty farmlands, once mercifully shaded by the trees of a tightly tangled forest, which hung over the sliver of track, brushed with monkeys and birds. Half the passengers, at least, risked cholera or dysentery to drink handfuls of water from a nearby stream. The rest waited patiently for the villagers, who always appeared as if on cue at sunset, to quench their thirst on tiny mandarin oranges. Everyone had diarrhea from the diet of radishes and fruit, and the bathroom was continuously in use, even after the other family had left. Rehman did not dare to think of all the people on the roof of the train or crammed into the third-class compartments, which by now must be so filled that most of the passengers would not be able to find seats on the wooden benches. At every major station new loads pushed hysterically onto the train, but only a handful got off. The stops were always late at night and as short as possible, with British and Indian police everywhere to hurry the process along.

The station at Allahabad was in the middle of the city and more filled with people than any they had seen so far. It was crisscrossed with tracks, and the monkeys who lived near the station were hysterical in the banyan trees, gaping down at the scene of pushing and shouting below. The train had to empty out all the passengers who were to connect here with the southbound train to Bombay. At the same time the train was being loaded with new arrivals, trying to push in so they could continue their journey east to Calcutta and Dacca in East Pakistan. Their direction depended on whether they were Muslims fleeing India or Hindus fleeing Karachi via Bombay. It was impossible to tell who was who, and everyone was crashing bodily into everyone else. The sky was lit with light.

"What's going on here?" asked Gappu.

No one seemed to know. They stopped a man who was pushing past them into the compartment they were vacating. "Are they setting the city on fire?"

"Don't you know," the man asked astonished. "Today is August 15, Independence Day. The whole city of Allahabad is having a celebration. Anyway, who would set fire to Allahabad? It is the home of Pandit Nehru."

Rehman was shocked at himself for losing track of time so badly. It should have been obvious, except that independence did not seem to have really come to them, with British soldiers lined up everywhere even as the new flag of India was being raised over the station and assuredly on every other official building throughout the country. Yesterday had been Independence Day for Pakistan. Rehman looked up at the new flag over the stationmaster's door. He did a double take. It was just as Gappu had told him in the early part of the summer. The symbol of Gandhi's spinning wheel had been replaced in the center of the green, white, and orange stripes, by another wheel, the ancient Buddhist wheel from the time of Ashoka which was supposed to represent the continuity and circularity of life.

177

Their hired English companion was ready to leave them, but he said for the price of one of the small valises, which was filled with ancient saris, he would see about their reservations and even scrounge up some food. Although he stood facing Rehman in the center of their tight family cluster, he had to shout to make himself heard above the din of people and movement that was pushing against them from every side. Trains clattered in and out of the station, their whistles echoing in the hollow dome. Occasionally the air popped with firecrackers from very close at hand. The Englishman was deeply tanned, but there was no mistaking him for Indian, with his pale brown eyes and slim bony features and his air of confidence and ease in his well-tailored pants and shirt.

He clapped Rehman on the shoulder. "Wait here. You will never find the train in all this mess," he said, and slipped off through the crowd of passengers and soldiers and porters, who were shoving trunks ahead of themselves like battering rams.

The family stood together for almost an hour, not daring to take a step away from their belongings. There was no room to sit down on the trunks which they kept upended and leaned against exhaustedly, too tired even to talk. Finally the Englishman reappeared out of the crowd and slipped a reservation form into Rehman's hand.

"You have to come with me to get this validated. You will have to bring everything you can carry as payment; otherwise, I am afraid, the officials will not give you a stamp. There are long lines, and you must offer more than anyone else or nothing doing."

Rehman looked at the still worthless slip of paper in his hand, and then at all the trunks which he would have to exchange for it. Apaji had turned away, and Gappu was peering over his shoulder.

"Abu, this is the wrong ticket," Gappu said, tapping the slip of paper with his hand. "Don't you see? It is for Patna and not Bombay."

"The Bombay trains are not stopping in Allahabad," the Englishman explained. "You have to go to Patna or turn back."

Rehman whirled around, and as he did so, someone brushed heavily against his shoulder with a valise. His glasses slipped from his nose and splattered on the ground. Apaji stooped quickly to retrieve the frame and held it dangling in her hand.

"That's too bad. I'm sorry about that," the Englishman said.

Rehman squinted back at him. "The glasses do not matter. I am only worried about going to Patna. It is so close to the new border which is just what we were trying to avoid. That is the whole reason we were going via Bombay and not directly overland."

"Well, you'd better make your decision now, or you will lose your place. Why don't you go to East Pakistan instead of West? In Patna you will be almost there."

Rehman caught Apaji's eye. He knew it was impossible to go to Bengal where the language, as well as the customs and the people, was completely different. Everyone they knew had gone the other way. There would be no hope for them to begin afresh there, and Rehman was determined not to attempt crossing the border by train, where even the small margin of safety they had gained by zigzagging through the center of the subcontinent would be lost completely. He knew Apaji was telling him not to go to Bengal. She was staring at him and holding Sara tightly against her chest.

"At any rate, your first objective is to get to Patna," the Englishman continued. "We had better hurry."

Rehman nodded. He realized he would have to learn to think step by step or his long-range goals, buffeted as they were by circumstance, would never be realized.

"We'll see about these reservations," he said. "Gappu take two of the valises and come with me." He put two cases under his own arms and clutched two more by the handles.

The Englishman hoisted up another three. "I'm afraid there won't be room on a train until morning. You will have to pay extra, but I can get you into a smaller waiting room where the children can sleep. Follow me."

The Englishman wove his way through the crowded station, with Rehman following behind and the rest of the family dragging what was left of their belongings in between. Of the twenty trunks and valises they had brought from Aligarh, only ten would be remaining, and at this rate, Rehman wondered if there would be enough to use as exchange once they reached Patna and then again in Bombay. He felt crushed beneath the weight of the valises he was carrying, and without his glasses he could hardly distinguish individuals or read the signs and advertisements hanging overhead, which were all a blur of color and motion. He could only walk behind, trained like a dog to obey, where always he had led.

Apaji and the children were deposited in a small waiting room which was dim behind a swinging screen door. It was crowded with Muslim children, and women sitting blank-eyed, their black veils dropped to their shoulders. Rehman was not permitted inside, because even here the women were trying to practice purdah. Furiously Rehman stalked off with Gappu and their English protector to finish the process of reservations.

It was well after midnight before the station quieted down. Apaji divided a long radish among the children and gave them each a portion of roasted wheat flour and gur. Despite the crowded conditions, with women pressed together among their luggage on the floor, all the children were finally falling into a drained and motionless sleep. The fans were working, and the air blew mustily around the room. Apaji sat erect and sleepless, watching over their little forms. Sara was whimpering weakly in her lap. For several days now, Apaji's milk had hardly come to her breasts. She tried to will them to flood full of liquid, to feel the throbbing sensation of the milk heavy in her veins, but the diet of raw vegetables and wheat flour and the lack of cow's milk had all but stopped its formation in her glands.

Most of the women and children in the waiting room were asleep, but several who were sick lay, perspiring and pale-faced, against the walls and in the corners trying not to contaminate everybody else, by turning their heads down into their clothes. One woman was coughing drily and seemed to be spitting up blood, while her children kept covering her face and shoulders with their hands and rocking her in their arms. Others were running constantly to the toilets, which had the stench of diarrhea and illness. From time to time, Apaji heard the soft shuffle of people hurrying past the vaiting room, their shadows reflected on the screening of the door, out mostly the station beyond was quiet and seemed deserted as if he trains had stopped running altogether.

Toward morning Apaji was just beginning to doze off when she heard a child sobbing outside the waiting room. Her eyelids had been fluttering drunkenly down over her eyes, and her head was nodding, and the crying seemed to be in a dream. She looked at each of her own children and thought she must have been mistaken, but the sobbing did not cease. She was certain a child was crying alone, close to the women's waiting room. Her body tensed, and she felt Raheel's head stir in her lap. Although she had promised her husband not to leave the room until he came from the men's waiting room to get her, she could not bear the incessant weeping and whimpering that assailed her ears. Gently she lifted Raheel's head from her knees, and shouldering Sara, stepped across the other women and children toward the door.

Raheel sat up, rubbing her eyes, bewildered. "Where are you going, Apaji?" she whispered.

Apaji put her fingers to her lips and motioned her daughter to remain seated and silent, but Raheel was scrambling to her feet. Apaji pushed open the screen door and saw a little boy of no more than four or five, black-skinned and fragile, dressed in a pair of old torn pajama bottoms without a top. His skin was mottled with sores and blemishes, and in his arms was a naked infant, scrawny and wizened, with tightly closed eyes and fists. As soon as the child saw Apaji, he dropped the baby on the floor and ran screaming through the empty station and out into the city.

Apaji called after him, scooping up the infant in one arm and holding Sara in the other.

Raheel was immediately at her side. "What are you doing, Apaji? Come back inside."

Apaji put her head against the baby's mouth and listened to its breathing. It was coming in such shallow spurts that it almost seemed not to be coming at all. Apaji lifted the edge of her short sari blouse and pushed the nipple of her breast between the baby's flaccid lips, but it was too weak to suck.

"What are you doing?" Raheel demanded. "You don't even have enough milk to feed Sara."

Apaji pressed the baby's mouth against her ear and listened again for the breathing. It was like a little rattle of air deep within the infant's throat, and prying her fingers through the baby's lips she tried again to make him nurse. Raheel was pulling at her arm as Apaji held the baby tightly against her breast and tears ran down her face. Again she listened for the breathing. "I think he is dead," she whispered to Raheel.

"Leave him, Apaji," Raheel pleaded.

"No. I can't do that. This is a baby. It could be anybody's baby. It could be Sara." She looked frantically around the empty expanse of the station under the beautiful dome. The ticket booths were shuttered, and all the screened doors of the waiting rooms closed tight.

"Go back inside," Apaji commanded. "I'm going to bury him."

"No," Raheel wailed, but Apaji already was running toward the tracks at the far end of the station. The morning was shadowed grayly over the pebbles and charcoals between the tracks, and hoisting up her skirts, Apaji flew over the rail lines and down the slope of the embankment, which was strewn with refuse and weeds. Across the narrow roadway was a row of barracks for the railroad workers. Praying that no one would come outside and see her, Apaji laid the dead infant down and stooped to the ground. Sara was screaming, and Raheel was still at her shoulder, begging her to come back inside before Abu noticed they were gone, but Apaji was scraping at the rough dry dirt, pulling up weeds and covering the baby as if she were crazed.

"I'm going to get Gappu," Raheel said and ran back down the track to the station.

All Apaji could hear was her own breathing and Sara wailing and monkeys scampering in the treetops. She was still digging when Raheel reappeared over the embankment with Gappu and Gerrar and Karim trailing behind. Why was Karim always coming where he did not belong? Apaji thought. They were calling to her and waving their arms. From the distance she could hear the high piercing whisle of a train. Her hand rested lightly on the infant's sunken chest half covered with sand, as she watched her own children slide down the rutted bank. Their voices were drowned by the approaching train. Clutching Sara under the fall of her sari, she jumped to her feet and started to run toward the station as the train they were waiting for passed heavily above her head.

The station had sprung to life. People were running out of the waiting rooms, and Abu was standing at the edge of the platform, cradling the trunk in his arms like a child and looking for Apaji and the older children in the crowds gathered outside all the bogies. Moïd, Mona, and Piari were standing bewildered among the remaining valises and sacks. As soon as Abu saw Apaji, he hurried them all toward the bogie where they had seats, but the reserved compartments had been filled to bursting long before the train had ever made it to Allahabad. Some said the train was coming from Calcutta. Others said it was coming from Delhi. None of it made any sense. The only point was to get out, get out of India.

There was no way to open the doors to the special compartments. The people inside said they had guns. The people outside said they had guns. They faced each other stalemated in this horrid game. The train was huffing, but there was no stationmaster to blow the whistle and no guards to decide the issue. Should they shoot and kill each other, and who, would they say, had done it the next day? Sikhs? Hindus? Muslims killing Muslims? It was impossible. The train could not move, and if it did, someone would pull the emergency cord, and the train would be stuck again for hours. Everyone was cursing everyone else.

One group of people was dressed in Western clothes, and another group was wearing turbans, but they all spoke the same dialect. Apaji searched their angry stony faces for some clue as to their identities. They couldn't be Sikhs. What would Sikhs be doing in Allahabad on a train bound for Patna? It was simply the wrong direction. All the women were huddled in corners in the rear of the train, and the men were leaning out the windows with the muscles on their forearms exposed. Apaji was still crying and holding onto the Koran and telling the children that all the people were friends.

"The people in the turbans are going to stop the train in the woods," Karim whispered. "It's their job to hijack it and loot the compartments."

"Shut up," Gappu told his brother. "You don't know what you're talking about." But he gripped Karim's hand in his own. He would rather have been holding Apaji's hand, but she was surrounded by the girls and Moïd, who was forever clutching onto the skirt of her sari.

Abu was searching the crowd for the white faces of the British police. He watched the conversation between the two groups of people, who seemed to be agreeing by shaking their heads, but they had a look on their faces that said they agreed to nothing at all. Finally Abu located one of the English soldiers. Gappu saw his father slip a fat wad of rupee notes to the officer, whose tan uniform was drenched with perspiration. He kept dabbing at his face and neck with his kerchief, as he led them down the platform to a different compartment. They were assured of passage again, because Abu had paid another British guard to stand watch over their lives.

After another journey of three days, stopping at night and traveling only between sunrise and sunset, the train pulled into Patna. They had waited all day in a station just outside of Patna, and it had taken only a half hour once the train had started moving. The whole family was still dizzy from the sun that had soaked into their compartment all day, and they were bitten with thirst. Police were running everywhere under the vast roof of the station with its mosaic of girders and garish advertisements. The unloading process was long and tiring, because the police and train officials had to check the tickets of the continuing passengers and direct them to the proper waiting rooms. There were two separate rooms for those bound for Bombay, and again men and women were segregated. Rehman saw

Apaji and the children to the door of the women's waiting room and gave her the firmest instructions never to leave. "Gappu and I will be right outside the door if you need anything. I don't think we will have to spend more than one night here. Remember, this is the state of Bihar, and there has been a good deal of unrest. We are very near to East Pakistan," he cautioned her.

Apaji nodded, and she and the children filed into the huge waiting room. It was a living cesspool. The children had to roll up their pants and skirts to wade through the muck that sloshed between their toes. The rows of benches had been pushed back from the center of the room, and there was no place to sit except right down in the middle of the urine and muck, which was slippery over the dark red tile floor. Apaji did not even have a rag with which to clean a spot for them. She took a fine cotton sheet from one of her bundles, and spreading it out on the ground, she squatted there on her haunches, like a farmer in a swamped paddy, with Sara in her lap. Moïd, Piari, and Mona pressed against her arms, but Raheel, Karim, and Gerrar stood above her, looking down, their faces knotted with nausea. Women and children were hunched shoulder to shoulder, and the hot air of late evening was filled with the heavy stench of human excretion and vomit.

The children had been brave up to this point, but now almost all of them were crying. It seemed as if finally they had been reduced to the status of cattle, and even Apaji was losing a grip on herself. It had been a long road, and everyone had been hanging on with their last ounces of emotional strength, through the riots, the blood, the loss of possessions, the raw food and diarrhea, the grueling heat, the uncertainty of being closeted in a train for hours at a time without knowing where they were, the constant threat of sudden violence, the sight of decapitated children, of mothers and infants dying of disease, the rerouting of trains that sent them whirling precipitously farther and farther in the wrong direction and deeper into India, which they were trying to escape.

Apaji thought it would all be bearable, but now her milk was drying up, and she wasn't going to see her eighth child die before her eyes. It was impossible. She was the daughter of the Darogaji, and none of her children died. She always had to hide her long hair from women who would try to snip it off and save it for good luck. Now her heavy braid of hair was in her way and hot against the nape of her neck. Her eyes were empty of visions except for her children who were clutching onto her clothes, and the tiny undernourished baby crumpled in her lap and defecating on the skirt of her sari.

Apaji had never seen such a tiny baby. Darogaji would not have stood for such a granddaughter. He would have rushed to the village of Milak to find a young mother with full firm breasts. He would have examined all the girls' breasts himself, and then brought the best nursing mother and her entire family to live on the estate in Nehtor, where they would be fed special dishes and the best water buffalo's milk to make the mother's milk sweet and strong. Darogaji's grandchild would never have been deprived of real mother's milk, or the feeling of a warm breast beneath the small helpless fingers. Apaji had always been proud that she never had to resort to the services of a surrogate mother. Now she would be willing to eat grass like a buffalo if she thought it would make her breasts flow with milk.

Other women were in the same plight. They sat all over the crowded hall, and their infants were red-faced with screaming. Some were already too weak to protest and lay limp and bloated across their mothers' shoulders, staring with tearless eyes at the commotion, which all seemed to be connected with the search for food. In the center of the room was a communal fire, built out of wood from the broken benches and with charcoal from the trains, and everyone was cooking rice and dal. The poorest were easy to pick out. They had taken off their black burkas, but still tried to conceal their faces beneath tattered scarves. Only the affluent women had had the time or money to disguise themselves in saris, which hulked around their bodies, inexpertly pleated and tied in the wrong direction. It was easy to separate those who swung the cloth comfortably over their shoulders and heads from those who had to clasp the edges in their hands and tripped over their skirts.

The nursing mothers were the most desperate, and they circulated through the room trying to hide their shattered faces beneath their scarves. "O Memsahib, Memsahib. *Dudh nahin hai.* There is no milk." Their chants were chilling songs punctuating the continuum of women's voices and children's cries. Others were reduced to stealing. Apaji, who was sitting directly across from the main door, could see them lurking behind the screening, emaciated silhouettes tensely pressing their babies against their sari blouses and shrouds. They waited inconspicuously in the dimly lit station among the men who were standing guard at the three arched doorways to see that their wives were not disturbed. Suddenly one of the girls would fly through the door, grab a few sections of fruit from a child's hand, and disappear again in the crowd of saris and squawking babies.

Apaji could understand their plight, but never would she take food from childrens' mouths. It was her greatest dilemma, because only by taking less herself could she assure herself that there would be enough food all the way to Bombay for her children, yet even the whole meal she fed them would not be adequate to sustain her milk and feed Sara. She could read the same desperation in the other women's faces, whose teething infants bit into their breasts. Apaji thought perhaps she could make the milk come with the power of her mind. Perhaps if she resorted to prayer, some miracle would make the milk strong.

Mona and Piari were pressing their faces into her lap and whining.

"Ummy, why can't we have pudding," Mona cried. "Why don't you make us some keer?"

Moïd just looked at her mutely with his round brown eyes.

"Raheel, take another sheet and rip it into strips," Apaji said. "The children can put it in their mouths to kill some of the hunger."

Raheel squatted alongside her mother and pulled out a sheet of fine woven threads and colors from one of the jute sacks. Apaji could see the soft pale skin of Raheel's arms beneath the sheer scarf across her shoulders. They had grown so thin, and Raheel looked tiny and lost in the trailing skirt she was wearing instead of a long blouse and pajamas, so that she, too, would appear Hindu or possibly Parsi.

187

Apaji looked up at Gerrar in his crumpled trousers and dirt-streaked shirt and Karim in his short shorts. They were still hanging back, scowling at the filth she was sitting in.

"You should sit down, or you will be too exhausted to travel," Apaji said gently.

Gerrar knelt on the sheet, but Karim stamped his foot. "I am going to stay with Abu," he said. "I don't like it in here."

Apaji lowered her head. "You can go if you wish, but don't get lost."

Karim picked his way through the women and children, sitting all over the floor of the huge room, and slipped through the door. The entrance was crowded with men hovering between the doorways. He caught sight of Abu standing with Gappu beside the ten remaining trunks and suitcases, all of varying sizes, and he could see Gappu talking to the other men like a grown-up. He hurried through the crowd before Abu saw him. Gerrar might be content to remain inside, helping his mother and Raheel with the younger children, but Karim could not stand it any longer. He wandered through the station which was wanly lit by naked electric light bulbs, breathing the air and looking at all the people in their strange costumes. They spoke a hundred different dialects and seemed to be going to a thousand different destinations.

Karim was puzzled how the rioters could tell everyone apart so quickly. How did they know they were killing the right people, he wondered, especially the babies who all looked alike. It seemed to Karim that more babies had been killed than anyone else. He could not forget all the blood he had seen, the baby who had been cut in half by a knife and spread out neatly in two pieces on the bed of the railroad track. The toes had been touching the head. Eyes closed. If you just saw the part above the chest, Karim thought, there was nothing wrong with the baby, and maybe through prayer it could be remade. He had once tried putting two pieces of cloth together on his Dadi's sewing machine. Maybe he could have done it with the baby. He knew it was childish of him to think so, but he had been desperate to ask Abu if the baby could be repaired. It had looked so perfect, so neatly severed. The only time Karim had seen death so close in his life before had been when his cousin Waji died of cholera, and that kind of death was different.

Karim wandered among the passengers in the perpetual twilight of the terminal. Patna was the largest station they had been in. It was used as a junction to field trains coming in from every direction, according to the Indian peace formula of 1947. One train, which had left hours earlier, had been turned back after traveling well over a hundred miles, because there was word that an ambush was set up farther along the track. Thousands of people had to be rerouted, and they were milling about in search of a new train, and there was a logjam at the station.

Karim wanted to announce to everybody, "I am from Nehtor. I am from the green fields of Milak. It is a nice little town, and the population is divided between the landholding Muslims and the merchant Hindus. There is even a minority of Sikhs, and we all play together, and we live in peace. There is one little road, and the nearest railway station is seven miles away. We must ride on horses or in tongas to get there. The road is lined with mango gardens, and every mile there is a little marker, which was put there in the time of Ashoka. A man sits beside each marker on a charpoy with a slingshot to keep the parrots out of the trees when the aroma of the blossoms fills the land. Outside the town are the houses of the Untouchables with thatch roofs which are the cleanest of all because they keep pigs to eat waste and to act as the entire sanitation department of the village. There is a canal which allows the Gangan River to seep over just enough to fill up the town pond, which is surrounded by banana trees, and the persistent reflection of their long green leaves shines in the water. The banana pods protrude from their stems and swing from side to side like a heavy udder. In the evening they turn into moving tusks of rouge with the falling sun behind the thousands of trees. At the end of the road is the little school with its white archways and the Mulvi bent over lessons from the Koran.

"My grandfather was the Daroga, or mayor of the district. He did not like his English title of Chairman, and only foreigners used it. Darogaji kept his original title even though he had long ago been promoted from the lesser position of Daroga. His name became

Darogaji, and he wore it with distinction. His tastes ran to silk handkerchiefs and white horses and greyhound dogs. To a Muslim, owning a dog was as bad as eating pork. If by mistake you brushed against a dog, you were supposed to wash your clothes immediately, take a bath, say a prayer, and go to sleep. Darogaji always justified his greyhounds by saying that the rule was made because most dogs were owned by peasants and were flea-bitten and died of fevers and madness. Some of the people covered their faces when they saw the greyhounds and muttered 'Islam khatra men hai,' which means 'Islam is in danger.' But the greyhounds were different from most dogs, and they strode around the courtyards of the house like Princes of Wales.

"Down the road from my grandfather's house, beside the mosque, is a well where all the young girls of the village come to draw water. We swam in the canal all summer and watched the girls giggling at the well and chasing each other with water from their clay pots, which sometimes would fall and break into tiny pieces at their feet and they would laugh. Thousands and thousands of songs and poems have been written about meeting the young girls of India at their wells, of watching them come and go with their shapely clay pots protruding from their hips, humming tunes between their lips and smiling under their scarves.

"This is the India I am leaving behind," thought Karim, as he walked back again among the hordes of strange people who, he knew, came from villages almost exactly like his own. No one seemed to know where they were going, and whole families were running back and forth along the quays, reading the destinations printed on placards in the windows of the trains. The hall was cluttered with refuse, and pools of turgid water lay in the empty tracks. Karim had to push through crowds of people who were trying to find room in a train that had already started moving. Women were leaping through the doors, tripping over their saris, or hoisting their children onto the roofs of the cars, which were supposed to be safer than the third-class cars where it was easier to be trapped. Karim could not understand what anyone was saying. Besides Urdu, they seemed to be speaking Bengali, and many dialects he did not recognize at all. They wore Madrasi dhotis and Bengali lengas and saris tied in a hundred different ways, caught tightly between the women's legs or draped loosely from head to toe. Karim had no idea who all the people were or where they came from, but he knew that they were homeless like himself, and going to foreign places. He wished he could know where they were going, and he wanted to let them know who he was. "I am Indian," he kept saying to himself. "I am a Nehtori."

Karim held his breath as he stepped back into the waiting room by one of the two side doors, so that Abu would not know he had been wandering around. It seemed to be even more filled with women and small children defecating and with crying and noise than before. Apaji was near collapse from the strain of feeding Sara. She was more saddened than her baby, and she was crying bitterly as the suckling and nibbling on her nipple made her cracked and drier, and no milk came. Sara's fists were clenched into two little balls against her mother's breast.

Apaji knew her husband had ordered her to stay in the waiting room, but the more the hours passed, the less her milk would come, and Sara's cries were becoming weaker, so that she seemed to moan like an old dying woman. The rice and lentils, the scraps of oranges, Apaji had been eating, were not enough to sustain her body which had been nurtured on the fattest meats, the richest butters, yogurts, and milks. Sara's thirst was the only thing that could lead Apaji to take risks, even more risks than her husband whose firm orders to stay in the waiting room until the train arrived kept ringing in her ears. Apaji had never before dreamed of being disobedient to her husband or her father whom she had always obeyed to the point that when the old Darogaji told her to sit facing a tree when a man passed her, she would do so, even if she was covered from head to toe in the suffocating black burka Muslim women were supposed to wear to hide their faces and their very beings. Apaji had always worn a burka in Nehtor during her years of engagement to her husband, even though she hated it and felt trapped and claustrophobic like a young animal caught in a hunter's net.

Now she was ready to break all bondage, and she jumped to her feet and hurried across the room to the door farthest from where she knew Abu and Gappu were standing. She was not going to let Sara die. The children leaped up and ran after her. There were so many people coming and going, it was easy for a mother even with six children and a baby holding onto her, to slip unnoticed through their midst. The men were standing guard for the very purpose of interceding in an emergency or to stop the fleeing women who could take no more of the stench and squalor of the waiting room, or the tensions of waiting interminably. However, by the time Rehman received the news from other women who whispered it to their husbands, that they had seen Apaji escape with all her children, including Gerrar who was supposed to come and tell him if something like this happened, he was helpless. He did not even know which way she had gone.

The children were following Apaji, despite the fact that they knew the horrible stories of the massacres in the towns and cities along their route. The younger children were screaming at the top of their voices for Apaji to take them back, but no one came to see what was the matter. It was already late at night, and the road beside the station was shadowed in pale electric lights. Not a soul was about, and they ran across the road and into a street of shops and medium-sized buildings. Raheel told Apaji that the Sikhs would kill them with their kirpans; but the children had to follow because otherwise they would be separated from both their mother and Abu, and end up alone in the deserted streets of Patna.

There were burned houses and a mosque half in ashes. There were broken windows and charred trees and dead animals. There was not a soul on the streets and no noise. The birds were gone. The flowers were gone, and the doors to most of the houses were gaping open. There were no mule carts, and no rickshaws and no sweet-meat salesmen. The shops were open but vacant, and there was no food, only thin black cakes of blood in small pools on the sidewalks.

Suddenly the children realized they had no fear. There was nothing to fear in an absolutely deserted city. They could walk, and they could see everywhere. The street was long and wide, and Apaji was walking ahead of them at a fast pace. Gerrar held Moïd and Mona by their hands. Raheel was carrying Sara, and Karim was leading Piari with quick little steps.

"Apaji is looking for food that she does not have to cook," they whispered to each other. "We must find milk for her. Look for a buffalo or a cow. Look for packages of biscuits and tins of meat and cheese. There must be a shop with something left where we can help ourselves."

Noises were coming from somewhere on another street. They all stopped frozen in their footsteps. They looked down the street one way and then the other, but in the darkness they could see nothing. Still, the voices and the noise of motors did not stop. It sounded as if many people were advancing in slow-moving cars and on foot. The younger children were becoming hysterical. They could no longer swallow the screams that came pouring out of them. Gerrar and Karim tried to gather them into a circle, but they did not know which way the noises were coming from or which way to move. Every corner as far as the eye could see down the long cobblestone thoroughfare was bisected by smaller streets, and any minute the whole horde of angry-sounding people would turn and flood into view. Apaji kept moving fast. She looked over her shoulder to make sure all seven children were there, taking them all in by instinct, because she did not have the time to count. She ducked into the narrow opening between two wooden buildings, and the children, still screaming, followed quickly behind her. Karim and Gerrar tried to put their hands over the other children's mouths to silence them, but there were too many mouths going at once.

They heard sirens, and several cars came rumbling past the alley, their headlights appearing like phantoms out of nowhere. They could see people running along beside the cars. Some were wearing loincloths, and others wore turbans, and many of them were holding long sticks. Ahead of them a group of Bihari Muslims, mostly women and children, were running and tripping, and there was terror.

"Where is the station?" Apaji whispered. "We have to find the station." Most of the cars had passed, and they could hear the sirens and the screaming fade into another street as fast as they had come. Apaji peered around the corner of the alley into the quiet street, but a black taxi whizzed around the nearest corner. Apaji ducked and pushed the children behind her, squeezing them under the side railing of a shop. They clung to the steps overhead with their fingers, and dead rats were lying at their feet in a dirty cesspool. They could hear the car stop beside the alleyway. Someone climbed out of the car and walked toward the place where they were hiding.

A hand was extended, beneath the white sleeve of a cotton blouse. Apaji took the hand and rose to the street level to stare directly into the white-bearded face of a Sikh under his turban. The children climbed up after her.

"You can't hide here," the man told her. "Where are you going?"

"I came from the station," Apaji told him, looking steadily into the gruff wide bones and deep-set eyes.

"What are you doing here? You could be shot. It is way after curfew." The Sikh continued to grasp her arm tightly in his fist.

"We are looking for food, Sardarji," said Apaji, using the respectful title for Sikh men. She could hear her own voice shaking, and the children were pressing against her, but she continued to gaze at the tall, white-haired stranger. The man looked over his shoulder at his companion, who was sitting in the driver's seat of a very old car. The driver nodded his turbaned head.

"We will take you as close to the station as possible," he said to Apaji. "We are not part of this, but there is not much we can do, or we will be killed. We will look for food on the way."

Apaji hesitated only a moment, sizing up the two Sikhs in the instant. Whatever their motives, she knew there was no alternative but to go with them. The children piled ahead of her into the car. They were all smiling now, despite their hunger and despite the tears still rolling down their cheeks.

The man turned to them from the front seat. "Where is your husband?" he asked.

"He is at the station. He does not know we left," Apaji answered.

The Sardarji shook his head. "The best we can do is to take you to a safer street where you can walk back to the station. Don't let anyone see you. Not the police, not even the English police, or they will take you to jail and you may never get out. People are jammed into the jails, and they are rotting there. You don't even have any papers with you."

They drove through many back streets, turning sharply and twisting down alleys. Although the children were crouching low on the floor and in the rear seat of the car, they could see the shuttered windows of the three- and four-story buildings squeezed together over their heads. Apaji had not realized they had walked so far, but time and distance had become meaningless. All she could do was trust in this Sardarji taxi driver who was smiling at her with his yellow teeth, his fat stomach going up and down with laughter as he tried to amuse the children and distract them. Apaji saw fire in his breath and the hottest of suns in his eyes and a skin of a thousand cracks, but a heart full of gold. He smelled of perspiration and garlic, but he was their savior.

He told the children about how his people had suffered exile and massacre three hundred years ago, when the Muslim rulers demanded that the Sikhs convert to Islam or face death and torture. The entire Sikh population hid in the woods, and their hair grew long, so that now they kept it washed and braided neatly beneath their turbans, and they carried long crescent knives, or kirpans, for their protection and survival, and always wore a miniature dagger close to their chests and an iron ring on their wrists to symbolize the captivity of their entire population by the kings of the Mogul Empire. He told them that his people had sworn to maintain the symbols of the long hair and the crescent knife and the iron ring in order never to forget what they had suffered for God, who has many names, who is Bahwan and Allah and Yaweh. It was the teaching of the Gurus.

"But now we are all suffering together," he told them, "who can understand why?"

The children had heard the story many times before, but in the car with the jolly man telling it, first coming close to tears and then making clown faces so that they would all laugh again, the story had a new sound, and they had a deeper understanding of it.

The car came to a stop, and the driver turned around and smiled. He was a younger man. His turban was a soft deep purple and his black beard was neatly combed under his chin and tied back around his ears. "This is the shop of a friend. He will not ask questions, and I will bring you some meat and cheese."

Apaji could not believe her ears; she was so filled with gratitude. She extended her hand with one of her finest brooches of gold and emeralds locked inside her fist. She had fished it up from the pouch of jewels she was wearing concealed beneath the waistband of her sari. The Sardarji pried open her fingers and stared at the jewel glittering in Apaji's hand, which was lined black with dirt, in the creases, and under her broken nails.

"There is no need for that," he said sternly. "What we will bring you is worth no more than ten or fifteen rupees at most, even in these days."

"You risk your lives for us," said Apaji. "Others want more for much less."

The driver closed her fingers back over the jewel and held Apaji's fist firmly in his long fingers. "Save something for your beautiful daughter," he said, looking at Raheel. "Soon many men will be asking for her, and she will need a dowry to match the sapphires in her eyes."

Raheel buried her head in her mother's shoulder and drew her thin little dopatta over her hair, as the driver climbed out of the taxi and disappeared into a shuttered and seemingly deserted shop. He was gone less than a minute, and when he returned, Raheel had regained her composure and smiled shyly back at his black piercing eyes which were staring at her appreciatively. He handed Apaji a small basket filled with tins of corned beef and cheese imported from England, as he had promised. There was also a can of butter and some halvah wrapped in a bit of newspaper, a box of powdered milk, and a package of noodles. It was truly a feast. The children could not express their thanks enough, and Apaji felt the tears flooding over the brims of her eyes and streaking down her face.

"We will never forget you," she said. "We will always pray for you."

"That is all we ask," said the older man. "If ever you are in Patna again, remember my name. I am Jit Singh Aluwallah."

The driver started the car, and they drove quickly off down the empty street. It was almost morning, but still no one was walking about in this section of Patna. All the windows were fastened tightly. They made several turns with the taxi's wheels screeching and the old engine straining as the car rumbled on with as much speed as the driver could muster, in and out of alleyways and across thoroughfares. Finally they turned onto a straightaway, and there was some traffic, with cars and bicycles and rickshaws weaving among the meandering cows. Goats were tied up along the curbside, and there were temples on every corner and shrines nestled in the folds of towering trees.

"Stay down," the Sardarji hissed, and everyone ducked. "It is only a few blocks, and we will be back on the street you came from. Don't turn around or speak when you get out of the car. I will open the door, and you climb out. You will see the station ahead of you, but don't run. I want you to walk casually as if you knew the street very well and knew where you were going. I do not think anyone will see you, but you must be careful."

Apaji nodded, although the Sardarjis could not see her hunched down and pressed as she was against the seat. Their broad shoulders were towering above her, and Apaji was amazed to realize how totally the sight of these strong masculine backs had changed their meaning for her. What only a few hours ago she held in the greatest fear, she now leaned against. The shoulders that once seemed to be knotted with angry muscles, tense with hatred, were now gentle and filled with fatherly concern. Apaji longed to caress them, to touch them with blessings and kiss them with prayers.

Rehman thought he was going out of his mind. The whole family, except for Gappu, had disappeared. He didn't even know which way to look for them. He left the luggage with someone he had met a bare two hours earlier and grabbed Gappu by the arm. He wasn't going to lose sight of Gappu for a single moment. His eldest son might be the only one left to him. Rehman gulped at the thought and tried to force out the ugly visions that barraged his mind and only confused him. He had to think straight.

Gappu was frantic, and Rehman could feel him trembling as they walked together through the crowds and out of the station. There was nothing to be seen. The dusty road was dimly lit and empty. Rehman had heard the curfew sirens whining all over the city almost an hour earlier. Apaji couldn't have gone outside during curfew, he reasoned, and he hurried Gappu back inside to make another thorough search of the station. They went up and down every platform and into all the waiting rooms, sometimes bribing a policeman to let them in without tickets, since each room was used for different trainloads instead of according to class. Gappu had to go into the women's waiting rooms, and even he had to explain that his mother was lost or the women practicing purdah would not let him in and told him he was too old to look at their daughters.

Apaji and the children were nowhere to be found. It was clear they had gone out of the station. Rehman stopped every official he could find and offered them money to take him into Patna to look for his wife and children, but everyone refused. They sent him from office to office, where hundreds of other passengers were trying to obtain information or help, exchanging money, gold, and valuables for tickets, and all talking at once. The railway officials kept him waiting for an hour, and no one could tell him what to do except wait. Still holding Gappu firmly by the arm, he ran out of the station again, and suddenly he saw the whole brood coming toward him at a run. They were laughing, and Raheel's arms were filled with a basket of food. He ran halfway to meet them and immediately went into a tirade.

"Why should I worry about you?" he screamed at them. "There are thousands of children like you dying all over India. Why should I worry about you when I can pick up hundreds more like you." First he screamed and then he cried, and he sat right down in the cobbled street, holding his family in his arms, hugging them all at once.

Apaji was the celebrity of the day in the women's waiting room. She was a heroine. So many wanted to, but no one else had dared to go. Now she was back with the food she had received from men in turbans. She offered to share what she had with the women around her, but no one would take any. They refused with silent bowings of their heads and averted eyes.

"Is it because the food was given by Sikh people?"

"No, not at all," they protested. It was just that no one wished to deprive this gallant lady, the bravest of them all, of the sustenance she had found for her family at such great risk. This was the law of survival, but they did rejoice with her, and they even allowed Rehman to come into the waiting room, the only man permitted in the whole place, because he could not take his eyes off his dhulan, his eternal bride, and her brave children.

Apaji divided the food for her children and felt the gentle touch of the Sikh on her hand when he extended the food to her. Karim was dancing all around Abu and telling him the whole adventure, and especially about their Sikh friend, Jit Aluwallah, and Karim laughed about his name, which meant potato man, and said he was kind and handsome with a flowing white beard and a pink turban. Karim said he wanted to wear a turban someday too. Apaji smiled at the thought of the kind ungainly man and the young attractive driver who was so nice to Raheel, making her smile even in the crushed dirty long skirt she was wearing. Abu placed his hand on her shoulder, and kissing the younger children, left them all with the admiring women. Apaji repeated the story of the evening a hundred times as women squatted down beside her to meet her and see what she had brought. After everyone had eaten, she told the children to lie down and try to sleep, but she spent the rest of the night bowing from her knees to the ground, deep in prayer for the two Sikh men who had procured food for her and tried to make a few moments of happiness for her children, at the risk of their own lives. She prayed until her knees gave out, and she had to squat again among all the women, who bowed and called her blessed.

Satisfied that all would now remain calm in the women's waiting room, Rehman retrieved his luggage from the stranger who had been guarding it and told Gappu to stay with it in the men's waiting room. He was determined to obtain information about the Bombay trains, and this time he took a whole pocket full of gold coins with him in order to be able to buy someone's attention. Handing over one coin to a *titi*, he was led into an inner room where the English stationmaster was gulping tea and a plate of chapati and meat. The stationmaster looked as if he had not slept in days or had the time to change his uniform, which was hanging tiredly off his long narrow shoulders. Rehman learned that only one train bound for Bombay was expected that day. The problem was that this train had already been cut up somewhere between Dacca and Patna. It was carrying a cargo of the dead, and it was not expected to stop.

Fired by his wife's bravery, Rehman's mind was clicking clear as a logician's. He decided that if the train had already been attacked once, it was unlikely that it would be attacked again. He was thinking that this was the kind of decision that his father had to make while fleeing from Dera Ghazi Khan when Rehman himself was only three. It required the weighing of probabilities and the likelihoods of fate. It seemed only reasonable, however, that a cut-up train would not be stopped a second time. He was hardly concerned with the news that it was filled with dead bodies. The stories of atrocities had become so casual, so matter of fact, it hardly seemed more than a matter of numbers any longer. All that was important was the survival of the family. The only thing he could think about was that they must reach Bombay intact and with enough money and possessions to secure passage on the boat for Karachi. After that, he could be empty handed—that was no concern. It only mattered that all ten of them reach Pakistan. The rest would take care of itself.

After giving a proper amount of gold, it was agreed with the stationmaster that Rehman and his family would proceed to a point about a hundred yards down the track beyond the railroad station.

As the last car was passing, the train would stop just long enough for them to get on board. The stationmaster agreed that it could be arranged if the train had not yet left the last station. He would wire and see that it was accomplished, provided that there was an equal sum for the train's engineer. They shook hands and it was done.

At a few minutes before noon, later that morning, the stationmaster appeared in the men's waiting room and signaled to Rehman to come quickly. He had brought several coolies to carry the ten trunks and valises, and Rehman called Apaji and the children from their waiting room. Rehman had not told Apaji about the plan to take a train full of corpses, and all the women looked up surprised as the family left with their belongings, and whispered among themselves that here indeed was a special woman. Apaji did not even have a chance to say good-bye as she followed obediently behind her husband and the stationmaster and all the porters along the platform and down some steps into the bright sunlight, which was glinting off the tracks and all the pebbles and bits of charcoal underfoot. Rehman knew that if she understood what they were doing, she would have protested, but there was no time for questions because they could see the huge black engine of the train coming at top speed along the track circumventing the station.

"That's it," the stationmaster shouted above the blasts of the whistle and the clattering of the wheels.

The bright green cars were whipping past them. It did not look as if the train could possibly stop. Rehman felt his throat tighten, and the palms of his hands were weak and wet with perspiration. Finally the train began to lose speed. It was an exceptionally long train and seemed to have so many additional cars that it snaked in front and behind them for hundreds of yards.

As the train slowed down, the children could see that all the cars in the front of the train were filled with the same frozen dead faces they had seen once before at the beginning of their journey, but for some reason the back cars were almost empty. The train did not stop completely, but as the last car approached, the station-master began hoisting the children through the doors. Grabbing Apaji and Sara, Rehman jumped onto the step in the last door before the caboose, and by the time he turned around the stationmaster and the coolies had been left behind, and he was looking down at the bed of rails that whooshed below and the houses and trees and temples of Patna.

People were sitting in quiet, dazed groups on the wooden seats, all facing each other but not speaking. There was a confused Parsi, intellectual-looking and solemn behind his glasses and Western suit. There were the saddened faces of a family of Sikhs with bundles perched on their knees. Rehman and Apaji sat on a bench with the younger children in their laps and leaning against their arms. Gappu, Gerrar, and Raheel sat erect and numb, facing their parents, while Karim curled up behind them on a vacant seat. No one asked what Abu had done to get them on board, as if any discussion might make the train disappear, as if the explanation of all the dead bodies in the front of the train would somehow change what was happening to them, force them back into the cesspool of a waiting room or out into one of the hot endless fields they were now passing.

For hours they held their breath, waiting for something to occur, but the train sped south through Bihar, and by the time they had eaten and the younger children were asleep, their heads resting on Abu's and Apaji's laps or against their shoulders, they could see the first hills of the Western Ghats rising from the flat land, and the lakes where fishermen chased the migrating geese from the water with the beating of their nets. Thunderclouds gathered overhead, and the rains came to wash away the blood from the first half of the train. They seemed to be moving faster and faster into the south, never stopping at stations, but only at water silos and in the black fields of coal where lines of almost naked workers with sooty faces fought through the rain to climb a steep incline to the train and feed it coal from baskets balanced on their heads. Gappu had the runs and spent most of the time in the toilet, the first clean one he had seen in days. It was only a hole in a block of cement over which Gappu had to crouch, but Gappu had used the Indian country-style toilets many times in Milak and at Dadi's house in Nehtor, and at least there was a door he could close and be alone with his thoughts.

Karim pressed his nose to a window, alone on his private bench, and sang with the wheels, "Half dead and half alive." He tried to count the number of nights he had now spent without a bed. There was the waiting room at Patna, one night and one day. There was the train from Allahabad to Patna, three nights and two days, and the overnight stop in Allahabad where the baby was buried. It was another three nights and two days from Aligarh to Allahabad and there were the weeks on the floor of Bashir's room behind the house in Aligarh. How many weeks? Two, three, almost a month. It was difficult to remember. He tried to imagine Nehtor and the beds in Dadi's sleeping room from which they incessantly tried to escape. He could not remember the last bed he had slept in. He could not remember if it was in Aligarh or Nehtor. Or in the chicken coop with Bashir trembling at his side. The ceiling light from the roof was dim in the deepening shadows after twilight. Most intriguing were the different lights as they fell through the window and across his own legs, the warm flashes of lightning and the eerie yellows as they sped through empty country stations. The sound of thunder and of rain on the roof almost drowned out the continuous lunging of the wheels. The train whistle blew occasionally to warn straying animals to get off the tracks. Riding through the rain, he thought of the peacocks of Milak that danced in the monsoons, bathing their tail feathers luxuriously and calling to each other in mournful screeches. They had slept in rows of beds at Tariq's wedding, listening for sounds of lovemaking in the bridal room next to theirs. There were a hundred ladies in one room. They had long silken bodies, and they slept on cotton sheets, wet with humidity. There was the sound of the Sikh's car horn in Patna as he wielded them through the disastrous streets with laughter in their aching mouths and tears in their eyes. There were tears for Milak and Nehtor, and sadness with the moving wind and the rain and the thunder that rippled all night around the rushing train and well into a dark gray morning, and everything was almost forgotten in sleep.

Karim felt pins all over his body, and thought he had just been gored again by the sharp horns of an angry bull after a race in Milak, and Moonah was running scared out of the field. He was hanging on to the bull's horn with his thigh. The bull was shaking him. Shaking and shaking. Abu was shaking him, and it was Bombay.

4

Partition II

Freedom. It was less an idea than a feeling. Rehman Hussain could sense its presence in every fiber of his body. It came up to meet him through the very boards of the ship as he stood looking out over the Arabian Sea. It seemed to elevate him in the air; for the entire day and a half they had already been at sea, he could not remember having slept or having sat down at all. He hovered over the water during the day, when the winds whipped the masses of waves on every side of him. He leaned against the railings at night, peering into the darkness deep below him, keeping company with the waning moon into ever longer hours of morning.

From the moment the S.S. *Shiralla* sailed from the port in Bombay, with a sighing of its ropes and a swaying of its broad white sides, Rehman grappled with the alternating emotions of joy and bitterness. Like a pendulum, he swung with the rocking of the Arabian Sea. First came tears of thankfulness as his eyes ran over the flaccid bodies of his children lying on the open deck. Each one was here. Each had survived a journey so dizzying that all of India, rushing by them in the green flowering of its harvest, seemed bathed in a screaming pattern of white cloth smeared with red blood. He could not believe that joy would ever be unmitigated again. As he closed his eyes, he dared to see the fearful images of burning homes and shops he had managed to repress throughout the entire last month: He saw Gappu, naked on the floor, beside the body of his neighbor's son. He saw Raheel stretched across a bed, raped, and bleeding between her legs. He saw Gerrar, insane and babbling with groping hands and blinded eyes. He saw his babies dismembered and his wife transparent, like a shadow, with her skeletal infant dead at her breast.

With every hour that passed, taking them closer to Karachi, Rehman pushed the visions further back into his mind from where he had fearfully let them spring. The family slept on the wooden planks of the open deck, unruffled by the chill in the morning sea air, unaware of the movement of the ship or their destination. They created a special enclave, nine strong, amidst all the other bodies, exhausted in the hiatus from suffering.

They had been lucky to find a corner of the deck where the other milling refugees did not climb about their legs and trip across their bodies. Apaji could finally rest. She lay with her head in Raheel's lap, while Sara's newborn head rolled drunkenly across her shoulder, filled with the first adequate milk that had come with peace. Raheel sat upright, her eyes half closed, her hand clutching her little sister Piari's, who slept by her side. Moïd and Mona also slept, tiny rolled-up balls, half covering each other. Gerrar sat with his back against a pile of rope, braiding and unbraiding the ends of twine with a studiously lost expression on his face. Rehman noticed that Gerrar's ankles and bare feet peeped out too far from his trousers, with the smallest growth of hair at the edge of the cuff. Gappu and Karim hung over the opposite railing deep in a whispering conversation. Rehman wished his three older sons would sleep and rest their minds. No matter, he thought. They were safe. India was an alien country now, and they were surrounded by ocean with no place to wander off to and perhaps never return.

The closer they came to Pakistan, the more Rehman sensed the old power creep back into his muscles, which had hung useless and heavy for too long at his sides. He had been built for a rugged life. Despite his education, he was a man raised for hunting, for coatless ourneys through rain-hung forests and treks across sun-scorched hills. As a young man, he had worked in the glittering, bare whiteness of the salt lakes near Jaipur, his body tingling with salt and his eyes aching from the sun's glare reflected on the metallic salt water. As an administrator of Darogaji's property, he had inspected stunted villages that hunkered alone in damp fields, seething with snakes that were chased from their holes and burrows by the monsoon rain, and where villagers did not know the meaning of the word *doctor*. His boyhood home in Nehtor had been surrounded by craftsmen whose ancestors were gun and arrow makers, and they taught him to shoot an automatic and build firecrackers when he was only a child. He had killed snakes with sticks and stalked wild boar and tigers on foot. He learned to swim in the canals and walk the endless footpaths through the plains and forests of the United Provinces while on tours of inspection, collecting taxes and deciding local issues. That is all very good, his father had often told him, but a man's strength is in his mind. Only your mind will protect you when the time comes. His father had been right. No strength of bone or flesh or even gun, although he was well armed with all three, could have brought him safely to this ship.

He watched the jagged shoreline slipping past the boat. It seemed deserted of life. The hills of the Western Ghats were silent with low-bending coconut trees twisted tortuously in the shape the wind had left them. Soon the coast of India became no more than a green blur on the horizon, the demarcation of a lifetime, left behind like a ghost in the teeming cities and among the gardens and fields.

Rehman looked out across the water. A thousand porpoises appeared, bucking the waves and playing in the wake of the ship. How mindless of time and place, of direction and turbulence, they seemed! Rehman found it a pleasant relief to watch them.

All the women on board were speaking of seasickness and sunstroke as they rose periodically from their long sleeps to retch over the side, or find an unoccupied corner to urinate beneath their skirts. They said that late summer was a bad time to travel on the Persian Gulf. People usually waited until winter, when nights were calm and gentle, to make the pilgrimage to Mecca and the Holy Land.

That was the time to travel, and the open decks would be filled with happy black-veiled Muslims going to pray at the Prophet's grave. Now was not the time. The sea lurked with dangers and monsoons.

Rehman could not be bothered with such talk—or, indeed, with any talk. For twenty hours, thirty hours, the boat moved soundlessly, bearing a blanket of curled bodies. Of all the voyages he had ever taken, this was the most momentous. For Rehman, this was no time to sleep. It did not matter that he wore the same shirt, deeply soiled from a month of sleeping on filthy floors, or that his once golden cheeks were yellow under a scraggly growth of beard, or that the new hairs that scratched beneath his chin were almost as much gray as black, or that his eyes were mere red slits from squinting without his glasses, which had broken weeks before. He felt as strong and directionless as the porpoises that materialized everywhere before him. He was boundless with joy and energy. He was free; Pakistan was free; India was free.

Rehman had never before thought about freedom. It was a part of his life. He had freedom to worship, freedom to work, freedom to move about from place to place and city to city. He had always believed he had freedom of choice. Then, suddenly, there were no choices in life anymore. Choice became a matter of ultimatums. Do this and maybe die. Do the other thing and maybe die. Leave Aligarh, leave Nehtor, leave India. Were these choices? Was there any other way?

Throughout the two nights and a day since leaving Bombay, Rehman grappled with the notion of freedom. While others slept in a deep stupor or milled silently among the crumpled bodies, his mind tried to put some order into the events that had changed the course of his life so suddenly. The images unreeled behind his eyes, and he saw himself fleeing for his life to the edge of India to a boat they clambered on like monkeys at sunrise. Until the decisive moment when the ship had sailed, his mind had been blank of any thought, any purpose, other than reaching that ship. Throughout the long journey from Aligarh, the trains, the waiting rooms, the rerouting and crisscrossing of India, the thousand-mile maze of rail tracks, his decisions seemed to come not from his mind but from elsewhere in his body. He was like a mechanism that shunted his family in blind, senseless directions, thinking only that somehow he must protect them and keep them alive. No God, no prayers, could do that. Only the man—Abu, the father; Rehman, the husband. When a train was cut down, he directed his efforts to shielding his children's eyes, but he knew they saw, nevertheless. He remembered Karim's voice saying, "Abu, Abu, do you see the baby without its head?" He had tried to ignore his son, as they stood on the station platform, pushed by the crowd on every side. It was all he had been able to do to keep his eyes focused on Apaji holding Sara with Mona and Moïd and Piari surrounding her. He had to pay money for seats. He had to keep gold money for the next emergency. He had to keep track of the trunks and suitcases and sacks. He had to make sure that the guards he had paid for protection were not spun madly away from him in the melee of frantic fellow refugees. He had to rub his hands together in order not to lose sensation altogether and fall dead away in a faint. He reminded himself constantly, "I am a refugee!"

The feeling of his helplessness still coursed through the heavy muscles in his arms. Over and over Rehman told himself that the children had not seen, that Apaji, his bride of jasmine skin and milk-bathed hair, had never crouched in a running sewer or tried to bury an infant under charcoal and pebbles. All he had allowed himself to think about for the past month was arriving in Bombay, the last port, and finding the ship that would take them to Pakistan.

The memory of Karim's hysterical voice continued to spin in Rehman's thoughts like a recurrent dream. He had pretended not to hear, but how could he forget Karim repeating the same phrase over and over, "Do you see the baby without a head, Abu? Do you see the baby?" Rehman had wanted to grab his son and shake him, silence him, wrap his hands around his mouth, his eyes, his ears. He wanted to suffocate the memory in Karim's mind of the warm, pink torso, quivering in death, the neck not yet formed, the head with puckered lips and unfocused eyes tossed against its grasping hand like a football, but he had no energy for anything except his goal of freedom. Bombay and the ship. The ship was freedom, and freedom was the difference between life and death.

The waters of the Arabian Sea lay blackened in the still hour before sunrise. As light tinged the air for the second time in the voyage, people began to stir with the sun. The long day-and-a-half sleep was like a pall which people were struggling to lift, one by one, weak and dazed. A tearful man stood up from the center of a mass of sleeping bodies, his face drunk with grogginess. He pointed to the sun that was suspended over the water in an otherwise empty and colorless sky. "Is that the sunrise or sunset?" he asked. Others, who had awakened here and there among the groups of families, looked out over the water. Most of them had never seen the sea or the clarity of the sun when it rose solitarily between the water and sky. As the sun nudged its way into the sky, the people began calling Azan—the prayer of greeting life at sunrise—and all the passengers who were awake bent deeply forward to press their foreheads onto the ship's planks.

A Mulvi came walking along the deck, calling the people to him in a high tenor song of prayer. He held a rosary in his hands, and the ends of his long flowing beard were neatly tucked into his trim white cap. He wore no shoes. They had probably pinched his sweating feet and been left at a roadside or sold for a few rupees' worth of lentils. The Mulvi stooped to bless the people who greeted him with handclasps as he walked. A small group of men followed him to the prow of the ship, where Rehman was standing. They were trying to decide where Mecca was, so that they could face in the right direction as they prayed. Rehman joined in the prayer. Although it was a sin to miss the Azan at sunrise or sunset, most of the passengers were either sleeping or still too dazed to pray. The fifteen or twenty men who had gathered in the prow bent forward to the floor seven times, following the lead of the Mulvi. "Allah ho Akbar. God is One," they responded.

After the prayers, the men continued to sit together, cross-legged, looking out over the water. There was a strong feeling of brotherhood among them. The prow of the ship had become a mosque where women were not allowed, a small masculine sanctuary for deciding important issues and exchanging ideas. As the ship pierced the water, the salt spray freshened their faces and the wind lew through their hair. They clasped one another's hands and in-roduced themselves.

There were several students in open-necked sport shirts that hung loosely outside the belt of their pants. Unshaven and raw-eyed, they had joined in the prayer which they had previously left to their parents to say for them. They were only slightly older than Gappu, and had the shaggy, fiery-eyed look Gappu was developing. All of them were busy finding out where everyone else had come from. Some were from Delhi and Bombay, and others from rural areas as far away as Mysore City in the south or Hyderabad in central India.

"It does not matter where we came from," the Mulvi inter-rupted their game. "It matters where we are going." He smiled as he spoke, and his fingers continuously worked the rosary beads because he said his prayers silently with his mind when he was not saying them aloud with his words. A callous ridge grown smooth and shin-ing across his deeply lined forehead from so much bending to the ground was a mark of his piety.

"We are going to the promised land, Pir Sahib," a young stu-dent said with fire in his voice, addressing the old holy man with the highest title of respect. "No one has to tell us that."

"Promises, promises. Who is giving you these promises?" asked a small old man dressed in soiled pajamas. "Lawyers and money-lenders are sending you to your promised land."

The student leaped forward on his knees and looked in the old man's face. "What do you mean by that, old man? Are you implying that Mohammed Ali Jinnah is not an honorable man? Are you saying Pakistan is not the promised land?"

The old man raised his open palms and retreated from the stu-dent. "I'm only saying that rulers come and go, and life is still the same."

"Not so old man," said a man from Bombay. He was a typical Bombay wallah who looked uncomfortable in his English suit and unaccustomed to the prayer, to the very voyage, and to suffering. "We have not all lived lives of hardship, you know. The lawyers you speak of have won your country freedom. It is not Mr. Jinnah's fault if the mobs run amok and decide to have riots."

Rehman looked nervously around at the faces in the group. He did not wish to witness an argument, and the student was growing angrier and red-necked under his collar. The Mulvi raised his hands. "Pakistan is an untouched land. We have been given a great gift, and we must treat it as God would have us."

"Yes. An eye for an eye and a tooth for a tooth," one of the students answered. "Just as it says in the Koran, just as God spoke to Moses." He leaned toward the Bombay wallah. "The riots you speak of will be revenged."

"No, brother," the Mulvi intervened. "This is not a time for revenge."

"I can answer this young riffraff for myself," the man from Bombay said.

"You may well speak," said a slightly younger man in faded pajamas with bloodshot eyes. "Anyone can see that you have not suffered for a hair on your head. Ask me about revenge. I lost a sister. People we had never seen before came to our house and took her away. Then they burned the house. In Pakistan I will kill three sisters for every sister that was killed in India."

Rehman could not resist entering into the discussion. "Surely, this is not the reason we Muslims have asked for our own country," he protested. "I cannot believe I am hearing Muslims talk like this."

"It is a jihad. A holy revenge."

Rehman turned around to see who was speaking. It seemed everyone had taken sides, each for his own reasons.

"We do not wish to kill for the sake of killing," one man said, justifying his position. "But it may become necessary. We have been promised homes in Pakistan. If there are Hindu and Sikh people occupying the houses, we shall force them to leave, just as we were forced to leave our houses."

Almost everyone seemed to agree with the point. "There will be no alternative but to find houses," they said. "How else will we live? Where will we find shelter in this new land which is not prepared for us?"

Rehman stood up to leave. "We will each have to make our own decisions," he said.

"What will you do?" the Mulvi asked him.

"I don't know," Rehman said.

"Remember," said a student. "It is our land."

Rehman agreed. The land was theirs. Whether they wanted it or not, the contracts had been signed with the British, and Pakistan was created by law. It was up to the people to decide what to do with it. He walked across the deck. Apaji and the children were still asleep, and he was glad. The charred remains of the fires they had built the night before lay scattered over the deck. The fires had been built against the explicit instructions of the Indian crew, who finally had grown tired of prowling among them to see that all was in order and had retreated to the innards of the ship. Each family enclave had cooked its own food over the fires, which were made from whatever they could find—bits of rope, charcoal hoarded in their pockets from the trains, pieces of wood they pried up from the deck. Now the embers were cold.

Rehman walked over to the covered portion of the deck, hoping to find a place to be alone, but it was crowded with people waiting on line to use what was left of the flush toilets. Hours earlier the toilets had been broken, but still people waited patiently to use the one room where they could close a door behind them, conceal themselves, and find some privacy, despite the stench and the floor running with muck and disintegrating paper. Many of them had never used an English toilet before, and they had tried to flush down anything they could no longer make use of—soiled rags, used tea leaves, old newspapers. Now the whole inner portion of the deck was being used as a toilet. The floors were greasy with urine and excrement, and many of the people in the close air inside were sick and vomiting what little food they had managed to put into their stomachs the night before.

Rehman left quickly and made his way around the deck for the hundredth time since the voyage began. Picking his way among the yards and yards of sleeping bodies, he wondered where all the thousands of refugees would go once they arrived in Pakistan. They surely did not all have homes and lands waiting for them. Rehman himself was counting on the chance that some relative had arrived safely in Karachi weeks or months before and would have a place for his family to live until he could get his bearings. It seemed impossible that so many people, fleeing for their lives, frightened and docile as sheep, could turn murderous and vengeful when the tables were turned. He could not imagine it, even if they quoted Islamic law about revenge and punishment, and even if they were in desperation to find homes. Houses and land—that was what this whole journey was about.

To the four hundred million people of India, Rehman thought, freedom was the land. They had worked to gain possession of it for an entire century. Ever since the women first glanced shyly from behind their veils into the broad-boned, sun-reddened faces of the wives of the British raj, they had cried for their land. The ministers of Delhi and Calcutta, as if awakening from eons of a cultural dream, wept to each other in the halls of parliament while they continued to trade away their myths of independence into colonial bondage. They accepted titles from the King of England while living in segregated hotels in Bombay. Young men went off to London to study law in the Inns of Court, while the judges of Bombay and Delhi created laws that defined Indian laws as illegal, laws that labeled Indians as treasonous who met to form their own government and make their own decisions, laws that forbade protest and called out armies of Indian soldiers to shoot down and club fellow Indians who demonstrated in public. The fishermen who scooped shrimp and mackerel out of the ocean with their nets and dried them for days on the sandy beaches sold them to exporters who carted them away in trucks to make into oil and fertilizer. Tenant farmers planted gardens of tea and coffee, orchards of mangoes and dates and coconuts, that they were not allowed to pick. Impassioned leaders in Bengal called for militancy and armed battle, but the deeply entrenched Indian individualism, the force underlying the religion of monkey gods and cobra gods, of one God and many gods, of God in nature and God in scripture, of Muslim God and the philosophical God that every man knew in different ways—the god of rivers accepting sacrifices of flower petals and fruits and seeds, and the god that was the river, denied that the land was not theirs. It was as if the Indian people had so much freedom they felt they had some to spare.

Rehman remembered the story of the Koh-i-noor diamond, which his father often told him when he was a child. His father always told parables of religion and history in the hours after sunrise when he curled up on his charpoy in the courtyard and sucked on the stem of his water-cooled pipe. Rehman had not always been able to separate fact from fiction, but the story had a special significance for him now. The Koh-i-noor diamond was owned by the Nawab of Punjab, and he wore it constantly in the folds of his brightly starched turban, where everyone could see that it was as large as a boy's fist. It was easily visible when he sat high above the heads of his subjects in the Diwan, or public courtyard, where they knelt before him.

The Nawab's palace had other treasures as well. There was a *shish mahal*, or hall of mirrors, which was made from a thousand pieces of cut glass. Frescoes scored the walls and arches, depicting ancestral princes whose crowns toppled with jewels and were as large as their entire bodies. The frescoes had been painted by anonymous artists who mixed their paints from crushed pearls, amethysts, and rubies, and all about the palace walls merchants sold gems from huge jute sacks. Emeralds and diamonds dripped from their hands like grain. Every inch of wall was slashed with marble latticework and bas-reliefs of flowers. Within, gardens sprawled about artificial lakes that were laced with miniature islands where peacocks and pigeons strutted. Courtesans floated across the gleaming white bridges or lolled about a private pool beneath their rooms. Their saris were so sheer the six yards of cloth could be folded and transported in a matchbox.

The Nawab of Punjab was a man of such delicate taste, it seemed his very being was fashioned from the softest silk and the most dazzling satin. When he held court, he reclined on mounds of velvet pillows, curled and sinuous beneath the frescoes of his ancestors, and he played host to the great men of India and the world with a smiling passion that proclaimed, All I have in my home is yours.

One day, as the story went, the Nawab found himself host to a fair-skinned Sahib from England, a titled man in the service of a great European King. It was a momentous occasion. After many years of disagreement, the English Sahib had brought terms of a trade agreement which the Nawab found eminently satisfactory. The whole principality turned out to witness the signing of a contract of friendship. For weeks elephants traipsed up the manicured paths to the palace, bearing guests for the celebration. Musicians tortured the air with their music, popping up in the gardens, drifting across lakes in oarless boats, escorting the elephants, and sitting beneath the terraces of every room.

On the day of feasting, all who had assembled filled the Diwan i Khas, hall of lords. Everyone sat cross-legged on the floor facing the Nawab. Young girls and graceful boys weaved among the guests with silver bowls and golden platters. They served dishes of cashews and pecans, and a variety of vegetables so abundant no one could identify them all. They poured drinks of rose nectar and water spiced with cardamom and cumin.

The English Ambassador had the place of honor opposite the Prince. They sat face to face—the one in his military uniform, metallic with buttons and medals; the other, flowing in chiffon scarves. A jewel-encrusted satin jacket flared over the Nawab's jodhpurs of creamed silk. In all the splendor, however, it was the Koh-i-noor diamond, shimmering with pale austere light in the center of his turban, that held everyone's attention.

During the feasting, the English Sahib rose to honor the new friendship between the King and the Prince of Punjab. "I know that in your princely state there is a simple custom one performs as a show and seal of lifelong friendship," said the English Ambassador. "In my country our customs are not quite so gracious as yours. We swear our brotherhood in blood, but we are a younger and far more barbarous race." Everyone laughed and applauded appreciatively. "In India there is a custom that I would be honored to share if, my dear Prince, you should give me leave."

The Nawab was delighted. "Anything you wish to make our friendship everlasting we shall perform," answered the Nawab. "What is the custom to which you refer?"

"The exchanging of hats," said the English Sahib. "You give me your turban, and I will give you my cap."

The blood seemed to drain from the face of the Nawab, and all eyes flew to the center of the cream silk turban where the Koh-i-noor rested among the folds. It was an impossible request, but the Prince had been taken off guard. His treasured diamond was reputed to be the finest in all India, but here in his ancestral hall, beneath the images and frescoes of so many holy men and before the eyes of all his relatives, ministers, important subjects, and friends, there was no way to refuse. With a slow and steady hand, the Nawab of Punjab removed the turban and exchanged it and the diamond for the Ambassador's military cap, and by so doing swore eternal friendship.

The story, which Rehman had heard many times, seemed more important now than ever before. The Indian people had given away so much for illusory gains, for honor, for wealth and prestige abroad, and now for freedom. Would all the possessions he had left behind really buy him freedom? Would the anonymity he had accepted in exchange for a heritage of centuries enable him to progress and enrich himself as never before, or would Pakistan smother him in the shabby, dusty poverty that had been swallowing the people of India, generation after generation, despite their noblest attempts?

Suddenly a loudspeaker crackled through the air and his thoughts. The message was garbled, delivered in a fast harrumphing English that was impossible to understand. An announcement in Urdu followed, high and excited and fast, and also impossible to understand. The ship had become a jumble of movement. It was as if a small town had been erected overnight and with the full light of day sprung to life. Everywhere things were for sale or exchange. Women, offering to sell shoes or bits of cloth for food, raised their hands to his knees as he pushed past them. "Bhai Sahib, the shoes are new. This shawl is hardly worn," they called to him and to every man that wandered along the deck seemingly unattached to family and need. Rehman brushed the hands away. Indian servants of the crew had materialized again for the first time since the night they left Bombay. They walked up and down the deck, hawking cigarettes and supplies from the ship's commissary where the refugees were not allowed to go. The chokidars were dressed in dilapidated khaki shorts and seemed even worse off than the refugees themselves.

217

A family of rich Bombay wallahs were buying cigarettes at a hundred times their normal price. Rehman noticed their incongruousness and stood watching their apprehensive faces. People from Bombay in their English suits and fine saris were easily distinguishable from the rest of the throng. They sat frozen together among stacks of valises that surrounded them like a fortress. Being from Bombay, Rehman realized, they had been able to leave India at greater leisure, making their decision to leave the country and purchasing their tickets with relative calm. They had probably been able to dispose of their properties with profit and arrive at the ship still dressed in tie and jacket. They were not like the rest of the people, Rehman thought, and he looked at them with curiosity almost as if they were foreigners. Their experiences had been so different from the rest of them. In fact, they had not become refugees at all until they were forced like everyone else to sit crammed together on the open deck, and Rehman recognized their expressions of horror and dismay. Bombay, after all, was not like Nehtor or Aligarh or the cities of the north. It was the most cosmopolitan city in India, and Rehman had always felt somewhat out of his depth when he stopped in its sophisticated hotels and dined in formal restaurants. It was ironic to see the Bombay wallahs now, sitting on the ship in their nervous attitudes. They had not been landlocked and forced to travel through India on sooty trains or been flung into riots or forced to leave their homes. In Bombay, the riots were only among the poor, where the city was cordoned off and the streets writhed with ancient chaos. The rich Muslims had not learned to scramble among a crowd for bits of food or to sleep in the open, pressed against strange bodies, listening to the cries of hungry infants, or to hold in their bladders for an entire day.

A group of children ran headlong into Rehman. They had begun running all over, tripping across people's legs, and climbing the wire gates over the stairs that locked the deck passengers below. They kept climbing up the fencing, shouting over the side of the next deck at the servants, hurrying back and forth with trays of fruit and tea in their arms, to let them come up and take a bath. There was much raucous laughter, but they were completely ignored by everyone else as their families were probably out of sight on the other side of the deck or further below.

Rehman hurried toward his family who were still sitting where they had slept. He was pleased to see that his children were orderly. Apaji was holding Sara in her arms, nursing her, while Raheel bent over a pot, sifting grains of rice to clean them of stones. The other children were clustered around Gappu and Gerrar, who were trying to amuse them with stories about the ocean. They all sat with their knees tucked under their chins like a sculpture frozen together.

"You can see that the world is round," Gappu was saying. He pointed to the horizon of water. "Watch the way the clouds come up over the water. You don't think they touch the water out there, do you?"

"I think they do," shouted Karim.

"Then how do you think we'll pass under them?" asked Gappu, hitting Karim lightly on the head.

"That doesn't matter to me," said Karim.

Raheel looked up from her rice cleaning. "Karim knows about that. He learned it in school."

"I learned it," said Karim. "But I think that when we get to those clouds, they will still be coming out of the water. No matter how far we go, forever and ever, we will always see the clouds coming out of the water."

Gerrar laughed. "Karim does not have a head for science."

"What do you think, Moïd?" asked Rehman, who had been observing his children.

Moïd raised his large brown eyes that were brimming with moisture. His lips were clamped together, and his chin quivered.

"What is the matter with Moïd?" his father asked.

"He's stopped talking," said Raheel.

"When did that happen?" Rehman asked Apaji, bewildered.

"It has been several weeks. You have not had time to notice," she answered her husband.

"What are you doing about it?" He was becoming red in the face with frustration and held out his hands to his youngest son. Gappu lifted Moïd in the air and passed him to his father.

"Are these the first scars?" Rehman asked, holding Moïd against his chest. He felt the small arms encircle his shoulders and the unshod feet press into his back. The boy was too frail, too small for five years. That was to be expected. That could easily be remedied with food and rest and the care he would give them once they arrived in Pakistan.

"How is it that I never noticed?" Rehman asked. "What are we going to do about it?"

"We will wait," said Apaji. "It will pass."

Rehman felt the old doubts creep back into his will. He could not have been so busy that he had not noticed his son's silence. All during the journey, it seemed, he had known his family only with his eyes, his mind being continuously elsewhere, thinking of past and future at once and ignoring the present, alert only to danger signs and to immediate physical necessities. He had guarded his family like a jungle cat. "Oh, this cannot be!" he moaned.

"When he tries to speak, he makes so many noises he cannot get a word out," Karim informed him.

"It is true, Abu," said Gerrar. "Try to speak to him."

Rehman felt Moïd's arms grip tighter around his neck and the nails dig into his skin. Moïd was quivering all over.

"No. Your mother is right. We will wait and it will pass," Rehman said decisively. "All will pass in Pakistan." He felt Moïd's grip loosen ever so slightly, and he sensed the child's relief. He sat down beside Apaji, who averted her eyes and adjusted her dopatta, so that her baby and her breast were doubly covered. The frantic attempts at nursing, when the milk would not come, were over, and she could regain the extra tokens of propriety that she had stripped away without thought when the screams and whimpers of her starving infant assailed her through long nights and torpid days.

"Where did you find the rice?" Rehman asked Apaji, trying to change the subject.

"We traded with a lady from Bombay who had many bags. It is good rice," she said.

"What did you trade?" he asked with wonder that there was still something of enough value left to buy rice.

"We had a little ring," said Apaji. "It was not an important ring. Prices are not so high on the ship as they were in India."

"If this were any other time or any other place, I would not eat this rice," said Rehman. "You know that, don't you?" he said to Apaji and all the children.

"We know that," answered Apaji, her eyes still averted from her husband whom she would not dishonor by staring at in public. "There are many on this ship who still do not have rice."

"Some of the people have had to beg," said Gappu.

"Why?" shouted Rehman, smashing his fist onto the wooden floor. "Even here where we are all brothers, all beginning a new life together, the people do not share with one another."

"They share," said Apaji. "But there is not enough to go around."

"Then everyone should eat a little less, so that all the people may have something."

"I have an idea," said Karim, jumping up.

"Where are you going?"

"I'll be back. I won't get lost, Abu. You'll see."

Rehman did not answer.

"Let me go, Abu," pleaded Karim.

Rehman nodded his head. "All right. But I won't come looking for you if you do not return here."

"Thank you, Abu," said Karim.

He picked his way across the circles of people sprawling and moving everywhere on the deck. It was strange to be in a crowd comprised entirely of Muslims. Karim felt as if they were all his friends. In Delhi, when he had sneaked off with his school friends to visit Connaught Place and to stare in the shops filled with ivory figurines and the bookstalls filled with musty manuscripts, he used to watch the great variety of people coming and going. There were Hindus and Muslims and Sikhs and Anglo-Indians and English people. There was every sort of person he could imagine, and it was important not to speak to any of them. Everyone knew stories of the child thieves that roamed around Delhi ready to kidnap boys at school and make slaves of them. It could be that man in the dhoti who loitered on the curb and peered at you from behind the colonnades encircling the vast market, or it could be the half-naked saddhu with his bag of puzzles and hashish who sat for hours on the road, or the heavy farmer with the rounded red cheeks of the countryside who was standing at the waterbearer's cart filling up glass after glass of water. The province was notorious for dacoits, bands of thieves armed with long knives, who murdered for pleasure. Karim had always been warned of crowds, but on the ship they were all Muslims and he was a Syed, the highest caste. His ancestry went back to the Prophet Muhammad himself. It made him not only a brother but a young Prince among the others. Dadi had told him often enough that the presence of a Syed was so important that village elders would offer lands and gold to get a member of the caste to live among them. If there were no living Syed, the next best thing was a dead one. His grave would be honored, and his name remembered. Karim felt he belonged to the people on the boat, and he was unafraid.

It was impossible for him to accept that there were still people starving. Had they not all been living as he had lived, a private room for every child to crawl into at the back of the house, a servant boy to carry their schoolbooks and fetch water? It was hard to believe some of the people could starve, or that many were worse off than he. The deprivation he had seen around him, peripherally, as he was growing up, did not seem like poverty. It was more an integral part of the land—the color of peasant clothes and rice paddies, the sound of singing in the fields. He had never seen starvation. All through the voyage of the last month, when things had seemed at their very worst, somehow there had always been food, something to fill up their gnawing stomachs. They always found a trinket to sell for rice, or someone kind like the Sardarji drivers in Patna who gave them bread and tins of meat. If Apaji did not find them food, Abu brought it, though it might only be a dozen rotten potatoes found wrapped in an old scarf left under a seat in a train by some previous family, or dried milk that was rationed in Bombay to all the refugees who squatted in mosques, waiting for ships and airplanes to cart them off to the promised land. Why were the others unable to find food as his family had always done? He knew where to find the best food of all on the ship, and he was determined to bring it back for the people who needed it.

Karim squinted in the bright sunlight and scanned the upper decks, glinting white and unapproachable. As far as the eye could see, the refugees swarmed below, trying to find food and cook it over one of the communal fires, and dickering with coolies who had finally come down from the upper decks where the first-class passengers were accommodated.

Karim stopped to examine the contents of a sack that was being sold. He pushed between the tangle of legs and shoulders surrounding the coolie and peered into the top of the filthy brown jute bag. It was filled with meat which was maroon in the center and blackened along the veins like soured blood.

The coolie plucked a fat slab of meat from the sack and threw it down onto the deck. The crowd pushed closer. It had been a long time since Karim had seen meat, but the stench of it burned his nostrils, and he covered his nose with the sleeve of his shirt.

"You expect too many rupees for such meat," a student was saying. He kicked the meat with his foot.

"How much? How much?" the women kept yelling.

"One hundred rupees," the coolie answered. "Final offer."

"We should kill you right here," the student shouted. "Your flesh would probably be better than this manure." The student kept kicking the meat, but no one seemed to care.

"I can give you seventy-five," said a woman in a sari. Her hair was blowing with the soft cotton folds of her skirts, and she picked the stinking meat up in her hands and held it close to her chest. She dug into a small pouch at the waist of her sari and brought out a crumpled bill, thin from handling and as limp as the meat.

"You can't buy that," said the student, moving closer to the coolie to prevent the exchange. "Where did you get this meat?"

The coolie backed off from the student until he was against the rail of the ship. "It's not my meat," the coolie protested, raising his open palms. "I got it from the Sahib Bhadur."

"Which Sahib?" asked the student.

"The one upstairs who speaks Git Pit."

"You mean the English," the student shouted. "Why are you working for them?" He yanked the meat out of the hands of the woman so hard that her sari flew off her shoulder. She grabbed the meat back, and they stood there holding it between them, glaring at each other. There was no thought of practicing purdah here.

"I'm buying this meat," the woman said. All shyness she had ever known, muzzled for years behind a Muslim veil, was gone, and she pushed her face close to the student's, her teeth gritted.

A crowd gathered around them, and Karim found himself pressed up against the coolie and the man and woman who were arguing and the jute sack with all the rotting meat smelling under his nose. He turned to escape, but on every side he was enveloped by shouting women in saris who shoved him deeper into the middle of the crowd. He looked wildly for a way to get out and run down the narrow passageway along the side of the ship. There seemed to be nothing but people's bodies, and he tried to peer between them. The terrified coolie kept glancing over his shoulder at the rail and the churning water below.

"Give us the meat," the student demanded, and he grabbed the coolie by the collar of his meat-stained shirt, which was tassled with threads and open on his thin perspiring brown chest.

"I can't," whined the coolie. "I'll sell it to someone else."

"He is probably a Hindu," the student said, addressing the women. "He won't touch the meat himself, but he tries to sell it to us."

"No, Sahib. I am Muslim. Oh, Bhai. Oh, brother. Please, don't hurt me." He pressed his hands to his chest as if begging and bent so far down to the ground that he was almost kneeling on his shaking knees, which were like two knots on a toothpick.

"We can strip him now and find out if he is an uncircumcised Kafir."

"No, no!" shouted the women. "We don't wish to see."

The coolie kept begging the student with his hands. "You can see my Koran. I am wearing it at my neck." He lifted the dirty string of his tabeez and kissed the pendant.

Karim turned toward the student. "Let me out of here," he said. The stench of the meat was overwhelming. It smelled like everything dead and clung to the dirty clothes of the poor coolie.

No one was interested in Karim. If the coolie was a Hindu, he should be forced to give up the meat. Rotten or not, it was real mutton. It would stick to the ribs of the husbands and sons as all the bread and rice and dal they had been eating could not. Its foul flavor could be extinguished by hours of cooking over coals, and it would be eaten with handfuls of fiery hot peppers.

The coolie turned toward his customer. "Oh, Mai. Oh, mother," he intoned. "I am a son like your son. I, too, have come on this ship to go to the new nation. I must sell this meat to pay for my passage. Otherwise, the Git Pit English will take me back to India and will not let me get off in the promised land."

The coolie was as skinny as a tree stripped of its foliage and showing signs of its impending fall. The tears rolled down his cheeks, streaking the grime and perspiration embedded in his skin. His hair was wiry and gray with dirt, and his teeth—the few that were left—were stained brown from old betel-nut juice. "I am hungry, too," he pleaded. "This is old meat, Memsahib, it is true. They brought it for the shipload of Hindus they took from Karachi to Bombay last week, but no one would touch it. Now the English are selling it to you because they won't buy new meat. The English Sahib is angry that the Hindus will not eat meat even when they are starving."

"I will buy the meat," said the woman. She spoke the finest Urdu and the cloth of her sari, although rumpled in a thousand creases, was of the best muslin, with hand-dyed circles of earth-green colors. "Leave this boy alone," she said sternly to the student. Her eyes were filled with tears.

"What about the rest of us?" the student persisted. "You take pity on the coolie, but you buy the meat at too high a price."

"I am buying at the price he is selling."

"If you buy for less, then those of us with less money can buy meat, too." Again the student grabbed hold of the meat.

"I will sell it for fifty." The coolie grabbed at the chance to

225

compromise. Since the woman and the student were arguing, the bargaining advantage was with him. "I can bring other things to sell from the English."

"I will go with you to get flour. Do they have that?" another woman asked.

Before he knew it, the coolie had people coming up to him from every side with special requests. "I want some glucose. My child is weak, and the doctor says glucose will give him energy. I will give you my best pair of shoes."

"Ah, Bhai," pleaded another. "Take this shawl. I never thought I would walk in public bareheaded, without my dopatta, but take it and bring me some milk."

Everyone was paying the coolie with personal possessions, and some had money. They stood back and made way for him to circulate among them and hear their requests. The coolie was their only link with the larder upstairs in the British commissary, the only hope of food for the next day. What the refugees had brought with them had been whittled down by division and redivision to a few mouthfuls apiece.

Karim was finally able to get away from the bargaining women and the arguing student and the poor coolie stowaway, who was trying to retain his last ounce of dignity while telling the women he was so poor he could not even begin to think of eating the food he was selling. Karim knew he could never eat such meat. He thought Apaji would cry if he brought it to her, and he was certain he could find better, without waiting for the coolie. He knew there was fresh fruit on the upper deck.

After they had finally boarded the ship, at the port in Bombay, Gappu had pointed to the European passengers who were going aboard the ship on their own gangplank. Gappu had said these people would sleep in little rooms with beds and wash basins and eat in a large dining hall with tablecloths and bowls of flowers. Karim and Gappu, standing on the open deck, had watched the passengers arriving on the quay, loaded down with cameras and neat little valises. European men dressed in casual open-necked shirts, stiff with starch, directed a trickle of coolies toward the waiting boat, and they eemed annoyed to have to show the coolies where to go. Their wives followed nervously behind in their little print dresses, legs showing everywhere, and sunbonnets on their heads. They seemed to be trying to avoid looking up at the deck mottled with refugees in their tattered clothing and brown faces. After the Europeans had disappeared hurriedly onto the first-class decks over their heads, a small group of Europeans, standing in the recesses of the customs shed, had come to the foot of the gangplank to wave good-bye to their friends and relatives and throw armloads of fruit onto the upper decks. Gappu and Karim had watched the oranges, small yellow melons, and even mangoes fly past them. Karim did not have to speak. He knew Gappu could taste the fruit as he could, remember its cool freshness on his deadened tongue and its sour sweetness stinging his lips and gums.

Fruit was what Karim now wanted to find. He imagined pears and the soft white insides of lychee and bright red pomegranate seeds, which popped in the mouth yielding up only the smallest trickle of liquid like a rare treasure. He was sure he would find all these and more on the upper decks. The Englishmen with their polite ways, eating only at prescribed times in dining rooms, as Karim was forced to do at boarding school, could never have finished all the wonderful fruit. The only thing standing between himself and the fruit was the wired-off passageways and stairs to the first-class decks. He had only to surmount this barrier, and the fruit would be his. He would bring it to Apaji, and they would disburse it to all the poor people who had less than they.

Karim felt that this was his responsibility. Distributing food to the poor had always been part of the routine of his home and his family. Daily surpluses of food were carted off by a continuous parade of servants, washerwomen, cooks, house cleaners, gardeners, workmen, and a dish was always set aside for a beggar, especially when there was a feast. In Nehtor, his grandfathers never ate if they knew of someone being hungry. Karim had seen celebrations on the festival of Id when full cartloads of grain and meat and fruit and sugar were given away by his family. Both grandfathers used to go from the hanging garden streets of their estates with much singing and happiness, and gave away sweetmeats and rice, vegetables and dal. Long lines of beggars came from the villages and countryside, people Karim had never imagined lived anywhere near Nehtor. He remembered seeing young girls so twisted with leprosy that their sheet-white faces seemed old and senile, and they walked on one side, using an arm as a second leg. All had to eat before either grandfather could eat.

Karim felt he was the grandson of Darogaji and Mubarik, and could not eat the rice Apaji was preparing when Abu said others were starving. He wanted to supply the whole S.S. *Shiralla* with fruit. It would definitely be the best food anyone had seen since they left home so long ago.

Karim surveyed the open deck. There seemed to be no stairway to the deck above. If he craned his neck to look up along the wire fencing, through the ropes and tarpaulins that hung overhead, he could see just over the high railing to the fresh white walls where all the little rooms were, but he could detect no movement or life. He imagined all the first-class passengers were sitting indoors away from the heat and the glaring whiteness of ship, sun, and water, taking midafternoon tea under spinning fans, sipping cool drinks, and tasting cakes with delicate fingers. Karim thought that there might be an open passageway from the inner deck or the deck even farther below, which all the women were using as a toilet. There had to be a way that the coolies had found to slip on and off the deck with no one noticing or making a commotion.

The air inside the narrow dark inner deck was rancid. It had the smell of animals, but not so fresh, not so tended and cared for, as a bullock shed where villagers collected the manure and used it like clay. This had the smell of bestial animals, hairy and grotesque and red-eyed with sickness. It was as if all the people up on the deck, splayed with sunlight across the colorful patchwork quilt of their clothes and refreshed by the sea and wind, still came surreptitiously down the stairways to do this secret and dirty thing. They had laid the floor with their bowel movements as if the new spirit of the ship were only a fantasy, and that other dark month of being huddled together like sheep in a pen, like goats trotting along a dusty road, quiver with fright, nostrils flaring, were the reality. In this room-toilet were the remains of those shameful days that would now be permanently with them, tucked away somewhere. Karim felt his confidence shaken anew by a terrible sense of foreboding as he witnessed this descent of his people. They were like all the uneducated farmers whom his grandfather led to a field and said, "Shit here."

He opened a door and found a man crouching at his feet. The man did not shout at him because of his intrusion. He just turned his head away, lowered his eyes, and pretended not to notice Karim. The man could not control his bowels, and as Karim stepped around him, a thick spurt gurgled from between his legs, splattering the floor and Karim's foot.

Karim ran down a long passageway flanked on either side by doors of thick wood with chains and double locks. He had been lucky not to have the runs. For two full nights and almost two days he had held his bowels tight inside him. Gappu sometimes had to run, no matter how he held his sides and strained with his mind to keep it in. He slunk off at night, without admitting it to anyone, to find a corner of this cesspool to eliminate in. Even in the deserted passageway, Karim found the walls streaked with urine and the floor slippery with muck. He turned several corners, leading farther into the passageways that ran through the ship like silent intestines. The corridors were quiet and gave only the slightest sensation of the movement of the ship, so that Karim forgot for moments where he was and then felt a grumble somewhere beneath his feet as if the sea were reminding him of their suspension.

At the corner of one passageway, Karim found a door slightly ajar, hooked to the wall by a thick chain, but the opening was just wide enough for his thin sticklike body to squeeze through. Behind were two stairways going up and down. He could hear the ship's motors and engines pulsating loudly through the cold cement walls of this back staircase. Karim prayed he would not have to go farther down into the ship, where the air might cage him in a heavy prison of vomit and feces into which he would faint and sink and never work his way up to the light again.

He climbed a staircase and pushed another door open a crack.

This led onto another long corridor, hushed and empty, with a row of neat, highly polished doors. The linoleum floor covering smelled of fresh disinfectant, and little electric lamps guarded each door. Suddenly two British officers entered the corridor from the other end. Their white shorts and open shirts seemed brilliantly washed and starched, and their soft pink knees and the inches of freckled thigh showing above their knee-length socks seemed to snap as they walked, laughing together, with hair as orange as sunlight and cheeks shining with down.

Karim felt his own brown shabbiness creep over his body like an invading shroud. His clothes, which had once been a proud schoolboy's uniform, were rumpled with dirt, slept in for a month, the shirt torn at the elbows, the blazer with its buttons gone, and the emblem of the Aligarh college blackened. He wanted to sink back into the churning silence of the stairs, run back to the deck and his people. If the English officers found him, there was no telling what they might do. Hadn't he seen them leaning over the railing like lofty carvings on the top flank of the ship, while Karim's people hovered below, counting their steps up the gangplank? Didn't they know that so many children in their own ship were hungry and that his own mother had to take her daughters into the public sewer of the lower deck, and cook lentils with her own long, soft fingers over used charred wood? Karim felt sickeningly that this was the reason they did not like him, and he wanted to tell them that he was not always like this, that his home was filled with flowering gardens and his family's celebrations were feasts of golden cloth and jeweled bangles, that his uncle had silver flowers thrown over his billowing pink chiffon turban at his wedding procession, and that his own school in Delhi was in the English style.

The officers seemed to notice him suddenly, as if he had just materialized out of the wall, and they walked up to him.

"It's a refugee boy," he heard one of the officers laughing. "What do you make of that?"

"How the devil do you suppose he got up here?" the other man said. "Do you think he speaks English?"

"I do speak English," Karim said. He was furious and would

not let himself be afraid. His father had so many English friends, these officers were nothing new. "I came up here to find fruit."

"You speak very good English, don't you?" said the taller fellow. He had a thin moustache, so pale it was difficult to see until Karim was very close to him. The shorter one was older and had a rounded belly straining the buttons of his shirt. He patted Karim on the head and kept smiling at him. "You want fruit, do you? What can we do for him, Clive?" he said, turning to the younger man.

They were both laughing at him and smiling all the time.

"What do you want it for?" the older one asked.

"That should be obvious," said Karim, and both men burst out laughing as if he had said something very funny.

"You really do speak good English," the officer called Clive said to him. "Better than I did at your age."

Karim thought he had to speak good English, or he would not be promoted at school. It was the most important subject that was taught from the very beginning—English grammar, English letter writing, English history, English stories from the *King's Reader*. Why should it be such a surprise to the English officers? Karim sealed his lips. "I only came for fruit," he said.

"What makes you think we have fruit?" the taller one taunted him.

"I saw people throwing it up on the deck in Bombay."

"But that's all gone, laddie," the stout one said. "Why don't you tell us what you want it for?"

"I want it for the people," Karim said.

"Not for your mother, eh?" the smaller officer continued. "I thought all little beggar boys want food for their mothers."

"I'm not a beggar," Karim said.

"No? What are you then?" They laughed. "He looks like a beggar boy, doesn't he? Why don't you ask us, 'Please, sahib, please, food for my mother,' and kiss your fingers and touch our sleeves?"

"He hasn't learned the tricks of the trade yet."

Karim felt like crying. He could not understand why they were smiling at him and laughing, with their heads thrown back and their teeth showing, or why they kept patting him on the head, if they thought he was a beggar. He could not tell if they were laughing at him or just being funny.

"I think we've frightened the laddie enough," said the shorter officer who spoke in a more singsong way than the other. "You must excuse us, lad, but we had a bit too much to drink last night. There is nothing to do on this trip except look for stowaways. I think I can find you some fruit. But not enough for all the people, mind you." He took Karim by the arm.

"Why don't you have food for the people?" Karim asked the officers, following them along the corridor.

"This may be very difficult for you to understand," the tall officer told him. "But this ship is a business. It is owned by a company—not by a church or a charity."

"It is owned by a British company, furthermore," the other officer added. "You people have won your independence. You can't ask for favors now."

"India has made a separation between meat eaters and non-meat eaters. That's why you're here. We have nothing to do with it."

It made sense to Karim, but something struck him as wrong. They had won independence from the English, but it was the Indians who were suffering. All through the years they had admired the British and hated them. Karim had been taught English, had it rammed into his mouth and down his throat. At the same time he had been warned not to like the English too much or to follow completely in their ways. Every schoolboy in India was taught to pray for independence, but no one had ever raised a gun or formed an army. Karim was still not really sure what independence was, even though he had seen the new flag of India raised and sung the national anthem in public. All he knew was that India had won something called independence from the British without ever firing a shot, and now Indians were killing each other. The British still rode above their heads like jewels in an untouchable crown, while the family of Syed Rehman Hassain Nehtori sat in filth below.

The officers ushered him into a sitting room with plain little couches and dark-red leather chairs. Shelves of books lined the walls, and a flat green carpet soaked up the little sunlight that came through the draped portholes. On several of the small tables scattered around the room were glass bowls containing three or four oranges.

"You take these to your mother, lad," the short officer was saying. "Is she pretty?"

"Yes," Karim answered uneasily.

"I'll bet she is," the officer continued. "She must be a pretty little Indian lass to have a nice son like you." Again both officers laughed out loud.

"Now, off with you. If we spent all our time on charity cases, we would never get our work done," the tall officer said, looking sternly over the curl of his pale moustache from cool and vacant eyes.

Karim quickly gathered up an armload of oranges from the bowls, feeling the English eyes staring glassily into his back, but again the men laughed, and Karim was thoroughly confused. He could not tell if these officers strutting like white whooping cranes were his friends or if, in fact, they were his enemies and not the other Indians from whom his family had fled.

Karim ran down the stairs the officers led him to and out onto the open deck. He did not quite know what the officers wanted of him, but he was content that he had obtained what he wanted from them. The oranges were securely balanced in the overlap of his shirt. The deck was still filled with sunlight, and activity continued everywhere just as Karim had left it. Groups of men sat together playing cards and gambling, and arguing heatedly over their good or bad fortune. Fires burned low on the deck here and there, and all that could be seen through the crowds of people, sitting and standing together, was gray drafts of smoke pitching upward and dissipating into the wind. Eating and bargaining for food was a continuous process, and the women had begun to make friends with each other and trade stories in monotone voices about their losses. Few wore dopattas concealing their faces, but the women remained expressionless with eyes that did not focus on strange faces, and mouths that neither smiled nor wept.

Karim saw that Apaji had found a friend. She was sitting where he had left her, speaking to a woman who sat cross-legged at her side, and both were continuously working rosary beads through their fingers as they talked. Karim had never seen his mother so religious before. Although she prayed at the prescribed times and observed religious holidays and the constant little rituals of wishing and thanksgiving that followed the flow of events, Apaji had never been so lost in prayer that she would pray for hour after hour like a Mulvi who never stopped repeating the Koran. She was praying now with her eyes and the muscles of her face, even while she was talking. Karim felt he could not intrude upon this deep meditation which he knew was because of himself and his brothers and India— and all Apaji had felt and seen over the last weeks.

He wanted to show Apaji the oranges, but he felt to interrupt her would be a terrible incursion, and for the first time in his childhood, he checked the impulse to rush headlong into her mothering arms with his prize. Furthermore, Karim realized that the oranges he had so daringly procured were not even sufficient to go around his small family. It would be impossible to decide which of the lean and hungry faces everywhere on the deck were most in need of his gift of fruit. Perhaps there was no family needier than his own. They had no meat, but only grains so hard to clean that they could feel hard bits of earth and tiny pebbles crunch between their teeth. Their only water was filled in small pots from dripping lukewarm faucets after waiting for hours on line with other refugees. Their clothes were in tatters, just remnants of what they once had been. It was too difficult to understand, but they were no different from the thousands and thousands they had seen traveling around them and with them. Karim opened one of the jute sacks lying on the sheet at Apaji's side, and deposited his six or seven oranges, so that Apaji would discover them at some later time and would not feel guilty eating them in front of the others.

Raheel appeared out of the crowd with the younger children trailing after her. She slipped Sara back into Apaji's arms and knelt before her mother. Her face was ashen, and Mona and Moïd and Piari were crying. "Where is Abu?" she asked, crouching next to Karim.

"What happened?" said Apaji, rocking Sara who was screaming and holding her red fists rigid against her mother's body.

"There is a case of smallpox. We saw the family. There is a child all puffy and red, and everyone is screaming to throw the family off the ship."

"Where?" shouted Karim, jumping up.

"Sit down," Raheel commanded him. "Don't go anywhere near that family. Don't you know how fast smallpox spreads. This whole ship may be contaminated."

Apaji was moaning gently as she rocked Sara back and forth in her lap. "*Aarre, aarre,*" she cried. "Is there no end in sight to our suffering? How will I protect my children now?" Moïd clung to her neck in speechless terror, and Piari continued to wail.

The other families around them also heard the news, and the restlessness of their activity seemed to increase as soon as they understood the reason for the commotion. The word smallpox traveled fast, from ear to ear, and each face was lit with panic.

"What do we do now?" many were asking. "Won't the English Sahibs come down now to give us inoculations? They can't just leave us here. Perhaps they won't let us get off the boat in Karachi."

Abu came rushing up, with Gappu and Gerrar behind him, full of stories about the family with smallpox.

"We have reported the case to the ship's officers," Abu told them. "There is nothing to do. The ship's doctor has very little smallpox vaccine. I tried to buy some, but it is not for sale. In any case, they tell me it is too late now."

"The people want to throw the family into the sea," Gerrar said, full of agitated excitement. "The mother is weeping and holding the child in her arms. The father is pleading with them."

"Most of the people on the far side of the deck are saying it is the only safety measure we can take," said Gappu.

"*Ai ai ai,*" said Apaji. "Are there no officers to protect them?"

Rehman was surprised to see Apaji fingering her rosary all the while she listened and talked to them and rocked Sara in her lap against her knee. He wished he could shield her from the shocks, but there was no way. She knew the story before he was even able to

235

reach her. Words traveled faster from woman to woman seated on the ground than he could hope to maneuver through the squirming carpet of bodies on the deck.

"Everyone is discussing the issue, trying to decide what to do," Rehman told her. "They have thrown all their belongings over the side, but I think the family will be saved."

"The father wailed and held his head in his hands," Gappu continued. "He was wearing a suit, but he got down on his knees and prayed."

"Everything was thrown overboard," Gerrar said. "He must have been a rich man."

"The important thing is that we are trapped here," said Raheel, bursting into tears. "It isn't enough that we have lost everything. Now we will lose our eyes and our ears and our faces and our bodies, too." She was becoming hysterical. Her skin was barely adolescent, still with the pink shine and soft rounded cheeks of her young girlhood. The orbs of her eyes were so white they were almost blue, and the silk of her body was untouched. Now the dreaded disease, the Indian pestilence, threatened to scratch her eyes into windowless vacuums, mar her skin in a bubble of red welts, and leave her a sheet of gashes before she had known the joys of love for which she saved herself. "Oh, Abu, Abu, please help us," she cried.

There was nothing Rehman could do. Even when they had been caught in the train riot or imprisoned in the servant's quarters behind their house in Aligarh so long ago, he had always been able to use his intelligence or his money to find a way out. He could not bargain with anyone against smallpox. There was nothing to sell for protection from contamination. He could only order his children to stop drinking water, even though the sun dried their lips, and order them not to eat, although their stomachs had shrunken into their clothes, lest the food and water be infected. All the refugees were in a turmoil of prayer, or discussion, or hopeless crying. They were surrounded by water with no means of escape, and no one to help them or offer advice. Most had never boiled their own water and had kept servants to clean, fetch, and procure everything. Even the poorest among them were still of a class to house at least one or two servants to do their chores. They sat overwhelmed in helplessness, looking out over the water they thought would save them and now might be their grave.

The chimes of the loudspeaker blared through the air. "This is your captain," the voice said. This time there was no difficulty understanding the clear, clipped English. Everyone was listening intently, frozen in their confusion in the hope of hearing words that would save them from the outbreak of the disease. The captain would tell them that it was an isolated case, though they knew that was impossible. Perhaps it was a mistaken diagnosis. If the English doctor looked at the sick little girl, he would know better. Everyone was asking everyone else for a translation of the English.

"This is your captain," the speaker repeated. "We have discovered a case of smallpox on the deck. The family in question has been removed to the stern of the ship. All deck passengers will observe strict quarantine."

There was much grumbling among the passengers. All this, they already knew. They wanted medicine and doctors and vaccinations.

"There is no need to panic," the captain continued. "We will be in Karachi in less than two hours. Thank you."

The final announcement left everyone stunned. Rehman threw up his hands in joyful thanksgiving. The whole ship seemed to let up a wail of relief. It was as if Pakistan were coming to them by divine intervention. No one had bothered to keep track of the time.

"What does that mean about the smallpox, Abu," Gappu asked his father.

"It means we are probably safe. We have had no contact with the sick girl, and there are no flies on the ocean to carry the contamination to our drinking water. There is not enough time for the disease to spread. I shall pray."

The children watched their father touch the ground with his forehead. Apaji joined him. They faced over the seaward side of the boat toward Mecca in the west. The children did not speak, and they noticed that a great silence had swept over the ship. In the absence of the usual din, they could hear the sea beating gently against the ship's hull. One by one, other families began to pray, kneeling and rising. First the fathers prayed, and then their wives, and then grandmothers and young men. In little clusters the children remained sitting in cross-legged tension, sniffing the air. Overhead white birds hung suspended like mobiles.

"They are the first sign of land," Gappu pointed out to his brothers and sisters. "We are in Pakistan." He rose slowly toward the west. "Allah ho Akbar," he cried and fell to his knees. The other children watched in amazement. Gappu had been the one who laughed at the Mulvis with their lucky prayers and holy talismans and called them doddering fools. He taunted the Nai who performed their circumcisions and taught Karim and Gerrar ways to trick their religious teachers and avoid going to the mosque. Now he prayed alongside Abu and Apaji who bent so low to the ground that Sara was completely concealed, clinging to her mother's breast, within the folds of the sari. Everyone on the ship was praying. Even Piari and Moïd crawled like little chimpanzees to their knees in imitation of their parents. The students were praying, and the Bombay wallahs in their suits and old grandfathers in Gandhi caps with a thousand wrinkles on their faces like dried brown figs. Finally, even Gerrar and Karim joined the prayer, reciting the words they had rebelled against all their lives.

The praying lasted a full hour. The ship rang with dissonant song as each prayer was raised louder and stronger against the others, until they all prayed with a single voice.

"Land. I see Pakistan," someone shouted.

Every head was raised and turned again toward the east. The ribbon of land floated alongside them in the distant water.

"Pakistan. Pakistan Zindabad," someone shouted.

"Pakistan Zindabad. Long live Pakistan," the people responded, and a great cheer went up from a thousand mouths on the deck. All the people began congratulating each other, and they started to move as if mesmerized to the landward side of the ship. The wind whipped their faces and scarves and hair. Some were crying and holding out their hands to the earth that stretched in an endless parched tongue, thirsty against the water. Others searched wordlessly the soft red dunes of clay, tipped with orange from the sinking sun, that rolled away into the horizon.

Rehman bounded across the deck to get a closer look at the land. There was a great crush at the rail.

A man at his side turned to him. "*Mubarik.* Congratulations," he said and clasped Rehman in an embrace.

"The land is barren now, but it is rich," he said. "I am an engineer. All it needs is a little irrigation, and the desert will bloom with fruit and wheat."

Rehman smiled at the fellow refugee with his educated speech. He was glad to see there was hope among the people of building new lives and a new nation.

"I know this land," Rehman said. "I was here as a child. My father was in the service of the Nawab of Bahawalpur."

The engineer began to speak, but he was jostled away by more and more people who were pushing as close as they could to the railing to see their promised land. A hundred arms grabbed Rehman and hugged him. "*Mubarik, mubarik.* Congratulations and good luck," they all said.

Again the loudspeaker broke through the babble of voices and shouting: "This is your captain. All deck passengers please move away from the starboard side of the deck. You are tilting the ship."

Still the people pushed forward. Rehman could see the deep list of the boat toward the water as two thousand feet pressed into the deck and a thousand bodies shuffled together, yearning with all their strength toward the land they had traveled so far to reach. Miles and miles of the Sind desert stretched along the coast. The boat had veered so close they could see occasional camel caravans sifting through the lakes of evening light as if floating in drifts of sand. Everywhere people were crying, half in jubilation and half for someone dead or missing whom they had left behind and would not be with them in Pakistan.

Again the loudspeaker blared. "I repeat," the captain commanded. "You are tilting the ship. All deck passengers move immediately back to their places."

"What do we care about this tub?" someone near Rehman called out. "Let the ship sink. We'll swim ashore." They all pressed forward with cheering. "Pakistan Zindabad. Long live Pakistan."

For the last hour of the voyage, the deck remained frenetic with movement and newfound energy. The people circled around together, shaking every hand they could find, and then came back to the railing to look long and lovingly again at the empty stretch of desert, until the last twinge of sunlight obscured the juncture of sky and land.

By nightfall the ship had eased slowly into the Karachi harbor. For the first time the British officers came onto the refugees' deck and circulated among them. The women had packed their pots and remnants of food back into their cloth sacks, and sat about with their bundles and families, waiting for the signal to disembark. The harbor was bathed in light from gas lamps, and a few large freighters clung to the wharves with ropes in the silence of evening. The quay was empty, and they were pushed quickly down the gangplank by officers who said the ship must move immediately to another pier, where a load of Hindus and Sikhs were waiting in a refugee camp to be carted back to India. Unlike Bombay, where only one gangplank was in use, the ship lowered several, and the officials shouted at them to move faster. They did not want any stragglers, they said, because they did not wish to run the risk of riots if the Hindus and Muslims should meet and clash.

Rehman watched his family run down the gangplank in their turn. Their possessions had diminished to a few sacks and bundles, the clothes they wore, and a few jewels and rupee notes hidden on each child and in Apaji's sari. The last remaining trunk was almost empty except for a few sheets and odd pieces of cloth which had not been traded. They were completely unencumbered as he felt his foot fall onto the cement of the quay and he breathed the first warm air of Pakistan.

The wharf was only a small tin shed, and the road was clearly visible from the quay on which Rehman and his family stood. Coolies ran everywhere trying to direct people to certain camel and donkey-cart drivers from whom they would get a kickback on the fare, while the drivers tried to hustle passengers for themselves and void paying off the coolies. The coolies guarded the shed which was their domain, and if they found an unt wallah, or camel driver, sneaking through the crowd with his desert scarf wrapped around his head, a heated discussion broke out, and the driver was sent back to his camel with warnings not to encroach on the coolies' business.

Earlier arrivals of refugees, the poorest of the poor, had already erected a shantytown in the street. Their makeshift huts of tin and bitterly soiled strips of cloth and jute spilled against the wooden police barricades that delineated the quay from the road. Children hunkered at the curb, washing chipped clay bowls and plates in water that flowed in the gutter from a single preciously regulated water tap. Other children were defecating in the street, their tiny brown buttocks exposed and straining in the air like quivering little goats. Within their tents, the women could be seen squatting in the light of low glimmering fires, grinding chick-peas into flour and heating thin black chapati. An occasional man slipped with lowered head in and out of the cloth flaps that separated one tent from another. The men seemed not to be a part of the domesticated scene of the street, as if this women's world was something shameful, and they tried to hide themselves within the anonymity of their pajamas and their beards. The refugee camp encroached on the very threshold of the wide-open, wall-less customs shed and seemed to lap up the new arrivals from Bombay in its muddy maw.

"Abu, will we have to stay here?" asked Gappu, his eyes wide with dismay as they entered the shed. It was one thing to be without a home when they were traveling and en route, but this was Karachi, their destination. Gappu had heard the people on the ship discussing the homes that would be waiting for them—large inviting houses with gardens and lawns and doors that would swing open and admit them to a carpeted world of beds and furniture, of clean cottons and linens and running water. Yet here was Karachi, greeting them at its miniature port, swollen to its very limits by the haunted faces of the homeless and destitute.

Gappu felt the hundred rupee note in his pocket. If he were to run, right now, and disappear into the city, get lost among the web of wooden carts and animal feet and the darkness of the night, he would never have to live among all the crouching outcasts of India that wriggled at his feet like worms. "I'm not staying here," he thought. "I didn't come to Pakistan to live in a refugee camp." The hundred rupees would buy him food enough to escape this city and flee back to the north where rivers brightened the land with fertility and harvests. Perhaps he would be able to sneak back into India and travel, along the roads like Bashir and Uncle Tariq, unnoticed until he reached Nehtor. He would be only another of the million shadows that floated along India's roads with distant purposes and remote homes. But Karachi was devastated by desert. He could feel the weighty dustiness of the outlying hills in the slow undulating rhythm of camel bells, the beige sand color of their mossy backs.

Rehman led the children to a corner of the shed. "You will not stay here long, I promise you," he said. "We will not even spend the night."

"What are you going to do?" Gappu asked him.

"Apaji and I have to find a place to stay," said Abu. "Your mother must come to look for her relatives."

"You can't leave us here," said Raheel, clutching Piari to her hip and looking small and frail.

"Your brothers will protect you. They have guns and money. I am sure you will not be in danger. This is Pakistan. It is our land. If you do not move, we cannot possibly lose each other."

The children watched Abu lead Apaji away with Sara in her arms. They had sat in so many stations, so many sidewalks and enclosures in strange cities, one more night was of little importance, but it was the first time in their lives they were left alone. The following day they would be home. Abu had promised to find a place to live before morning. He had promised as he had never promised before. "This is Pakistan," he said. "This is your home."

They sat forlornly staring at the entrance to the shed where Abu and Apaji had disappeared into the milling street of the camp. There was no ayah, or nurse, to supervise and comfort the babies, no stern teacher as there was at boarding school monitoring even their hours of escape and mischief. There were no uncles or Dadis or Nanis, no servant boys like Bashir and Moonah, or familiar shopeepers to mark their comings and goings. The whole city attacked their nostrils and their senses with new perfumes and foreign sounds wafting through the open shed. Traffic outside was a slow and dreamy hum of pedestrians on quiet bare feet and a clattering of bells from a hundred different carts drawn by animals through the littered lanes of the refugee camp. They could hear the drivers' voices calling to each other in the strange guttural Sindhi dialect, and the light tinkling of donkey carts which hauled ten times their size. They were being loaded with refugees who climbed atop mounds of belongings. Camels gracefully navigated carts as large as barges that wove away from the wharf, stacked with cartons and people. Horses of every size trotted or walked in different rhythms—old mares, ponies, and mules. Larger horses with jangling bells proudly led immaculate Victoria carriages, in which richer people carrying neat valises seemed set to go riding along the paths of a New Delhi park. The coaches were black and open in the English style of the last century, but the colors of the desert people bedecked the horses. Each tonga-wallah decorated his cart as if trying to compensate for the unrelenting brown of the terrain. The horses wore multicolored blankets, and their reins were studded with pounded silver ornaments, silver and brass bells, and proverbs from the Koran. Orange and green and red feathers fluttered on their heads and flowered patches obscured their noses.

There were no cars as there were in India, and only an occasional black taxi waited incongruously at the curbside. No motor scooters or bicycles or motorized rickshaws were zipping everywhere as they did in Delhi and Bombay. The children thought even the familiar animals were missing. No Hindu cows meandered among the tents. Wiry donkeys and sour-faced camels took the place of the water buffalo and bullocks that plied India's lush green roads with mud shining on their backs. In Karachi, it seemed, there were only dry clipped sounds, and the pasty foam of old, stored, half-digested food that dribbled from the camels' mouths. It was also strange to see only Muslims in the street. Even the chokidars and coolies were Muslims. Everywhere else in India the Sikhs had a monopoly at the wheel, but here the drivers were Muslims too. Gappu had to keep reminding himself that Karachi had been India only a few week before. It had been India for two thousand years, but it did not seem like India at all. There was something different—something in the desert animals and something in the uniformity of the people that was India and was not India at the same time.

The children waited silently for many hours for Abu to return Slowly the shed emptied out, and the sidewalks and road of living humanity fell whispering to sleep. Indians were routinized and slept quickly after the setting sun. Even in the cities a deep Indian mistrust of night was lodged in the souls of the people. Gappu, Raheel and Gerrar sat watch around the smaller children with wakeful uneasiness. They tried half-heartedly to make a game of teaching Moïd to speak, but he was cranky and preferred to sleep. Even Karim joined the younger ones. He felt it was his prerogative to shift roles between the younger and older half of his family, since he had been smack in the middle until Sara was born. This was the first time he did not know assuredly that either Abu or Apaji would be waiting for him in the same secure spot he had left them. Gappu tried to talk to the children so they would not have time to wonder.

The few people remaining in the shed were families like their own, not the poorest, but not able to whisk off in a Victoria to the custom-ready house Gappu had imagined was waiting for them Some of them snored, and a child awakened by the barking of stray dogs began to cry. It was late at night, and no other noise could be heard from the streets. The families in the shed eyed each other shyly and uneasily from where they sat on benches and piles of cartons, or curled up gracefully on the floor, children's heads sleeping in their parents' laps.

The night was, otherwise, quiet. The wind carried the odor of fish and sea. Even the chokidars had gone home or disappeared off somewhere to nap, for sleeping was the chief occupation of Indians after dark, and those who were employed to stay awake still could not resist the lure of sleep. Nighttime held all the possibilities for the realization of the stories that were told during the day—of dacoits who stole children and looted whole villages, of souls that roamed the earth at midnight and especially on Thursdays, of diseases that ttacked with sudden fevers after dark. At home, in Nehtor, Dadi never forgot to light the oil lamp in her dead husband's room, because at night it was possible that his spirit would come back for something he had forgotten.

Although Gappu was old enough to laugh at Dadi's beliefs, the Indian night was still a mixture of the myth and the hazards of reality. Gappu felt the presence of all the people he had seen killed around him since the rioting first broke out in Aligarh. From all he had heard and observed of fellow refugees, those who fled with him and those who fled from him, killing had taken place on both sides, recent killing, continuous killing. The refugees hidden in their huts at the entrance to the customs shed were testimonials to his fears. Their squalor, their exposure to the night and the roaming dogs, the chaotic quilt of their brown rag tents, seemed to lie in wait for Gappu and his family, like a drugged beast ready at any moment to spring from its stupor and claim them in its grip of poverty.

He could not believe that so many people could live together in passivity and not hate anyone who did not have to join them, not want to fight and kill. There might even have been killing in this very shed, just days before. The British officers had said there was an island in Karachi harbor filled with Hindu and Sikh refugees who were waiting to go back to India. Gappu could see their fire lights flickering across the water. Who knew how close those refugees had come to blood and severed bodies on their journey to Karachi from the innards of Pakistan? He wished Apaji and Abu would hurry back, and he tried not to watch the large clock that beamed over the customs desk. Abu had said that in Pakistan they were safe. Gappu tried to tell himself he had nothing to fear from the empty shed, from the harbor islands where refugees were waiting, or from the shantytown that seemed to beckon like a graveyard of the half-dead.

Suddenly four of the chokidars reappeared as if returning from dinner or a long smoke. They carried clubs in the belts of their petty officer police uniforms, and they looked very well fed and muscular.

"We have been assigned to move the refugees out of the hall," they said, walking from family to family. Three women, who were without their husbands or any other men, started to run. The police officers ran after them, grabbing them around their waists or by the cloth of their saris as they struggled and screamed like small caught birds.

"You can't send me out there," a man in pajamas pleaded as a chokidar pushed him toward the door. "I am waiting for someone. We will get separated. We will never find each other again."

"You can wait outside," said the chokidar.

"But I can't go out there into the refugee camp," he said, peering out into the street that lay like a rubble of human waste.

"Why not?" asked the policeman. "Who are you?"

The answer seemed to stick in the refugee's mouth. "I tell you I must wait here," he repeated. The chokidar gave the man a kick in the butt and sent him spinning out of the shed. His wife and children watched mutely, then followed behind as if they had not seen. If they were not important enough for someone to come and get them, they had to go to the refugee camp.

Gappu and Gerrar stood in front of their brothers and sisters, who were huddled in the corner. A police officer approached Gappu and held him by his arm. "You boys will have to leave. The wharf must be cleared. Are your parents dead?"

Gappu was shaking with fright. "No," he said. "We are waiting for them. They will be right back."

"Have they abandoned you?"

"No. I tell you they will be right back."

The policeman looked over Gappu's shoulder at the children. "They must be crazy, leaving daughters alone."

"They are coming right back," Gappu repeated.

"Wait in the street; they won't miss you," the officer said.

"My sisters can't go into the camp," Gappu protested. "It is filthy and filled with dogs and men."

The chokidar smiled. He was quite willing to be accommodating where young girls were concerned. "I will take your sisters back to my house. You can meet them when your parents return."

Gappu knew the signal well. This was no kindness to be mistaken for concern or respect for the status of his family. This was the anger signal he had been waiting for. All the stories he had ever heard of child thieves and slave trade of young girls pounded in his head, the images of red-light districts he had seen and pretty girls as little as seven or eight with rouge powdered on their sallow cheeks, stacked together like a full house of cards waiting to be picked and played. He knew what the chokidar with his substantial healthy Arab face wanted. Raheel, cowering behind him, held Piari even more tightly in her arms.

This chokidar was the first real Pakistani they had talked to, and he looked heavier and stronger than the Indian police, who wore shorts and had dark-brown skins. The Pakistani policeman was a paler olive. He had quick darting eyes that moved over Raheel's body. Gappu knew that Raheel could easily bring five thousand rupees in sale to a house of prostitution. Even in Aligarh a girl was not allowed to walk alone to school without a servant to protect her, because danger in the cities could be anywhere.

"I can take all three sisters home," the chokidar repeated. Gappu did not know what to do. He felt frozen in his indecisiveness. The chokidar kept tapping his stick in his hand. "Otherwise, I am clearing you from this shed. We must observe the law."

Gappu grabbed hold of the policeman's stick. "I thought there would be homes for us in Pakistan. My father told us we are *maha-irs*, like the Prophet Muhammad when he escaped from Mecca, and that we would be treated like guests."

The guard seemed embarrassed. "Don't talk to me about religion, Ghai. This is my job, and I have to keep order."

Gappu straightened himself to his tallest and faced the policeman. His thin body felt new to him and strangely gangling, with his wrists, too long and narrow, hanging out of his small blazer's cuffs, the lightest of shadow beards above his upper lip and at his overgrown sideburns. "We are Syed," he told the policeman. "We are descended from the Prophet."

The chokidar laughed. "Partition Syed. Everyone coming from India says they are Syed. The Prophet must have had a thousand grandsons."

"You don't believe me?" Gappu asked incredulously. He thought, as Dadi always told him, that a Syed was an honored, almost holy man.

"No, I don't believe you," the guard said, yanking his stick from Gappu's hands. "You have tried to be very clever, but I am going to see you out that door." He pointed with his stick, and Gappu grabbed at it again. The guard reacted suddenly, and Gappu felt the edge of the stick sharply against his cheek, which had never been hurt or slapped, never known personal abuse, before. His hands flew to his face, and he felt the tears smarting in his eyes. Gerrar leaped forward to his side, waving Abu's little metal pistol in his hand.

"We have this," Gerrar shouted wildly, his voice breaking. "Let anyone throw us out, and we'll see."

The chokidar backed off. He did not like real violence and did not wish to be the cause of an incident. It was impossible to tell who a refugee might really be. "You can wait an hour longer," he said. "Your parents had better be here by then. It is after midnight."

The rest of the shed was cleared. The four chokidars sat sullenly on benches across the room, napping and talking together. Gappu's head was pounding with pain. He rested it in Raheel's lap and let her massage his temples and his neck. The other children were deeply impressed with their two oldest brothers, and could not wait to tell Abu about their courage and intelligence.

By the time Abu and Apaji finally returned, all the children had fallen asleep. Apaji roused them, and Abu had to carry both Moïd and Piari in either arm, rather than awaken them fully from their red-faced drunken drowsiness. The guard who had threatened them watched grimly as the family walked out of the shed.

Abu was full of news. "I found my older sister, your Phopi Fatima," he told them. "We had to go to an all-night officer who keeps lists of new arrivals so that people can find places to sleep quickly and not be in the streets."

"Who is that?" Mona asked, rubbing the sleep from her eyes with her fists.

Apaji pushed the hair out of Mona's eyes. "She is your father's

.lder sister. You have met her many times at your Dadi's house, but he lives in Delhi, and you forget."

"Phopi is the one Dadi does not like," Raheel told Mona. "Dadi .eeps her in the kitchen and does not allow her children to play."

Abu looked sternly at Raheel. "You will not speak of your el- .lest aunt that way. We are going to live in her home, and you must)e thankful. Phopi has been here for a month. She came from Delhi n an airlift. Uncle Tariq is with her. He never made it back to Nehtor, although he sent Bashir on."

Raheel examined her mother's face for any expression, but Apaji remained tight-lipped and resolute as she had been ever since heir ordeal began. Raheel knew that Apaji never went to Phopi's nome in Old Delhi, because Phopi was not nice to her.

She was the bad one, the first child to be born to Dadi and Mubarik. Dadi resented her for this. Not only was it a very bad)men, in Dadi's opinion, to give birth first to a daughter, but this)articular daughter was dark-skinned, and disparagingly called Kali,)r Blackie, for short. From infancy it was clear that Phopi Fatima would be difficult to marry off, which was Dadi's first thought when he newborn baby was placed in her arms. At that time Dadi was fourteen and had been married less than ten months. She turned away from the black wizened daughter there and then on her natal)ed, and wept bitter tears.

Dadi's prognostications about the infant had been correct. She was a bad omen. For the next seven years, not only had Dadi failed to bear a son, she did not conceive at all. Of course, Phopi Fatima received all the blame. Dadi cursed her and covered her in veils of shame at the age of five and put her to work at the age of seven, as soon as Rehman, the first treasured son, was born.

The whole family despaired of ever marrying Phopi, and so her best place was amid the ashes of the stove and in the service of her younger brothers as each was born. Dadi never forgave Phopi Fatima for the seven years of anguish before Rehman was born, or for all the prayers that she had made and all the riches poured into lucky mizars, or all her fears that Mubarik would take a second wife if she did not conceive a son.

Dadi did not like girls, period. For this reason Raheel had never liked to go to Dadi's house. Neither did Apaji, and when they were in Nehtor, she always slept at Nani's house instead. Apaji and Raheel did not believe in hiding their faces or in total submission to the men and boys of their family. On the contrary, Apaji had been the Darogaji's prized daughter and favorite child, and Nani regaled her daughter and granddaughters with jewels and clothes, with wreaths of flowers and with lessons in poetry, music, and embroidery. Nani never permitted them to work or even enter the kitchen.

Raheel felt very uncomfortable around Phopi Fatima. Although Fatima had surprised everyone by marrying and moving to Delhi, she remained a shadowy figure of the kitchen and dark inner rooms, appearing voiceless in her deep purdah, ensconced in black shroud from the tip of her head to the floor, observing everyone sourly through a little caged window in her hood.

Raheel was very disappointed. It was their luck that the only relative to arrive in Karachi, out of all the hundreds who were fun loving and educated and gay, would have to be Phopi Fatima, but she followed Apaji out into the street, past all the hovels of sleeping refugees, to a camel cart that was waiting for them. Raheel did not like the idea of driving through the city in an unt gari. She thought of it as the vehicle of the peasants. Its wooden planks were rough and sandy, and the camel had a strong musty odor. Abu and Apaji silently helped the children onto the cart.

The camel drifted along the dark quiet streets. The waning moon was just coming up and lit the small clouds that puffed in from the Arabian Sea. The bell clanging hollowly at the camel's neck made the only sound, as the wharf area gave way to broad boulevards lined with huge elegant houses, sweeping circular driveways and lawns. The camel driver acted as guide and kept calling over his shoulder to Abu the names of the different buildings they were passing. The church belonged to the British. Many of the most beautiful homes were now embassies since Karachi was to be the capital of Pakistan. On the left was the Indian High Commission. It was strange to see the familiar Indian flag, which they were no longer supposed to honor but to despise, fluttering in front. There was no traffic, and the slow, even movement of the camel through the long uneventful streets lulled the younger children back to sleep.

Gappu, Gerrar, Karim, and Raheel sat up with their parents watching their new city unfold. The spacious houses everywhere were reassuring, and even if it was only Phopi Fatima's, there was a home waiting for them in this once beautiful, former resort city of beaches and desert. They felt free and almost giddy with the rocking gait of the camel and the warm desert wind blowing against their faces and in their hair. There was no need to cower low to the bottom of the cart or to keep their eyes trained on every doorway to see if some danger was lurking there. It was the first time the family had been alone together. It took more than three hours for the camel to walk through Karachi, and by the time they reached the edge of the city a pale shadowless light was stretching across the sky, and the air sang with the call of prayer from the minars of the mosques that dotted the streets and squares.

The cobbled streets of the city ended abruptly and were met by new ill-defined roads, rutted and blowing with dust. They seemed only recently to have been carved out of the dry red hills of the desert, which rose in the distance billowing with sand, and blasted rudely away to expose their veins of clay. As far as the eye could see, rows and rows of tan cement barracks with flat tin roofs had been erected for refugees. Each square little house was separated from the next by a few yards of sandy earth, and occasionally they could see young vines beginning to crawl over crude wooden arbors tied together with rope. Here and there pale tomato plants or stalks of maize corn were fighting their way up through the arid soil. Everywhere in the streets and in the long narrow alleys that ran between the houses, people were sleeping on jute charpoys.

Phopi Fatima was waiting in front of her little house on Martin Road. It was a corner house, the same size and color as all the rest, and the moment she saw the camel cart turn into the long road, she jumped from her chair and ran to meet them. She even forgot to pull the veils of her coarse black burka down over her face, and the cloth hung around her shoulders and flew in the red dust as she ran, holding out her arms to them. Tears were streaming from her eyes, and with a whoop Karim leaped from the back of the cart and threw himself into her arms. Gerrar and Gappu followed him somewhat less exuberantly, and Rehman carried the babies down from the cart and into Phopi's outstretched hands.

"I can't believe it. I can't believe you're really here," she repeated over and over again. All the neighbors sat up on their beds to look at the new arrivals, and Phopi's four daughters flooded out of the house, covering their faces and shoulders with their shawls as they came to meet their cousins. They were barefooted, and the hems of their flaring white pajamas were rimmed red from the sand. Phopi's husband, Sharif, who was shorter than she, followed his daughters into the street, his dark, narrow, little face bursting with smiles behind his long feathery moustache. He clasped Rehman's arms and laid his hands over each of the children's shoulders and heads in blessing.

"Ai Allah, ai Allah, I never thought we would see you again," Phopi wailed over and over. Her high loud voice was reaching a pitch of hysteria, and her large chest was heaving with sobs. "But my son is missing. My Achan is gone. God has brought us together, but he has taken my son. Ai, ai, ai," she cried.

Phopi's husband pushed her toward the house, and ushered Rehman and the family into the barracks. "Some say that these houses were built for the army," he explained. "There is a flush toilet and running water. But no one knows which army, since the British are gone and Pakistan has no military to speak of."

"We are lucky they are here," Rehman said, nodding.

"Yes, and already they are all occupied. The newest arrivals must go to camps and build their own huts, if they cannot find a relative to take them in. We are very crowded." Phopi's husband led Rehman and the family through the house. There were two rooms, side by side, with a kitchen and bathroom in the rear. They were completely bare except for charpoys, and two large tin trunks in which all Phopi Fatima's possessions were stored.

As they entered the dim cement room, filled with the shadowy light of early morning, Tariq appeared from the rear of the house, looking wan and ten years older than the handsome bridegroom of

Nehtor. He made a frail attempt to smile, continuously rubbing the cloth of his black shervani jacket, which was caked with dirt and crumpled. His eyes darted restlessly over the faces of his relatives, and no one dared approach him. "Sit, sit," he said in a shaking voice. "I'm glad you are safe." His voice seemed to choke, and he looked nervously around the room, not focusing on anybody. "I was just leaving. I am looking for work. Please stay seated." He backed out of the room. "I'm afraid I'll be late. Thank God, you are safe, but I cannot be late."

Rehman stared at his brother in amazement, but Phopi Fatima offered no explanation. She grabbed Apaji and Raheel by the hand and pulled them into the kitchen, where her daughters were already making chapati and dal over the brick stove. She kept her daughters and herself as confined as possible to the kitchen, but even Phopi Fatima could not impose purdah in the new quarters. The men and women had to live on top of one another without any private room or garden to retire to.

"There is not enough food to go around," Fatima said, as she squatted beside her daughters and began slapping the balls of dough from palm to palm to flatten them into breads. "We will have to make an arrangement, but for now eat and sleep. If only my son could be here to see this moment!"

Raheel stood quietly behind Apaji and tugged on the skirt of her mother's sari, but Apaji shot her a warning glance and sat down on the earthen floor to help Phopi Fatima prepare the chapati, while all her nieces smiled shyly and bent their heads away.

After breakfast, the children were deposited in the rear alley and on the street to sleep, two to a charpoy. The boys were in front, and the girls had to stay in the rear along with their cousins whom they hardly knew. Inside was for eating and the adults. It was mid-morning, and the roads were filled with people and animals. Camels and donkeys dragging cartloads of produce moved steadily among the pedestrians, and local salesmen in the voluminous earth-color pants of Sind called out their wares in melodious singing voices. The heat was unmerciful, baked by the desert and weighted by moisture from the sea, and the sun reflected off the tin roofs like a drum and shimmered in the red and orange mirrored caps of the Sindhi people. The children were warned not to wander out of the quarter, because the Sindhi desert tribesmen who lived nomadically in the hills were coming into Karachi to steal children. Gappu thought these were only stories, but he promised to keep watch over the younger children. He did not care about the desert, or the barracks, or the scanty breakfast, or Phopi Fatima's backward ways. All that mattered was that they were in Pakistan. Their family was together. Life could begin anew.

Rehman wasted no time in beginning to look for a job, but in two long weeks of hunting there was none to be had. Everyday there were promises, and every night he returned home empty-handed to live off his sister's husband. Rehman was beginning to know the city like a map. The official buildings carved great archways and courtyards into the city streets. They housed the many departments and agencies bequeathed by the British bureaucratization of their lives. He stopped each morning and each evening at the refugee office in the Customs building to look for familiar names among the lists of thousands that were mounting into stacks of forms. Refugee faces lined the walls where they sat for hours and even days in the courtyard of the office building, waiting for relatives whom they would not believe were lost. They sat in orderly fashion, beneath the stares of the clerks and police officers who came and went out of the building with official poise. Rehman strolled among the refugees, wiping away from each one the threads of familiarity in their swarthy features and their questioning expressions. He thought he recognized a hundred faces, but he knew none. There had to be a Nehtori among them, a face he had not seen perhaps since childhood, or only occasionally at a wedding or funeral. He prayed someone could tell him what had happened in Nehtor, whether the riots had spread that far, burning their estates and villages to the ground and forcing Dadi to leave her house for the second time in her life and arrive in

he city with her country dress and farmer's ways. He dared not
conjecture. It was better to wait and ask for news. Everyone was
waiting. His sister Fatima waited for news about Achan, her son,
who was lost in Delhi. Tariq made his own search during the blinding hot daylight of Karachi afternoons. It was only a matter of time
before someone would arrive.

Rehman joined the line of men waiting to enter the small cubicle of the refugee office with its heavy wooden desks and piles of thin
frayed papers that were bound together by ropes. The papers were
stacked to the ceiling and strewn on window ledges and across the
desk. The officer in charge was a familiar figure to Rehman by now,
but the officer did not seem to reciprocate the recognition.

"Be sure to check everyday," he warned each man who leafed
through the big ledger of signatures lying open on the table. "You
must keep up to date if you hope to find whomever you are looking
for. Only newcomers may see the back dates."

Rehman took his turn in the line and read through the names,
tracing the pages with his fingers as if in the contact he might bring
to life one name that belonged to his own people from India. He
smiled at the officer, whose thin face and narrow eyes pressed him to
finish faster.

"There will be someone soon, I am sure," Rehman said.

"Yes. There is always someone sooner or later," the officer said.
"Just keep looking. If you don't find friends, they may find you."

Rehman fumbled helplessly against his shirt for a small gratuity
with which to buy the officer's recognition. Day after day they
exchanged one or two sentences—always the same. Rehman knew
that a little baksheesh would ensure some kind of comfort from the
man. Perhaps he would then be on the lookout for a special name
Rehman would tell him, although there were so many names he
could give, it would be impossible to choose. The men in line were
peering over Rehman's shoulder, trying to see in advance if one signature would light up for them among all the rest. They formed a
semicircle around the table. Rehman looked up at the row of eager
faces awaiting their turns. He shrugged. "It's all yours, brother," he

said as he did every day, and walked off down the corridor where all the other little offices were jammed to overflowing with refugees behind the screen doors.

Time weighed heavily on Rehman's head. The whole morning stretched ahead of him, until his appointment at the ministry of mines where he hoped to find work. In the past two weeks he had already been to the department of civil engineering, the tax collector's bureau, and the tobacco mart, hoping that his background in one or another of these fields would qualify him for a position in Pakistan, but every afternoon ended in fruitless search. Each morning, daylight forced him off the charpoy where he lay shivering under a cloth in the desert night outside the barracks. Hunger swirled him through the city, a forest of languages and second-hand merchandise curtaining the marketplaces and lying in bundles on street corners. Nothing was available. Rice was as much stone and grit as it was grain. Tea was a lifeless mud-brown, and sugar was nonexistent.

After making his morning stop at the refugee office, he haunted the streets, poking into the bazaars where he could not buy. His arms were useless weights hanging from his shoulders. Since he had abandoned all his suits of raw silk and brushed cotton, the vests and boots, the scarves and leather purses, he held his forearms folded across his chest as he walked. He bought and wore immediately the thin cotton blouse native to the region of Sindh, which he alternated with his Western suit, the one he had worn in his escape from India, the one that permanently held the lingering odor of his perspiration, the gray tint underlying the cloth from weeks without bathing and the incessant rain of charcoal-filled air from trains and waiting rooms.

It was not the expensive cloth he missed, or the slim fitted lines and neat creases wrought by his Delhi tailor. He would never again need or want such luxuries, he assured himself. There was no honor or merit in the yards of imported flannel, or the smiling tailor who measured Rehman's expansive shoulders with gentle admiring fingers and a sideways clucking of his bald perfumed head, or the tape measure deftly encircling his groin and running up and down his legs. The shirt and pants from those days hung on his body like someone else's lost skin. The only thing he missed, he admitted, was his attaché case. He carried his meager belongings in a handkerchief. All his possessions consisted of a few rupees and a lunch of bread and onion that Apaji prepared for him. He also carried the few deeds he had managed to bring from Aligarh. They were his sole identification.

Rehman wandered through the Sadar Bazaar, where the half-empty stalls still bore the names of departed Hindus and Sikhs on large signs. Many shops were closed altogether, waiting for merchants to come from India and stake their claims. If Rehman had been a shopkeeper before, he could have opened one of the doors and set himself up in business, but as it was his fortune had been land, his skill management; his deeds were for mines and hotels, and these were unavailable.

The Home Ministry was his second stop. The offices were slightly larger than at the Customs Building, and he sat alone on a bench in a long corridor, waiting nervously for the appointment he had made days before with the Minister of lands and mines. He had worked his way up through the bureaucracy of department secretaries and commissioners, producing the precious deeds that were cracking along the creases where he folded them to pocket size. Each official had referred him to a superior for the ultimate approval of his claim. Each saw no reason why the next officer would be unable to grant him the mines he asked for. His deeds were bona fide. Pakistan needed his skills.

"The Minister will see you now," a young office boy told him. Rehman rose slowly off the bench with a deep sigh, and followed the boy into the office. A fan rotated overhead, and the office was a dark cool oasis of polished furniture and files. The Minister rose from behind the desk and shook Rehman's hand.

"I understand you have a claim to a mine," he said in clipped English. "Please sit down."

Rehman remained standing. The Minister's well-pressed suit was of fine dark cotton, and in his cuffs were two black star-sapphire stones that glinted in the half light from the window.

"I have these deeds," said Rehman. He unwrapped the small

handkerchief that belonged to Apaji, and spread the old faded documents on the Minister's desk, unfolding each crease gently and smoothing them with his hands. "You can see how old the paper is. These deeds have been in my family for many generations."

"Let's have a look," said the Minister, sliding his glasses slightly down the bridge of his nose. He scanned the papers quickly and handed them back. "I am afraid I do not read Urdu very well," he said.

Rehman was embarrassed. "These mines in Rajputna were inherited," he explained. "My own deeds are in English, but they were left behind in India."

"Quite," said the Minister. "What sort of mines were these?"

"Salt mines. Actually they are lakes. They are near Jaipur in Sambhar District. I have managed them for over twenty years. We do refining and exporting—the whole process."

The Minister rose again from his desk. "The government of Pakistan would like to honor your deeds." He smiled. "I am afraid, however, that I cannot give you such permission here. You must go to the regional offices in Multan."

"I don't understand," said Rehman. "Isn't this the central office? Multan is six hundred miles from here."

Again the Minister smiled. "I know how you must feel, but you have to understand that refugees are flooding Pakistan along every inch of border. They come through Punjab and through the desert. Many, many millions have come to Lahore, even more than to Karachi. It is impossible for the head to know what the tail is doing."

Rehman gathered up his deeds and folded them back into the little hanky, which he tucked into the waistband of his pants. "Where do you suggest I go?"

"As I said, you should try Multan. There are salt mines in southern Punjab that I believe are vacant."

"I don't know how we will get there. I have eight children and little money." Rehman could not admit that he had no money at all, that whatever little he could scrounge up from selling off their belongings, all the way down to the lucky talismans his children wore around their necks, was immediately spent on food. He could not even afford to take a trolley every day to and from the barracks on Martin Road and walked the several miles through the city instead. How could they find the money for a train? It was impossible.

"I am sure you will like it there," the Minister continued, ignoring Rehman's statement, so that Rehman felt his skin flush even more—to the roots of his black hair. "It is closer to India. More like home than Karachi."

"Will there be homes for my children?" Rehman asked.

"Why don't you leave the children in Karachi until you are settled?" the Minister suggested.

"No. That is impossible." Rehman wondered that the Minister did not know what it was like along the roads and in the towns all over India, on both sides of the borders. He did not seem to understand that the family was his strength.

"Can you at least write a letter of introduction for me?"

"Certainly," said the Minister. "I will dictate an excellent letter to my secretary, and you can pick it up next week." Again he shook Rehman's hand. "In the meantime, find a job. Make some money. The trains are crowded and inexpensive," he advised. "Maybe the railway department will give you a free ticket."

The Minister escorted Rehman all the way to the street. "You will see. It will all work out in the end," he promised Rehman. "I am a mahajir myself, but I came last year, before the trouble started. That was the wise thing to do."

Rehman wandered through the streets again, looking for a shady spot to eat his bread and onion. There was nothing left to do until the end of the day when he would again check at the refugee office in the Customs Building. All week he had occupied his time in petitioning commissioners and subcommissioners, with the ultimate goal of meeting with the Minister of the entire department. Now that was achieved, and the illusion he had cherished all week vanished. The feeling that he had been involved in meaningful work that would succor and sustain his family was no more. There would follow another journey and a second uprooting, but normalcy which for so long had been attached to an image of Karachi was now attached to the image of the salt mines.

Rehman never expected to identify himself as a miner. The lakes in Sambhar had always seemed a side affair to him. His presence there had never been necessary for more than one month out of the year. He had inherited the mines along with their highly organized functioning. The nomadic harvesters, called banjara, came summer and winter to load the salt that had been dredged from the lakes, with their black skin streaked and cracked with scars of white from the salt. The miners, the guards, the village itself, belonged to him in an ancient serfdom exactly like the farmers of Nehtor who belonged to the fields. There was no need for the landlord and owner who appeared generation after generation, the embodiment of the same man, descending from the city to collect his profits. There were already supervisors and inspectors, and they also belonged to Rehman in a way. His only job was to check the accounts. As a young man he had spent one year learning the business, which was a shock to the managers of the village, because no one had done even that much before him. Rehman's continued interest in the mines had only been through the chance that his yearly visit to the salt lakes was a favorite vacation for his entire family. The children loved the villages and cities of the state which was divided into the principalities of many Maharajas. They loved the hills and fortresses, palaces and gardens, that surrounded the crystal lakes where the salt raking was done, the roads where elephants and peacocks walked, and the pink-colored city of Jaipur. It was only fortuitous that Rehman had grabbed those particular deeds from his bureau drawer when he escaped from the bedrooms and sitting rooms and terraces of his Aligarh house. He had not particularly expected to use them. He had expected to find a house in Karachi. Probably, he thought, he would be given some vacant government post in the city. It was the least he could expect, but he had been wrong. That was what everyone expected, and now suddenly his mines had become his most precious possession and his only selling point.

Again Rehman had to consider making a move. Since there was nothing left for him to do in Karachi, he started back toward home. If he decided to go to Multan, he would have to find a way to make money without delay or someone else with a mine claim might arrive before him and take away his last hope of a decent survival. Otherwise, at his age and with nothing in his pockets, what position could he fill, what business could he build, and where could he begin?

As Rehman crossed from the streets and boulevards of the city, he noticed many people walking faster than the usual meandering Indian gait. The streets were changing to the newly blasted dirt roads. In the distance the barracks that housed Rehman's family, along with half a million refugees, stretched out until the city ended in desert. The people were all hurrying in one direction, and Rehman followed them. They turned a corner, and he saw a huge field of red dirt filled with thousands of people. The wind was blowing sand across the open dome of the hill, and everyone was quiet, listening to a speech over a loudspeaker. Mostly there were men, rough Sindhi farmers and camel drivers from the outlying desert and villages, and refugees in pajamas and old shirts.

Rehman pushed into the rear of the crowd. "Who is speaking?" he asked.

"Brother, it is Quaid i Azam, the father of our country, Mohammed Ali Jinnah."

The words of the speech were barely distinguishable, from the wooden platform where the small form of their leader stood, but that did not seem to matter. Everyone was listening intently to the voice of the man they all revered, like a hum of wind falling on their ears and caressing them. Rehman's weakened eyes could just pinch out the slim gray coat and Persian fedora hat Jinnah wore, cocked on the side of his long lean head. Anyone would recognize him even at this distance. He looked like a prophet. Jinnah standing there, slim and ephemeral, was holding the multitudes by the web of his presence. All questions Rehman had about the politics of the last decade, about Nehru, Gandhi, and Jinnah, the troika of lawyers, and about the division of the country, seemed to fade from his mind, and only Jinnah remained, forceful and articulate, promising them democracy, promising them equality, and offering them hope.

In his speech Jinnah requested the people of Pakistan to stop rioting. He spoke of the Indian people as brothers, and many times the word Pakistan trembled off his lips and shimmered in the bright air. Rehman could hear flags snapping all around the field, above the high crackling of Jinnah's amplified voice, the crescent and star of Islam graceful on a fertile field of green cloth. The speech was long and in English, and although Rehman was certain few people were able to understand it, they stood in awed silence and let the sound of the words waft over them like a prayer.

"Faith, Unity, and Discipline—that is our motto," Jinnah shouted, and the crowd waved and roared its approval. The three words reverberated in Rehman's mind. It did not matter that he had not heard the whole speech, the spirit was clear to everyone gathered along the crest of the hill. Their leader was here in Karachi with them, and he understood their suffering. Jinnah was their father, their high priest, their ultimate Mulvi. Our brothers, he called them, brothers in Islam, brothers in Pakistan, and brothers in suffering. The words were like a personal message to Rehman. From this day forward there would be no more killing in the villages, no more uprooting of fellow men in order to steal their homes and possessions, and for the refugees, hard work. Rehman vowed no longer to moan and weep over lost privileges and luxuries. There were sure ways to survive. They lay in Faith, Unity, and Discipline. It meant grasp opportunities, never leave the side of his wife and children, and work at anything and everything that offered itself for the betterment of himself, his family, and Pakistan.

The crowd surged forward as Jinnah stepped off the platform and walked swiftly erect through the people. Men were screaming with religious frenzy and running toward the path Jinnah was taking. "Father, father," they screamed. "Long live Quaid i Azam. Pakistan Zindabad."

Rehman ran from the crowd, shoving his body against the tide of cheering, shouting men who blocked the road on every side. There was one sure place he knew where he could make money fast, one place where he had seen money exchanged freely, abundantly, even desperately. There was one occupation where no questions were asked and every man took what he could get—the wharves. Rehman was fired with the idea. He had paid thousands of rupees himself to have his belongings and his family loaded onto trains and onto the ship in Bombay. Now he could earn the same; even with fair prices, he could earn at least enough for food and passage to Multan. He ran all the way back through Karachi to the docks.

Every wharf was astir with activity. It seemed easy to find customers. It was midday, and crew members and passengers were embarking and disembarking with trunks and luggage and a thousand bundles. Rehman ripped off his shirt. He tied it around his head like a bandanna, and slipped along the quay unnoticed into a gang of coolies, who were hauling the ropes of a massive passenger ship onto the wharf and securing them to metal girders. His whole body strained with the effort, and he joined in the chanting to relieve the tension in his tight muscles as the men heaved and dragged the heavy ropes. He followed the coolies up the gangplank and onto the decks of the ship. He kicked off his sandals to get a better grip on the plank and watched the flowing motion of the coolies' bodies. He was determined to learn the business with his mind, to make up for the exercise his body lacked.

On deck the coolies made a mad dash for the first-class cabins, and they invaded each room like a swarm of bees in a hive. The passengers all seemed to be European, and they stood about in their rooms ordering the coolies where to go and what to pick up and dickering over prices. Without waiting for commands, Rehman swooped up a large leather valise and balanced it on his head. A young woman came up to him and stuffed two more bags into his arms. "Carry these carefully," she said. "Bahaut, breakable." She spoke half in Urdu and half in English with a flat nasal accent.

Rehman nodded.

"How much?" the lady asked him.

How much? How much? Rehman had no idea. In Bombay he had paid a thousand rupees for a coolie to carry his daughter Piari. "One rupee," he said. "For each bag."

The woman gave him a sidelong glance as if to say too much.

"Madam," he said. "I am the best coolie in Karachi."

The lady laughed. "Fair enough then," she said and led him down the gangplank and off the ship.

Rehman worked all afternoon. The sun beat down on his head,

and the perspiration gathered under his bandanna and trickled down his face. With every valise he raised to his head, his arms groaned and his head throbbed. Each trunk knifed into his shoulders, and he felt his legs would give way as he galloped up and down the gang-plank. "Faith, Unity, and Discipline," he reminded himself, and the words made the pain in his back and his legs bearable. "I am a coolie now, and I will be the best coolie in Karachi. Then I will think about tomorrow."

Rehman was amazed at how quickly the rupees amassed in his handkerchief. The bread and onion went uneaten until the entire day's work was finished. Then while he was walking home, he re-membered it and gobbled it in three or four swallows, while he counted again the pile of rupee notes. He felt like a boy who had just earned his first wages. In less than a week he would have enough money to go to Multan. He vowed not to tell Apaji until it was a fait accompli, and never would he tell her how the money was earned.

While Rehman was out looking for work, Apaji was closeted in the kitchen. In the two weeks they had been in Phopi Fatima's house, she had not even had time to go outside and see Karachi. All she knew were the barracks and the hills and the Sindhi people who flowed in from the desert to sell their mutton and milk, cloth and clay pots. The children were restless, but she could not watch them as carefully as she would have liked, because Fatima did her best to keep her imprisoned in her woman's place, while she berated God and the fates for their misfortunes and cried for the loss of her son. Apaji listened to her for hours as they bent together over the fire of coal and bits of wood, and mashed peppers into paste on the mortar and pestle. Her sari was blackened with soot, and her eyes stung with smoke.

Phopi Fatima was annoyed that her brother Rehman had brought his whole family to her house without money, and she could not hide her impatience. She eyed Apaji nervously, trying to hold her tongue, but she was worried. Rehman had so little money he could not afford to feed his children for another week, and then Phopi's husband would have to support them on his meager salary of sixty rupees a week. The job was so new he had only been paid once, and the first salary was eaten up as soon as it came in. She still owed money to every street vendor that passed the barracks door. Phopi's brother Tariq was enough of a burden, but he was a baby still and could not help himself. She had known that she would have to support Tariq when he accompanied her from Delhi, but what could the poor boy do when all his gold and jewels had been stolen by a band of thieves? Tariq had returned to her from Rehman's home in Aligarh and told her how they were living. The big man, who had all the wealth of their father and all the wealth of Darogaji combined, was squatting in the servants' quarters of his big Aligarh house with his snobbish and spoiled children, quaking in his shoes and begging for food.

Phopi did not demand money from Tariq. He was the baby of the family and was only married that very summer in Nehtor. Phopi had not gone to the wedding because she could not get along with Dadi, but she felt she was as much a mother to Tariq as Dadi was. He had told her how he tried to run from Aligarh to Nehtor, but was stopped on the road by a band of Hindus who stole his money and all the jewels from his bride's dowry. He had crawled back to her in the refugee camp at the Red Fort in Delhi and cried at her feet. "Oh, sister, Bahin, they left me nothing," he wept. "So shortly after my marriage, I am reduced to a beggar. I cannot reach my wife who is surely pregnant. Where can I go?" She looked at the crumpled form of her baby brother. She had been married and a mother herself by the time he was born, and she had carried him in her arms along with her own children, cooked his food, and bathed him.

Although Phopi's only son had been missing in Delhi for a month, she agreed to leave with Tariq and her four daughters and her husband for Pakistan. They all prevailed upon her night after night within the confines of the Red Fort. "There is no point in staying imprisoned here," they told her. "If Achan were in Delhi, he would come to the Fort. Perhaps he has safely reached Nehtor. Maybe he went ahead to Pakistan and is waiting for us there."

"Maybe he is dead," Phopi wailed. Every night she moaned and cried. All day she searched among the new refugees who flooded into the Fort in the hope of news of her eldest child. Each week the refugees came from greater distances, from Lucknow in the east and Amritsar in the west. The farther they had traveled, the more hopeless and tired they were. There was less and less chance that anyone had seen her son, but still she asked and prayed. There was no water, and cholera was breaking out everywhere in the camp. We are leaving, her husband told her, and Tariq had pleaded that they would soon all be wasted by the disease and dead. Think of your other children, they said, and finally Phopi Fatima yielded, and they left by airlift for Karachi.

Apaji listened for hours as Phopi talked about her only son. "He is not in Karachi, but maybe he went to Lahore."

"If he is alive, I am sure you will find him," Apaji said.

Phopi was furious. "You speak of life and death, you who have never lost a child. You do not know what it is to suffer."

Apaji rose to leave the little room where they sat cross-legged by the stove. Everyday they sat together from sunrise until the evening meal, interminably cleaning rice and grains. Phopi's fingers worked with amazing speed, darting from under the folds of her long black cape. She wore the burka constantly and only lifted off the hood when she was certain no man would barge in on her sanctity. Apaji worked much more slowly. She was unused to the work and often mistook shafts of rice for stones. Her eyes felt strained as she stared day in and day out at the little yellow and brown grains. Her knuckles were growing sore and tight against the skin that seemed to be wearing thin over her hands, as she ground hard little lentils into massala on the mortar and pestle. Phopi watched Apaji's progress with a slight smirk, all the while talking and praying for her son. Her speech was constructed almost totally out of aphorisms from the Koran. She rocked back and forth on her haunches continuously as she spoke, as if everything she said were an incantation. Apaji felt hypnotized by Phopi's incessant talk, and was relieved that she was rarely called upon to respond.

Every day, however, Phopi's tongue was becoming looser in her

266

head. Now that the first shynesses of respect were over and the children and Apaji had merged into the routine of the quarters, Phopi had more to say which Apaji did not wish to hear.

"You have always had it very good. Now you know what it is to cook for your children," Phopi sneered.

Apaji turned to leave the kitchen.

"Where are you going?" Phopi said. "There is too much work."

"I do not have to take your abuse," Apaji said, pulling the edge of her sari over her small head. Her masses of hair were gone, and the remaining she tucked into a bun at the nape of her neck. She had been cutting it shorter and shorter ever since they left Aligarh, and now it barely reached her shoulder blades.

"Abuse you." Phopi Fatima laughed. "I house you. I feed your children and care for Rehman Bhai like a nursemaid. If this be abuse, I would like to receive it."

"I did not think you felt you were offering us charity," said Apaji. She was close to tears, but she did not know if she should run from the room or sit down again by Phopi's side in acceptance of her position. She could not anger her husband's older sister. Not only would that be the greatest dishonor to Abu, there was no place else for them to go. Crowded as the quarters were, it was still so much superior to the little hovels of the city, the mud-brown huts of refugees, like dunghills dropped into the sewers they created. Here on Martin Road, the barracks were of cement and truly separated from one another by squarely defined plots of earth that at least gave the illusion of space. Even though the men and sons had to sleep on cots on the street, there was still a bedroom that adults could share on a rotating basis and a toilet and running water.

"It is only that relatives from my husband's side would like to come. Since there is no room, they have offered to pay gold as a contribution to the house. Otherwise none of us will have enough to eat."

Apaji felt speechless. There were no words to express the deep insult that Phopi had heaped upon her firstborn brother by the suggestion that they should pay their keep. Her lips quivered, and she nervously pushed the short wisps of hair up under the fall of her sari. Phopi did not look at her but continued to stare into the bowl of chick-peas she was washing.

"We have no gold to give," said Apaji. "But your brother is looking for work. Surely he will find something soon."

"Tell him to look for a house, too. There must be many available better than this. In Rehman Bhai's position he must know some high official who can give him the empty house of a Hindu. Why does he want to stay with us?"

Apaji did not answer, but stood hesitating on the doorsill of the kitchen.

"Perhaps we can agree to marry two of my daughters to Gappu and Gerrar. Such ties will bind us closer as a family than my husband is bound to his."

Apaji was shocked. "I can't do that. I have vowed not to marry my sons to their cousins, no matter what. It is not healthy or good."

Phopi threw her hands up into the air. "You may stick to your old ways, little sister, for as long as you can. You will continue to live on charity."

"It is something I cannot do. Your daughters are much older than Gappu and Gerrar. They would never agree."

"You think you are still a fine lady like your mother. You have always been too good to stay with us. Rehman Bhai married the daughter of the Darogaji; there should be someone better to take care of you. Have you no relatives here, sister? Your relatives were among the most important Muslims in India. Your mother used to wear gold on her feet when she went to the shit house."

"Your feelings for me and my family are not new to me, Big Sister," Apaji said. "Still I did not believe that you would let them so blind you at a time of all our greatest need."

Phopi kept looking down into the hard peas as she picked them from her lap and soaked them in the bowl of water at her side, but her dark face grew even darker with crimson. She and Dadi had always discussed Apaji behind her back, her haughty ways, her refusal to wear the burka even in the village, her unwillingness to cook or live in Dadi's house when Rehman Bhai was away, but they had never dared to criticize Apaji to her face.

"I will discuss what you say with my husband this evening," Apaji said and left Phopi sitting in the kitchen.

It was late afternoon, and there was no one else in the house. It was still too hot indoors under the tin roof, where the sun beat down so hard she could hear it crackling overhead. Clouds always passed high over Karachi, but they never stopped until they reached the Himalayas in the north. It was the best time of day to be outside, and her children had scattered in all directions. There was no water until six o'clock when it was rationed by the city and released in the pipes for an hour. Without water the house was of little use to her sons. They ate and slept outside. They played in the sand of the alleyways and roads. The only time they came indoors was to bathe or use the toilet, since that was the best thing in the house.

Apaji found Gappu sitting outside in the street with Moïd and Uncle Tariq, who appeared to be sleeping. The street was full of activity. Children played in the sand. An endless stream of hawkers navigated their pushcarts around the children and the beds where older boys and men were taking their naps. Women walked always in groups or at least in pairs, like a religious order of sisters, talking madly to each other from behind their veils.

Moïd was crying, and when he saw his mother, he buried his head in Gappu's lap so that she should not notice.

"Why is Moïd crying?" Apaji asked.

"It is nothing important," said Gappu, rising to give his mother a seat. She picked Moïd up and held him in her lap. She could feel his small body tense against her legs, and he kept his head lowered.

"Kya hai, Beta? What is it, son?" she asked.

Moïd pressed his lips tightly together and made a sputtering sound. "B-b-b," he strained. Apaji looked at Gappu for assistance.

"He wants to buy a biscuit from the biscuit wallah," Gappu explained.

"No," Moïd screamed. It was the only word he had no difficulty saying, but it was marked progress from the days of the trains when he could say nothing at all and had refused even to try.

Apaji wished she could figure out what vision was clogged in his mind, which sight or sound on their journey had locked the words in

Moïd's throat. She bent down and removed her sandals. "Take these," she said, offering the shoes to Moïd. "Perhaps the biscuit wallah will agree to exchange some biscuits for these shoes."

Gappu looked horrified, Tariq sat up on his charpoy. "You can't do that," he said.

"The shoes are no use to me here," said Apaji. "My feet are hardened, and shoes are just in my way."

"Moïd needs biscuits less than you need shoes. I can't let you give them away," Tariq protested.

Apaji was not interested in Tariq's opinion. She felt sorry indeed that the young bridegroom had lost everything he had so recently gained, but it was not his place to be with them in Karachi. Even if he was the baby brother of the family—the petted and spoiled young man who wore nothing but silk suits and studied Persian poetry and art—his place was with his wife in Nehtor, and not moping in Karachi like a shadow of his older sister and brother. She handed Gappu her sandals. "Take Moïd to the biscuit wallah and try to get enough for all the children," she ordered.

"You don't know how to handle your children," Tariq accused her. "It is insanity to give your shoes for a handful of biscuits."

Apaji ignored Tariq's outbursts. Her small hand modestly covered her mouth when she spoke to her brother-in-law, but she would not be ruled by him. "It is almost six o'clock," she reminded him. "Wouldn't you like to take a bath?"

Tariq shot up off his charpoy. "There is no need of a bath."

"Bhai, I think that you have not taken a bath in the entire two weeks we have been in Karachi," said Apaji. "Let me draw the water for you."

"How can I take a bath when the children are always running in and out? I cannot bathe without absolute privacy."

"No one is home now," Apaji said. "I will see that you are not disturbed."

Tariq ran his hands over his long black shervani which had grown gray with dust and rust-colored from sand. Beneath the jacket, his once soft muslin shirt was jagged with pulled threads and runs, and so entirely soiled that the stains merged together in one pasty mixture of old sweat and food. His fine beard and moustache which once had been his pride, always combed and waxed and contoured to the sculptured shape of his delicate bones, climbed wildly over his sallow cheeks that had begun to break out in acne. His face and bloodshot eyes gave him the over-all look of someone lit red with madness. He was embarrassed that Apaji spoke to him of his appearance, but of course, it was obvious. He must give a very strange impression, and people must think him odd. Indeed, he was odd, Tariq thought. Did they notice how he could never sleep at night and prowled about among the barracks when there was not even moonlight to mark his way? Did they notice that he sought out darkness and obscure corners to weep away the hours that pursued him with thoughts and remembrances of all he had loved? Did they realize that all the while he lay immobile on his charpoy he swore he would do anything at all to go back, plotted ways of decircumcising himself and sneaking across the border to the university and his books, to his new house, his motorcycle, and his bride? Had anyone seen him sneaking away during the day and hailing a Victoria, which no one else could afford, and just riding for hours through the city, looking at the fine old houses of the English and the Nawabs while he tried to decide what to do? Had they guessed what he had hidden under his shirt and in his trousers and shoes?

Instinctively Tariq hugged his body with his arms. He felt himself shudder and saw Apaji raise a hand toward him as if to comfort him. He shrank back with a twitch of his shoulder.

"I know I need a bath," he mumbled. "Do you promise me you will keep everyone away?"

"No one will disturb you, Tariq Bhai," Apaji promised.

"I will draw my own water then," said Tariq, and he backed away into the barracks, watching Apaji closely.

For a few precious minutes Apaji could sink alone onto a charpoy. She buried her face in her sari and blotted out the frantic movement of the pedestrians continually streaming past her and the sounds of the vegetable and peanut salesmen and clay-pot man calling out their discordant songs. Her sari smelled strongly of soap as she washed it every day, juggling the petticoat and cloth intermina-

271

bly into a dual wardrobe as she had observed so many peasant girls do. In retrospect she admired their artistry and grace. She felt herself clumsy and exposed, wearing one half of her dress while the other half hung in the alley to dry in the hot Karachi wind.

Since it was six o'clock, everyone in the quarter was heading toward home. Children who were too old to defecate in the street ran holding in their diarrhetic bowels which they had waited twenty-four hours to relieve. Women carried kicking babies inside to give them precious baths before the water gave out. If it were not for the bathrooms, they would all have been living like swine in a running sewer, Apaji thought with a shiver of horror. There were so many millions forced to do just that, the poorest and most unfortunate, who had lost homes in villages they had never really owned, who understood even less than her children what the anguish and suffering was all about.

Even in Nehtor where there was no modern plumbing, the bathroom was a clean and spotless place, swept everyday by bhangis, the Untouchables who lived beyond the town and whom they thought of only as sylphlike figures, beneath communication. She did not blame Tariq for his frenzied desire for privacy, the boy who had lived alone in his own flat in Delhi with a servant to tend to his needs and a cook to feed him. Life was a shock to them all, but Tariq seemed to be the worst. He was completely undone, not just his appearance, but deep within his concave body that shook and shivered and was wracked with pain. Apaji had heard him groaning late at night and seen him run from the house, holding his sides with pain. When she asked him, he said it was kidney pains, but Apaji felt it went deeper than that into his very soul. He said he was going to a mizar where there was a certain ring that would cure the pain. The only trouble, he said, was the fact that the Pir would not let him kiss the ring unless he paid a large sum of money. "I have no money," he would wail. "No money at all." Everyone in the family tried to let Tariq go his own way.

"Apaji, Apaji," Karim's voice called to her. He came leaping through the house, his arms waving in the air. Even Karim, Apaji

272

noticed, was growing taller than she. All her sons, it seemed, had inherited Abu's genes.

Karim threw his arms around his mother's shoulders, and buried his soft dark face against her ear. "Uncle Tariq is taking a bath," he whispered.

Apaji laughed and struggled to get loose from her son. "What is so odd about that?" she said.

Karim jumped in front of her and stooped at her feet, hugging her lap. "It is the first bath he has taken in two weeks. You can smell him a mile away. Raheel says he has lice."

"How would Raheel know a thing like that?" laughed Apaji, giving Karim's wrist a gentle slap.

"Raheel looked in Uncle's hat," said Karim, and he danced around the charpoy.

"Why are you so happy today?" asked Apaji.

"No reason. Just because Uncle Tariq is taking a bath."

Apaji was very happy that Karim seemed to be faring best of all her sons now that they had arrived in Karachi. It did not seem to matter what kind of a place they were living in as long as it was a home and it was theirs. Perhaps it was his age. Moïd at only five had been quietly traumatized back into babyhood. Gappu and Gerrar were adolescently sullen and morbid behind the young black growths of hair over their upper lips. Karim kept himself in high spirits and exceedingly busy. He explored the entire city from bazaars to wharves to the private houses along the broad boulevards, and reported everything to Apaji in the evening. "I am never returning to school," he had announced much to Abu's annoyance. "I am learning more this way," he had argued heatedly and went stamping out of the barracks.

Apaji smiled at Karim. "Just leave Uncle Tariq in peace," she warned her most rambunctious son.

The road was almost empty now since everyone had gone inside to take their daily baths and use the toilet. Raheel appeared around the corner of the house, holding Sara in her arms. "*Hsst*, Apaji," she called. "Come here."

"What is it?" Apaji asked, motioning Raheel to come forward. Piari and Mona trailed behind her, and she placed Sara in Apaji's lap.

"Uncle Tariq is taking a bath," Raheel whispered.

"Why are you whispering?" said Apaji. "We already know he is taking a bath. What is the matter with all of you?"

Raheel wrinkled her brow and seemed very concerned. "Gerrar has found something in Uncle Tariq's clothes."

"Oh, no," said Apaji, jumping up. "What are you doing in Uncle Tariq's clothes? I promised him he would not be disturbed. How did everyone get into the house?"

"We came in through the back, and we didn't go into his clothes," Raheel protested. "We were only waiting our turns for the bathroom, and his clothes fell off the hook, and something fell out."

"What is it?" asked Apaji.

"I can't tell you," said Raheel, and she burst into tears. "Come and see quickly."

Apaji rushed into the barracks, with Karim, Piari, Mona, and Raheel running after her. There was a great racket going on, with Gerrar pounding on the bathroom door and yelling that Uncle Tariq should come out and Tariq holding the door to the bathroom and sobbing.

"What is going on here?" Apaji pulled Tariq's pants out of Gerrar's hands, and a huge overstuffed money belt fell to the floor. They all stared at it horrified. Tariq continued to moan.

"See what he has been concealing from us," Gerrar hissed. "It's filled with jewels and money. A quarter of his wife's dowry must be in there."

"Ai Allah," said Apaji. She heard Tariq wailing behind the bathroom door. "Forgive me, sister. Forgive me," he cried.

"I don't think we should tell Abu," Apaji said to her children.

"I think he should pay us for all the food he has been taking from our mouths and the money he borrowed in Aligarh to get back to Nehtor," said Gerrar.

"You gave him the best bread while Abu ate potatoes," Raheel whimpered.

274

"No, no," said Apaji. "He is your father's youngest brother."

"Sister," Tariq pleaded from the bathroom. "Forgive me."

"Then when the going got tough, he left us in Aligarh and came to live off Phopi Fatima," Gerrar argued. "We should have no part of him."

Apaji was shocked. "Gerrar, he is your uncle. You must respect him."

"No," said Karim, joining the argument. He felt close to tears. This was the uncle who had taken him on his wedding horse, the uncle of chiffon and satin, rings and paintings. He could not bear to think that this uncle had cheated them so. "He stole from us," Karim lashed out. "I am telling Abu."

"It is better that you should not," Apaji advised. "Let Uncle come out and get his clothes."

They turned around and found Abu standing behind them in the room. His long body was bent and darkened with dirt and perspiration. The whole family gasped to see their father like that. They did not know what the body had been doing, but they would not ask. Obviously he had been doing something all afternoon that lengthened his face in fatigue and caused his shoulders to stoop further than they had the day before. They all decided right then and there not to tell Abu about Tariq's money belt. Apaji and the children faced him guiltily.

"What is this all about?" Rehman asked.

"It is nothing," they told him.

"What do you mean nothing? Why is Tariq hiding in the bathroom? Why is everyone all upset?"

The family stood with their lips sealed, looking at Rehman. He lunged toward Gerrar, who was holding the money belt behind his back.

"You don't have to tell me," Abu shouted. "I can see with my own eyes." He shook the belt loose from Gerrar's hands and spilled the contents out onto the floor. A tangle of gold jewelry, brooches, chains, rings, and coins clattered to the ground. Rehman screamed at the top of his voice. "You had all this gold. I fed my children less while you ate more. Come out of that bathroom immediately."

"No, Rehman Bhai," Tariq said in a trembling voice. "I will die in here first. Take the money. Please, I beg you."

"Open the door, and let us see your face," Rehman insisted.

Tariq opened the door a crack and peered out, concealing his wet naked body. His face was pale, and his cheeks were streaming tears. He had taken the jewelry his mother had given him. It was not as if it were stolen. He had not touched a single earring that belonged to his bride, but had left them all in the big new house in Delhi, abandoned in a wall safe, along with his books and paintings and the Lodhi Gardens where the house stood. The jewels he had brought were his own, given to him to wear over his wedding clothes. There were pins to fasten his pink chiffon turban to the gold-threaded gota that wrapped around his brow and the crowning headpiece which had hung over his forehead like a Japanese beaded curtain when he rode through the streets on his bridal horse in the gaslight.

Apaji and Raheel turned their backs, hiding their faces with eyes closed. Rehman pushed his face into the crack of the door that Tariq had opened.

"Why did you do this?" he asked his brother.

"These were jewels to be cherished, Bhai Rehman, not to be sold and bartered. They are works of art," Tariq cried. "They are heirlooms that have been in our family for generations. I took nothing that was new, nothing to sell—only these."

"What about the gold coins?" Rehman shouted.

Tariq flung wide his arms and fell to the wet cement floor of the bathroom, crouching at his brother's feet. "Take the coins. I prayed they could be saved to build a house. It is so important to have a house. Now you take them. Build your house. If we had spent the coins before, there would be nothing left to build a house."

"I am building four houses. My sons are my houses." Rehman kicked the jewels that lay scattered on the floor and threw the money belt at Tariq. "Keep your jewels. I am taking the family to Multan, where we will build our lives anew. There are things more important than houses."

He turned to Apaji and the children. "Come! We have nothing more to do here."

His family looked at him in surprise. It was the first mention Abu had ever made of Multan, and no one knew anything about it.

"Abu, must we leave Karachi?" Karim wailed. "Why do we have to go to Multan?"

Rehman did not answer. It was not something they could discuss. He knew that as soon as he had saved enough money working as a coolie, they would leave for Multan. He knew he could take Tariq's money and not have to work. They could even stay in Karachi and invest in a new business and build the house that Tariq dreamed of, but he felt that to take Tariq's money would be to put a curse of ill fortune on whatever he tried to do with it. From now on, Rehman vowed to himself, whatever I give my children will have to be the result of my own work and intelligence.

"The only thing I can promise you is that when we go, we will travel in a first-class compartment in the train. We will take no risks, and there will be no more hardship."

A calm settled over the house of Phopi Fatima on Martin Road. Phopi Fatima could no longer nag Apaji about work and money. Tariq guarded his jewels, but now he could take a daily bath without the anguish that when he disrobed, his secret would be discovered.

Gappu, Karim, and Gerrar passed the days wandering through the streets and alleys of the strange desert city. Everyday the tattered refugee huts of the poorest of the poor seemed to advance over the land and into the hills like a rapidly growing cancer, and they feared to think of what unknown thing awaited them in Multan.

Apaji told them that the important thing was to have faith in Abu. Gappu was willing to give him faith for one more time, one more promise of a safe journey and a home. The family was moving again, and no one was quite certain if this were a blessing or a new

277

misfortune. They did not ask Abu what date they would leave, but watched him come home each day at six o'clock to bathe the dust and grime from his face and limbs. Apaji washed and rewashed his tired pants and shirt and an old piece of cloth he now wore as a bandanna. In the morning he awakened with the first rays of sunlight to bathe his nostrils, his ears and feet delicately before his prayer. He used the water sparingly, which was reserved in buckets for daytime use when the rationed water in the pipes was still.

Gappu watched his father coming and going deep in fatigue. He barely glanced their way or spoke to them, and once Gappu found his father alone in a room talking to himself, Gappu looked at him with shock. Abu's spine curved into his shoulders. His neck seemed to sag under the heavy weight of his head, and his thick black hair was streaked through with gray. Gappu was frightened to find himself thinking, "Abu is old and the promises cannot be kept." Each time he saw Abu at the end of the day he was surprised by the pinched look of his eyes without his glasses, by his haggard skin and the tired shuffle of his gait. The man had been young only yesterday.

It was also a shock to Gappu when he looked at his brothers as they walked together through the city. They were stretching out of their clothes lengthwise, but fading into the cloth as their flesh shrank against their protruding ribs. Occasionally Gappu caught sight of himself reflected in a mirror in a shop or in a pane of glass, and he blinked quickly back at the image of the stranger that met him. He was no longer a child in that reflection, but a man who should begin to shave his upper lip, whose sideburns grew heavily down his cheeks and whose hair flew thick and unruly.

They walked aimlessly through the bazaar. They had lost the frantic need to learn the language of Sindh and the locations of various shops, and Gappu no longer led his brothers in reading aloud the shop signs in their new dialect. The houses of the central city were no longer something to aspire to and plan for, because they were heading north to Multan.

Gappu, Gerrar, and Karim spent the afternoons lying on charpoys in the street, watching the pedestrian traffic go by and discussing politics. They knew the trains in Pakistan were attacked just as the trains in India were, but no one dared to remember the visions they all tried to repress. There was news of riots still going on after almost two months, but Abu had gathered them around in the evening and promised they would not affect their train.

"How can he promise such a thing?" Karim said angrily to Gappu and Gerrar, but his brothers did not wish to discuss the trains.

"There is no way of defying Abu's edict," Gappu explained. He only prayed that their train would not be attacked in the darkness of night, stopped somewhere along a rolling field and sky, and that they would never have to hear again the screams of mothers and children or the pleas of men being castrated by knives.

"I've heard that in India Gandhiji is fasting for an end to the rioting," Gerrar tried to reassure them.

"To hell with Mr. Gandhi and India," said Gappu, affecting the colloquial English speech of Mohammed Ali Jinnah which had become popular. "In Pakistan there will not be killing. Faith, Unity, and Discipline—those are the words of the father of our country."

"On Abu's birthday," Gerrar said. "I am sure there will be peace."

Abu's birthday was approaching fast. Karim was surprised. He had not realized that it was only a week away, for there had been no preparations, no vats of sweetmeats cooking or presents hidden in Apaji's closet. Usually the tailor came weeks in advance to measure everyone for new clothes. Abu's birthday was almost as big a celebration as the Muslim high holy day of Id. Abu was born on the new moon of the month of Ziquaad. It was at the end of the month of feasting for Muslims, but this year there had been no Id. It was as if Ramadan, the month of fasting and atonement had never come to an end. Abu's birthday seemed that much more important, and in a very real way the deaths and sorrows of the last month for India would soon have to come to an end. It was impossible to think that so many millions could be forced to live in deprivation forever. If this had been a curse on them for the cruelties of their country, the rising moon of the new month would signal the end of their atonement.

They had not seen the moon since the ship voyage when it was just passing its fullness, but in a few days, the children would take up a vigil, watching for it at sunset, straining their eyes to catch the pale outline of crescent. That would be the time to run to Apaji and tell her the old month was over, and it was time to begin the feasting. They had seen the moon rise in many different settings. Abu's birthday, like all important occasions, rotated from season to season, blessing each time of year with its festivities, since the Muslim calendar had only twenty-nine or thirty days to every month. Sometimes his birthday was in the spring, and they watched the moon rise over the salt lakes of Jaipur. The past few years it had been in the summer, when they were all in Nehtor, and the entire extended family gathered in Dadi's house. In Karachi the September moon of Ziquaad would rise to the exact position that was pictured on the flag of Pakistan, cradling a star in its shape, and it would have to bring peace. No one mentioned the usual festivities, the gifts, and the preparations. If peace came, that would be gift enough.

Every afternoon the postman came to Martin Road, lugging huge sacks of mail across the wheels and handlebars of his bicycle. Several people were always waiting for him at the corner of the road, tense with excitement, hoping for news of someone feared dead, and anxious that the postman not forget their names and new addresses. Mothers and grandmothers with babies in their arms squatted in the dusty road, gossiping and calling to their children, who chased each other around the houses and played with stones. They kept cupping their hands over their eyes to look into the sinking sun that seemed to be hanging parallel to the road. As soon as the postman appeared, wobbling along the rutted road on his heavy black bicycle, the women jumped to their feet and besieged him with a hundred questions. He had to get off and push the bicycle because they left him no room to keep his precarious balance.

"I promise you I won't forget to come to your house," he said to each of the women. "But I don't think there is anything for you today."

Gappu raised himself on one elbow on the charpoy. This afternoon the postman seemed to be heading directly toward Phopi Fatima's house, and he held up his hand in greeting. The postman never stopped at their barracks, although Phopi had begged him a hundred times to bring her a letter from her son, as if he had the power to create as well as to deliver news. Gappu thought it impossible for anyone to know where his family was, but the postman stopped in front of his charpoy and held out a letter.

"There is an envelope from America which I think might be for your aunt. I can read the word Syeda, and you are the only Syeds I know of on Martin Road. Can you read English?" he asked.

Gappu swung his legs over the side of the charpoy and grabbed the letter. Karim and Gerrar leaped up and pressed against him to read over his shoulders, and all the women in the road looked curiously on.

"It is for Phopi Fatima," Gappu shouted. "Get Phopi. Hurry! Run!"

Karim and Gerrar ran into the house and returned pulling Phopi Fatima by her arm. Apaji and all their sisters and cousins and Moïd came running after her. Phopi looked as if she were about to swoon, and she did not bother to pull her burka over her head as Gerrar supported her and Gappu handed her the letter.

"My God, my God! It is from my son. I know it is from my son," she gasped, holding her hand against her ample bosom, which was heaving for breath, and she covered the envelope with kisses. She was shaking from head to foot, and Gappu had to wrench the letter out of her hand in order to read it to her. The women were surrounding them on every side, trying to get a look at the letter from America with its big Red Cross stamp, and in the center of the crowd the postman was beaming as if he were a messenger from God. Phopi shrieked as Gappu ripped the envelope open and kept touching the paper as he tried to unfold it and read.

"It *is* from your son, Phopi Fatima," Gappu said.

"Ai Allah," Phopi breathed, and Apaji cleared a place for her on the charpoy because she could no longer stand. Gappu sat down beside her and began to read.

"Blessed mother, Assalaam Aleicum and congratulations on your arrival in Pakistan. It is I, your son Achan. Thank God, you are safe."

Phopi burst into tears and tried to take the letter to kiss it again, but Apaji rubbed her shoulders and forehead and tried to keep her calm. Gappu continued to read: "I cannot tell you all the details of how I arrived in America until we are together again, but when we were separated in Delhi, I took the wrong lorry and arrived at the airport. I wanted to come back for you, but the airlift for Karachi was leaving, and I had to decide very quickly what to do. I could not get back to Delhi, and I thought I could help you better from Karachi."

Phopi Fatima jumped up from the charpoy. "You see how good my Achan is. You see how he always thinks of me. Thank God for such a son!"

All the women nodded their heads in agreement and began muttering among themselves. Gappu smiled at his aunt, who reached out for his hand and held it against her cheek.

"As soon as I arrived in Karachi, I looked for a job, and took an examination for a post in the foreign service. Among thousands of others, I was selected, and I have been made secretary to an important attaché."

"Ah, my son, my son," Phopi Fatima cried, still sobbing and shaking all over.

"I have learned through the Red Cross of your address and see that my prayers for your safety have been answered. I pray for my father and my sisters and salaam my uncles and my aunt and my cousins. Soon I will send money. If any of my cousins would like to come to America, now is the time. I will take care of them. Pray for your son and for peace. Your loving son, Achan."

Gappu relinquished the letter to his aunt, who pressed it against her face and lips, held it outstretched to the sky and again against her eyes and cheeks and bosom, caressing it and streaking it with her tears. The letter was passed from hand to hand, and all the women ook turns examining the fine Urdu script, which half of them could not read, and praising the stationery, the stamp, and most of all, Phopi Fatima for having a son in America.

Karim and Gerrar reread the letter together, and then Raheel read it aloud again to Phopi Fatima. It seemed as if the whole street had come to listen to the letter and celebrate the news with them. Phopi Fatima was kissing Apaji's hands and all her daughters, and everyone was hugging her and giving her their blessings. It was truly a gift for Abu's birthday and an end to the month of mourning.

The children waited for Abu to rise on the morning of his birthday. He had been up at sunrise all week and disappeared into the city without breakfast before the rest of the family began to stir. It was not like other birthdays when everyone would be up before dawn to get new clothes from Apaji to go to the mosque and exchange gifts with relatives and neighbors, who always descended on them and greeted them with handshakes and bear hugs. There was no fresh paan, wrapped in real silver leaf, piled high on filigree trays, or the smell of rich butter simmering on the stoves to make sweetmeats and curries, and no two and a half pound sacks of grain waiting in the living room for each person to distribute to the poor. But it was the first time that Abu had slept late, and everyone was happy. Abu was always very gay on his birthday. He would laugh continuously and give ten times more presents to his children than he received. The children made a game of asking for extra treats and money. All day they would try to find out who got the most, and then go back to Abu and demand an equal share.

Abu was smiling in his sleep as if sleep were the greatest gift he could ask for. No one dreamed of disturbing him, and the children tiptoed around the barracks, smiling at each other and whispering. "Congratulations on Abu's birthday. At least, we are alive." They reminded each other, as Dadi always did, that Abu had been born after seven years of infertility. Gappu did not mention the motorcycle he had been promised on the last birthday, or Raheel, the ten extra rupees Abu always gave her, which no one ever found out about, and Gerrar did not speak of Nehtor and the year before, when he had kissed Jilla for the first time and promised to come back every year no matter where he was or how old he grew.

Apaji said her prayers all morning. She was only required to kneel thirty-four times, but it seemed as if she was praying continuously, bowing and prostrating as if she were transfixed. She began with prayers for her children and for Abu, and then went on to pray for Nani and Dadi in Nehtor, and for her dead father and her brothers and their wives and their children, and for Phopi Fatima and her son in America, and for all Abu's relatives. Her chanting voice rose so loud that finally Abu was awakened. He came bounding out into the sunlight, calling the children.

"How long did I sleep?" he shouted. "Why didn't someone awaken me?"

"Abu, you slept so peacefully," Raheel said, curling against his shoulder. "You can say seven prayers next year and make atonement."

"It is not prayer I'm worried about. We are leaving today for Multan. Look! Here are the train tickets. It was supposed to be a surprise. They are for first class."

The children grabbed the tickets out of his hand and danced in the street, cheering so loudly that all the passersby stopped to look at them.

"The tickets were not easy to get," he laughed. "I'm glad you appreciate them."

"Oh, Abu, were they very expensive?" Raheel gasped.

"Not too bad," he said. "The problem was finding a legitimate ticket agent. The black market for tickets is so big that there are many people disguised as *titis* selling bogus seats. Now we must go quickly. Gather up your things."

Everyone started to run around the house and yard, collecting old pieces of cloth and pillows, pots and pans they had saved and accumulated, and the few precious possessions like Apaji's tikka and Dadi's Koran, and some trinkets that still remained, like the silver flower from Abu's wedding veil—one of hundreds—which Apaji had managed to keep pinned to her sari. They moved so fast that they barely remembered to salaam Phopi Fatima and Uncle Tariq and their cousins, who had burst into tears and were trying to kiss them all good-bye.

The railroad station was jammed with people. Families were camped along the platforms and in the terminal under old advertisements for movies and a variety of British goods. The inevitable refugee shacks sat shoulder to shoulder beside the tracks and spilled over into the road among the waiting victorias and animal carts. It was as if the people had come as far as they could go and did not have the energy to board another train.

The slow third-class awami, or people's express, was filled to overflowing and ready to pull out of Karachi. People sat everywhere, in the doors and on the floors of the cars and on every inch of roof, regardless of the fact that injuries and mangling from falls were a daily occurrence. It was difficult to see the train through all the bodies swarming over it. Smoke chortled out of the engine, and suddenly the train gave a lurch. All the people pitched forward calling out, "Oh-ho" and "Hai Allah."

The faster "one up" train with first-class compartments was waiting dark and quiet on the outer track. As the awami express pulled out of the station, the doors to the "one up" were dropped open by shouting *titis* in dirty red and white uniforms, and the crowd of people on the platforms broke loose and started running for the compartments. Already a family had lodged itself inside the compartment that Rehman had reserved. At least fifteen women and children were crowded into the space that was meant for only eight, and they closed the window and bolted the door. Rehman banged on the door and waved his ticket over his head.

"That is my compartment," he shouted. "Come out of there immediately, or I will have you arrested."

One of the women raised the window and shouted back, "We are not coming out. We are alone and cannot ride on the roof."

Rehman looked around in desperation. The children looked pale and nervous. "What can we do, Abu?" Gappu asked.

There were policemen everywhere. They ran from car to car, waving their sticks and pulling people out of the cars through the windows and off the roof. Rehman grabbed an officer, who was running past, by the sleeve. "Bhai," he said, "I have tickets for this compartment, but these squatters won't let us in."

The officer stopped and examined the tickets closely. There were many pages stapled together for each person, including Sara, because Rehman wanted to be sure that this time there would be no mistakes as there had been on the ship. The officer read each page carefully with all its stamps and signatures. He snapped upright and handed the tickets back. "Ji Hazoor. Yes, sir. I will have them out in no time."

Gappu sighed with relief that Abu had purchased the right tickets. His promise was good. They really would travel first class, and not among the pushing shouting mass of refugees sprawled along the rooftops, under the desert sun, or closeted into a breathless third-class car like cattle.

The officer raised his pistol and banged with it against the door. The women raised their windows again and started to beg and plead.

"Oh, mother," they called to Apaji. "If we do not make it to Lahore, our brothers will give us up for dead."

"You will have to ride in another compartment. This one is reserved," the officer shouted through the window.

Apaji hung her head as the women climbed down from the compartment, for it was Abu's birthday when everyone in their family traditionally gave two and a half pounds of grain to the poor. In Nehtor her father had always given cartloads away on his birthday, in the name of his vast family, legitimate and illegitimate. No one ever knew exactly whose names were represented, but the poor came from miles around and were able to survive for half a year on the food he gave. Now she was giving nothing to the poor and was also depriving the terrified women and their children of such a trifle as a train compartment. Not even seven times seven the amount of grain they were supposed to give the next year would atone for the shame she felt. She looked at Abu with her protests frozen on her lips.

"This day shall curse you," the oldest woman hissed in Apaji's face as she gathered up her skirts and jumped from the train into the crowd on the platform.

Apaji looked straight ahead as the police officer escorted them into the vacated compartment, but the curses of the women stung her face like a slap. She vowed she would pray throughout the entire journey, for the ill wishes of the women lingered in the air and on the green-plush upholstered seats. For as long as Abu had rented the seats, the compartment was theirs, and she felt she had turned hungry guests out of her home.

Once they had installed the luggage under the seats and in the overhead racks, and the children arranged themselves in all six seats and the upper berths as well, the officer took Abu into the corridor and gave him instructions.

"The train may stop between stations," he said. "These refugees cannot be controlled, and they continuously pull the emergency cord if they want to get off. Sometimes they let other passengers on in a prearranged spot. A whole village will come. Do not open your doors or windows under any circumstances—not even for a minute."

Rehman nodded his head.

"There may be Hindus and Sikhs who are trying to reach India. Many still remain in Punjab, and chances are there will be a riot in Serghoda, since that is the last point for fleeing into India. If you keep yourselves locked inside, you will be safe. Even if they say they are Muslims and pray to God, do not open the door. Otherwise, there will not be enough officers to protect you. Do you have a gun?"

Rehman nodded.

"Then do not worry, Bhai. Most of these are harmless refugees, looking for a home. Ai Allah, but they would have been better off in India." The officer sighed, leaning against the bars of the open window. He turned around and lowered the double screen and wooden shutter that the British had built into the trains years ago for their own protection.

"Keep them locked like this, Bhai Sahib, especially in a station. Even while you are in Karachi."

"Thank you," Rehman said and then remembered the officer

would be expecting his baksheesh. He fished a rupee note from the small remaining supply in his pocket, and the officer disappeared.

For several hours the train stood in Karachi, awaiting its scheduled time of departure. Then there was delay after delay, and much shouting and arguing could be heard outside. Still Rehman would not allow anyone to open the window even a crack to see what was going on. Since the electricity had not yet been turned on, they could not use the fans, and the children were tired and restless in the cramped stuffy compartment that was meant to seat six and sleep four.

Occasionally a fist would pound on the bolted door, and voices would plead with them, proud articulate voices. "I have been here three months, and I have space in this compartment. My wife made it to Lahore. I have heard from my brother. She thinks I am dead, but she is living in the waiting room to see if I will arrive."

"Khuda ke waste. Forgive us," Rehman cried back.

"She will never find me. I have heart trouble."

"Forgive us," Rehman repeated.

"Rem karo. I will, I will."

As the train began to glide forward, one voice that sounded familiar pierced through the shuttered windows. "Bhai Rehman, where are you?"

Rehman threw open the window and leaned out. He saw Tariq running along with the first-class compartments, all of which were shuttered like their own. Rehman leaned all the way out of the window and waved.

"Bhai, where are you? Don't leave me. Take me with you," Tariq cried, but his voice had become distant, and his cry was the last to be drowned by the moving train.

The train passed through the desert, speeding through the whooshing and twirling sands that baked in fleeting mirages along the horizon of hills. On both sides of the railroad track, an endless procession of humanity was walking barefoot to Lahore. Tall women and young girls in long orange peasant skirts and violet dopattas, half covering their faces, balanced huge bundles on their heads and clay pots and babies on their hips. The men, all in flowing white, padded continuously forward with tin cases atop their vibrantly colored turbans. It was impossible to tell if they were Muslims arriving or Sikhs departing—emptying out their villages to go to Lahore, city of the holy Sikh Guru, and then across to the Indian side of Punjab. They streamed by without glancing at the train that sped along, as if too many trains had passed and they had been walking for days.

Most of the children were asleep. The overhead berths had been lowered on their chains over the bottom seats, and Piari, Moïd, and Mona lay curled up together on one of the planks. Karim had the opposite berth all to himself, since Raheel, Gappu, and Gerrar preferred to sit below with Apaji and Abu like adults. Karim leaned over so he could see out the window, wishing there was some way he could have the books he had left behind in Aligarh. Geography and History were his favorite subjects. Even if he studied nothing else, he knew all about India and the land and the British Empire. Karim wanted to look on his maps for Multan and the state of Punjab, land of the tall lassy-drinking Sikh people, and their capital Lahore with the broad mosques of sandstone and the golden steeple of the Gurdwara, second holiest shrine of the Sikh faith. The only thing Karim knew about Multan was that they made Multanni there, the clay that every schoolboy in India used as his slate. Karim vowed he would not go to school unless he was allowed to study only Geography. Abu bribed the teachers so that Gerrar would pass his difficult subjects. Karim decided he would also have his own room, no matter what. It would be the room farthest away from the others, preferably a smaller room on some staircase.

Karim could see his father sleeping with his head against the frame of the open window. Abu, the tall man, the dark man, the brave man, who wore Italian shoes and suits with plus-fours when he took them hunting, the lucky man who had eight children born and living, was limp with exhaustion. The dust and charcoal were settling in the curls of his thick graying head. His stomach was sagging, and for the first time since they left Aligarh, he was snoring.

Karim had always despised Abu's snoring, but now it seemed like a beautiful sound. Abu was half sitting in his seat and half lying against the window and outer door, and the ivory sheath that concealed his pistol was protruding slightly from his clasped hands. New glasses were balanced on his nose, too small for his big long face.

Across from Abu, Apaji repeated her prayers as she had promised. All through the evening when they awoke to eat the bread and dal that Abu had brought, and through the night when they slept again, Apaji prayed, as the train tooled by station after station in the darkness, and stopped only to quench its thirst under great wooden tanks and to eliminate its belch of steam.

It was a sight to behold. There was the rising sun, and the children could still hear Apaji praying as they rubbed the sleep from their eyes and stretched their cramped limbs. Apaji looked at her children with embarrassment. "I will just finish with the shortest prayer of morning," she told them.

Karim climbed over Gappu, who had joined him during the night on the upper berth, and sat in front of his mother. The land had changed during the night from the rough desert of Sindh to the low-lying fields of Punjab, green with crops and the waters of canals. Footpaths wound everywhere in the morning shadows. There was a cool breeze coming through the massive banyan and peepul trees and over brown fields just emptied of their biannual cotton crop.

The train was pulling into a small country station. There seemed to be no reason to stop. Abu got up to close the shutters, but he noticed that an old man had jumped onto the running board with a fluttering of his clothes and was holding onto the train for dear life.

"Don't turn me away," he cried, looking through the window. Abu tried to close the shutters, but he did not want to crush the old man's fingers, which curled over the edge.

"We must let him in," Apaji cried, touching her husband's arm. "Please! We have not much further to travel."

All the children joined in a chorus to let the old man in. Abu knew if he opened the door the streams of people moving past them would flood into the compartment. As soon as he pushed back the iron bolts, they did just that. Women and men carrying their belongings, children and toddlers dragging infants, overran the small room and the corridor until there wasn't an inch of space for a single other body.

The overcrowded compartment meant that there were as many newspapers as there were people. All the newcomers had stories to tell, speaking in Punjabi which was difficult to understand. It seemed as if they were speaking the same language, until suddenly they were lost in the colloquialisms of the new dialect. Still, everyone understood the essential things—the stories repeated over and over again about sons who were lost and children who were murdered. Rehman did not want his children subjected to more news about killing and bloodshed, and he tried to change the subject, but everyone kept talking.

"There is rioting in Bahawalpur," the old man said. "We could not reach Lahore if you had not let us into the compartment."

"There has been rioting for several days," another man added. "Many trains are being hijacked to India, and Jinnah has ordered the stopping of all refugee trains before the border. I do not know how they will go across, but it will be best to keep all the windows locked in Bahawalpur."

The children shrank into the depths of the upper berths. Below them, the people in their compartment were sitting on the floor and standing shoulder to shoulder in the hall.

Karim kept saying, "I want to go back to Dadi in India."

"Keep quiet," Gappu warned him. "It is not nice to say that in Pakistan."

"Maybe the train won't stop in Bahawalpur. Maybe they will skip the station," said Raheel, but nothing like that seemed possible.

The hot sun of Punjab, from which the only respite was a tall glass of lassy, was pounding down on the train roof with its cloth of bodies stretched from one end to the other. The mothers on the roof were trying to shield their childrens' heads with their dopattas and their eyes from the piles of bodies that lay decomposing in rows along the approach to Bahawalpur. They sat like monkeys holding their brood, the hot wind scorching their faces. In the distance was

291

the reflection of fire, like the fires of Aligarh that had gutted their neighbor's house, fire within the fire of the day, and no residents were about, except merrymakers and looters.

Abu slammed the shutters closed, but not before the children had seen the two silent trains parked along the track, on either side of their own train, and the piles and piles of bodies, so that it was hard to figure out which hand belonged to which arm, and the deep red gashes in the stripped and torn figures, which seemed to be lying in the deepest sleep. Abu pretended no one had seen, but the people all nodded Yes with their heads. In the flash before the window was closed, they saw the bodies of the men stripped to disclose their swollen genitals which they recently cut in order to pass as Muslims, but the gesture had not worked. The Muslim killers had swept down upon the trains and ripped the clothes with their swords and found the new telltale circumcisions and done away with them. The police who had just been sent by Jinnah to guard Bahawalpur were running back and forth between the trains like a confused flock of birds.

"Who did the killing?" Gappu demanded from his father.

"Oh, the same ones who are doing it in our villages in Serghoda," said the old man casually. "One village kills another, and there are roving bands."

"Where are they?" shouted Gappu. "I want to see who they are."

"They are right outside," the old man said. "Where else would they be? If you open the window, you will see them cleaning the blood from their swords in the canal. It is like that everyday from town to town and village to village."

The children shuddered together and closed their eyes.

"Only this should be the end. There are no more Hindus and Sikhs left in the villages. They have been routed out one by one, picked off, and gutted by fire. The Muslims are already saying they should not have let them go. Hindu Lala-ji is gone, and there is no one to lend them money. Sikh Sardarji has left his small shops, and the farmers cannot find trucks to take their produce to Lahore. After this, there is no more cause for riots. You will see. It is the end. We have purged Pakistan of our brothers. Their blood is dripping on our heads."

The train did not come to a full stop in Bahawalpur, and quickly regained speed as it withdrew from the station, and the images everyone had seen fleetingly mirrored there like the recollection of a dream. There was no more opening of the window, not even as the train sped through the open fields, whistling every minute to clear the track of whatever blocked them. No one knew if it was the usual animals—herds of goats and camels—or people fleeing and half dead. They did not look outside until they hard the *titi* call Multan.

The station was quiet in the heat of the afternoon. The air wafting in from the countryside was heavy with the odor of soil and growing things.

Multan was so small that one could easily see the surrounding fields from the station at the edge of the city. Gaily colored tongas drawn by miniature horses were the fastest mode of transportation. They stood listlessly on the streets and roads, poised on alternating feet, their noses buried deep in feed bags, waiting for the lazy commerce of the town to hire them.

Very few people got off the train at Multan, since Lahore was the main destination. Rehman blinked in the first blast of white sunlight and drank in the heady smells of animals and moist fertilized fields as he unfolded his cramped limbs. He immediately found a coolie to lead them to a place to sleep. There were two choices, he learned. Since all the Hindus had been chased from Multan weeks ago, empty houses were plentiful, and Rehman could have his pick. Otherwise, many merchants were renting vacant rooms over their newly acquired stores, since business was almost at a standstill. Supplies were meager, and few people had enough money to purchase anything other than food.

The coolie offered to lead the family to a fine house. He looked

Rehman and Apaji and the children up and down, and decided that even though their clothes were ragged, they had seen better days and would have no problem claiming a Hindu's house from the municipal inspector.

"Let me show you an excellent house, Sahib. One on the banks of the canal with its own deep well that produces the coldest water. There is even a flush toilet." The coolie raised both hands benignly to his chest. "I do not even ask money for the information. A man like you, Sahib, will remember me when the time is right."

Rehman was pleased that there were so many houses available he could actually pick and choose. He beamed at his children who clamored to go. The coolie was so well fed and tall, the air so fertile and shining, the fields and animals of Punjab so clean and overstuffed, it was like Nehtor, like home.

Only Apaji held back, her sari concealing most of her face, which was trembling at the thought of taking a Hindu house. Rehman peered at her over the heads of the children. "What is the matter?" he asked her sternly.

Apaji lowered her head and cooed at Sara, who was in the cradle of her arm, in an effort to look indifferent.

"Do you have something to say, bride?"

"No," Apaji said. "We will go where you say."

The children cheered and pushed Abu forward to take them to a real house. Apaji trailed hesitantly behind them. The coolie first led them to a house close to the station. It was ringed off by a brick wall from the street of shabby shops and two-story municipal buildings. The iron gate was slightly open, as if someone had just gone out for a walk, but there was no stirring or sounds of life in the neat garden behind the wall, with its rows of unwatered shrubs and grass just beginning to burn brown and spotted on either side of the cobblestone walk. Hundreds of tiny sparrows hopped gingerly about, as if for many days they had been undisturbed in their pecking search for insects and worms. As soon as the family entered, they fluttered to a large banyan tree beside the house.

Several lawn chairs and a charpoy lay scattered about the lawn, and clay pots stood tipped here and there against a water faucet.

Apaji felt they were intruding on more than a house. It was as if the family still lingered there, watching her as she walked among their things to the little altar beside the door. Dried offerings of Prashad—brown flower petals and leaves—still lay in the tray held by the god Hunaman's monkey hands within the miniature pagoda-shaped temple. A bowl of water, used to wash during prayers, was filled with fine sand that blew in from the desert beyond the fields.

Apaji stepped aside in front of the sacred statue. It forbade her to enter the house. Even though Muslims were told to despise images and they prayed Allah ho Akbar, God is One, five times a day, Hunaman was still a god, a god of hundreds of millions, and not to be disrespected. Apaji's own stepmother, Darogaji's second wife, was a Hindu and had taught her the stories of the gods. Bhagwan and Allah—they all meant the same thing. She watched the children dance ahead of her, ringing the tinkling votive bell above the door. They went running in and out of the house and across the grass, wild with excitement, and Apaji tried to close her ears to their cries of playing which she had not heard in so long.

Karim ran outside, waving his arms. "Apaji, come inside and see what we have found." He dragged his mother by her sari into the large front sitting room. A carpet on the floor was slightly frayed from much use. The chairs and pillows looked sat in, and a hookah perched on a small brass stool was partially filled with burned tobacco. Karim pulled her forward through the house and out into the inner courtyard where Rehman was examining a row of cactuses in clay pots. A cow was tied to a pole and had eaten all the grass she could reach and had denuded a nearby bush of leaves. She was mooing with hunger, and Moïd and Mona and Piari were gathering large handfuls of leaves for the cow to eat.

Rehman saw Apaji and smiled at her. "Well, what do you think?"

Apaji burst into tears. "I can't stay here," she cried, and she gathered up her skirts and ran through the house. Rehman and the children ran after her into the front garden where the coolie was waiting for their decision.

"We must stay here. Why can't we stay here?" they clamored.

"It is a very good house," Rehman said.

"It is the best house," said Gappu. "We must live here."

Raheel started to shout at Apaji. "You wouldn't prevent us from living here. You couldn't. Not after all you have put us through already."

"Quiet. You cannot talk to your mother like that," Rehman boomed. "All of you be quiet."

Apaji sank to the grass. "I know you cannot forgive me, but we will not live in this house." She sobbed and sobbed into her sari. "The linens are still untouched on the beds, the closets are filled with clothes and pots for cooking. In the kitchen are sacks of grains and spices and vegetables half eaten. I am not going to move into this house. I do not want to inherit someone else's pain."

"We want it anyway," said Raheel.

"It is ours by right," Gappu said.

Apaji looked at Abu. "We are entitled to the house legally," Rehman added, but he knew his wife had to prevail. She was adamant.

"This house was left in misery as we left our house in Aligarh. I want no part of it. Only take the cow. It needs feeding."

"If we cannot have the Hindu house," Gappu said, "I am going back to India. I will leave right away and go with all the Hindu refugees over the border."

"Oh, no," Apaji cried. "Do you not see? There are eight of you. I will help you to have better than this house, but we cannot begin by taking the house and land of someone else or a curse will be on us. I want no more curses."

The children glared at her. Even the coolie seemed disgusted as he leaned against the iron gate, chewing paan. He spat as she glanced at him.

"Tell Apaji that we are taking the house," Raheel pleaded with her father.

"I cannot go against your mother's wishes. She comes first," he said. "We will find a better house. You sons are my four houses. She is right. We cannot sleep in the bed of those who by the stroke of the pen and the creation of this country might not be alive. If they are alive, the family might come back and throw us out as squatters when all this insanity is over. We cannot take the house."

The children accepted their defeat in shock. They could not believe that both Abu and Apaji would desert them and be united against them in something they wanted so much. They followed their parents, tight-lipped, out of the garden.

On the street the coolie scratched his neck under his turban. "Sahib, you wish to see more houses?" he inquired. "If Memsahib is afraid the Hindus will come back, I know a better house where the family was all slaughtered—the one by the canal."

Rehman shook his head. "Show us some rooms to let. We will take a house when we can pay for it."

The coolie sauntered across the street to a small shop that opened onto the sidewalk. A wiry little shopkeeper, dressed in faded black cloth from the tip of his turban to his bare feet, sat hunkered on the wooden floor. He peered at them sideways. There appeared to be no merchandise in the shop other than a few tins of raw sugar, some sacks of flour, and knickknacks stolen from the empty houses. The merchant folded and unfolded his idle hands continuously.

When the coolie asked for rooms, the shopkeeper's mouth cracked into a thin toothless smile, and a glob of greenish-red paan juice gurgled on his lip like blood.

"See for yourself if you want it," he lisped, pointing to a flight of stairs that led from the shop to a small apartment on the second story of the brown brick structure.

Raheel's face went white to think of having to walk past the leering creature in the shop everyday, up the pitch-dark stairs that smelled of urine, and calling the four rooms home. Two tiny cubicles opened onto a rooftop courtyard that served as a kitchen. On the other side were two more rooms and a bathroom with a crouch-style toilet.

"It's unbearable. Unthinkable," Raheel complained, touching gingerly the dusty walls.

"That's enough," Rehman barked at her. "It will do for a few weeks that is all."

Raheel vowed silently that she would never forgive Apaji for turning down the Hindu house. Through the shuttered windows she could see the Hindu house that should have been theirs. Over the surrounding wall, its white brick facade was bathed in sunlight that underscored the brown shoddiness of their new apartment.

Apaji tried to enfold Raheel in her arms, but Raheel jerked her shoulders away. "How long are you going to make us wait?" she shouted. "First, you make us leave India and sit in filthy trains and beg for food like wretched street people. You take us to city after city and make us live like foundlings in places we are not wanted. Now when we finally find a house, you will not let us live in it. The smart ones never left India."

She turned on Abu, flinging her hands down at her sides and stamping her small foot under the folds of her cotton skirt. "You are ruled by women and silly stories," she accused.

Rehman and Apaji looked at their daughter in mute amazement. Her loving nature seemed torn to threads like the thin dopatta she wore over her head and draping her narrow shoulders and heaving chest. Gappu grabbed her by the hand. He felt the cuts and abrasions scored across the little palm and knuckles. "I am right, Gappu. Why don't you say something?" she pleaded with him.

"All right. I say that we must give Abu another chance. Let him build a business and a house. He says he will send us to school. We will have again all the things we left behind in Aligarh and Nehtor. We are staying in Multan. There will be no more moving."

"I've heard that before," said Raheel. "Even you abandon me."

Abu threw up his hands. "All you think about are your dresses and your trinkets. Do you not thank God that you are alive?" He looked around the dark little sitting room with its dilapidated armchairs and cold tile floor, at his other children who were sitting cross-legged on the floor. They stared blankly back at him. "What do the rest of you have to say?" he boomed.

Gerrar hung his head. "Show us God, Abu. I think God has left the earth."

"Not the earth, but your minds. Are you my children?" he asked.

Apaji touched softly the sleeve of his shirt. "It is not fair, Abu.

They have been so brave, so good. They are right to be angry and impatient with me. We ask too much of them, but we do not consult them when we make decisions."

"Since when does a father consult his children?" he complained, but the answer was clear—since children were forced to see the things of adults, since they learned that life did not always bring them platters of food and chests of clothes, that sometimes bodies were protected only by a single piece of cloth and that nourishment was whatever one's fist could scoop up off the ground and shove into one's mouth, that even the rich and powerful sometimes learned hunger and fear, and that the poor inherit the earth. Fathers consulted children when they learned that death is sudden and unremitting.

"All right. We will make our next decisions by democratic vote."

"You mean when we move again, we will all decide?" said Karim, jumping up off the floor. "We can vote on the house and the school and everything?"

"We will even vote on my business," Rehman conceded. "The whole family will decide. Piari and Moïd will have one vote between them, and Apaji must have two because she is carrying Sara. It will be absolutely parliamentary."

"But you will be the prime minister," said Karim, happily joining in the game.

"Yes, but I want no unfair politicking among the younger children. Piari and Moïd and Mona will vote as they see fit, and bribes will be punishable. We will have no more fighting. Only discussion."

Piari and Moïd started dancing around the room because they were included in the game, too, and Mona ran timidly after them.

Rehman looked at Gappu for approval. "There are many issues to discuss. Will you draw up an agenda?"

Gappu smiled. "When will the first meeting be?"

"Tonight," said Abu, clapping his hands. "Now I want tea. Bring me my tea."

Apaji dragged her bundle of pots and utensils across the floor and out onto the small square rooftop courtyard between the front and back rooms. The stove was only a chullah, made of red bricks piled on top of each other forming an oven that was covered with fine powdered ash and sand, which drifted across the clay floor that was baking-hot under her bare feet. She turned on the rusted water pipe that climbed up the shoulders of the wall from the street. The first droplets that coughed out of the pipe were hot and steamed on the floor, but in a short while the water turned cold, and she splashed the entire courtyard with it. An earthy dampness refreshed the air that was blowing dust across the rooftop. Swollen gray clouds sailed high overhead. Apaji lined up all her metal dishes, her mortar and pestle, and paring knives neatly along the wall. Until they came to Karachi she had only used such a stove for amusement in the village, learning from the servant Saddiquan how to regulate the heat and tend the logs with a poker. She used to enjoy the feel of moist stretchy dough clinging to her fingers, as she slapped and kneaded it into breads, and the sizzling of butter and the burned-wood flavor of country food. Her fingers were soon covered with soot as she leaned over the chullah and swept it off with the jute sack in which she carried her kitchen equipment.

Raheel stood in the doorway looking at her mother's slender form, the sari askew between her legs. "I have brought the tea, Apaji. Shall I fill the pot with water?" she asked.

Apaji held out her hands for the dented metal teapot, and Raheel came to her side, lifting the old cotton of her skirt above her ankles with her hand.

Karim and Gerrar bounded up to Apaji and offered to search for wood or coal to be used as fuel. Apaji gave them a rupee from the purse she wore in the waistband of her sari and warned them not to spend the whole thing. They ran down the unlit stairs past the shopkeeper, who perched immobile on the threshold of his shop.

"Where can we find wood?" they asked him.

"Hah! Ask me where you can find a yard of silk. These days it would be easier." He spat a stream of red betel juice and just barely missed the cuff of Gerrar's pants.

They turned away from the railroad station toward the center of the city. Like most refugee houses, theirs was near the tracks at the edge of the city, peripheral to the already established order of life and business. A dust storm was brewing in the fields, and they could feel the grains fine in the air sifting through the streets. Shopkeepers in the nooks and crannies of the brick buildings were lowering shades over their stalls and covering their merchandise with cloth against the daily descent of sand that painted Multan an earth brown.

Gerrar asked at shop after shop where he could find a rupee's worth of wood, but there was none available. "Go to the railroad station and pick up coal," one merchant told him. "It is lying all around, and it is free. You won't find wood for a rupee in Multan unless you go to the villages and chop it down for yourself. Where do you think we get wood with the trains not stopping and the population doubling every week?"

They made their way to the bazaar. It was a huge open-air market, several blocks long and flanked by stalls and shops. Villagers and farmers who came to town to sell their produce, squatted on carpets among piles of vegetables, sallow green lettuces, and skinny pale fruits. Meat, thick with flies, hung from iron hooks against the market walls and lay across wooden benches. Dogs sniffed among the skinned corpses of goats and beef. Crows swooped down among the passersby and called frantically from trees and rooftops, their beady eyes swiveling in their heads. It seemed as if the meat and vegetables had been standing for days with few people coming to the stalls to buy them. Karim and Gerrar turned down an alleyway and saw a long line of women and children formed in front of a booth where milk was being rationed by a foreign charity. The children were clutching clay pots that dangled at their skinny legs. Little wide-eyed girls in long torn skirts carried struggling brown naked infants, whose eyes looked bigger than their heads. A tiny shrouded lady at the front of the line raised her baby high overhead as she took her turn, the folds of her faded shawl slipping beneath her elbows. With pleading eyes she pointed to her impassive sparrowlike children standing behind her and asked for a little extra for a child who was sick and could not come.

Gerrar and Karim shouldered their way through the line that stretched across the thoroughfare and down another alley of the market, where the stalls were mostly shuttered and Hindu lettering proclaimed the Gold Mart, the Shop of Sapphires, Sri Gupta's Hall of Emeralds.

"I don't think there is wood in all of Multan," said Karim, scanning the long brick street. It was crammed with pedestrians, but the shops were almost empty of merchandise or customers. The usual beggars that haunted the bazaars of every Indian city were nowhere to be seen, because now there were ration lines and everyone was a beggar.

"We'll just keep looking," said Gerrar. "We can't bring Apaji anthracite coal."

The boys pushed out of the bazaar through the jostling crowd of people walking quickly, always in pairs or family groups. Beyond the main marketplace, old Multan twisted off into a maze of streets that circled in upon each other and tangled together in a collage of multistoried buildings at every angle and growing out of one another like the roots of a banyan tree. As they walked, the brick streets became narrower, and every inch of space was inhabited. People spilled out of the wooden doorways and hung from windows and rooftops. The brothers turned into a street of columns and arcades where whole families were living beneath the archways, protected only by strips of cloth strung from column to column, and cooking at sputtering fires over kerosene stoves on the sidewalk. Shops had been turned into houses, and even the little three-wheeled carts that normally served as tobacco and paan stalls were being used as beds and kitchens.

Karim and Gerrar could see people sleeping on charpoys that were crammed into every imaginable nook. They had to walk in the middle of the street, because the sidewalk was a mass of activity—of cooking, cleaning, gossiping family life. It was as if the whole city had been turned into a gigantic house with the walls stripped away, and the boys felt like trespassers, spying on the exposed intimacies of this bustling preoccupied world. Children darted across their path, and women chattered incessantly in a hundred different dialects as they went about their chores, squatting in every inch of space, from the curbside to the columns of the arcades, to the three-wheeled carts enfolded within the niches in the buildings, to the rooms of the buildings themselves. Only the mosques and mizars seemed to be uninhabited. Every corner and every street had a mosque, jutting from the facade of buildings at oblique angles, for they all faced toward Mecca. They seemed cool and vacant oases with their glazed bricks of royal blue and date green that were shaped like leaves and lotus flowers.

People respected the mosques even when housing was unavailable, and women did not dare to enter, but the miniature Hindu temples scattered among the holy Muslim buildings had not been spared. Karim stopped and stared at the cluster of a family that was using one of the pretty little shrines as a home. Their dark bony faces shimmered in the fire within the shadows of the inner sanctum. The icons of the Hindu gods had been desecrated. The jeweled and silver screen before the altar was ripped open and stripped to metal, and the faces of the animal gods were smashed, noseless, and blind. The neat white walls still freshly painted with figurines and stories of the gods were streaked with stains and urine. The sacrificial altar was being used as a stove, and the greasy smell of cooking meat regurgitated through the portals of the temple that forbade killing or the eating of flesh. The sacred cows that once lived beside the temples were no longer wandering through the streets.

Karim felt sad to see the lovely shrine shamed and naked. It seemed to weep with pain. "I don't think the people should destroy the temples like that," he said.

"People need houses," said Gerrar. "What do you expect them to do?"

"Then why don't they use the mosques as well?" Karim demanded.

Gerrar slapped him on the back of his head. "Hurry up. It will be evening soon," he said. "Apaji needs logs or Abu will never get his tea."

The sky was overcast with clouds that were growing larger and denser. The wind picked up fistfuls of sand and blew the dust into their faces and matted their hair. Lightning flashed soundlessly from cloud to cloud rolling in metallic waves on their journey from the sea to the hills. The boys saw the rain coming like the rippling of a silk veil, and they ducked into a building behind the temple. It was a schoolhouse for Hindu children, and each room on the bottom floor was occupied by families, napping and cooking among the desks and chairs. The blackboards had been torn from the walls and were being used as large double beds for children. At the end of the long hall they ran up a flight of stairs and found the second floor was completely unoccupied. Karim and Gerrar liked the idea of an empty school, and they ran noisily along the corridors, since no one in Multan seemed to care what anyone else was doing. Gerrar flung open the door to a classroom and ran inside.

"Do you see what I see?" he called to Karim, who was rummaging through the books and maps that lined the shelves and walls.

"What?"

"Desks—wooden desks. We could not have more wood if we had stumbled into a forest." He picked up a chair, swung it over his head, and smashed it into the wall. As it splintered into pieces, Gerrar cheered and began to pry the legs loose.

Karim jumped with all his might onto a little desk and laughed, skipping aside as it split down the middle. They broke off as many limbs of wood as they could carry and ran down through the school and out into the bazaar.

By the time they arrived home, the flash rainstorm had moved on toward the north, and the brick streets and clay roads were smelling with freshness and tinged with the rose colors of evening reflected in rivers of water that streamed through the cracks of earth and cobbles. Apaji already had her fire going, since Gappu had collected coals from the tracks that ran only two blocks away from the little apartment.

"We thought you were lost," Gappu complained when they dumped the wood at Apaji's feet in the courtyard. "You should not go running off like that. Abu has already had his tea."

"We brought the wood," Karim protested, but Gerrar laughed and whispered in Karim's ear that Gappu looked like an unt, or camel, with his long sullen face and his thin droopy body.

"Unt," Karim squealed at his brother. "Gappu looks like a camel."

Gappu jumped on Karim and pummeled him with his fists. "Don't call me that," he shouted.

Karim skipped away, screaming back at him, "Unt, unt, unt." Instantly Gappu picked up a coal and hurled it into Karim's face.

Abu came storming into the courtyard. "Why are you fighting? Don't you know how to be nice to each other any longer? Haven't you seen enough fighting and killing?"

Karim and Gappu hung their heads. "How can we have a family conference when you do not treat each other with respect? I think I should call the whole thing off."

"No, Abu. It was my fault," said Karim. "Let us have the conference now."

Abu nodded his head and called the rest of the family around him. They sat in the courtyard where the hot wind of the day had changed to a cool breeze filled with the scent of the nearby fields and the whistling of parrots that fluttered in the date tree beside the roof.

Gappu read the agenda from a torn piece of newspaper, which he had scribbled with a crayon whittled out of charcoal. "First order of business is a house. Second is dividing up the chores. Third is school."

"Aachaa. Very good," said Rehman. "But I think you have things a little backward. You have forgotten the most important thing of all."

Gappu glared at his father for interrupting him.

"What about business? Do you think without money we can even consider these other things?"

"How do you know I wasn't getting to that?" Gappu snapped. "Were you?"

"Yes. Number four—Abu's business."

"Thank you. Then that is what we will discuss."

"I thought this meeting was supposed to be parliamentary. You can't tell us what to discuss."

"Yes he can. Abu is Prime Minister," Karim reminded him.

Gappu put down his paper disgustedly. "All right. What about your business?"

Abu produced the deeds to his salt lakes in Jaipur along with the letter the Home Minister had written for him in Karachi. He unfolded them neatly on the clay earth, which covered the wooden ceiling of the house, as carefully as he had on the Minister's desk. The children moved closer to Abu and looked at the delicately scrawled Persian on the antique papers. Even Piari and Moïd were listening intently as Abu explained.

"These deeds to our salt lakes in Jaipur are transferable here in Pakistan. There are mines in Punjab—not lakes, but hills. Still, it is all the same as long as no one makes a counterclaim. The problem is that even when the deeds are honored and signed over to us, it will take money to produce salt, to mine it from the hills and sell it in the cities. We can go to the mountain, but we cannot bring the mountain to Muhammad. How do you propose we do that?"

The children looked at him blankly.

"There is nothing more to sell, Abu. Do we find jobs?" said Gappu.

"No. I have looked on a map, and I realized that Multan is only a short distance from Dera Ghazi Khan, where my father was in service to the Nawab of Bahawalpur. I was only a child of three when we had to run back to Nehtor, but I am sure you have heard the story from your Dadi many times. Now the old Nawab's grandson is Nawab. His father, with whom I played as a toddler, is dead, and the title has fallen to the grandson. I will return to Dera Ghazi Khan and speak to him about loaning me the capital to start working the mines."

"Isn't that dangerous, Abu? Dadi told us how the Nawab and his men tried to carve your flesh and wear it around their necks as good-luck charms because you are Syed. Suppose they try to do it again," Karim cried.

"Those things don't happen in 1947. The tribes are peaceful now. This Nawab was educated in London and he owns a yacht large enough to sleep two hundred people. He sails it on the Indus River. I have questioned the shopkeeper, who knows the Nawab's reputation very well. I am sure he will be happy to see me. There can be no objection to my plan. So let's vote."

"You will leave us alone?" asked Raheel.

"You can help Apaji take care of the children, and Gappu will care for Apaji. I will be gone less than a week. There is no other way, unless you want to live here forever. Now what is your vote?"

Apaji and all the children voted in agreement with Rehman. Even Gappu reluctantly raised his hand.

"Good," said Abu. "I will leave tomorrow. The meeting is adjourned."

"What about the house?" asked Gappu.

"First things first," said Abu, rising and going into the inner rooms for a nap.

"Some conference," said Gappu. "He is not Prime Minister. He is still a dictator."

During Abu's journey to Dera Ghazi Khan, Gerrar and Karim felt free to roam about the city and the nearby fields and villages of Punjab. Gappu was always too busy, taking Apaji to the bazaar to buy supplies and helping Raheel watch out for the younger children, to notice what they were doing. Karim and Gerrar quickly did their clean-up chores, morning and night, and then escaped for the whole day to the farms and canals that reminded them of Nehtor. Despite the proximity of the desert, Punjab was very much like their own state, only here people did not recognize them and call to them wherever they walked, or invite them as honored guests to take tea and sweets.

Every morning they washed down the dark and musty outer stairway, so that the lingering odors of chickens and cats that once must have been kept there began to dissipate under the bucketfuls of water they lavished on the walls and ceilings and even on the sidewalk and street.

The shop merchant who lived downstairs watched them morosely over his folded arms. He seemed to try a new business every day. One morning he was preparing lassy out of milk which he boiled in a large vat. He would then take it to the railroad station

307

with a single unwashed glass, where he sold it in the heat of the day to the hordes of people who descended from the trains to stretch their legs and arms on the platform while the trains released their steam. Another morning he was busy tying bundles of grain, which he had hauled in from a village on foot and planned to take to market to sell. Consistently his supply of bric-a-brac and furniture grew along the walls and hung from the beams of the ceiling. It was all booty from his nightly rounds to abandoned Sikh and Hindu homes, where he stole whatever he could carry. The shopkeeper was always on the lookout for a sale, and he tried to enlist Karim and Gerrar as carriers to take his salted lassy to the station, so he could sit about his shop and guard the growing hordes of looted goods.

Karim and Gerrar tried to run out of the house when the shop-keeper wasn't looking so that they could quickly turn the corner of the Hindu house, run around the cesspool, and cross the tracks before the old man could stop them. They did not like the smirks and winks of the crude black little Muslim and his toothless aphorisms.

"Running off again," he gurgled through his thin cheeks plumped full of paan and tobacco leaf. "You are farmers and seek pleasures like goats. Why don't you work for me and make your father proud?"

"We are not farmers. We are Syed," said Karim.

The shopkeeper laughed, thinly parting his jaws. His almost toothless gums were stained reddish brown. "Hah! Partition Syeds. I know better. All Syeds have money. Where is yours? The Syeds did not have to leave India. If you worked for me, you would earn the kind of living you deserve."

"We do not work for chamars," said Gerrar haughtily. "This was not even your shop before Partition. The whole street and alley were owned by the Hindu, and you sat at his feet and ran his messages. You were not even allowed to bring his water with your hands."

The merchant waved his long bony finger at them. "Remember your respect," he admonished them. "You are living in my quarters."

Gerrar was ready to fight, but Karim pulled him away. It was not like Aligarh where the small shopkeepers in the godowns that surrounded the walls of their house and gardens treated them like little brothers and gave them candies whenever they stopped to chat. Multan was an alien city, and Punjabi was difficult to understand. It was better to stay away from unfriendly people and walk together in the countryside and through the villages that nestled in field after field.

Not far from the house was a canal. It was visible in the distance, and Karim and Gerrar always walked along the track toward the train trestle that spanned the canal in order to avoid the station that was always too crowded with refugees. Some had been waiting for days for train connections.

The hot golden grasses crackled with the dry sounds of grasshoppers, and were lit with the motion of orange butterflies and pale lizards as slender and transparent as reeds. The deep green of the paddies adjacent to the canal was reflected in the water. Water buffalo and cows were bathing. Little boys, naked but for a strip of cloth around their loins, waded among the animals. They carried shaved twigs that stung the buffaloes' shining black backs, as they clambered along the sloping stone walls of the canal as agile as monkeys. Farther along, young girls were washing clothes and bathing, their wide pants drawn up above their knees. The wet cloth clung across their tiny buttocks outlining them like small melons as they squatted in the shallows and washed their hair, unweaving the thick braids and calling to each other with taunts and laughter. Karim and Gerrar could hardly understand a word they were saying, but Gerrar did not miss the young girl who smiled at him secretly with dancing eyes and bright white teeth shining in her smooth dark face when her older sister was not looking.

A flock of ducks hobbled across the brothers' path. A boy and girl of not more than four or five were chasing them with sticks, trying to make the birds walk straight ahead instead of in circles as they constantly tried to do. It seemed just like Nehtor, where the canal of the town tumbled into the countryside, and the banks were a tapestry of red, yellow, and purple wild flowers. The sweet fruit trees were cluttered with parrots that merged with the foliage until Gerrar threw a rock and they rose off the branches in a swarm seeming to denude the trees of half their leaves. The village girls were like the girls of Milak, like a hundred, smiling, gossiping Jillas, like the farmers' daughters, their tiny rounded hips snapping with every step of their firm brown calves, and their blowing hair.

Only no one called them Mir Sahib as they passed and no one wished them salaam, and instead of the mango orchards, which they owned and on which they gorged themselves during the long lazy afternoons of summer, these were fields and fields of date groves. All the other children who played along the canal were munching dates, but Karim and Gerrar were not allowed to touch them.

An ancient-looking man dazzling white from his beard to his toes sat with his dog in the thickest part of the shadow of a tree, enjoying his retirement by eating fistful after fistful of dates. He was so expert that he shoved the fruit into one side of his mouth while extracting the pit from the other, his hands in constant motion.

Gerrar could stand it no longer, and he pulled Karim deep into the thickest grove. Greedily they stuffed themselves with as many dates as they could, hoping no one would pass and catch them in their theft. They tried eating the way they saw the old man, but the skill was great and took years of practice. The old man ate so fast he looked like a machine. He could even wrap the fruit in the *tokri*, or date leaf, while he was pushing it into the corner of his mouth. When Karim and Gerrar tried, the dates got stuck in their cheeks and they spit the fruit instead of the pits, but they giggled joyously together trying to smother their laughter so that no one would hear.

Once they had found the date grove, Karim and Gerrar returned every afternoon to stuff themselves full of dates, despite the stomach cramps they suffered every night. They wanted to carry home dates for Apaji and all the children, but they were afraid the farmers would notice their bulging pockets and have them arrested or beaten. Instead, they contented themselves with the secret of their treasure. With stomachs full and hunger abated, they would wait out the daily thunder and duststorm, which was often accompanied by a flash of rain, beneath the sheltering trees. At sunset, when the whole

310

earth was glowing fresh, they washed the stains from their shirts and lips in the warm water of the canal and started the long walk home.

Often on the return trip they braved passing through the railroad station in hope that the small gauge train from Dera Ghazi Khan would arrive with Abu on it, but also the station intrigued them. They were frightened and fascinated at the same time. They knew there was only one train Abu could take since the railroads traversed Pakistan from north to south and only small gauge lines spindled out to the west as far as the Indus River where they could go no farther. The river had no bridges and could only be crossed by boats. Some days the train from the Indus River did not come at all. When it did come, it was filled with refugees who arrived from across the unharnessed river, showing signs of having walked through the desert for days in their haggard faces and dust-scorched hair. Each evening that the train arrived, Gerrar and Karim searched the restless anxious faces for Abu, but even on the seventh day he had not come.

In the early evening of the eighth day as they walked homeward, Karim and Gerrar thought they saw edges of flame leap against the glowing amber of the sun sinking to the horizon. It was just the hint of flame, as if the sky had been torn at the edge like a jagged cloth. Perhaps the sun was playing tricks on their eyes, lying so low to the flat fields with its meandering footpaths and crisscrossing of animals on their way home after plowing.

"Is something burning?" Karim asked.

Gerrar felt a twinge of fear leap through his blood, and he cupped his hands over his eyes, straining to discern some object that might be on fire in the rippling glare of orange sky and green rice paddies. "I don't know," he said to Karim. "I think it is coming from the railroad station."

Karim grabbed his brother's arm. "Hurry up. Let's go see," he said. The boys quickened their steps, and as the arches and spires of the city came into view, they could see the railroad tracks sliced across the earth on a rise. A long express train, miniature in the distance, was bitten through with flame and standing half in the station and half out. Karim clutched Gerrar's hand tighter. It was an all too familiar sight. They could not yet make out any people, but the sounds of distant screaming leaped into their ears on wafts of wind, and Gerrar stopped frozen, shaking in his tracks.

"Oh, God," he whispered to Karim. "There is a train riot."

"How will we get home? Must we cross the tracks?" Karim asked.

Gerrar looked all around. They could walk several miles along the track, and cross down where the train would be out of sight, but by then it would be dark, and they might come upon the rioters again farther from home and safety. There was no way to get back home without crossing in the thick of the riot. A bullock cart was racing toward them, straight through the paddies. They could hear the bull snorting wetly through its hot nostrils, as the driver beat his back incessantly with whistling lashes of his stick, and the bull's back was scored with cuts and spurting blood and mud.

"What is happening?" Gerrar called to the farmer, who was standing up in the cart and swinging his arms frantically.

"The refugees of Multan have attacked a Hindu train," he shouted as the cart rumbled past them. "Hide, hide. Do not go there," he warned, but Karim and Gerrar continued to run. Their legs felt malleable as paste, but their feet were directing them inexorably toward the tracks, and their only thought was to reach Apaji and home on the other side. They could see the cars of the train becoming clearer and clearer as they ran. Flames were pouring from the windows and engulfing the roofs where hundreds of people were standing together and trying to leap through the fire. Men in white pajamas were running toward the station from the trestle over the canal, and along the road adjacent to the tracks, all converging on the parked train, while others poured away from the train in great waves, mothers and young girls screaming and clutching their children against their saris, which twirled from their bodies in a frantic unfurling of cloth. Everyone was running past them, with arms outstretched as if gasping at the sky and fields for air, their charcoal-streaked and bleeding faces lit with terror. A battalion of carts raced back and forth beside the train, horses and oxen braying and rearing up on their haunches as smoke swirled around their heads and stung their eyes, but the drivers kept beating the animals. Hundreds of men were pulling valises and bundles from the fleeing Hindus, knocking their heads with long sticks which they waved wildly overhead and piling the carts full of the looted belongings.

People were running in every direction, and Karim and Gerrar tried to skirt them as they came tripping into the fields. A band of Muslim men in white plunged past Karim and Gerrar from behind. As they ran, they drew knives and guns from their belts and brandished them in the air, grabbing the Hindus like fistfuls of booty by the hems of their dhotis and the ends of their saris, and plunging their knives into flesh with cries of "Hai Allah" as great gurgles of blood washed over their bodies and screams pierced the earth and sky and fields. A burly man with face flushed red ran beside Karim and Gerrar. "You are not Hindu children. Arm yourselves," he shouted. "This is a jihad. It is a holy war. It is your duty as Muslims to fight."

Gerrar stared at the man's heated face, choking a scream in the bursting pockets of his lungs. He led Karim at a run to the front end of the train, where clouds of steam and smoke obscured the track and the large iron engine. The engineer, blackened and greasy with coal and oil, stood overhead in the cabin frantically jiggling the train's levers to make the train move, while the guards and *titis* ran up and down the track, splashing buckets of water on the burning cars and looking for the car where the emergency cord had been pulled that stopped the train. On the other side of the train, ten times as many Muslim men were streaming out of the city. Several came with torches, which trailed yellow streams of fire in the failing daylight, as they leaped into the mob and hurled them onto the roofs of the train and against the shuttered windows of the compartments. The hundreds of families locked inside were screaming and beating their bodies against the walls. They were trying to stay inside the train, but as a car caught fire, the windows were heaved open and fathers threw their children onto the tracks while the Muslim rioters pushed them back through the smoke and flames or greeted them with the edge of a blade, slicing their small bodies, gouging their heads and faces with the random whiplashes of their knives.

More and more men were flooding out of the city, and Gerrar pushed into the crowds, dragging Karim with both his hands and looking into his brother's reddened eyes. Gerrar was screaming frantically as he ran, "Make them stop. Make them stop," although he did not even hear his own voice, and Karim kept pulling back like a frightened pony, so that Gerrar had to yank his arms to keep him moving into the mobs running across the station platform and around the path of the cesspool that was between them and their house. The rioters running past them were shouting prayers and slogans and curses all at once. They seemed drunk with excitement, passionate with hysteria, as if participating in a mad carnival of carnage. "I will get their jewels before they steal them from our country. I lost a sister. I am going to kill five sisters," they shouted to each other. "I want the testicles with which they raped my wife. I want their fingers which stole from my house. I want their tongues which preach against Muslims and their hearts which hate God."

Karim and Gerrar crossed the platform and pushed into the crowd of men who were running in the opposite direction. They could not believe they were seeing everything repeated here in Pakistan. The Muslims who were their brothers, the lambs with whom they had fled from India and killing, with weeping in their throats and tears in their eyes, were the lions of Pakistan. They were doing to the Hindus what had so recently been done to them, but they called it a holy jihad. Behind them, they heard the sound of drums beating hollowly, stridently, only this time they were Muslim drums, and the calls of "Allah ho Akbar. God is One," were triumphant. Instead the Hindu prayers were desperate and piercing.

"Oh, Mata."

"Oh, Bap."

"Mere Lal."

"Mere Sunder."

"Mere Pritham. Oh, mother, father, brother, sister! Oh, my darling. Oh, Bagwan. Oh, God."

Gerrar and Karim stood at the edge of the cesspool between the station and their house. They could see bodies floating facedown in the shallow muck, their white robes splayed among the weeds and growth like fallen sails of a ship. Hundreds of men were running around them with curses on their lips. Karim and Gerrar ducked off the path that had been beaten around the cesspool and into the narrow alley that enclosed them between its walls of windowless brick. Gerrar pressed his back against the bricks and stood riveted to the wall.

"What's the matter?" Karim screamed at him. "We're almost home."

Gerrar looked up at his brother. They were both covered from head to toe with black soot, and stains from the smoke blotched the faded cloth of their pajamas and old school jackets. Karim could see Gerrar's chest heaving spastically against his shirt.

"I can't go any farther. I've brought you this far. Go home yourself."

Karim grabbed Gerrar by the shoulder, but Gerrar shoved him away, and turning his face to the wall, bit onto the bricks with his lips and tongue, cutting himself but feeling nothing in his numbed flesh.

"Stop it," Karim screamed. "We are almost home. Don't you understand?" Karim thought he was going to vomit, and he reeled dizzily looking into the long shadows of the blind alley, which turned in darkness at the end against another wall. He felt Gerrar's hand wrap around his chest. "What's that?" Gerrar hissed in his ear.

Karim listened, and in the silence of the alley with the screams of the Hindus and the rioters muffled by the brick, he could hear low deep moaning coming from around the corner of the alley. Hand in hand they crept along the wall and peered around the corner. A young girl lay in a pool of shadows, her sari spread-eagled over the ground.

"Sister," Karim whispered, and the girl leaped up with a screech, exposing the body of her father which she had been concealing, and the front of her sari and her long mat of black hair, which covered her face, were smeared with thick globs of blood.

"Oh, Bhai. Oh, brother," she cried. "Where is my father's head? Oh, my father! What will I do now? You were just talking." With hands outstretched, she hurled herself between the walls of the two buildings like a trapped bird. She fluttered from one wall to the other, her fingers groping frenetically in the air. "I am blind," she sobbed.

Oh, my God. The vultures were in Pakistan, too. Is this what Mohammed Ali Jinnah promised us when he carved Pakistan out of India? Whom did he do it for? Did he do it for us? Did he do it for this man who was the only eyes of his blind daughter, leading her to the land purified by the Ganges? Gerrar could see the decapitated head gaping out of the corner, tilted up slightly as if resting on one ear and blood bubbled from its neck. A blood-spattered bandanna was still tied securely around its crown.

Gerrar stared at the head as if hypnotized by the trickle of blood at the edge of the ear and the ooze that seeped from the neck. The girl kept running back and forth, tripping over the father's body with her tiny feet, and her fingers waved madly in the air before her arched form and raised distorted face. No tears could flow from the wells of scarred skin where her eyes should have been, and the edge of her sari trailed streams of red blood across the sandy path. Karim tried to grasp her by the arms, but she wrenched herself from his grip, crying hysterically. "Where is the head? I must find the head."

Karim looked wildly at his brother for assistance, but Gerrar walked slowly to the corner of the alley and stooped over the head. Karim stared at him in disbelief as he lifted the bleeding head in his arms and held it in his lap "What are you doing?" Karim screamed at him. "The man is dead."

"Maybe we can save him," Gerrar said slowly in a hushed voice.

As soon as the blind girl heard Gerrar's voice, she lunged for the body and started dragging it through the alley, its arms and hands clawing heavily in the dust. Gerrar ran after her with the head dripping in his outstretched hands. He could feel the cheeks still warm and the bulbous lips seemed ready to talk to him. He was sure he could save the man, though his clothes were dripping with the human blood of the Indian soil.

Karim looked at Gerrar stunned. "You're crazy. Do you hear? You don't know what you're doing. Help me with the girl."

Gerrar seemed unable to respond, and for long seconds he stood breathing heavily in the dim evening light in the alley, his blood thumping with the distant drums, and the head inexplicably resting in his hands, his doctor's hands, the hands he thought would bring cure and healing and were now holding a warm sculpture of death.

Karim despaired of his brother and grabbed the girl by her arms. He tried to stop her from making noise, but she kept jerking her face away from him. He was afraid someone would hear her sobbing and babbling, "Where is my father's head?" but she was not in her mind, anymore than Gerrar was. She wanted to escape. She never wanted to leave her father's body. The bright face of the moon had no eyes, and she had lost the head of her father who had been her eyesight, and now she was hitting the wall with her forehead.

Karim twirled her around and unwrapped her sari, leaving the girl in her brown petticoat. He ripped off an edge of the fragile threadbare cloth and tied her hands which would not stop fluttering ahead of her. Gerrar was staggering toward them and stopped over the body with the head still in his arms.

"Drop the head," Karim ordered. "Drop it now." Gerrar released his fingers and watched the head flop onto the body with the neck jagged and the long gray strands of hair tangled in the web of raw flesh and veins. "I can do something if I take him to the hospital," he said, staring at Karim.

"He is dead, he is dead," Karim kept screaming at Gerrar, who did not seem able to comprehend. "You are crazy. He is dead."

"Dead, dead dead," the blind girl chorused and collapsed in Karim's arms. He felt the slight weight of the girl's body trembling against his shoulders. She was several inches shorter than he and as fragile as a kitten. Gerrar looked at Karim with the blind girl draped in his arms and the corpse of her father at their feet, and all the tears of the afternoon, of the riot in Multan and the riots of the trains, and of India and of Aligarh flooded from his mouth, his eyes, and his nose. Gerrar realized the man was dead, that there was nothing he could do but continue to witness the fratricidal frenzy of the people. With a sense of drowning in his tears that wet his face and stung his eyes, he wrapped the head in the sari that Karim handed him, and

317

together they dragged the girl in her petticoat and the body back to the house, a nice present for Apaji.

Both their weights combined were less than the body alone, and Karim was trying to keep his free hand around the blind girl's mouth and push her with his knee. They peered around the corner of the Hindu's house, across the street from their own, and into the empty brick street. There was no movement from their apartment, and even the Muslim merchant had closed his shop and gone to see the riot. They stumbled hurriedly across the open street and into the darkness of their building. They tried to drag the body up the pitch-black staircase, pushing the girl ahead of them. Blood still gushed from the head that was tied up in the sari, and the man's feet bounced along the stairs behind them with a thud.

Abu came running down the street. His train had arrived in the thick of the riot, and he had come home to find that Karim and Gerrar were gone. He had been looking for them. "Thank God, you are here," he said as he ran up behind them. "The police are handing out guns and rifles to anyone who wants them." He squinted up at them through the darkness of the stairwell. "What have you got there?"

Karim and Gerrar stared down at Abu guiltily, afraid of what his reaction was going to be when he saw the blind Hindu girl and the dead body they were dragging. Irrationally they tried to conceal the body behind their feet. Karim had his hand over the blind girl's mouth. Abu started to climb up the stairs, but immediately tripped and fell on the thick slippery blood that still percolated out of the warm body, although the torso was getting cooler and stiffer by the minute.

Gappu opened the door at the top of the stairs and looked down. "What is going on?" he asked. He saw Abu lying at the bottom and started to run down the stairs past Gerrar and Karim and the girl behind them in the pitch darkness. Gappu also tripped and fell. Apaji peered out of the doorway, stunned at the sight of Gappu and Abu lying on the ground. She struck a match and the whole staircase lit up. Apaji gasped at the sight of her sons bathed in deep

318

maroon blood along with the feather of a girl, stripped to her brown petticoat and midrift blouse, and the corpse partially concealed by the soaking wet sari. Gerrar was holding onto the body and crying hysterically, "I want to go to Nani."

Apaji raised her voice. "First, I want Abu to come up, but this time walk carefully." She told Gappu to take the dead body and put it in the closet under the staircase beside the shop. Karim and Gerrar and the girl were sent together to the bathroom where Apaji stripped them and gave them a bath, heaving buckets of water in their faces and over their bodies. Raheel ran back and forth with the buckets, filling them from the waterpump on the roof and handing them to Apaji. The girl fell moaning to the floor to conceal her naked body, and Apaji touched her frail brown shoulders. The skin was taut over the bones, and although the tiny girl seemed no more than nine or ten, her small buttons of breasts showed she was in early adolescence. Apaji raised her gently, smoothing the long masses of wet hair across her head so that she could wash her face. Apaji looked into the eyes of the girl for the first time. She had not realized she was blind and could not stifle her cry of shock. "Hai Allah," she breathed. "They have killed the blind girl's father. The doers will have a curse on them forever."

Apaji took charge. She wrapped her sons in old sheets and sent them to the roof so that Raheel could give them tea. The blind girl rested limply in Apaji's supporting arms. Apaji turned to Abu who was watching the scene dumbfounded. "You run and get help. Clean the blood from the stairs and the street."

She tried to feed the rosebud of the Sind, but the girl was still sobbing too much. She seemed to be from a nice family, the way she was trying to hide her face in her hanky.

Rehman had to move fast. He got a load of wood from a store for which he had to pay ten rupees. With Gerrar's help he took the body out of the godown and spread it out in the middle of the street on the blind girl's sari, over the logs. He took out three guns, so no one would question his authority, and called the family outside to light the funeral pyre. Everyone stood in the empty street. The

319

sounds of screaming and chanting from the railroad station were dying out, but the full moonlight that filled the street seemed to be tinged with blood and flame and the groans of the dying.

The whole family stood in the middle of the street, holding their guns around the dead body. There was no one to light the match to the pyre. Abu laid the head neatly at the shoulders, but there was no neck, and he covered the body in a wreath of dried date leaves. "Only the eldest son is supposed to light the ghat," he said. "But since there is no son, my son will do it." He handed the matches to Gappu.

"I did not find the body. Gerrar should do it," Gappu said.

Abu turned to Gerrar, but he was still shaking all over and trying to contain his tears. Karim took the matches from Gappu. Abu sprayed the body with kerosine from a gallon can. Karim lit the whole matchbox and threw it onto the dry date leaves, and fire sprang all over the body, which had been throbbing less than an hour before.

"You have to say the prayer," said Abu.

"Bismillah ir Rehman nir Rahim. But I cannot say that. He is Hindu. O Ram, O Bagwan, O Khuda, O Christ, give this man peace, and make me such that I shall always be in a position to stop the suffering of my people."

The family watched in the street for hours as the flames ate into the flesh. The whole street was infused with the acrid smell. The fire lit the faces of the children watching behind Apaji, who cradled the softly sobbing blind girl in her arms. Everyone was crying.

All night Abu and Gappu watched the bones and flesh crumple and smolder into ashes. Holding their guns akimbo across their knees, they took turns sleeping in the street, while Apaji put the others to bed and sang psalms and prayers to erase the sounds and visions of the day from their dreams. Just before sunrise Abu gathered the dying embers into a large clay pot. He brought them into the girl who lay on a charpoy on the roof with Raheel and the babies. He touched her gently on the shoulder, and she shot upright with a sob.

"Someday I will take your father's ashes to the Holy Ganges.

Or one of my sons will do it. Your father's soul will rest in India. Someday when the madness is over, I will send you back, too. This I promise." He put his hand on the head of the Hindu girl, Rukmani.

5

Diaspora

OCTOBER 1947

After the riot of Multan, the children slept all morning. Raheel moved indoors with Piari and Mona because they were shivering from the dampness of the predawn air. They slept near to Abu and Apaji, whose room was the smallest and overlooked the side street. Gerrar and Karim slept on the carpet in the front room because it was the closest to the outdoors and easiest from which to escape.

Gappu was too tense to sleep. He shared a room with Moïd and spent the morning trying to teach his baby brother to speak, as Moïd would not leave the charpoy for his own bed. He held Moïd between his legs while the frail five-year-old wriggled from side to side trying to avoid Gappu's eyes when he stuttered out a word.

Gappu had not played with Karim and Gerrar since they arrived in Multan. There were more important things to do than wander in the countryside and steal dates. He had to guard Moïd who was afraid to be alone. Every afternoon he took Apaji to the market where she stood in line to get rations of soap, clay pots, strips of cloth for blankets. Anything that the government or charities could think of to send to Multan, they needed. Apaji never said a word to him when they went together, and he could have cried to see the tiny lady, whom he towered over, concealing her dancing

323

face beneath her shawl and raising her soft delicate arms to the uniformed disbursers in the booths. Apaji would not let Raheel go with her to see the ration lines, and did not want her to know where the supplies were coming from. Only Gappu could go with her. Alone, the official would take him for a young man without family and turn him away. He could not take Karim and Gerrar with him because they always teased him and called him camel.

Gappu was embarrassed enough about his appearance and was glad there were no girls he knew in Multan to see him. His face was big and pointed at the chin, and his legs were almost as long as Abu's but thin to ugliness. Obviously his nickname, Gappu, was no longer applicable. The name, which meant "fatty," referred to some other being—a child Gappu could hardly remember. It was the name of the curly-haired pink-cheeked boy whose belly was always loaded up with sweetmeats, almonds, mangoes, and watermelons, and whose hands were always carrying schoolbooks, when he stopped to eat in the markets of Aligarh. It was the name for the happy prank-playing boy, the favorite child of Darogaji, the leader of all the brothers and cousins and sisters in the games of Nehtor. He was the heir, and his brothers called him Prince of Wales. His real name, Marouf, meant "favored one," but now Gerrar and Karim called him Unt whenever he came near them, and laughed and had silly secrets.

Moïd laid his head in Gappu's lap, and Gappu stroked his brother's neck and forehead, trying to make him sleep, as their grandfather Darogaji used to do for him when he was Moïd's age. "Soon we will go back to school, and you will find friends to play with. Now sleep, little brother, chote Bhai. Do not think of India and what is past. Sleep."

Outside on the rooftop courtyard between the rooms, the blind girl, Rukmani, was prone on the tiny charpoy near the fire. She stared sightlessly up at the cleansed white sky of the new morning, her thin brown arm draped over her forehead. Apaji sat quietly at Rukmani's side, stitching the children's old fragile clothes that were always tearing and growing too small. It was as if nothing had happened the night before, except that Rukmani lay in her petticoat under a thin sheet as a reminder that the Muslims had cut down the Hindu train, and all their clothes that had been smeared with the blood of Rukmani's father were draped over the brick walls and drying in the hot wind. Otherwise, everything was as usual. The pot full of lentils, ground onions, and peppers was simmering on the coals for breakfast. Apaji heard passersby on the street below talking as they walked, and the occasional tinkling of a bicycle bell, and the sound of trains rattling in and out of the station with long crying whistles and gasps of steam. Crows hopped from rooftop to rooftop, and a flock of ducks sailed overhead.

Abu came to the door of their room in the corner of the court-yard and signaled her to come. He had already bathed from the bucketful of water she had drawn the night before and left to cool off in the shed that concealed the bathroom from the roof. He was wrapped in a sheet, and his heavy mass of hair was matted across his forehead.

"Come, bride. We must talk," he said.

Apaji laid down her stitching and followed him into their room, which was bare except for the blanket and pillows they slept on, and the jute sacks containing their remaining possessions, stacked in the corner against the wall. Since only the front rooms were tiled, the floors were of the same clay earth as the courtyard and felt cool under her feet.

Abu pulled her down onto the blanket and cradled her small body against his own, which was warm and sweet from the bath. His hands went through the hair she wore pinned into a knot over her head, and let the shortened black strands sift through his fingers and cover his face. Once the hair had been a yard long and smelled of perfume instead of soap. It was the hair that Apaji had to hide from the superstitious women of Nehtor and the villagers, because they always tried to snip it and eat it for good luck. Apaji's abundant hair had been the symbol of her fecundity, of the health and survival of four strong sons, and the fact that she had never experienced the death of a child. Women who wished a son would sneak up to Apaji when she slept on a verandah, or beneath a tree in one of the villages, and cut off a swatch with scissors to take home and burn into a powder and eat with rice so that good luck would come to them, too.

Now Apaji had cut her hair. It had been too long for such tasks as cooking and washing, and Sara pulled on it with her fists. There was no nurse to relieve her or admiring servants to spread the hair across a chair and comb out the thick tangles, but Abu was still intensely in love with her. She was even more beautiful now than before, though the rouge that daubed her cheeks was washed away with the flowers and perfumes. The jewels that circled her neck and arms, her head and ankles, were lost, but her eyes were fiercer, her skin darker and more mellow, and her small body infused with a sleepless strength no one ever guessed she had.

Rehman pressed the little hands against his bare chest, the hands that had buried a stranger's child. He covered the eyes that had seen too much with deep wet kisses, trying to devour away the visions, drink the tears. Her breasts were firm and heavy with Sara's milk beneath his arms, and he dared not touch them with his hands. With each child she nursed, a barrier of mother and infant was erected that Rehman could not cross in body or fathom in mind.

"Dhulan, bride. When all this is over, we will have another child. A Pakistani child who has seen none of the suffering and war."

Apaji buried her face against his shoulder. Her nose and lips were pressed so deeply against his skin, she was barely breathing. Abu stroked her arms and back, the hair that lay across his eyes, and the small rounding of her hips curved beneath the coarse cloth of her sari.

"Our moments alone are so few," he whispered.

"We will be together forever," said Apaji into the flesh of his neck. He pushed the hair across her forehead and tilted her face up toward his to look into the voluminous eyes.

"I have the money, Dhulan, for a house, for a business, for food," he said softly, his lips moving against her cheek. "The Nawab was kind. Twenty times he asked to hear the story of his grandfather and the day we crossed the River Indus. He gave us money and said it was reparations for his grandfather's primitive ways. Of course, I would not hear of it, and I accepted the money as a loan. 'It is an in-

326

vestment in my business,' I told him. And he said, 'It is an invest-
ment in Pakistan, a country of brothers.' "

"We are very happy for you," Apaji said, and Rehman could see
the tears swimming in her eyes.

"Now we will move away from here, from train stations and the
houses of refugees. I will take you to the country where you will not
see fires burning or hear the cries of people who have no homes. Our
sons will go to school. It has been too long since they have seen a
teacher or a lesson. The Hindu girl, Rukmani, will stay with us until
it is safe, and then I will send her to India. Afterward, in a year or
two, we will have a Pakistani child—if you wish it. Tell me if you
can bear another child?"

"Yes, my dear brave man, there will be another child."

Rehman swooped her against the full length of his body with a
rush of feeling as new and powerful as the first time he held her
alone in their bridal room, unwrapping the gold and silver jewels,
the satin skirts and chiffon veils from her flowering body. She
yielded against him, and he felt the stomach that had housed all their
children soft and fertile beneath his chest, and her breasts rushed
wet and warm with milk.

"You are the brave one," he said. "Without you I would have
fallen from the trains. I would have faltered on the ship. I would
have died a hundred times."

A quiet knocking on their bedroom door interrupted their love.
Apaji sat bolt upright on the carpet.

"What is it?" she called.

"Apaji. I am sorry. Come quickly," Raheel called to her.

Apaji leaped toward the door and flung it open. Her hair was
flying at her shoulders, and her sari was all askew. Raheel's trembling face met her own, and Apaji grabbed her daughter's hand.
"What has happened?" she gasped.

"I don't know," said Raheel. "Come and see. I think Piari is
sick."

"Oh, God!"

Apaji ran out of the room with Raheel. Rehman followed
wrapping his sheet around his waist like a dhoti. Piari lay on a char-

poy in the next room, whimpering in perspiration. Apaji gently placed her hands on Piari's forehead and face and tiny body, and Piari tossed and turned under her cool touch. All the children surrounded the bed, and Rukmani was keening on the floor, hitting her chest with her hands as if crazed.

"Gappu, take everyone out of here," Abu ordered. "Someone run quickly and find a doctor. Tell him we can pay."

Moïd was clutching the edge of Piari's cot, and Gappu had to pry his hands away and drag him from the room.

"Ummy, Ummy," Piari cried holding her hands up to her mother. Apaji lifted Piari in her arms and paced the floor. She could feel the child's hot tears falling on her face and shoulders, and she rubbed the small of Piari's back where she said she had pain. Then Piari coughed violently and vomited all over the front of Apaji's sari. Still Apaji did not put her down, but tried to wash her feverish face with a damp cloth that Raheel brought from the pump, and whispered and hummed in Piari's ear to quiet the coughing and choking and sobbing of the child.

Apaji instructed Raheel to boil some water for at least twenty minutes and to sterilize the plates and pots and everything they would use for Piari.

"What is it, Apaji? What is wrong with Piari?" Raheel cried, wringing her hands.

"It is too soon to tell. It is probably food poisoning. Now go and do as I say." Apaji was trying to be as calm as she could be in front of the other children. When she was alone, she wept and prayed and asked God to give her whatever it was that caused her baby's head to swirl with fever and her body to heave.

Abu kept walking in and out of the room anxious for reports. Gerrar and Karim had been gone for over an hour, looking for a doctor. He should have gone himself. There was no way he could help Apaji, and he watched her helplessly as she walked back and forth across the floor with Piari in her arms. He was too nervous to sit outside with Gappu and the other children, with Moïd stuttering and Sara screaming for her milk. Apaji told him to help Raheel feed the other children, but he did not have the patience to do that, and continuously ran into the street, looking for his sons and the doctor. Finally he saw them walking quickly with a gray-bearded man in a black coat. He hurried them along, waving his arms and thanking the doctor for coming.

"You don't have to worry. We can pay your fee," he assured the doctor, as he rushed him up the stairs, through the courtyard, and into Piari's room. The doctor saw the distraught look on Rehman's face and placed his hand on his shoulder.

"At a time like this there is no question of fees," the doctor said. "You will give me what you can. Let me see the little girl."

Apaji lay Piari down on the bed. She was limp with fever and perspiration poured out of her as if her flesh were melting away. The doctor bent over the bed and felt Piari's glands and stomach. With long experienced fingers, his hands glided up and down the little girl's body, and her long legs that always danced around the house but were now distended and weak.

"Has there been diarrhea?" he asked Apaji.

"No, but she vomited once."

"If no one else is sick, it is probably not food poisoning," the doctor said. He hesitated.

"Tell me what you think, doctor? Don't hide the truth from me."

"It is too early to tell for sure. There are so many diseases—epidemics everywhere. We will hope it is only measles and not smallpox or cholera."

"Oh, no! Oh, God, please save my baby!" Apaji staggered backward, almost fainting. Abu caught her and helped her to sit on one of the other beds. Apaji jumped up again and held Piari against her chest.

"What can we do, doctor? Tell me what to do."

"The most important thing is to isolate the other children. Can you do that?"

"Yes, yes. I will take them to another house immediately," said Rehman. "But what can we do for this child?"

"For the time being, be calm. You must observe her to see what develops. If there is diarrhea, call me immediately. It might be cholera, but the new treatments are simple."

"It is not cholera," said Apaji. "I know the symptoms of cholera. My nephew died of that disease in our house in Aligarh."

"Oh, you are from Aligarh," said the doctor with a mark of respect in his voice. "I have been there to see the university. I should think then, if you don't mind my saying so, that you would know better than to live in this street so close to the cesspool and the trains with people coming from God knows where."

"Yes, doctor, but now what do we do for our little girl?" Rehman asked impatiently.

The doctor hung his head. "I'm afraid there is little we can do at the moment, but keep her comfortable with compresses and watch her vigilantly. There are so many possibilities. I see children every day who have come from every corner of India. They have brought a hundred different diseases with them. I will come to see your child each morning and evening. We will watch her progress carefully. You must check her skin for a rash. If there is spotting on her stomach, it is measles, but if you see eruptions on her forehead or wrists, it might be smallpox. The other children must have inoculations and leave the house right now. I know a rest house only three miles from the city. It would be the best place to go, and there are many houses along the canal which you can rent or buy very cheap. I will help you."

Abu rounded up the children, who were sitting nervously in the courtyard. He told Apaji that he would find them a place to live right away and then come back to keep vigil at Piari's bedside.

Leading his children, hand in hand, Abu followed the doctor away from the apartment along the railroad track, which served as the main thoroughfare for pedestrians and animals as well as trains. A gang of coolies were sweeping the station as if there had been no slaughter there the night before. The only reminders of the riot of Multan were the dark stains on the street where Gerrar and Karim had dragged Rukmani's father and the blackened spot where his

330

orpse had been burned. Bullock carts were drifting slowly in and
out of the station crammed with the startled faces of new arrivals.
Raheel carried Sara. Gappu held Moïd by the hand, and Gerrar was
leading Mona. Karim trailed behind, holding Rukmani's strange
small hand as she stumbled along in her brown patched petticoat
through the tall grasses and fields of wild flowers. The children were
weeping, torn between the need to flee again and the fear of leaving
Apaji alone with Piari and the terrible illness that was burning fe-
verishly out of her skin.

They crossed the fields where Karim and Gerrar had come all
week to explore and play among the date groves, looking back over
their shoulders at the turrets of the city until they were no longer
visible.

A row of ten or twelve single-story houses stretched from the
train trestle along the embankment on the far side of the canal, about
two miles from the station. Abu wanted the house farthest from the
tracks. They had been pursued enough by riots on trains which were
hijacked and waylaid, and came bearing their cargoes of murdered
and murderers, hunger and disease. It was enough. Why, he asked
the dead white sky, the still warm waters of the canal, the rattling
leaves of the date trees and palm fronds, did death haunt every nook
and cranny in which they sought shelter? Why did it follow him no
matter how he labored and loved? Death seeped out of the Indian
soil and mushroomed in the brilliance of her flowering fields. Like a
snake it twined within the foliage of the sweetest bushes and hid
among the fruits of the most luxurious trees.

The last house on the edge of the fields was vacant, as were
most of the houses in the so-called suburbs of Multan. Some had
belonged to Hindus and Sikhs who had fled, and others to Muslims
who had left for bigger homes and better positions in the cities of
Lahore and Karachi, which had become available at the moment of
Partition. The house was close enough to the city so that Abu could
walk back and forth between Apaji in the apartment and the children
along the canal.

Its white brick walls rose out of the canal where the impassive backs of water buffalo glistened, like stepping-stones, half submerged. The uncut grasses of the fields spread right into the garden and up to the front door.

Rehman examined the rooms cursorily to make sure that all was in order. Since the house had belonged to a Muslim family before Partition, the furnishings were sparse. The family had left behind only what they did not value or could not carry. No carpets lay on the cool tiled floors, or linens on the wooden beds. The cupboards and closets were empty, and the curtainless windows gaped nakedly out onto the surrounding countryside. The children traipsed after him from room to room, not saying a word and barely looking at the few belongings someone had left behind.

"The house will be sold at auction for next to nothing," the doctor told Rehman. "It is a simple matter of making an application which I can arrange for you. It is much better for the children here than in the city, don't you agree?"

Rehman nodded his head. "There is very little choice." He looked at his children who gathered around him gloomily on the verandah. "What do you think?" he asked them.

Raheel opened her arms wide as if in supplication. "Must we stay here, Abu? Why can't we be with Apaji and you?"

"You won't be alone. I will come back and forth every day and every night. It is only a two-mile walk. There is no other way."

The children continued to stare at him, a row of faces accusing him. Why was every promise broken? Why had he not protected them better? Why was every house only temporary, every decision a compromise?

"Gappu, tell me. Do you see any other way?" he pleaded. "How can I protect you and Piari at the same time? Do you want your sister to die? Do you all want to die?"

"I don't know, Abu. We can discuss it later when Piari is better."

The doctor touched Rehman gently on the sleeve. "It is not a decision for children to make. They will have to understand."

Rehman turned back to his children. Their faces were gaunt. The house he had promised for so long, which he had gone to the

Nawab of Bahawalpur by train and boat and camel to get money for, meant nothing to them. They did not care about the fields, the trees, and the fruit, which were so reminiscent of their home in Nehtor. They seemed drained and lifeless. He wished they would argue and scream, only not regard him so, with quiet obstinacy and disbelief.

"Gerrar, Karim," he pleaded. "Have you nothing to say?"

Karim looked away.

"What can we say?" Gerrar asked. "You must go to Apaji and Piari. There is nothing more that can make us afraid."

The children nodded.

"Go, Abu. We have seen the trains, the people without homes, the dead and dying, Rukmani's father without his head." Gappu took a deep breath. "Now Piari. It is the end." He looked almost like a man now, his eyes shining beneath his heavy black brows, his once-soft cheeks hollow against his bones. Rehman had the sickening feeling deep within his churning stomach and heavy chest that he had lost his children, that it really was the end, no matter what he said or did or promised them. The faith was finally broken. He wanted to gather them all to his chest and coddle them back into the childhood and security he could find no way to give them. He wanted them to have the peace and undisturbed sleep his father had always given to him, but here on the threshold of yet another home, with the hot sun of Punjab flashing on their immobile faces and farmers calling distantly to their animals like some forgotten dream, there was no way he could assure them that rest and happiness would come again.

"I will go only for a short while," he told them. "I will see Apaji and Piari, and I will bring you food. Will you be all right?"

Again the children nodded, and the doctor pulled him on the sleeve to follow. He watched the children as he walked away from them, lined up along the verandah facing the canal. Each small and pallid face tugged at him not to go: Gappu, tall and lean, the first and favored son; Gerrar who was supposed to be a doctor, the Chosen One; and Karim, the Fighter, his indomitable companion; Moïd, the last son, stricken with speechlessness; Mona, fragile and timid and forgotten between the older children and the babies; and finally Raheel, his flower, whose dowry of jewels and cloth had already filled two large trunks in India, with Sara in her arms. Rukmani stood darkly behind them, the girl they had to save. He held them with his eyes as he left them behind in the new unfurnished house, which still belonged to no one and least of all to them, until he crossed the rail line and they were out of sight.

For three days there was no change in Piari's condition. Apaji sat continuously at her bedside in the silent house, praying to God that the fever would fade, that there would be no diarrhea, and that spots would not appear. Every hour she changed the compresses of cloth soaked in water. She applied them to Piari's brow and neck and arms to keep the fever down, and examined her wrists and forehead as the doctor had advised. Abu came during the day but returned at night to the children in the house along the canal with eggs and small rations of meat and powdered milk for Sara who at only two months of age had to be weaned by Raheel and fed by spoon. In order to quiet her insistent screams of rage, Raheel had to plug the baby's mouth with a wad of cotton dipped in milk.

The house was in chaos. Dirty pots lay scattered around the kitchen crusted with dal and fried eggs that none of the children bothered to clean. They complained that they did not like Raheel's cooking. The rice was lumpy; the vegetables were burned. Why didn't Apaji come home if nothing serious was happening to Piari?

Gerrar went to the library in the city and brought home a big basic medical textbook. He showed the pictures of all the illnesses to the children, faces bloated with so-called rare tropical diseases. He was certain he could diagnose Piari's illness better than the doctor or anyone else. He caught frogs and dissected them in the garden, leaving their skeletons along the path that was overgrown with weeds in the dry cracks of earth. Raheel complained to Abu that Gerrar kept showing the frogs to her and making her sick to her stomach, but Abu never seemed to hear what any of them were saying. He just

ppeared at night like a ghost, and would not eat any food or settle
heir disputes.

At night, when they slept, they could hear him prowling
hrough the house, and in the morning he was gone before anyone
:lse woke up. He left for the apartment at sunrise and burst in on
Apaji with his haggard and frightened face, asking her without
words if Piari had shown any change. Once Gappu nagged him
:nough to let him come along. He promised not to touch anything or
:ven enter the room where Piari was lying delirious in her fever. He
hung about the rooftop courtyard wide-eyed and red in the face.
When Apaji came near him, he backed off as a Syed would treat an
Untouchable, and ran away embarrassed. He never should have
:ome.

It was during the fourth night when Apaji unwrapped the compresses that Piari's eyes popped open and stared clearly into her
own. "Ummy, I am thirsty," she said. Apaji laid her hands all over
Piari's face and throat and narrow little chest. She was cool and dry.
The fever was in remission. Apaji hugged Piari to her and ran to
bring a glass of water from the pump. The warm air was filled with
light from the full moon, and she could hear the calling of cuckoos
and other night birds. She brought the water back into the bedroom
and bent over Piari, who sat up and gulped the water, grasping the
glass with both hands. In the light of the candle she was holding,
Apaji could see small red bumps littered across Piari's wrists like a
poisonous bracelet.

"Oh, God," Apaji breathed, and she clasped her hand over her
lips to stifle a scream. The bumps were there. No matter how she
blinked and held the candle, they were shining across Piari's forehead and on her cheeks. She brought Piari glass after glass full of
water, and finally curled up on the bed beside her daughter. She
held Piari all night in the curve of her chest, whispering her prayer
over and over until she was hypnotized by the drone of her own
voice, "God take the disease from Piari's tiny body and pour it into
me. Oh, God, who is kind. God who is merciful. God who is one."

Before sunrise, Piari woke again and cried out that she was

thirsty. Apaji ran to the water pump but could not fill the glass. She stared at the water which poured onto the earthen floor and over her feet, and in the darkness it seemed to shine with squirming, insidious organisms, which danced in the air and crawled across the floor. She knew she was half-crazed, but she dashed the glass against the stone wall and saw the splintered pieces gray with filth. She breathed the heavy dust of the nightly sandstorm and backed away from the wall, which was alive with weeds and moss growing in the cracks. Everything was contaminated—the water, the air, the city, the earth. She did not know what to do or where to touch. There was no meat or vegetable, rice or wheat, to feed Piari that might not have a pestilence lurking in its veins.

Apaji ran back into the bedroom and sat Piari in her lap. The only thing that was not diseased was Apaji's own milk. She pulled up the edge of her blouse and fastened Piari's mouth around her breast. Piari beat Apaji's arms and face with her fists and tried to move her head away, but Apaji held her firm. "Drink, daughter. Drink," she murmured into Piari's thick straight hair. "This is the best milk. It will make you strong." Piari tossed her head back and forth and tried to scream.

Abu arrived just as the morning broke into shadows, and he could hear Piari's muffled screams floating out into the street. He bounded up the stairs and threw open the door to Piari's room.

"What are you doing?" he shouted. Apaji turned her frantic face toward her husband. Her hair was tumbling out of the knot at the nape of her neck and the long fall of her sari lay in her lap. Piari jerked her head away from Apaji's breast, and Rehman could see the red bumps livid on every inch of her face. Rehman fell to his knees on the clay floor of the room and burst into tears, while Apaji stared at him because she had no more strength for words.

Later in the morning the doctor came and confirmed the diagnosis of smallpox. Looking woefully at the distraught parents, he wagged his head and clucked his tongue. "Ai Allah. Disease follows fast on our sins."

"What sins?" cried Rehman. "What has this child done?"

"I am not a man of religion, only a doctor."

He gathered up his instruments, a worn black stethoscope and a flashlight, his small bottles and vials of balms and herbs, and placed them in the beaten and torn satchel he carried. "What can I say to you? It is the children who are dying in Multan. Every day I see two hundred cases of measles, a thousand of smallpox and cholera. The dispensaries are full, and they are all children. Thousands more never even see a doctor. You can see them playing in the streets. Their stomachs are swollen with malnutrition, and their naked bodies are wracked with sores. It is the children who are suffering." He handed a bottle of medicine to Apaji.

"It is only for the pain," he explained. "The rest is up to you. When the sores break, you must daub Piari's skin and see that the pus does not spread into her eyes. You must keep her hands tied to the bed. I need not tell you how important this is."

Abu saw the doctor out into the street and tried to pay him, but the doctor refused as he did every day. He had enough money, he said. He did not need to take food from the mouths of the refugees. The doctor salaamed, and Rehman climbed back up the dim stairs to the apartment. He shivered despite the heat of the day, and his perspiration felt cold and clammy on his arms and back.

For two weeks he watched with Apaji the progress of Piari's smallpox. He returned to the house at the canal only in the evening and did not sleep there with the children any longer. He did not have to explain why he left them every night. They could see in his bloodshot eyes, the distracted look of his face, which could not concentrate on anything, that Piari was passing through the worst stages of the illness and that Abu never slept and rarely ate.

His mind was preoccupied with the vision of his daughter's body swallowed in the acrid, rotting odor of her sores. There was not an inch that was clean. They seeped along her arms and legs, stomach and face, neck, shoulders, ears, fingers. Apaji and he watched each red and swollen bump erupt like a crater with the poisonous yellow liquid cupped within and spilling over, as they daubed her frantically with compresses and sour-smelling medicine. They counted each sore that crusted into a yellow scab and knew every time another broke, as they peered nervously into the soft brown eyes that pleaded with them from behind the bloated aching mass of flesh and face. Rehman had to pick out with his fingers, the pale wriggling worms that festered in an open wound on Piari's knee where she had scratched too much despite the cloth wrapped around her fingers like gloves. The pain was great, and Rehman fed Piari finely powdered spoonfuls of opium to keep her in a fitful half sleep. Throughout the scorching hot days, Apaji fanned the air over Piari's bed until her wrists were numb, and she splashed water around the room to settle the dust that swirled in through the windows and seeped through the cracks. They seemed to be battling everything but the disease itself which grew and festered and followed its malevolent course with a will all its own. At night they spread a blanket across the floor and only occasionally drifted into sleep, to be awakened with a start by Piari's whimpering as she strained to move her arms that were bound to the bed by strips of cloth.

For nine full days and nights the smallpox drifted liquidly up and down Piari's skin and consumed her flesh. The finished sores dried into scabs, and by the tenth morning Piari was encased in a brownish crust. The swelling had subsided, and her body was so thin her ribs and knees protruded from the wasted flesh. The danger was over, but the disease would last forever in the still livid scars that scored Piari's limbs and checkered her face.

The doctor told Apaji to spread a layer of finely sifted ashes all over Piari twice a day to prevent further contamination, and to take Piari to the countryside. Apaji wrapped her in a blanket, and Abu cradled her in his arms. Without speaking, they left the apartment, and Apaji breathed the perfumes of the air through her nostrils that seemed permeated with the sour-smelling odor of pus and disease.

Abu led Apaji along the track glistening in the sunlight and across the limpid green fields and rice paddies. Together they carried the wasted wreck of their beautiful daughter back to the children waiting in the house at the canal, thanking God that she was alive and that the smallpox had not spread into her eyes and that the other children had been spared. Now they could be a family again.

Raheel saw them coming. She was sitting on the shoulder of the canal, weaving flowers into bracelets for Mona and Rukmani who ere lying at her side. Her face, browned again from sunshine and full of blushing cheeks, burst into a smile. "Apaji is here!" she cried, and picking up her skirts, she ran barefooted through the rippling grass. Gerrar and Gappu came flying out of the house and ran along the path toward their parents, their arms waving madly in the air.

"Abu! Apaji! Piari!" they shouted.

Mona walked shyly behind them, leading Rukmani by the hand.

Abu raised his hand in greeting, but they all stopped in their tracks when they saw Apaji's wan smile and the bundle in her arms, not moving.

"How is Piari?" Gerrar asked.

Abu peeled back the edge of the blanket that was tucked around Piari's bald head, and the mottled face rolled toward her brothers and sisters and stared at them from deep black orbs of eyes that were rimmed with shadows and the scars where her eyebrows should have been. Her head had been shaven hastily, and the once long silky hair stood on her scabby scalp in patches. Gerrar withdrew his extended hand in shock, and Raheel swayed on her feet almost in a swoon.

"Ai Allah, my baby sister!"

Mona was trembling, and Rukmani burst into wails, although she could not see.

Gappu and Gerrar supported Apaji into the house, and they laid Piari gently on a bed, clearing it quickly of the clothes and sheets that lay crumpled all over. Apaji looked about the new house with a deep sigh. "I will put everything in order," she said. She did not ask whose house it had been before Partition, whether the former occupants had been forced to leave or what had been their suffering. There was no room in her for those considerations any longer. She asked Raheel to bring Sara to her, and she pressed the infant to her breast which had been denied to her for yet another two weeks in her short life.

Abu cleared the other children out of the room. "Piari still needs months of rest, so that she can regain her weight and her hair will grow again. You must guard her and watch to see that she does not pick off her scabs before they are completely healed," he warned, leading them outside to the bank of the canal. "You must be very quiet and play far away from the house."

The children sank around him on the grass. The sun was high overhead, and the clouds were just beginning to bank in huge white fists for the daily rain. Abu noticed for the first time the date trees filled with fruit and parrots, the flowers trembling in the warm movement of the air, the brown bodies of village children snaking through the paddies with bales of thrashed wheat and grass piled on their heads. The farmers were hurrying along their plow-oxen to get home before the rain. Rehman breathed deeply and filled his lungs with the fresh perfume of fertilizer, animals, and green growing things. All the children were together again. He held their faces in his eyes and said their names to himself as they watched him quietly, waiting to learn what he would ask them to do next. He looked along the expanse of fields, and in the distance he saw Karim coming along at a run, leading a goat and her kid by a piece of rope.

"Where has Karim been?" he asked, suddenly realizing that the third son had been missing.

"Karim has gone crazy," Gappu informed him. "He won't stay at home and goes wandering around the villages. He won't do any work, and he is fighting all the time."

"Yesterday he brought home a duck," said Gerrar. "Do you want to see? It is tied up in the back, and he is planning to build a duck pond."

Abu watched Karim running through the fields, his skinny legs sticking way out of the short shorts. His long, shaggy hair bounced across his forehead and hung into his eyes. The two goats trotted at his side, tugging at the rope with their chins and whimpering loudly. Karim came up to Abu and the children breathlessly and fell down on the grass. "Abu, you're back! Where are Apaji and Piari?"

"They are here, but you mustn't disturb them," said Rehman. "Where did you get those goats?"

Karim petted the wiry brown-and-white back of the tiny kid. "The she-goat will give good milk."

"I'll bet he stole it," said Gappu accusingly.

"I did not," said Karim, jumping to his feet. "I took the

undred rupees Abu gave me in India and bought the goats from a
armer. I didn't think we needed to keep the money anymore."

Gerrar stood up, thrusting his fists into the pockets of the old
chool blazer he still wore all the time. "It's not the money that is
mportant," he explained to Abu. "Karim wants to keep these filthy
nimals in the house. They breed diseases. Isn't one smallpox
nough?"

"I will have to think about it," Abu mediated.

Karim was close to tears, and he petted the kid which continued
o whimper and totter back and forth at the end of the rope, poking
ts face at the she-goat's udder which was wrapped in a cloth to pro-
ect the milk.

"If I can't keep my goats and duck, I am going back to Dadi in
Nehtor. I hate living here. Gerrar can't tell me what to do. He is
always dissecting frogs and lizards, but nobody tells him to stop."

"I am going to be a doctor," Gerrar shouted. "I am going to do
something about smallpox and cholera and the Indian plague."

Karim swung his fist at Gerrar and grazed his arm. Abu raised
his hands. "Children who fight cannot be trusted alone. If this is
how you behave when I am gone, I do not think I can go to the salt
mines in Khevera to start my business. We will sit here and eat up
all the money the Nawab of Bahawalpur has invested in us, and then
we will be very fine."

"Oh, no, Abu!" Raheel wailed. "You are not leaving us again!"
She looked at him with her deep soft eyes. They had lost the mis-
chievous shimmering of the days when she sneaked away from the
mahalla in Nehtor to go to the movies and flirted with young boys
from the colleges in Aligarh. Her hair was strewn with wild flowers,
and her cotton skirt was shabbily brown. Rehman could see the
rough red marks on her fingers, which she curled and uncurled in
her lap. Washing clothes and cleaning rice had stripped them of their
plump satin texture, and her nails were broken and chewed. "I can't
stay here caring for children for the rest of my life."

Rehman frowned. "Have you not learned what surprises there
are in life? Can you complain when you are sitting in the country
with eggs to eat and flowers to smell? Your brother has brought you

341

a goat, and now you will have milk and butter. Do you resent th▪ little things you do, when your sister lies inside almost dead an▪ scarred for life? Is fighting and complaining all you children can d▪ when millions of others have no homes?"

The children looked ashamed and could not meet Abu's eyes "How does Gerrar expect to be a doctor if I have no business to pa▪ his bills? How does Raheel think she will stop working and hav▪ new dresses stitched and saris and jewels for her dowry, if I canno▪ leave the children in her hands so that I can put our little money t▪ use? Does Karim think he will always have a hundred rupees t▪ spend on animals, if I cannot trust him to help his brothers instea▪ of playing in the villages all day when I am away? Must I ask per▪ mission from my children to do what I have to do?"

"Abu, you promised that we would decide everything by demo▪ cratic vote," Gappu reminded him. "We have many things to te▪ you."

"It is different now. We have no choices. I must invest th▪ Nawab's money in the mine. He has put his faith in us, and you wil▪ have to do your parts here."

"What about when you return from Khevera and you hav▪ money to give us? What will you do then?" Gerrar insisted. "Wil▪ you send me to medical school? I am almost fifteen. Gappu will b▪ sixteen next month. Will we make a better life or will we always live like refugees with the dead and dying?"

"A-A-Abu," Moïd stuttered, raising his small brown hand ti midly behind his older brothers, who always seemed to ignore him with their towering backs and fast tongues. Everyone turned to look at their little brother, who had not spoken except to Gappu since they left their house in Aligarh. "I w-w-want to go b-b-back to Neh tor," he stammered painfully.

Rehman scooped Moïd in his arms and stroked his hair. "I see your hatred of this country is so strong it will bring words to the mouths of mute children."

"It is not a question of blaming Pakistan," said Gappu. He looked out over the fields and paddies of Punjab, the banyan and date trees filled with green parrots and the canal lazily washing its

aters over the black backs of the buffaloes' humps, the silhouettes of
he last farmers of the afternoon riding home on the stems of their
wooden plows behind lumbering bullocks and oxen. "To me this is
ndia. It looks exactly the same. The farm girls sing the same songs
on their way home from the fields. The children play gilly-dunda
nd fly their kites. The old men sit on their charpoys and smoke
heir pipes in the evening. Tell us, Abu, why did Kanti Lal Shah
ake our house—so that we could come here and take the house of
omeone else? Why is there killing, and why are there refugees when
othing changes? Why is there suffering when everything stays ex-
ctly the same?"

Rehman rocked Moïd in his arms. "These are not questions I
an answer. I can only work to give you choices. When I return
rom Khevera, and if there is money, each of you may choose to go
where you please. It is the most I can offer you. I cannot force you
o live in a place where your questions may never be answered. My
amily will be divided, but that is the price for dividing the country.
ndia was divided, but that is the price for our independence."

He placed Moïd on the grass and rose to his feet. "If there is
profit in the salt business, Gerrar will go to medical school. Raheel
may buy dresses, and when the border is safe again, Moïd may go
back to Nehtor if he still wishes. And I will send Rukmani to her
people. The rest of you decide for yourselves. Gappu and Karim
may go to study where they wish, only give me the peace of mind to
go to Khevera and see what I can do."

He walked away from the children and back into the house.
They could see the stoop of his shoulders settling into a firm hump.
His head was thrust forward on his strong neck as if the weight of
his responsibilities had bent his back but not his mind, which
plunged ahead just a little faster than their demands and fought a
little harder than the events that attacked them. The only change in
his face was the pair of thick plastic glasses that he could hardly see
out of and the shock of graying hair that curled across his brow.
Karim eyed Gerrar over the back of the nanny goat and dragged the
animals to the rear of the house where he was building a fence. Gerrar marched off in the opposite direction. Raheel took Rukmani and

Mona by the hand and led them along the canal and into the dat grove beyond the house to pick fruit.

Gappu dangled his feet over the edge of the canal. There was n sense in running away. He could understand that Gerrar wished t be a doctor. It was the prophecy from the moment of his birth, an no one ever doubted that it would be fulfilled. Still that was n reason to harass Abu about things no one could control. Karim wa always fighting, and refused to do any of the chores assigned to him He would not talk to anybody since the night of the riot and onl cared about going to the villages and playing with animals becaus he said it reminded him of Nehtor. Gappu wished he could decid what he wanted to do himself. It was Abu's dream that he becom an engineer, but Gappu did not think it was right for him to go t school and study when the ten members of his family had only thre eggs to divide among themselves once a day and their only clothe were those they had worn on the trains and ship. He thought tha the best thing for him would be to go to Khevera with Abu and hel build the salt business. "Let the other sons go where they pleased, he decided. "I am staying with Abu until all this is over. I am man."

Rehman spent the next ten days preparing the family for his depar ture to Khevera. He was determined to provide them with everything necessary to eat and wear before he left them alone It appeared that it was truly the end of the rioting in India and Paki stan. The police from Karachi were permanently installed in Multar and the other cities along the border, to see that the last evacuation of refugees be without bloodshed and that the new arrivals be settle into the city in an orderly fashion, despite the scarcity of houses, food, and medicine. The police had taken up quarters in the old can tonment of the British army, and they prowled the streets in their khaki uniforms and heavy boots at night, enforcing curfew and send ing stragglers quickly on their way with curses and threats of beat ings and arrests. After a while, even the most recalcitrant and illiterate vagrants knew the sound of the curfew drums being tolled through the streets, and at night Multan became a city of ghosts.

Rehman saw the refugees every day when he passed the railroad station. They descended from trains, flooding the station house and the platforms, trying to decide if they should stop in Multan or continue pushing north to the mountains or west to the desert and the foreign hill tribes of the frontier. The police tried to push the people back onto the trains, shouting, "There is no more room in Multan. There are no houses. Go somewhere else." Those who remained were herded together in open lorries and bullock carts and taken to a dispersal office for assignment to one of the camps that filled the city's alleys with ragged tents and outhouses.

Whenever Rehman walked the two miles to the city, he was beset by the thin round-eyed faces of children recently taught to beg. They extended their frail, dirt-encrusted palms to every passerby but were too shy to offer prayers or call out curses as the more seasoned children of professional beggars learned to do at the earliest age. Rehman always gave a few coins to the children and to the mothers, crouching over their stoves in the street with nothing to cook on them but onions and peppers, and perhaps a wilted vegetable or the head of a fish found discarded in the market. He filled his pockets every day with dates from the grove behind the house on the canal. Otherwise, he could not walk through the city, visit officials to discuss his mine claim and his plans, or search the market for cloth for new clothes. He could not see the vague begging faces if he could not give them the little dates that nobody else claimed as their own or the few paissas change that would hardly buy a handful of rice.

New shops were opening every day as Muslims took over the premises abandoned by Hindus the month before. There was little merchandise to sell, and the new shopkeepers sat idly on their stools in the streets and slept there at night with their entire families, so that no one else would come to usurp their claims. The carpenter from India became a carpenter in Pakistan. The bicycle-repair man from Delhi hung his sign on the bicycle-repair shop in Multan and lived among the blackened tools and tires that hung from the ceiling like heavy ropes, waiting for business that some day soon would have to come.

The people seemed to be in a dream, waiting for life to begin. On every corner crowds of men gathered to listen to radio broadcasts that were piped through loudspeakers. The bazaar was filled with the high whining sounds of old scratchy recordings of Indian film music, and the pulsating wail of recorded wedding pipes mixed incongruously with the busy chattering of the people bargaining for food and arguing with the vegetable salesmen over quality. Each song was interrupted by announcements from the police, who warned continuously that all troublemakers would be shot and that anyone seen loitering near the railroad station or the tracks would be arrested and whipped.

Rehman scouted through the bazaar to learn all he could about the price of salt. He discovered that it was a much-needed commodity throughout Pakistan. With supply trains hijacked and not running, or at best unpredictable, all commodities, except what was grown locally, sat unharvested and unexcavated in the earth, without workers to do the labor and without businessmen to export them to the cities. Rehman was certain that the mines in Khevera would yield a generous living. Salt was totally unavailable, and the farmers were complaining that without salt lick their animals would wither and dry out in the sun. Rehman felt there was nothing more for him to learn in Multan. If he did not leave as soon as possible, he would exhaust his capital, and his family would be doomed to join the hordes who had not been lucky enough to have a business claim or to know an important person in the state, as he knew the Nawab, to invest in their future.

In order not to upset Apaji too much, he did not tell her he was leaving until he was certain that the godown beside their house was filled with enough grains of wheat and rice to last a month. He brought huge sacks of eggs, cushioned in moist sawdust that would preserve them for weeks, and other sacks full of peppers, onions, garlic, cumin seed, and turmeric. There were cans of kerosine and logs for fuel piled behind the house. On the last day he scoured the market for sugar and, gritting his teeth, bought it at too high a price,

nd from a stall nestled among a row of empty tailor shops he
ɔought a hundred rupees' worth of cloth, three yards for each child,
ɪncluding Rukmani, whose only clothing was her petticoat.

He carried his bundles back through the fields under his arms.
The brown sugar and raw cotton cloth were his first presents, the
ɪrst luxuries, he could give to his family, and he was beaming with
ɔride as he crossed the train trestle over the canal and turned toward
he house.

Raheel and Mona saw him coming and raced along the canal's
retaining wall to pull him by his arms and take the packages, full of
ɛxcitement that there were gifts to take to Apaji. They threw the
ɔackages down on the verandah and unfurled the yards of cloth in
the air. Each bolt was a different color. There was pink and yellow,
green and violet, for the girls, and dark blue, white, and tan for the
boys. Raheel danced around the verandah, singing with pleasure and
wound the cloth around herself and Mona and Rukmani like Salome
dancing with her veils. Everyone came running to see why Raheel
was so happy. Karim appeared from the rear of the house where he
had been feeding his goats. Apaji poked her head through the open
window of the front room. She could not believe her eyes. The
verandah was covered with the bright shining cloth, and all the
children were jumping and running up and down the steps of the
wide porch. Sara was propped in the crook of Apaji's arm, her small
brown head with its new soft fringe of hair rotating on her tiny neck,
and her long almond-shaped eyes darting back and forth to see the
excited movement and colors of the cloth flying in the air.

"See what Abu has brought," Raheel called to them.

"So much noise will waken your sister Piari," Apaji said.

Rehman looked at her sheepishly. "I have brought cloth for all
the children. Tomorrow the tailor will come to have them stitched."

Apaji adjusted Sara onto her shoulder. "I know what else will
happen tomorrow," she said, looking at Sara but speaking to her
husband.

"What would that be, bride?" Abu asked, realizing that she had
already guessed the truth that he was leaving for the mines.

"I have seen these signs before, many times. When you know

347

that you are leaving us, the godown is suddenly filled with a month's supplies. The tailor always comes, and you have your pockets full of presents for the children." She wrapped the edge of her sari around her head, encompassing Sara completely. "We are happy, Abu, that you can do so well."

Apaji withdrew from the window and swung the heavy wooden shutter closed. Rehman could hear her fit the latch and recede into the dim emptiness of the house. He knew she had gone to cry in the bedroom alone, where no one but the youngest child could see her. He did not go to her because he knew she would return as soon as she regained her composure. It was almost like normal, like all the years before Partition, when he came and went on business and Apaji cried at his departures. She always had a young baby to carry off with her, in whom she could confide and receive the comfort only an infant could give.

Rehman waited on the verandah where he liked to sit, watching the farmers hurrying home through the fields before the afternoon rains came. The washerwomen gathered up the bright dhotis and saris that were spread along the sloping ghats of the canal. The brown-legged children were trampling through the shallow water, waving their sticks at the buffalo to get moving. Rehman's children were playing in the grass.

Apaji returned to him, after crying, and put her hand on his shoulder. "You see our children," she said. "They are growing like bamboo. I am glad you have brought them cloth. I must soak it for shrinkage before the tailor comes tomorrow." She began gathering up the yards of cloth in her arms and called Raheel to help her.

"Rest a moment," said Rehman. "There are many important things to discuss. I want all the children to come and sit quietly, so that I can tell them what they must do."

Apaji called the rest of the children to come up from the grass. They all sat around Abu on the charpoys and the railing of the verandah.

Rehman raised his hands, palms open, like a teacher. He sat on the only armchair on the verandah. It was reserved for him. Even when he was not at home, no one else thought to sit in it.

"Since the riot of Multan, more than two weeks ago, there has not been any disturbance in a single village or town of Pakistan. The people are waiting for life to begin again. The bazaars are waiting for merchandise, and the factories for raw materials. The farmers need fertilizer and salt. It is time to begin our business, and therefore I am leaving you."

Everyone was listening intently to Abu. Over the children's heads he could see streaks of lightning from cloud to cloud that heaved up out of the distance, and great drops of water began to splatter on the dusty earth like balloons. "While I am gone, you must be on exceptional behavior. You must take care of Apaji and mind Piari closely because she is fragile and frightened. Karim may collect more animals, but he must see that they don't stray into the house, and Gerrar will not hurt them. When I return, I hope I will have the money to send each of my sons where they wish. Have you given any thought to where you would like to go?"

Gerrar looked closely at Abu but was afraid to speak now that he was actually being given his choice.

"I know you want to be a doctor," said Abu. "Have you chosen a medical school?"

"I will go to Lahore to prepare. Then I would like to go to England. The M.B.B.S. is the only medical degree of any value."

Rehman nodded. "And you, Karim?"

Karim hugged his knees to his chest. "I want to go to America, Abu. Phopi Fatima's son will send me to school."

Rehman nodded again and pointed to Gappu. "What about you?"

Gappu stood up. "I am not returning to school just yet. I gave it very careful thought. I would like to go to Khevera with you and be in your business." He thrust his hands into the pockets of his blazer.

Rehman looked at Moïd. "I suppose you have ideas, too. Do you still want to go to your grandmother's in Nehtor?"

Moïd nodded his head.

"Just as I expected," said Rehman. "Each of you has said what I least expected you to say. Gerrar dreams of London, when the schools in India and Pakistan are perfectly fine. Suddenly our degrees are worthless, and he must go to England, although we have just won our independence. Karim hears the word America, and now that is where he must go. What do I know about America? have hardly ever heard of it. Gappu, who of all my sons should be in school, thinks that suddenly I am in need of his assistance to take care of my business." He rubbed his hands through his thick graying hair. All three boys glared at him, and Gappu turned to protest.

Rehman raised his hand. "Nevertheless, I promised I would send you wherever you chose. Gerrar can go to Lahore Medical College and make his applications for England. Karim wants to go to America, which must be very expensive. But if we have the money his cousin will receive him. I will write to Phopi Fatima to inform her son. Moïd, of course, can go to Nehtor as soon as the border is open. Probably Uncle Tariq will also go, and they can take Rukman with them. Gappu can come with me, and perhaps someday he will see that he needs the university. At least I will have one son remaining to me."

"Why do you think only of sons?" said Raheel, bowing her head. "I have been thinking myself where I would like to go."

Rehman looked at Raheel in surprise. "Do you think there is a better place for you than in your mother's home? You will not find a husband in a school. Apaji will make your marriage arrangements and collect your dowry here."

"I don't wish a husband," said Raheel, bowing her head deeper and blushing. "I think there are enough children. Mona and Piari and Sara will give you grandchildren. I will be a teacher."

Rehman jumped up from his chair. "What? I won't hear of it," he boomed excitedly.

"Apaji," Raheel wailed. "Tell him."

Rehman looked at his wife. "You know about this?"

Apaji also blushed and covered her hair with her sari. "I have discussed it with Raheel, and I think she must do what she believes is important."

Rehman was amazed. "It is very un-Islamic. Islam Khatra men hai."

"Fatima, the Prophet's daughter, was a teacher," said Apaji.

Rehman folded his arms across his chest. Women had their defender in the Prophet's daughter and could always resort to her name in an argument.

"It is you who must collect the daughters' dowries," said Rehman, avoiding a religious debate that Apaji always won. "I cannot tell you what to do." He saw Apaji and Raheel exchange little glances of affirmation.

"The only child left is Mona. Has she already decided her fate?" Mona threw her arms around Apaji's waist and buried her head shyly in her mother's lap. "Are there any other ideas?" He scanned the faces of his children, who all shook their heads. "Well, then, tomorrow I leave for Khevera."

He looked out over the fields and breathed deeply the rain-drenched air and the sweet perfume of the wet dates that blew in the shivering branches of the trees. The green of the rice paddies was translucent behind a curtain of rain, and across the fields white whooping cranes were stretching their feathers with deep-throated cries. He thought that if the salt business proved profitable as he expected it would, he could quickly go to Lahore and make all the arrangements for his children, and in a flash of recognition, he wondered how old he would be before they all sat together again in their own home, and where would that house be?

"Punjab is a beautiful state," he sighed. "I wish you could all be happy here."

Gappu and Abu were ready for their departure early the next morning. Apaji said her final farewells inside the house and closeted herself in the bedroom to say her prayers. Piari was still sleeping at her side, doused in a thin layer of herbs and ash to help the scabs slowly to heal. The older children burst out of the house and followed their father and brother to the railroad station.

It was quiet and warm in the soft light of dawn, and the melodious sound of men at prayer drifted across the fields and out of the city. The station was almost deserted, except for the police and the coolies who stretched out along the platform chatting over their breakfasts of hot tea and chapatis. The tall Karachi policemen, armed with rifles and revolvers, patrolled back and forth like a paramilitary force. When the *titi* rang the bell for the Lahore train, the police took up positions along every few feet of track and held their bayonets ready. The children felt their muscles tense as the train rolled heavily into the station, its great iron engine obscured by blasts of charcoal-filled smoke. Men were sitting on the rooftops of the cars, wrapped up in cloth, with scarves across their faces and on their heads like turbans. All along the platform the men were jumping from the roofs, and women pushed through the doors of the bright green compartments, and tried to run to the women's waiting room. Everyone was talking or shouting, and the police tried to grab everyone to check tickets.

Gappu looked anxiously at Abu. There did not seem to be an inch of space on the train. He thought that possibly Abu was mad, taking him back into the crowded refugee trains. Each bogie was guarded by several Pakistani police officers, and the faces of the passengers crowded every window.

Rehman put his arm across Gappu's shoulder. "Don't worry about the crowds. There are many, but they are all travelers like you and me. The Sikhs and Hindus are all gone from Pakistan, and the looters have been arrested. Come with me now."

Rehman located their first-class compartment in which two other men were sitting. He presented his tickets to the policeman and then to the *titi*, and they were permitted to enter the bogie. Raheel handed him a tin tiffin carrier full of chapatis and sweet rice, which Apaji had prepared from Abu's gift of sugar, and the children gathered outside the window to wave good-bye.

It was an eight-hour journey to Lahore, where Gappu and Rehman would have to change trains for the small gauge line that would climb the hills to Khevera. By midday it was scorching hot, and the fans in the compartment did not seem able to move the heavy air by their turning. The train sped through the state of Punjab that was all fertile fields crisscrossed by rivers and canals. Gappu kept dozing off, but every time the train crossed the trestle of a canal, he started upright in his seat and glanced nervously out the window.

Abu watched his face. "What is the matter?" he asked.

"Nothing, Abu."

"I know what you are thinking."

"I am not thinking," Gappu protested. Rehman moved next to his son and sat close to him with his strong body. "I don't like the trains," Gappu said. "When I hear the wheels go over a bridge, I keep thinking of all the people I saw floating in the water, and the bodies lying on the bridges, and the train going so slowly." He closed his eyes.

"I don't want you to think about those things anymore. You were very brave, and now it is all over. You want to be a business-man. You should not think of all that has passed."

Gappu nodded his head and tried not to sleep. It was only in dreams that he froze half awake and half asleep in the memories he had somehow to repress. He sat up and tried to enjoy the ride. The train made only fueling stops all the way to Lahore, and gradually the outskirts of the city appeared, and the train lost speed to enter the mammoth station of Pakistan's largest metropolis. As soon as the train had slowed a little, coolies jumped on the steps below every compartment and asked through the windows for luggage. Overhead the roof riders were stirring, and their feet echoed in the compart-ment like thunder.

Announcements of train departures were being made over loud-speakers, and hawkers glided through the crowds of people, selling lassy and terra-cotta gharra pots full of the coldest water. Abu guided Gappu quickly across the overhead pass and away from the refugees unloading themselves from the roofs and compartments of the express train. The police were there to round them up and take them to camps the government and charities had finally combined to give them. Gappu felt their own arrival in Karachi had been tame compared to this. Another whole trainload was coming from Delhi after weeks of travel. Their own train had just been preceded by a slower train which had made every stop from Karachi to Lahore and had taken eight days to arrive. Rehman pushed Gappu ahead of him through the crowds. He kept talking to Gappu in a low voice to keep him calm as they passed through the pushing, shoving people who were being hurried along by the police to waiting lorries.

"Lahore is the capital city of Punjab. All the Muslims on the Indian side of Punjab want to come here. The police are showing them where to go," Rehman explained. "There is nothing to worry about. Jinnah is seeing to it that there are no more raids in Pakistan, and Gandhi is doing the same thing in India. The trains do not even cross the border any longer, but stop to let the people walk across and catch another train, so there can be no more hijackings. The villages between Lahore and Amritsar on the Indian side were the scenes of the worst riots because no one could agree where the border would start until weeks after Independence Day."

Gappu looked uneasily around as Abu steered him over another pass and down onto a narrower, empty track at the farthest end of the station. Their small gauge train was waiting at the platform while its engine was being hooked up with much gesturing and shouting from the engineers. Across the station, the refugees were a whirl of motion, with luggage flying from hand to hand and being carried on people's heads because there was no room to hold it in the crush of bodies. There were many tearful reunions and shouts of recognition as families separated for months without news rushed into each other's arms. The police ran back and forth and over the roofs of the three trains and along the tracks and platforms, trying to keep order.

Rehman slid Gappu into the wooden bench of their tiny two-seat compartment. He closed the miniature curtained window, lowered the blinds, and turned on the fan, so that the noises of the crowds outside were muffled. Rehman kept talking, trying to reassure Gappu, who was sitting on the edge of his seat and attempting to smile uneasily at his father: "You must realize that Lahore was the tensest city in all of western India. It was rivaled only by Dacca in the east. When Lahore was given to the Muslims and Amritsar only fourteen miles away was given to the Sikhs, all the people in the villages in between did not know where they belonged. One day a predominantly Muslim village burnt a predominantly Sikh village. The next day a Sikh village retaliated. No one knew where the border would be—before this village, or after that. The Sikhs were running eastward from Lahore, and the Muslims were running out of Amritsar to the west. It did not matter what it said on paper. The people in a village do not understand borders. That is why the police must be here. Everyone wants to come to Lahore. You should be grateful that now they can come. The border keeps opening and closing to let them in. You should not look so worried."

"I understand," said Gappu, but he kept lifting the slats of the blinds and looking out across the tracks. "There are so many people," he said. "I have never seen so many people except in a procession."

Rehman opened the door of the compartment and called the *titi* who was busily checking passengers' tickets with the record book he kept under his arm. The *titi* bustled over, pushing his official cap off his perspiring forehead, and Rehman ordered a dinner to be brought to the train. As soon as the food arrived, piping hot on a round metal tray, the train began to move and slide away from the station. Gappu ate hungrily, stuffing his mouth full of *rotis*, rice, vegetables, and chopped mutton *koftas*, which were floating in curry in little china dishes. There were even hot pickled condiments. It was the best meal Gappu had tasted in two and a half months. The grease ran down his chin, and he licked his fingers as he worked the rice and meat and curry into little balls.

The terrain changed quickly from fields to hills of rock and clay, where canals had not yet brought the waters of the rivers and the rains, which blew in a narrow stream from the sea to the Himalayas, did not fall. Rehman threw the window wide open and let the dry wind and sunlight pour into the compartment.

Before the train began its circuitous climb to Khevera, it stopped at a base station and a second engine was attached to the rear. As they wound through the brown-colored hills, the tribal children of the salt caves jumped along the running boards of the train, laughing and peering through the windows and asking for paisa. Many of the children were completely naked, and the men and women climbing alongside at almost the same speed as the struggling train were wearing only the scantiest loincloths.

The train veered away from the footpaths where the people were climbing straight up the steep hills among the stunted shrubbery. They were lost in a maze of rugged hills. The hard rocks were so rich in salt that very little vegetation could grow, and some of the peaks were so high that Gappu had to open the door and lean all the way out to see them. The train knifed through the hills, climbing steeply at every 180-degree turn. A paved road ran alongside the track, but it was completely empty of traffic since the villagers preferred the steep direct routes to which their wiry bodies were accustomed. The cliff walls were scored with the blank faces of salt caves, some discarded two thousand years ago as the salt mining advanced higher, century after century. Families of monkeys inhabited every cave. They ran along the walls of rock and squatted in the mine entrances, picking lice out of each other's fur and only lifting their heads from their chattering conversations to glance at the train that passed them once a week. Some playful male monkeys jumped on the train exactly like the tribal children and looked in the windows for food. It seemed to Gappu that there was only the slightest difference between the lives of the monkeys and the tribesmen who also lived among old mines and in huts scattered in the hills.

Gappu was surprised to find the salt deposits in Khevera so different from the flat plateaus of Jaipur, where the salt was gathered from hundreds of lakes that glistened in the land. Compared to Khevera, the mining village of Sambhur in Jaipur had been a paragon of modernity. It seemed that Khevera had been left behind by time and history, and the years could be counted only by the height of the caves.

It was a four-hour climb, although Khevera, halfway up one of the tallest hills, was only seven miles from the base station. Khevera itself was hardly even a town. Beyond the small wooden station, gracious little bungalows and rest houses clustered in the jigsaw puzzle of identical surrounding cliffs. Adjacent to the tracks was a large British chemical company compound of buildings, gleaming white and displaying the company flag. Young men were playing cricket on a lush lawn in the last light of day. The cricket field was the only green in the whole vista of brown hills and stone buildings. Several tousle-haired, solid-built English women were walking tall slender horses along the road that bisected the town.

Rehman took Gappu to a rest house, which was across the road from the chemical company and its group of houses with generous verandahs. Everything except the lawn of the compound was on a slant. Each building perched slightly higher than the next, and everything seemed to be built out of the rocks themselves. Another road climbed from the center of the town up along the hill toward the entrance to the mines. Gappu wanted to explore the town, but he was too distracted by the luxury of the running-water shower and he joined Rehman in a bath immediately. They sat together on the porch of the rest house as evening fell, and watched the monkeys running over the pointed roofs of the buildings and dashing across the road in the dim yellow of the compound's electric lights.

The next morning Rehman led Gappu up along the road a half mile to the entrance to the mines. The railroad track went right up to the mouth of the cave, so that several cars of the Lahore freight trains could be detached and brought up for loading. Workers in short shorts and turbans were riding in and out of the mine entrance on handcarts, which ran along a still smaller track. The miners had the lightest skin since they rarely saw the sun, and their faces were streaked with salt. They were seated atop piles of salt rocks like jagged white slabs of marble. Since the carts had to be pushed manually, the mines were dug from the bottom up, and the carts descended with their loads by force of gravity. A dilapidated stone powerhouse, put up by the government of India for the official rest houses and the chemical company, was still functioning, but its electric power had not been extended to the mines where abundant manpower and the ancient system of tunneling still sufficed.

On either side of the mine entrance, the shantytown of the workers sprawled darkly among the rocks. Women were washing clothes right on the earth outside their huts from pots of water that they collected from the condensing steam of trains. Since no freight trains had arrived since Partition, the women had to wait for the weekly passenger train, and hence everyone was using the little extra water they had gathered the night before.

Rehman walked through the shantytown looking for the quarters of the foremen and watchmen of the mines. Narrow dirt roads dipped downhill among the tents and huts where dogs and children scavenged for food. At the edge of the shanties were the barracklike buildings of the managers and minor mine officials. When Rehman inquired, a chokidar came to the door and pointed to a wooden structure which served as a teahouse. "The senior officer of the mines is there nowadays. He does not know whom he is working for, so why work?"

Rehman followed the guard's directions and entered the teahouse. Groups of men were sitting cross-legged on the floor and at tables in the dark interior, drinking thick tea and smoking their clay chillums, which they wrapped in the edges of their long turbans and cupped in their bony fingers that were ridged white with salt. The air was filled with the perfume of charcoal and sweet tobacco.

Rehman found the senior officer of the mines in his petty officer's khaki uniform, seated at a rough wooden table with several other men. Rehman introduced himself and nudged Gappu onto the bench opposite the foreman beside a row of men who squeezed together to make room. The foreman immediately ordered tea, smiling and salaaming. "I would have come to meet you myself, Sahib, but I wished you to take your rest. It is a happy occasion for us that a salt dealer has come to Khevera."

"How do you know I want to buy salt?" asked Rehman.

"This is a small town, Sahib, and news travels fast," said the foreman. "We have been waiting for someone to come. The mines are working, and the salt is piling up, but no one has come to buy the salt and export it. The British potash company still takes its quota, but that is only a fraction of our production. What do we do, though, when there are no trains? For two months I have had no order to fill, and no one to talk to. I sit idly in the teashops hoping he government of Pakistan will remember that in Khevera is the world's largest deposit of salt." The foreman sighed deeply.

"Is this your son?" he asked, pointing at Gappu. Gappu smiled and salaamed the foreman. He was watching the man with intense interest, his face all dry and lined with white salt like the veins of a leaf. He was flanked by two men on the bench who were passing a chillum with a wrought-silver handle. When the foreman's turn came, he waved the chillum on to the next man who wrapped the stem of the pipe in a strip of cloth which he moistened in a glass of water. The cloth was all stained and greasy from the tobacco and charcoal it filtered. The man sucked several times on the chillum, which he held clasped tightly in both hands, and the charcoal lit into a small flame that went out as he inhaled deeply with a shiver of his shoulders, and the veins on his neck stood out with the effort of the man's skinny chest. The men smoked so much in one breath that the chillum had to be cleaned and refilled after every round. Gappu thought that they must be smoking charas in the tobacco because his head was feeling light and dizzy in the heavy smoke.

The foreman noticed Gappu's slightly faint expression and waved at the smoke in the room with his hand. "This is not the place to talk," he said. "Would you like to see the mines?"

Rehman nodded his head, and they walked back out through the shantytown and up to the entrance of the mine. Rehman explained about his business at the salt lakes in Jaipur to the foreman, who kept saying how happy he was that someone with knowledge of business had finally come. "This is the largest and richest salt mine in the world," the foreman repeated over and over. "There is so much salt in this mine that it can feed the population of the world for a thousand years. The problem is not that we cannot get it out. We cannot ship it out."

Rehman asked a hundred questions about the number of men in a gang, the weight of one cartload of salt, the amount of blasting necessary to mine a ton of rock, and how much salt was yielded. Gappu followed at his father's heels, avoiding the cesspools and refuse left by dogs in the dirt. He tried to pay attention to all the details Abu was storing in his mind that seemed able to record hundreds of statistics and ideas all at once. Rehman already knew the current market price of salt and the uninflated prices before Partition.

The foreman stopped a cart that had just been unloaded and ordered the trainman to take them to a blasting site. Gappu and Rehman stood in front of the foreman in the cart as they rolled into the forty-foot-square entrance. The trainman pulled the cart from the front, and several others pushed from behind. The air was almost immediately cooler, and they were engulfed in pitch darkness.

Only the flashlight on the trainman's forehead thinly lit up the track directly ahead of them. They heard the voices of workers brushing past them alongside of the track. They seemed so accustomed to the dark that they were able to see perfectly where they were going. The cart traveled several hundred feet and then curved into chamber after chamber, slowly climbing uphill. Gappu could hear water dripping all around him as if it were locked within the walls. It was so dark that Gappu could not even see his father's form which he felt beside him.

"Is there any possibility of getting lost?" Gappu asked.

The foreman laughed. "The trainmen know the mines so well they can work without light altogether. Since they were born here, they prefer to be in the caves, and sunlight bothers their eyes. If someone who does not know his way gets lost, he can tap on the rail line, and he will be heard in every shaft of the chamber, and the trainmen can locate the sound to perfection. Stop here," the foreman ordered the trainman. "And I will turn on the light for the sahib and his son." He lit the gaslamp that hung from the cart, and the chamber burst into a bedazzling mirror of white lights glittering like diamonds overhead and on every side. It was the purest light, and as the foreman swung his lantern, the salt crystals seemed to shower like a thousand falling stars. "Kings and princes have come to Khevera to see the salt diamonds," the foreman said proudly, and the trainmen, all smiles, lit up their sweet-smelling *beedie* cigarettes.

The cart continued climbing until it reached a solid wall that was rigged and wired for blasting, but no one was at work. The foreman explained that no blasting had been done since months before Partition, when the former Sikh salt exporter had disappeared and no one came to take his place. "Of course, there are rumors that he was trapped in a chamber and killed, but I know that is not true—not in Khevera. He was my friend," the foreman said.

"When is blasting done?" Rehman asked.

"Whenever I can get a gang together. Most of the gangs you see working now are employed by the British potash company. All that salt is processed here and taken to England, but that is not a fraction of the salt that is mined. The whole town sits idle, because there is no salt being produced for Pakistan. The grinding mills are closed, and the foremen who were Sikhs are gone. There were threats among the villagers when Partition came, and the Sikh foremen left before there could be a fight. Now the people are sorry, because no one knows who will take over the mill. My ancestors have lived here for a hundred generations, but the millworkers are different. They come and go. You will have to choose a new foreman and workers."

Rehman asked their guide to take them to the mill and to the loading sites. The cart clattered back down the track with all the trainmen using their weight on the rear for braking. The main shaft was lit with crystals shimmering in the gaslight. Every hundred feet or so deep chambers bit into the rock surface and drowned in the black darkness.

"Many of these chambers have been here for over a hundred years, since this shaft was begun. We only go a mile deep into the rocks, and then we start a new chamber. Some of the shafts stretch over a hundred miles with their chambers." The foreman pointed to one chamber which appeared no different from the rest. "No one goes into that chamber."

"Why?" asked Gappu.

"Souls live there," the foreman said matter-of-factly. "A hundred Englishmen have tried to go to the end of the mine. None has ever returned."

Abu was laughing, but Gappu felt a chill as he peered into the black emptiness of the chamber.

"It is said that the emperor Ashoka left his treasure there when he gave up his earthly goods to become a Buddhist. A cobra with seven heads guards the treasure to keep the Englishmen from getting it."

"How do you know the snake is in there if no one ever comes out?" asked Gappu.

"It is known, Bhai Sahib," the foreman persisted. "The snake has been there for two thousand years. Since he has seven heads, when one heads gets old it dies and falls off, and the cobra eats his head. Another young head grows in its place, and hence he keeps himself alive. There are no other living creatures in the mines. Only the Namak ki Samp, the Snake of Salt."

"These are silly stories," Rehman said firmly, but Gappu was shivering as if a frozen wind blew through the already cold and sunless mines.

A blast of light greeted them at the entrance of the mines, and the hot air poured over them like a bath. The foreman led them up the hills to the mill where the rocks were cracked and processed into powder. Although the machines were idle, a whole trainload of processed salt was waiting to be taken to Lahore.

After Rehman made a thorough inspection of the machines, the foreman motioned him to follow farther up the hill. "You must meet the wise old man of the mines. He can tell you more than anybody all there is to know about the tunnels and chambers." They climbed the road past huts and shanties made from gunnysacks and separated by running sewers that flowed into a central cesspool.

They stopped at the last house along the road before which a man with a long white beard sat on his charpoy, which was covered with a bright orange sheet. Beside him was a clay pitcher filled with clean water. The old man's clothes were as white as his beard, and his eyebrows seemed to be clouds that moved up and down with his stomach. He was fanning himself continuously with a wooden fan. He was a Mulvi, because he had memorized the Koran and repeated it constantly, even in his sleep.

"Assalaam Aleicum," Rehman greeted the man of religion, but the old man just motioned with his forehead for Rehman to sit on the charpoy beside him as he continued to work his beads with one hand and the fan with the other. His eyes barely moved in their direction. In a few moments he stopped, and said something to the foreman in a dialect Gappu could not understand. The foreman nodded his head, and the old man got off his bed and took a trunk from under the sheet. It was filled with old maps and notes.

"This is all you need to know about the mines," he said, handing the maps to Rehman. "My ancestor was the first surveyor of the mines, and these maps are as good today. The length of feet and inches has not yet changed, has it?" he asked sternly.

"No, Pir," said Abu respectfully.

"So many people are hungry here. If you help them, you can have the maps for nothing. I have outlived my sons and grandsons. You must promise you will put the maps to proper use and give the people work. That is all I ask. God will bless you."

Rehman bowed to the Mulvi. He did not know what to say. He could only assure him that their purposes were the same. The Mulvi raised his hand. "You need not speak. I know who you are and how far you have come with your son. Take the maps and remember me in your prayers."

They left the house at the edge of the road, and the foreman took Rehman next to the power station which continued to supply electricity almost of its own accord to the mill and the compound. All day they explored Khevera, and by evening it seemed the whole town knew who they were. As they walked down the road toward their rest house, the women in the shanties stopped cooking to stare at Rehman and his son. Barefoot workers passing them on the road salaamed and welcomed them to Khevera. All the men in the dark smoke-filled teahouses lowered their saucers, from which they sipped hot tea and milk, and called prayers for Rehman's success and for many days filled with work.

Gappu was exhausted, but it seemed that Abu had more energy than when they started. He smiled at anyone and boomed in his huge voice that there was going to be good work for everyone. He rubbed his hands together with glee and kept throwing his arm around Gappu's tired shoulders as he walked with long bounding strides.

All Gappu wanted to do was sleep, but Abu ordered a huge meal of mutton shanks and lamb, which came from the hills that dipped into valleys and soared up again as far as the eye could see. In the fading light, Gappu could hear the sound of cricket players in the chemical company's compound at their daily afternoon match. It seemed the tall white Englishmen in their short shorts and knee-length socks were in another world, and had nothing to do with salt or mines or the rugged hills of Pakistan, far from vegetation and inhabited only by the people of the ancient tribes. All during dinner Abu talked about salt, but Gappu was distracted by the hazy calls of the Englishmen, the crack of the balls on the wickets, and the polite, restrained clapping of wives and children who were watching on the lawn.

"It is perfectly simple," Abu was saying. "Do you see how we are going to take the salt to Lahore by tomorrow?"

Gappu looked annoyed at his father. "I don't think there is any way for you to come along and start the mine blasting, the mill working, and the trains running just because you order it."

"Not trains," said Rehman, laughing. "That's just the point. Don't you see any other way of moving the salt to Lahore? Just look around."

Gappu scanned the Godforsaken, isolated hills. They seemed dead in the nightfall, like a rock jungle inhabited only by monkeys and hooting night birds, and the cricket players like a remote dream of England mirrored within the walls of the chemical company's compound.

"Just use your eyes and think. That is the art of being a businessman. That and money, which we are also fortunate to have."

Gappu was determined to pass Abu's test. He walked to the corner of the verandah and scanned the road that led down to the wooden station house and the houses of the stationmaster and railroad clerks. He looked over the rooftops where the road looped around the hill and joined again with the tracks. Gappu started. A lone truck was huffing around the bend and toward the chemical compound with barking brakes. "Trucks," he shouted. "You're going to use trucks! When did you think of it?"

"On the train, of course. You saw everything from the window just as I did—the monkeys in the hills, the children who can climb faster than the train, the road. But you did not think, as I did, only of salt. That is our reason for being here, and we will do very well. Tomorrow I will see about renting a truck from the chemical company, and we will take our first shipment of salt to Lahore. I calculate we will earn enough money from the salt to buy five trucks in Lahore, and then we are in business."

Gappu sat at his father's side. Abu seemed to be glowing with energy, and his eyes sparkled as if they still mirrored the chamber of salt crystals in the mine.

"Have you learned anything today?" he asked Gappu. "Do you still want to be a businessman?"

"There is a lot I don't know," said Gappu.

Rehman arose. "You see, Gappu. You would be better off in school," he said gently. "But we need not talk of that now. You have made your decision. Come. We must say the evening Namaz, and then we will get some sleep."

Gappu followed his father in prayer. He felt strange kneeling and rising behind his father, saying the words he only used to say at lessons in the mosque or on special occasions. Abu said a rosary for each of his children and prayed that he would be able to fulfill his promises to each one. He prayed that Gerrar would become a doctor, even if it meant study in England, and that Karim could join his cousin in America, if only he would go to school, and that Raheel could become a teacher since Apaji had proved that it was not un-Islamic to do so. He prayed that Moïd would stop stuttering and Mona lose her introversion and that Piari would grow strong and well and that Sara should never remember the suffering of her first three months of life. "And my eldest son, Marouf, whom we call Gappu, lead him into manhood with his eyes open and his mind clear. I think he also should go to school."

Gappu waited until his father had finished the prayer with the repetition of the Namaz, "Allah ho Akbar. God is One. The Prophet is One. The Prophet Muhammad was the last of his prophets on earth."

Gappu leaped to his feet. "Why do you want me to go to school?" he demanded. "You have brought me here to be a business-man, not a student."

"Even business has its students," Rehman said.

"I thought you would be happy that I wish to stay with you when all my brothers and sisters choose to desert you."

Rehman sat down again on the steps to the verandah. The last traces of sun had left the sky, and the only lights in the hills were those of the chemical company compound. "They do not desert me, Gappu. They go because they must go. There is no more Nehtor to keep the family together—no more lands and factories for the sons to inherit, or Nanis and Dadis to care for the grandsons. No matter how hard we work or how much money we earn, that life of India will never be again. The borders will open, but there is no going back. Even if it seems possible to go back, life cannot be the same. The world is catching up with India, and your brothers choose wisely to understand that. I can only work for my sons and pray they will not forget me too soon. I do not need them here."

Gappu did not argue further, and Rehman left him sitting on the verandah and went to bed. Gappu was enveloped by the night of the hills. He could hear a static radio from the shantytown about a half mile away, blaring the music of All India Radio from loud-speakers over the teashop doors. It seemed impossible to Gappu that he could hear India but might never see India again, or live in the gentle manner of her villages and market towns. Abu wanted him to go to school because he insisted that the India he loved would wel-come him no longer. The salt business would not prepare him for life; it would only pay for his preparation. Gappu did not want to go to school. It was not that he disliked school the way Karim did. It was only that leaving again, leaving Multan and Apaji, leaving Abu and the ancient mines, was only to find another way station. It was to be a refugee forever.

After breakfast and morning prayers, the foreman ran up to Rehman on the verandah. He had come with a message from the Mulvi, he explained breathlessly. "The wise old man was impressed with your son, Sahib. He wishes him to take an offering to the mizar as a prayer for good luck."

"I don't like mizars," Gappu protested. "They steal the people's food in exchange for dreams."

"There is nothing wrong with dreams," Abu reprimanded him. "I would go myself, but I must see about renting a truck. Business will not wait. Take a hundred rupees and promise more when your wish is fulfilled. You must go and do as the Mulvi says."

The foreman instructed Gappu to follow the road past the Mulvi's house and up into the hills where he would see the mizar. Gappu did not want to go alone, but there was no arguing with Abu once he made a decision.

It was a walk of four or five miles, uphill all the way. The sun glinted off the desolate rocks and hammered in the still air like a fist. Stiff little cactuses and the thorny hair of low-lying shrubs protruded through the cracks of dry clay. Gappu felt his perspiration running over his forehead and stinging his eyes with great droplets as he walked, and he could taste the metallic saltiness of the clay which had formed over the miles and miles of unmined salt deposits. The hills hummed with the chirping of lizards, and scrawny black buzzards sailed overhead scavenging. Sometimes the road became so steep and narrow that Gappu had to use his hands to haul himself forward. He could not imagine how the road could be traveled except by mountain goat. There were no other roads or even a footpath connecting the terrain of ridges.

Gappu felt as if he were climbing a never-ending ladder into nothing but empty hills growing out of hills. His eyes caught mirages of snakes coiled in the shadows of rocks, which caused him to stumble forward faster with a dry, choking sensation in his throat. He remembered the foreman's story of the cobra with seven heads, and at every twist of the road he looked for the hissing snake form to rise like a genie from the earth, spitting tongues and glinting eyes. He could hear his own breath coming from his mouth in short spurts, and his heart knocked furiously in his chest and in the veins of his neck and temples. When he tried to sit down at the side of the road, the oppressive stillness of the unending hills seemed menacing and propelled him forward. He had no idea how far he had walked. It seemed hours had passed, and at the same time only minutes. Gappu could not guess if he had gone half the distance to the mizar. As the road turned, he looked hopefully up each stretch of hill twisting above him, but no mizar appeared on the horizon. He wondered how long he would have to be gone before Abu would begin to worry about him. He pictured his graying father scrambling up the road to search for him at night, calling his name and swinging a lantern to search for him under the rocks. He imagined himself bitten by the Snake of Salt and limp with fever as his father walked past with a party of men, calling to him, and unable to shout back, "Abu, I am here!"

Gappu thought it impossible that a mizar would be on this road, although he knew that they were often in the most deserted places. They were erected in deserts and on mountainsides, wherever a martyr died or a miracle was performed. Gappu knew that Dadi had gone to a hundred mizars, before Abu was born, to pray that she might have a son. She had traveled hundreds of miles from Nehtor to leave a sacrifice and make a wish during the seven years of her infertility. The more far-flung the mizar, the holier and more shrouded in mysterious power it was, but the mizar of salt had to be the most isolated, the most veiled in death, of them all.

Finally, in the distance, he could make out the brick structure of walls like a small fortress, sitting on a plateau against a sheer backdrop of cliff. The road wound up to an open archway and stopped before a gate. There was no sign of life as Gappu pushed open a smaller door. He could hear the high whistle of a flute monotonously piping one note, and the sickeningly sweet, dead-flower smell of incense hung in the air like a curtain. The dark archway was several feet thick with bricks. It opened onto an outer courtyard filled with sheep that were heavy with wool and dragging their tails of naked pink fat. Their bleatings echoed in the courtyard along with the one-note flute. Chickens flapped back and forth over the bricks, picking at the manure of the sheep while leaving a circular trail of their own liquid droppings all across the floor.

"Hello! Is anyone here?" Gappu called, startled to hear his

own voice, and instantly the flute music stopped chanting. Gappu waited, then called again, "Hello!"

In response, the flute excitedly blew its droning one-note wail. Gappu scanned the row of straw and jute huts that leaned against the walls, yellow in the haze of sunlight, and tried to figure out which one the flute sound was coming from. He was half afraid to look since the otherworldly music might not be made by a man at all, although he kept telling himself that Abu would not be proud of his childishness. He walked over to the hut the music seemed to be coming from and lifted the flap of jute.

The flute screamed. Gappu froze, the white light of the sun dizzying his head, the goat bleatings and peals of laughter ringing in his ears. A great orb of a mouth, red-lipped with betel juice like blood and toothless, gushing drool, laughed and chortled, protruding beneath narrow slits of eyes and a pinhead that was completely bald.

Gappu backed away from the shed. His legs felt weak like rubber, and he could not run. The creature rose on spindly legs and drifted toward him, flapping his arms like the chickens that screeched and scattered at his feet. He wore only a dirty loincloth, and his brown flesh hung in calloused wrinkles over his knees which were growths between his equally thin thighs and calves.

"Oh, God! What are you?" Gappu shouted. "Are you a spirit?"

Again the creature laughed, and saliva fell from his lips in a long red stream. Gappu continued to back away. "Old man, tell me where is the Pir of the mizar? I have brought a sacrifice."

The creature waved his arms, grunted and hissed. He seemed to want Gappu to follow, and clutching his hundred-rupee note in the pocket of his shirt, Gappu walked through yet another wooden doorway and into a colonnaded inner courtyard. The huge expanse of brick was patterned into walks, and in the center, like a charming gazebo, was the white-domed, marble tomb. All about the footpaths, the fat pink sheep meandered among springy goats and plucking chickens. They were tended by a harem of young boys. Over a hundred of them were lying among the animals, as still as frescoes, and each child was strapped into an iron bonnet, like rounded black pots on their heads. Their slit-eyed faces were compressed beneath the restricting weight of the heavy metal hats. The boys ranged in age from infancy to adolescence, but they were all dressed alike in faded white loincloths, and the iron hats. Their thin sticklike bodies were a deeply bronzed brown from hourless years of sitting in the sun. Older boys and a few men among them no longer wore the iron caps, but their hairless skulls were as dark and rounded and gleaming smooth as the helmets. The flute player who had led Gappu in was the only really ancient person among them, but even those who seemed to Gappu to be his own age wore a ridge of wrinkles in their narrowed brows.

They were all sitting mutely or sprawled on the ground or curled up in sleeping fetal positions. As soon as they saw Gappu coming on the heels of the bowlegged old man, a great clattering of tongues went up among them like the babble of some strange unreasoned language. They began to struggle to their feet as if the weight of the helmets held them down, and they stumbled and slithered toward Gappu with their wagging hands extended before them in exaggerated attitudes of begging. They supplicated Gappu with the drooling, incoherent speech of their twisting lips, and knit their faces spastically in their efforts at communication.

Gappu was shaking so badly he felt the muscles in his legs cramp as he tried to run from the swarm of boys. They seemed to be rising wraithlike out of the ground and surrounding him, and he was running in desperate circles to free himself from their oozing mass of bodies without touching the dried, leathery skin or the spittle that bubbled from their mouths. A scream of sheer terror ached in his throat, and tears sprang to his eyes. He was so dizzy he thought he would faint as the visions bombarded him and the old man's flute took up its one-note cry like an eerie counterpoint to the language of shrieks and moans. Gappu tried to pray with all the energy of his mind that he would awaken from a hallucination. He thought that these must be the children of mad souls, crazed by premature death. He felt that they were dragging him into their midst, trying to claw the life out of him and claim it for their own. He thought wildly that perhaps he was already dead, but he could taste the salt of his own perspiration, which dripped out of his hot heavy hair and slid onto his lips and over his chin. His nostrils stung with the wafts of incense that blew across the courtyard.

Suddenly there was a sharp clacking noise, and the horde of boys looked around bewildered. The Pir of the mizar stood beneath its marble dome. He was dressed in glaring white from head to toe, and the bright sunlight glinted off his starched shirt and flowing pajamas and his cocked fedora cap. A white, thinly trimmed beard hung in fine wisps over his chest. In his hand he held two long, highly polished sticks of Kashmiri birch, which clacked as he beat them together.

The children wobbled off like trained monkeys, lines of disappointment twisting their stunted faces.

"Welcome, pilgrim. Assalaam Aleicum," the Pir pronounced. "Do not mind the children. They are taught to beg. It is many months since we have had a wanderer, Mahajir."

Gappu stared speechless at the pure white form of the Pir, who gestured with his arm for Gappu to enter the delicately laced marble archway of the mizar.

"Why do you stand there? Do you not have a wish?" the Pir asked him.

"Who are these children?" Gappu demanded in a choked, shaking voice.

"They are the eldest sons of barren women, the immaculate conceptions of God and his martyr of Khevera, the salted waters," the Pir intoned majestically, and his whole form quivered as he spoke. "They are the living miracles of the mizar."

Gappu backed slowly away from the mizar, his eyes pinned on the statuesque form of the Pir.

"Where are you going?" the Pir called. He frowned deeply and raised the birch sticks in his hands. "Where is your gift? Where is your sacrifice?"

The Pir clacked his sticks together, and again the hovering boys sprang to life and tripped and slithered toward Gappu. The flute music was playing furiously. Gappu threw his hundred-rupee note into their waving, outstretched arms, and turned on his feet and ran. He ran faster than he had ever run in his life, through the courtyard of sheep, out the brick gate of the fortress, and down the twisting road. He leaped over stones and cactuses that sprouted in the cracked clay, tripping over his feet and rolling to an upright position without ever stopping his frantic descent. His shirt was torn, and his hands and face bruised and covered with a coating of clay dust, which clung to his wet skin. He ran over a mile until he fell in the middle of the road in an exhausted heap. The road was never ending, and he raised himself on all fours like an animal licking its wounds, and listened to his gasps and his head beating with the hooting of the flute that seemed to be imbued in his brain in the silence of the omnipresent hills. The shriek of a buzzard startled him, and he leapt to his feet again and stumbled down the sharply twisting rutted road.

When he finally arrived at the first houses of Khevera, it was late afternoon. The women at their cooking and the barefooted children carrying water on their heads and defecating in the cesspools stopped to stare at the sight of Gappu's tattered clothing and panic-stricken face. They bowed their heads furiously together and whispered that he had been to the mizar.

Gappu burst in on Abu who was dozing on the verandah of the rest house. Gappu fell to his knees and heaved with sobs. Rehman jumped up at the sight of his son and tried to ease him into a chair. He called the servant of the rest house and ordered him to bring a bucket of water with soap and towels. Gappu could not speak while Rehman delicately wiped his face and tried to soothe him by rubbing his back and neck. Only when Gappu was calmer, Rehman asked him what had happened.

"Oh, God, Abu! I don't know. The mizar is filled with mad souls. There were children wearing heavy iron helmets who could not speak, and the Pir looked like a devil. He is the keeper of their souls."

"What is this nonsense?" Rehman demanded. "I can't understand what you are talking about."

The servant who was bustling about with tea and refilling the pot with warm milk stopped politely before Rehman, the set of china cups balanced in his hands.

"It is a very evil mizar," the servant explained. "The wise man should not have sent your son alone. I do not understand his reasons."

"Tell me what you know of the mizar," Rehman said.

"It is the mizar of a martyr who fathered five hundred sons in the hills of Khevera a thousand years ago, without the benefit of a woman. It is the holiest mizar in all of India for women who cannot bear a son. They come here to wish, and as a sacrifice they promise to give their first son to the martyr. Those are the children you saw," he explained, turning to Gappu. "But, Sahib, I do not think it is the martyr alone who fathers the children. I think the soul of the martyr enters the body of the Pir. Myself, I have seen some of these women, high-caste women who come from Persia and Hyderabad bearing caravans of gold and fruit, silks and jewels. They stay for weeks, sometimes months. At night their screams and wails can be heard in the hills over the prayers of the Pir. When they leave, they no longer wear their burkas, and their eyes appear transfixed. I have seen these women, Sahib. A year later an infant son is carried here by a single servant and camel driver and left in the mizar."

Gappu buried his head in his hands, and Rehman rose to his side. "You mean the Pir drugs the women and rapes them!" said Abu angrily. "There is no supernatural mystery to all of this. These are the abuses of religion."

"I am sorry, Sahib," said the servant, backing into the rest house. "What you say may be true."

Rehman was pacing the floor. Gappu jumped up and walked after him. "Abu, what am I going to do?" he wailed.

Rehman looked closely at his son. Gappu seemed half child, half young man. His high cheekbones and long chiseled nose were still too large for his face, and his black hair was as unruly as lamb's wool, but his dark eyes were burning and bitter. Rehman had not wanted his children to learn so soon about life. He would not have exposed them so early, but in the last three months the world had exposed itself to them, inch by inch, peeling off its veils like a prostitute revealing her haggard body and scars. Even now, with the salt business so promising, the truck rented and drivers hired, newly employed gangs of miners gratefully back in the caves, and the migrant workers operating the mill and loading the truck, there was still no way for him to offer Gappu safety.

Rehman had always said there was time to learn about the world. Children should play and go to school. Now that life had been seen, it was impossible to tuck it away again behind half-hearted explanations and fantasies. If he could hold Gappu's head and squeeze out the vision of the crazed, retarded children between the palms of his hands, he would do it. If he could hypnotize Gerrar and Karim with pretty stories, he would talk forever and obliterate their memories of Rukmani's father's severed head in their hands, and he would cut out his own tongue to give Moïd the clear speech he had lost somewhere among a rubble of corpses lying in a railroad train or floating in a river. He would buy Raheel a thousand dresses if that could erase the feel of her tattered clothes from her body or the ache of hunger from her tiny stomach and budding breasts. How could he restore laughter to Mona or security to an infant like Sara after the weeks of frustration when Apaji's milk was insufficient, and how could he repair for Piari the face she had lost to a disease of filth and open sewers? What could he say to Gappu about the millions of Rukmanis who lost their fathers during war and after war, the hungry and blind children, the beggars and lepers, the sacrificial lambs of the mizars? He put his hand softly on Gappu's shoulder, but he did not know what he could say that Gappu did not know himself except that he was sorry.

Gappu looked at Rehman steadily, searching his eyes for an answer. "Tell me one thing, Abu. Where should I go? If I knew for certain like Gerrar that I wanted to be a doctor, I would go to medical school. If I were a silly child and had no thought in my head, I would go dancing off to Phopi Fatima's son in America, like Karim. Moïd is a baby and can go back to Dadi's and Nani's laps in Nehtor. Raheel is the only smart one. She refuses to marry, and she will do something meaningful in the world. What will I do? Where is my place if it is not with you?"

Rehman grasped Gappu in his arms and stood for seconds awkwardly holding the adolescent body that was almost as tall as his

374

own but twice as thin. He pushed Gappu away and continued, pacing. "I think you should go to school in Lahore," he said as he walked. "Study anything you like until you find what you want to be. Take ten years to graduate, I don't care. You can still help me in the salt business from the Lahore side. Our first truck is already being loaded, and tomorrow we will sell our first shipment of salt in the Lahore market. After this we will have a whole fleet of trucks going back and forth, and you can check the shipments when they arrive."

Rehman was becoming excited. Gappu did not argue, and Rehman thought they had decided the best thing for his oldest son. Already Rehman's mind was formulating and planning, reorganizing the money he had calculated and budgeted. He would arrange everything in Lahore, enroll Gerrar in premedical school, and Raheel and Gappu in the arts and sciences. He would send Karim by plane to Phopi Fatima in Karachi where his Uncle Tariq could help him obtain the proper papers from the Americans. By the time all the arrangements were made, he would have enough money to wire to Karim in Karachi for boat passage and foreign exchange.

"Promise me one thing, Gappu," he said, interrupting his private calculations. "You will try to be happy. I don't care if you don't learn a thing at school as long as you come out knowing who you are, what you want to be, where you think you fit. Is that clear?"

"Yes, sir," said Gappu, beaming. He drew himself up to his fullest height and felt instantly that something had been renewed. He was full of love and pride for Abu, who had nine burdens compared to his own single one. It all seemed so simple. When Abu came out with his plans—orderly, efficient—everything fell into place. Gappu had never realized before what constituted the pieces—the traveling in the dead heat on trains and walking over hilly footpaths, the quick assimilation of facts gathered on the road, in smoke-filled teahouses and in casual conversations with workers, porters, servants, drivers. The alert piecing together of details so that mill machinery would run, salt mines would function, trucks roll to market, so that Abu could take home so much for school, so much for the house and food, so much for cloth, and so much for dowries. Gappu was amazed, and although he felt very old in a hundred ways, he was not yet prepared to face what Abu did. Perhaps he never would be.

The truck Rehman had rented from the British potash company was waiting at the door to the rest house by sunrise. The air was very still and clean, and only the monkeys were moving about, prancing on the road and railway tracks between the rest house and the compound. A crew of ten men were lolling on gunnysacks of salt in the open back of the brightly colored truck, which was decorated with metal flowers, crescents, and Islamic proverbs in Arabic. As they finished breakfast on the verandah, Rehman explained that the gang was coming to unload the salt and then to drive the trucks he planned to buy back to Khevera. The men waited comfortably, smoking their dark brown *beedie* cigarettes, which were made from unaged tobacco wrapped in a leaf.

Rehman paid the rest-house bill and slid into the front seat beside Gappu. One of the drivers jumped up to open the door and take his place at the wheel, but Rehman motioned him to the other side. "I'll drive this time," he said. "I want to get the feel of the road." He rolled up the sleeves of his cameez and started the engine, which barked and coughed exhaust. The truck lurched and bounced over the bumpy road, so that Gappu kept flying out of his seat, but Rehman held steadily to the steering wheel, and Gappu noticed the strong muscles on Abu's forearm, which he leaned against the window.

The ride to Lahore was almost entirely downhill, and the barren hills changed abruptly to green farmlands when they reached the plain of Lahore. The fertile land extended only as far as the canals could go because there was almost no rainfall west of the path of the monsoons. As they neared the city, the roads were filled with refugees still walking to their Pakistani Mecca—Lahore. They walked beside their bullock carts, which were loaded with wooden furniture and charpoys, pots and household equipment. Children came leading a buffalo or a cow on a rope, and young girls carried babies in their arms. Anyone who could walk traveled by foot, and even toddlers followed behind their buffalo, pushing them along with sticks through the dusty roads. Only old women covered from head to toe in burkas, despite the glaring heat, and old men, white-haired and wizened brown, sat in the carts, skinny and bewildered like ancient children. They all followed the roads adjacent to the major railroad lines, and as the truck jolted onto the larger roads, more and more people could be seen converging on the city. All around were bird-filled fields and canals where buffalo were bathing. Oxen turned the heavy wooden waterwheels and sprayed the crops from the deepest wells. Along the roadside, impeccably white mosques stood beside jewellike Sikh gurdwaras that combined Muslin archways and minarets with Hindu sculpturing on the walls and domes. Many had been partially burned or mutilated and seemed to stand screaming from raw wounds in the lush peaceful fields.

As they neared the city, they were joined on the road by traffic of every possible description. Carriages and rickshaws drawn by horses dodged among occasional trucks and taxis, and bicycles teetered under a load of four men or an entire family draped over the handlebars and standing on the wheels. The vehicles and pedestrians bottled together to clatter over the bridge of the River Ravi. Along the river's banks were the dhobi ghats of the washerwomen who beat their clothes against the river's stone steps and spread them out to dry in front of their huts in the surrounding miles of mud-moist fields. A little farther along the river were the abandoned ghats of Hindu crematoriums, cold and out of business.

Gappu could see the minars and domes of the Shahi Mosque shining above the rooftops of Anarkali, the old city of Lahore. Anarkali looked just like Delhi, only the fort of the Mogul dynasty was not as rundown as the one in Delhi, and the mosque, an exact replica of the Jama Masjid in Delhi, was set in a park of billowing trees. All the narrow streets twisted together within the ancient surrounding walls and gates of the city, and the lacy balconies and colonnades of the graceful buildings were concealed behind every kind of sign imaginable, written in a conglomeration of languages and scripts, from Arabic to Urdu to English. The only thing that marred the beauty of the city, studded at every turn with mosques, gardens, and temples, were the refugee camps. The black little huts were the signature of Partition. Shantytowns and cesspools had created their own subcities beneath and between the walls of Lahore.

Rehman maneuvered the heavily laden truck through the narrow brick streets, jammed with pedestrians. He leaned out of the truck's cabin several times to ask directions to the salt markets, and finally located a large brick warehouse on a street of almost empty shops and offices. The only shops that seemed busy were the crowded offices of doctors and apothecaries with their old, unlabeled vials and dusty bottles full of herbal juices.

Rehman disappeared into the dim warehouse. Gappu waited in the truck with the drivers, who were chattering excitedly about the city, while Rehman inquired within. He reappeared with the warehouse manager, a heavyset smiling businessman in an open-necked Western shirt and pants. The manager rubbed his hands together with pleasure at the sight of all the bales of salt bulging in the gunnysacks and all the raw bricks of salt rock loaded in the rear.

"I am glad you brought rock salt as well. The market has been bare for weeks and without salt lick animals will die all over Pakistan. It has been months since the trains carried salt." The manager was so excited he could not stop talking, and he kept shaking Rehman's hand and patting him on the back.

"We are buying a whole fleet of trucks that will make daily runs," Rehman explained.

"You are a blessing from God, my friend," the businessman laughed, tugging at the belt of his pants. "You see how much weight the businessmen of Lahore have lost because of Partition." He waved his arm at the street. "My brothers may have gained many shops, but there is nothing to sell to fill up their stomachs." He laughed again, inspecting the gang of drivers in their dhotis and patting the sacks of salt with his hands.

"This is fine," he said. "I am glad you came to me. I can give you the best price. Any price you ask."

Rehman knew that salt had become such a rare commodity that the warehouse manager did not even care to haggle over the price. Salt was necessary for everything, for animals, for food preservation, for daily consumption. In the dry heat of Punjab, salt was used in yogurt and tea instead of sugar, because it kept the body at the coolest temperature and was the only antidote to the scorching sun. Rehman asked for five thousand rupees per truckload, and the manager immediately agreed. He even wanted to sign a contract. Rehman felt that a binding agreement could wait, but he immediately ordered the men to unload the salt, with much congratulations and welcome wishes from the manager.

All week Rehman went methodically about his business, while Gappu enjoyed the luxury of their small hotel at the edge of the Anarkali section of Lahore. From the balcony he could see the complex of holy buildings, the sprawling stone Shahi Mosque, the Golden-domed Sikh Gurdwara, and a needle-shaped Hindu temple. The streets and park were a continuous motion of people, bicycles, and rickshaws. Refugee huts clung to the walls of the mosque like suckling kids to a she-goat. They were aswarm with women cooking and washing clothes, children defecating, and men prowling the alleys and byways.

Within the hotel was a small garden courtyard, filled with birds and flowers where Gappu liked to sit drinking tea and resting his eyes from the dizzying scene of the old streets. The truck drivers were installed in an even smaller hotel, which was actually one floor of rooms above the teahouses which they haunted, staying high on charas and strong tea all week.

Each day Rehman accomplished one of his missions. Gappu accompanied his father early every morning, but often by midday he was hot and exhausted and returned to the hotel to sleep. Rehman visited the colleges of Punjab University to enroll Gappu, Raheel, and Gerrar in classes. He inspected the student hostels and found them lodgings. He spoke with bankers about obtaining foreign exchange for Karim, and every day he went about the business of buying trucks. There were hundreds of trucks available, sold for almost nothing, that had been left by fleeing or dead Sikhs. He was able to buy five trucks for under fifty thousand rupees, which was less than what remained from the Nawab's loan and would be re-earned in three shipments of salt.

Gappu went with Rehman to the undergraduate college of Punjab University where they had to stand in a long line of enrolling students that stretched through the courtyards and under the arcades of the academic buildings, which looked like a sandstone Mogul fort. Young moustached men and studious-looking girls holding heavy books against the soft pleats of their wide *shilwar* pants were applying for every course imaginable, with their Indian diplomas and report cards in their hands. The university had become so crowded with new arrivals that classes overspilled onto the garden lawns and walks.

Gappu filled out form after form which he handed to other students working at desks set up in a big hall, but none of the student-clerks bothered to speak to him or even met his eyes as they detached one questionnaire and attached another with staples and affixed stamps. In Aligarh, when Rehman was enrolling his sons at the university before Partition, he had done all the red tape through his cousin Zamir with whom he personally discussed their educations. Aligarh Muslim University had been an intimate institution of fraternal clubs and neat school blazers, of professors and artists who were close relatives and neighbors, of school songs and proud emblems. Gappu looked around the huge courtyards of the city university bustling with students of every description, from poor young men in Western shirts to rich boys in blazers. Gappu fingered the emblem of his own blazer from Aligarh which Apaji had washed and rewashed, sewn and mended over and over for him. She had even found new buttons, although they were no longer of silver. Occasionally he noticed other boys wearing the Aligarh blazer, and he wished he could call out to them and greet them.

After the enrollment was completed, Abu had to go back to Anarkali to take the drivers to the trucks, which were all bought, tuned up, and filled with gas. Gappu wanted to stay at the university and look over his new hostel which was in another direction toward the burned-out Hindu section, Krishnagar. He walked away from the large university buildings along a broad thoroughfare that was crowded with traffic; people were walking in the street as well as on the sidewalks.

The midmorning sun was growing hot despite the first coolness of late October, and Gappu felt pangs of hunger gnawing in his stomach. Abu had given him five rupees for lunch. He turned off the boulevard into the cluster of little streets that were so crowded, everyone was walking shoulder to shoulder, and he often had to sidestep for an ox cart to push by. He entered a lunch shop where men were eating at rows of long tables. Gappu squeezed himself into a seat and immediately a busy waiter leaned over to take his order along with several others, and returned almost before Gappu could look around with a stack of dishes in his arms which he dispersed around the table in no particular order. Gappu sorted out his dish of mutton, his stack of chapati, and a tall glass of sweet lassy from the center of the table and gulped his food down hungrily.

Refreshed from his meal, he walked out again into the streets of Anarkali, turning into alley after alley, which connected through archways, so that Gappu sometimes could not tell if he was in a courtyard or on a street. Everywhere there were shops and stalls, and women walked heavily veiled among the men in their open shirts and pajamas. Gappu turned into a long street and realized he was in Hira Mundi, the red-light district, where women, brightly rouged and dressed in boldly printed skirts, were lurking in doorway after doorway and hanging from the windows overhead like parrots in a tree. The streets smelled of hashish and incense, and the sweetest mogra, jasmine, and musk from perfume stalls at every corner combined with the warm smell of bodies and of sheep that were tied up at the curbsides and in courtyards.

The prostitutes waiting in every doorway far outnumbered the crowds of men strolling through the streets and calling out remarks.

Behind the women, Gappu could see charpoys in all the inner rooms, separated from each other by paisley sheets or beaded curtains, and occasionally he would catch a glimpse of a man's bare arm or leg dangling from a bed. Most of the rooms, however, were filled only with hollow-eyed children and infants with dirt-encrusted mouths, who sat patiently on the floor waiting to be told by their mothers to move over for a customer.

When Gappu looked closely at the women, he could see behind the makeup and brightly colored clothes that many were girls even younger than Raheel, girls without breasts or hips, who could have been no more than nine or ten, while still others could have been grandmothers and were fat and low-hipped from childbearing, but the makeup and clothes obscured their individualities, made them all one. They looked out onto the street with indifference, but at one doorway Gappu felt the deep brown eyes of a tall willowy girl riveted on his own. He stopped. She had lipstick smeared in a wide arc over her mouth, and her long hair was slick and shining with oil. An ugly skirt of garish red was drawn tightly between her thin legs and exposed her blackened hard-skinned knees, but Gappu was frozen by the mascara-smudged eyes staring out from the prostitute's cage. He knew the eyes, and he could not move, looking at her, and jostled by the men on the street flowing past him.

"Jilla?" he breathed.

"Gappu *mian*," she cried. But that was all she sould say. The tears streaked through the thick layer of powder on her face.

"Oh, God, Jilla! What are you doing here?" A tall husky man in wide Punjabi pants and velvet slippers broke away from a little group on the corner and yanked Jilla by the arm. Gappu grabbed her from the other side. "Leave her alone. She is my cousin," Gappu shouted.

The pimp brought his face close to Gappu's. He smelled strongly of perfume. "Tell your stories to someone else," he said. "I saved this girl's life, and now you will pay the same price for her as everyone else."

Gappu threw what was left of his five rupees at the pimp's feet and dragged Jilla, who was sobbing and shaking all over, into the small room where they sat together on the charpoy. She looked so much older with all the cheap makeup and the dress of a prostitute. Her long fingers were clutched in her lap, and she leaned against Gappu's chest until her sobbing stopped. He could feel her thin shoulders beneath the coarse material of her tight midriff blouse. The bare cubicle was only large enough to accommodate the charpoy, and Gappu could see feet passing back and forth beneath the curtain on the door. Rumpled gray sheets were on the bed, and burning incense could not conceal the odor of the bodies that had passed in and out of the bed.

Gappu bathed Jilla's face with water from a clay pot that stood beside the bed. Slowly the golden-brown skin of Milak reappeared beneath the caked white powder and rouge of crushed flowers, and the whites of Jilla's eyes swam like pools of goat's milk.

"Dearest Gappu, do not tell Gerrar Sahib that you have seen me here. Do not tell anyone that you have seen me. I pray you to be that merciful."

"I must tell him. My father will take you away from here. You are our cousin. In Nehtor you were a domestic, but everyone knows your father was Darogaji. How can we permit such a thing?"

"No, no!" Jilla cried, jumping to her feet and shaking all over. "I am going to have a baby. I am married to this man. He owns me as well as his other wives. There is no way, no possible way, you can take me from him. I do not even know who is the father of the baby. Can this child in my body be the grandson of Darogaji?" Her voice rose to an hysterical pitch. "Can such a child be brought into your father's house?"

"I am not thinking of your baby. I am thinking of you."

Jilla turned away. Her eyes were overcast, and her mouth creased with bitterness. "This man owns me," she stated matter-of-factly. "There is nothing you can do."

"But how did you get here? Why did you leave Nehtor?"

Jilla laughed. "It is a wonderful story. I will tell it to you. I will tell you how your servant Bashir came to Nehtor from Aligarh to tell us that you had left for Pakistan, and every day your Nani sent him to the railroad station at Dhampur to see if there was news. I wanted to go with Bashir. They told me not to go. Your Nani ordered me to stay in Milak, but I sneaked away with Bashir, and the day I went to the station there was a riot."

Jilla kept laughing and crying at the same time. "Do you really want to hear?"

Gappu nodded his head.

"We saw that there was rioting, but we were too late. The Muslims and the Sikhs had drawn their swords, and the Hindus were burning the station. In every direction we tried to run, there were fires and men with knives. I was running, and I thought Bashir was behind me until I heard him scream. 'Jilla, Jilla,' he called, but when I looked back, I could not see him. I went wild shouting for Bashir, and people's hands were pulling me and grabbing hold of my skirt and my dopatta. I could not see Bashir anywhere, but I heard his voice. He said, 'Jilla, Jilla, I am dying. Help me. I am dying.' But I could not find him. His voice faded, and this man you saw scooped me up in his arms and carried me into the train. I kicked him and scratched him, but he told me not to be stupid, he was saving my life. The train moved, and I never even saw Bashir. I do not know if he is dead or alive, but I know about myself. I know that I am dead."

"Jilla," said Gappu, extending his arms.

"No," shouted Jilla, stamping her foot. "Get out of here. Promise me you will tell no one you have seen me."

"I can't do that," said Gappu, rising from the bed. "I promise not to say anything to Abu, but Gerrar and I are returning to Lahore for school. We will come to see you. We will arrange something."

Jilla stopped crying, and her lips quivered. He grabbed both her thin hands in his own. "I promise you, Jilla. There is hope. I will tell no one else of your sorrow, but Gerrar and I will come."

"Perhaps," said Jilla quietly. "But *he* will always make you pay. He is my husband in the eyes of God."

Gappu nodded solemnly, and quickly left Jilla standing in the center of her cage like a fallen bird. He ran all the way back to the hotel and collapsed on the bed. The musky scent of Jilla's perfume seemed oiled into his perspiration, and the heat of her body clung possessively to his skin. A desire to sob and curse was lodged in his throat, but he clenched his fists and thrashed impotently on the bed. Gappu knew that Jilla loved Gerrar above all others, and that Gerrar belonged to her in some special way. But he, Gappu, loved her, too, without ever having realized it. He loved her with an ache in his hands that were growing big and clumsy, and with his whole mind and heart, and in the pit of his stomach, as a brother would love a sister, a father a child, as a man loved his life. It was impossible to think of Jilla standing there in her cage, a garish painting of the village girl like a ghost in a new dress. Bashir dead, and Jilla raped, over and over again, a thousand times a day. Jilla, who was full of the breath of Milak and Nehtor, now filled with a stranger's child.

Gappu sat upright on the bed and stared at the soft white walls of the hotel room. He could not get his bearings. All the shining wood fixtures, the deep maroon Persian carpet on the floor, the long French windows that opened out onto a narrow terrace with iron grillwork, the hum of the city wafting up from the streets, seemed so benign, so unfitting to the scream that was in his chest and the image of Jilla, her mouth slashed with red lipstick, beckoning in a doorway. He vowed he would not breathe a word about Jilla to his father, but would bring Gerrar back to her when they returned to Lahore. Gappu would be sixteen. They would be college students, living in a hostel and free to do as they pleased. There would be some way to rescue Jilla.

Gappu swung his legs over the side of the bed and slowly dragged himself to the bathroom where he stripped and let the icy water of the shower pour over his body and stream into his mouth and eyes. He showered for almost an hour, trying to regain his composure, so that Abu would guess nothing about what had happened that afternoon and Jilla.

By the end of the week, Rehman was able to send the drivers back to Khevera with the five new trucks and continue on to Multan with Gappu in the truck he had rented from the British potash company.

Rehman was tingling with excitement at the thought of seeing Apaji and the children after a separation of almost two weeks. He loaded the truck with sacks of rice and wheat, almonds and spices, and an armload of Punjabi dresses he had had stitched for Raheel to wear to school. Rehman could not wait until morning, and as soon as the five trucks were dispatched to Khevera late in the afternoon, he set out for home. Empty of salt, except for a few rocks he remembered to take for Karim's goats, the truck raced and bounced over the flat roads through the Punjabi farmlands. Late at night Rehman stopped at a small country rest house to eat and sleep, and Gappu could hear him up before sunrise, pacing restlessly in and out of the stone building.

He hurried Gappu through a breakfast of chapati and fresh butter, and they were back on the road before the fall chill had left the air. They flew past village after village stirring in the pale morning light, where farmers were relieving water buffalo of milk and women were preparing *parathas* over the charcoals of their sunken *tandoori* ovens.

When they reached Montgomery, the town before Multan, Rehman burst into popular songs of the day, songs from Hindi and Urdu films and of Saigol, the Indian Caruso. Gappu looked at Abu in amazement. His brown face was scrubbed and shining, and surprisingly, the trimmed shock of curly hair streaked with gray made him look younger than before, with his regained weight and muscles firmed from work.

"Come on and sing with me," laughed Rehman, grabbing Gappu by the scruff of his neck. "We're companions, aren't we?" Gappu was embarrassed, but he joined in singing, too, and by the time they reached the canal of Multan, he was laughing and singing at the top of his voice, bouncing out of his seat as they turned onto the footpath and pulled up at the door of their house with a great jolt.

Raheel ran out onto the verandah, waving a spoon in her hand. "It's Abu in a truck!" she shouted. "Abu and Gappu are home!"

Everyone spilled out of the house at a run. Gerrar and Karim climbed all over the truck, and Moïd and Mona attacked Rehman's pockets where they found fistfuls of candies. Apaji appeared on the porch with Sara, observing brightly, in her arms. Apaji smiled and raised her hand to bless her husband and embrace her eldest son. Piari stood quietly behind Apaji, her thumb in her mouth and her almond eyes lowered shyly. She was so thin and fragile, she was lost in the long ruffled skirt and knee-length cameez blouse Apaji had sewn for her. A new growth of silken hair fringed her face, and she had the smallest studs of gold in her ears, which Apaji had had made from her last gold coin so that Piari might have the only jewelry in the family while she recovered from the shock of the smallpox. Rehman scooped Piari into his arms and fed her gaunt body with kisses, while she buried her silken head against his broad shoulder.

Rehman found the house filled with the spicy scents of cooking. Apaji had brought the little house to life with flowers and curtains. She had covered Abu's armchair with a paisley sheet, and in the dining room unmatched china dishes were set on the table at every place. Rukmani was seated alone on the floor of the sitting room, listening to the commotion with ears perked. Rehman blessed her, touching the thick black hair that fell down her back in a braid. "It will not be long before you can go home," he told her. She raised her sightless eyes to him as if to study his face and kissed his hands with gratitude.

The children surrounded Rehman in the living room and bombarded him with a thousand questions about the truck and Khevera and the salt business. They were amazed as Gappu told them all that Abu had done in two short weeks—that they had already sold a shipment of salt in Lahore, bought a fleet of five trucks, and enrolled Gerrar, Raheel, and himself in school. He described the mines of salt that looked like diamonds, and the city of Lahore so much like Delhi, and the university crowded with students, some of them even from Aligarh.

Rehman let Gappu tell the whole story. He leaned back in his armchair and listened, apprehensively watching Apaji as the realization that she would soon be losing her three older sons and her oldest daughter washed over her face. He saw her look at each child, and her lips were quivering.

"Abu, is it true?" "Are we really going?" "When will we be be leaving?" they all asked, sitting at his feet in a circle.

"There is no reason to wait longer than a day or two for you older children to start school which is already in progress." He spoke with bluster, but he was afraid of Apaji's reaction, and he looked at her from the corner of his eye, but she did not speak.

"What about me, Abu?" Karim complained, kneeling in front of his father.

"Unfortunately you do not see fit to return to school this year. You have ideas about going to America. Is that still your decision?"

"Yes, Abu. Phopi Fatima has answered your letter. She says she is happy to send me to her son in America. Will you let me go, Abu?"

Rehman looked at Apaji, who was staring at Karim with aching eyes. "I do not know anything about America, but if going there will make you go back to school, that is all I am interested in," Rehman said.

"It will, Abu," Karim promised. "I know all about America. It is the land of Thomas Jefferson and Lincoln who freed the slaves. That is the country I want to learn from, so I can free the people of India."

Rehman raised his hands. "Already you have ideas I do not agree with. Remember, the Prophet Muhammad was the last Prophet of God. Only he did not need an education because he received God's word. Remember when you are in America, if you forget your religion, there will be no home for you in Pakistan or India when you return."

Karim nodded his head solemnly.

"What do you think?" Rehman asked Apaji.

She wiped her eyes with the edge of her sari and stroked Sara's cap of hair with her cheek.

"When are you leaving?" she asked.

"My trucks are already back in Khevera, and I must go immediately to supervise the next shipment of salt. Since I cannot delay, I think we should leave tomorrow. We will send Karim by plane to my sister in Karachi where she can make arrangements for America.

Raheel, Gerrar, and Gappu must enter their colleges. I cannot stay away more than a few days, or I will lose the business."

Apaji rose slowly from her chair. "No mother is happy to lose her sons, but I do not question your wisdom. I will pray for the success of all your decisions. I will prepare for the journey and make a wish this evening."

Apaji worked all day to prepare the last meal for her sons. Tears kept springing to her eyes as she simmered curries of vegetables and meat over the wood-fuel stove. The children were busy gathering together their possessions and running in and out of the kitchen to ask her advice about what to take, so that she had to pretend the tears that fell across her cheeks were from the sharp smoke of the burning wood and not from the pain that constricted her chest as she tried to hold each child's face in her eyes and squeeze tens of years from the one day she had left to be with them. Gappu would be a man when he returned again. Even after only two weeks away with Abu, she could see the difference in his gaunt face, the beard growing heavier like a shadow along his cheeks, his uneasy posture as if he were already a guest in her home. Gerrar would go on to England and become a doctor before she could touch the years of his adolescence. Raheel would live among strangers and take up a profession, and Karim was going too far for her even to imagine. They told her America was farther than England, but to her the separations were not measured in distance, but in time and in the strangeness of the lives her sons would be leading.

At dinner she listened to their laughter and their plans, but did not speak until the meal was completed and she brought out the *keer* puddings. Each pudding was prepared from rice and milk, cardamom and sugar, in separate clay cups. She handed one to each member of the family, including Rukmani. "I want all of you to make a wish and eat the pudding until the cups are clean. Then I will save the cups so that when you tell me your wishes have been fulfilled I may say prayers of thanksgiving and prepare another *keer*.

My cup will remain until all eight children sit together again at my table." She could not look at them as they consumed the *keer*, and she wept in the kitchen, praying with her moving lips that God would let her live long enough to see the manhood of her sons and the marriages of her daughters. Abu stole into the kitchen to comfort her, to tell her not to take it so heavily on her heart that the sons were leaving. He promised that they would have another child, as they had discussed, a Pakistani child who would belong to their new lives and their new country, but his words held little consolation for her.

That night Apaji prayed on the carpet of the living-room floor with the children camped around her in languid slumber. She kept them all within arms' reach but held Karim particularly near because he was going the farthest away. In the still, darkened room, she imagined Karim climbing into the shining steel cylinder of an airplane which she had seen only in pictures, and she tried to visualize the miles of ocean he would travel by ship, but her mind became lost among the unfathomable emptiness of the waves, and the brown-skinned boy from Aligarh and Nehtor was an eternal refugee, continuously arriving knickered and sandaled on foreign shores. Apaji knew that Nani and Dadi would not have approved, but had her children been able to live like the generations before them in Nehtor, such questions would never have arisen. Only fifty years ago, there had not even been a university in Aligarh, and schooling in the sun-drenched courtyards of the mosque and at the feet of poets, musicians, and tutors sufficed. Grandmothers cared for grandsons while fathers inherited the land from which they harvested their food and their songs, their martyrs, and their miracles. But who was she to question what she did not understand? All decisions had been hers as much as Abu's and she must remain a stranger in her native land. She would never go back to Nehtor, never return on a train through green and orange fields that had locked behind her like a bamboo curtain. Apaji could see her mother's head, bowed beneath a shawl in prayer, and Dadi, turning from gray- to white-haired, stooped beside her brick stove, mourning deeply the loss of their children as now Apaji mourned the loss of hers, because she could no more follow them than go back to what was left behind. Pakistan was her final resting place, this corner of India that had been given to her people and divided them from half of what they knew and loved best. Still this promised land was India. What else could it be? It was India just three months ago, three years ago, three thousand years ago. It was India, governments, borders, nations notwithstanding, and she would never leave it.

All night Apaji prayed on her knees, wrapped in the coarse white cotton of her sari. Her thin brown fingers, working a rosary of one hundred beads, were knotted at the joints and throbbed with cold numbness as the hours passed. With the first drifting of light through the blowing curtains, she went out onto the verandah where she could hear the call to morning prayer sung across the fields like a bell. Abu's dusty truck was parked beside the house. She could hear Karim's ducks squawking and the she-goat bleating frantically as her kid tried to nurse at the milk bag that encumbered her udder. Already Karim had forgotten his animals, and Apaji walked barefooted through the grass to release the she-goat's bag and do the milking herself, as she had seen it done a thousand times in Nehtor, so that the children would have the freshest milk and the kid could nurse. She poured the milk into an iron pot and blew on her logs to kindle a fire.

As soon as the children smelled breakfast cooking, they were up with excitement, tearing through the house to gather their meager possessions and arguing over who should take what. Apaji tried to freeze their voices and their laughter in her thoughts, to shore them up against the emptiness she knew would drown the house once they were gone. They ate their chapatis and their eggs on the run, and each came to her in the kitchen to ask her not to be sad, but their activity whirled around her head, and she could not answer them. She could neither smile nor weep, but only watch them, memorize them with her eyes.

The morning flew by relentlessly, and still she could not speak to them. They were grabbing her by the arms and folding her in a hundred kisses and embrace after embrace. Their tears were flowing profusely as they led her, barely walking, out onto the verandah, climbing in and out of Abu's truck to kiss her again. Raheel sobbed uncontrollably; Karim and Gerrar were filled with tears; and Gappu was shaking. They scooped up Moïd and Mona and Piari in their arms, and the younger children were wailing. They blessed Rukmani a hundred times each and kissed their baby sister Sara, who looked on bewildered in Rukmani's arms. Abu pressed his lips to Apaji's forehead. "You are the bravest one," he told her. "I will come home before I go to Khevera and find someone to help you. Do not be afraid. Our children are strong and blessed."

Finally they were leaning out of the truck, their arms clutching hers and practically lifting her off her feet, as Abu turned the motor on and the truck started moving, until only fingertips were trailing and touching, and she ran alongside of the truck on the pebbles and sand of the footpath, the hundred yards or so to the road. The long grasses in the fields slashed her ankles and the edge of her skirts as she ran all the way across the train trestle and onto the road where the truck stopped to turn. The children all extended their hands to her. "Apaji, Apaji! Do not be sad. Remember us. Think of us. Apaji, we love you. Apaji, Salaam va Aleicum."

She watched the truck lurch forward again, and the children waving frantically, calling to her from the rear of the open truck and sobbing all together, until the truck was out of sight.

Apaji looked out across the fields of paddies and the village of clay huts clustered on the horizon like grazing cattle. Children were driving herds of buffalo into the canal, and young girls in orange and yellow shawls stooped to the earth to plant a new crop. The date trees were heavy with yellow fruit. Parrots fluttered in between the banyan trees, and doves cooed in the fields. From the date groves, Apaji could hear a flutist blowing on his pipes to ward off birds from the flowering fruits. High over the horizon a lone airplane sailed south to Karachi, glinting in the sun, and Apaji could hear the distant moan of its propellers. She cupped her hands over her eyes and looked at the machine, which she had never seen before, drifting lazily from cloud to cloud. She could still hear the flute, and she was reminded of an Urdu verse she had heard as a child: "O refugee, May the world be your house, May strangers be your brothers, May God be your pillow."

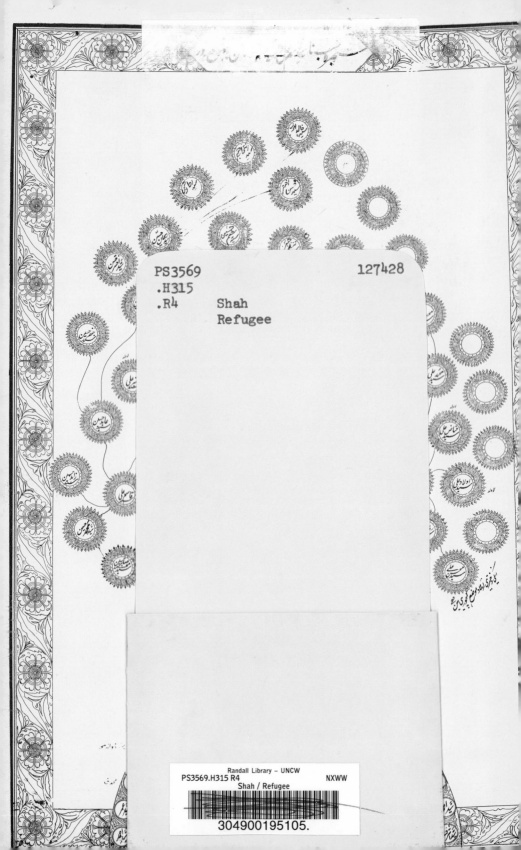